Forged
from
Shadows

by Ariel J. Schaub

PublishAmerica
Baltimore

ISBN: 1-4241-5977-6
PUBLISHED BY PUBLISHAMERICA, LLLP
www.publishamerica.com
Baltimore

Printed in the United States of America

To my husband, Michael,
who has always seen
only the best in me

Worlds Apart

John would much rather have just skipped this painful process of good-byes and slipped off, but there was still one more person he must not neglect to speak to before boarding the train. His arm was around his mother's shoulders, but his eyes were scanning the bustling platform. There she was. He could see her forest green bonnet bobbing as she wedged her way through the crowd.

John was especially dreading this farewell. There were so many things he had intended to say to Elizabeth during his visit, but he had not. Now there was no more time.

All the way to the station, Elizabeth had been willing herself not to cry. But now that she was standing in front of him, gazing up at his tall form for what was perhaps the last time, she felt her resolve falter. She pressed her lips together and stared hard at the scuffed toe of her old, brown shoe, until her naturally strong spirit reasserted itself and she was able to look up with a clear face.

"I'm sorry to rush up at the last minute like this," she apologized. "But father insisted the cows must be milked first, and then I spent forever squeezing through this crowd."

"It's alright." John's voice was reassuring as he took both her hands, but there was something distant in his gray eyes today. "Don't be sad," he said. "How many times have I left and always come back?"

"I know. But just promise me one thing, John, promise that this time you will come back, that you'll come back to me."

John knew her meaning. She was asking for an assurance of more than just his return, but his only response was to squeeze her hands and drop a light kiss on her cheek. One last hug to his mother, and then there was no more time. He jumped onto the train just as it started to move. He stayed in the doorway for a moment, hanging onto the railing as he waved to the rapidly shrinking forms of his parents, his two young brothers, Curtis and Lawrence, and Elizabeth.

The ten days he just spent with them had flown by unbelievably fast, and now he was on his way back to the army again. John had joined the Union cavalry at the outset of the war, and now in early May of 1864, he had just made the rank of 2nd lieutenant and been given leave to return to Maryland for a visit with his loved ones.

As they disappeared from sight, he found his way to a seat. Shoving his hand into his pocket, John drew out a plain silver ring. On the inside of the band was neatly etched the phrase, "semper fidelis". What was wrong with him? When he had stepped off the train ten days ago, he fully intended this ring would reside on Elizabeth's finger by the time of his departure, yet here he was leaving with the words still unsaid.

He marveled at his own hesitancy. It wasn't that he had found fault with Elizabeth, nor was it due to any natural shyness on his part. It was just that horrible, nagging thought, insisting he had no right to make a promise to a woman, when he had no certainty he would be able to keep it. Woman wanted promises—security.

He loved Elizabeth, or at least he thought he did. He had known her from infancy. There was no one else he would rather make a promise to, but who knew what the future held? During the three years which he had served, he had seen plenty of heavy fighting and hundreds, thousands of men had died. He had been fortunate so far, but what were the odds that would continue? He would have liked to simply get engaged, enjoy the time he had with her, and not think about the future. But John was just too conscientious to ignore the all too real possibility he might not return.

He sighed as he watched the light shine off the smooth edge of the ring he held in his open palm. Elizabeth's words rang in his head to the same monotonous rhythm of the train. "Just promise me one thing, John, promise me that this time you will come back, that you'll come back to me." And now as then, he had no answer.

In Washington John switched trains and headed south. As he walked down the aisle searching for a vacant seat, his face suddenly lit up at the sight of the young man vigorously waving to him.

"Arthur Connly, I'll be a flying mule. What are you doing here?"

"I got leave same as you." The young man flashed him one of his contagious smiles.

"I thought you said you lived in southern Kentucky."

Connly laughed and his dark eyes laughed with him. "I do, and what do you know, they're sending me from southern Kentucky to southern Virginia by way of Washington. There's nothing like a little sight seeing."

John had met Connly only a few months before, when they were both sergeants, but it hadn't taken long at all before they felt as if they had known one another their entire lives. John paused for a moment to look at his friend before he sat down. There was something about Connly which was absolutely magnetic.

He was small and wiry with thick, black hair, deeply suntanned face, and eyes sparkling with life and mischief. At only eighteen years of age, he was still a little wet behind the ears, and John fully enjoyed the admiring way the younger man looked up to him. But whatever Connly lacked in experience he made up for in enthusiasm. John settled down to enjoy the rest of the trip, knowing he would have no more time for troublesome reflections.

"So what do you think they have in mind for us when we get to Virginia?" Connly was asking. "We're meeting up with Grant's army, aren't we?"

John nodded. "But I doubt we'll stay there. Since we're cavalry, they'll most likely dispatch us on over to Sheridan."

"I hope I get a chance to meet Grant," Connly said eagerly.

"Ahh, he's not that much to look at," John said with a dismissive wave of his hand. "So small, something like yourself," he added and laughed at the reproachful look he had known Connly would turn on him.

"Come on now, President Lincoln says he doesn't care how long a man's legs are, just so they can reach the ground," Connly objected.

When the men finally arrived at their destination, the train full of soldiers was met by Corporal Higgins, a short, retiring fellow, with almost the whole lower half of his face covered by an enormous drooping mustache. He escorted them to Grant's camp, where after a few days of inactivity, John was summoned to report to Grant himself.

Despite the disparaging words he had spoken to Connly, as John hurried to the small stone house the General was occupying as a temporary headquarters, his heart beat with anticipation at the thought of actually speaking face to face with the great general.

"Lieutenant Fairfield reporting, sir." John's posture was perfectly erect and his salute stiff as he greeted his superior.

"At ease, Lieutenant. I'll get right to business. There has been no end of comings and goings lately, and now it's been brought to my attention that a number of cavalry have arrived at our camp—two dozen, thirty, something like that. At present I'm not prepared to fully utilize your talents, and as you seem to be the only officer among them, I'm giving you the responsibility of leading the group over to join Sheridan and his men, where your time can be put to much more efficient use."

"Yes, sir."

"I have a small map for you here. It's not going to be easy traveling so close to Richmond. I've marked several spots where you may have interference, but move cautiously and be prepared for anything. That's all, sir." Grant acknowledged John's salute with a casual one of his own and turned his attention to other matters.

John's head spun as he left the house. This would be his first mission where he was the sole leader; everything must go perfectly.

*   *   *   *   *

Elsa glanced pensively at the dark mountain of ominous clouds looming in the western sky and threatening to at any moment bathe the landscape in torrential rains.

"Sparrow, we must hurry," she addressed her horse. "Why are you plodding along so slow today? Come on." Elsa reached back to give him a gentle slap on the rump. "Do you really want to arrive home soaked to the bone? When this rain comes, it's going to be fierce. What's this, a limp?" Elsa sighed. "If I could fix it I would, but Sparrow, you know what a terrible time I have digging stones out of your hoof. Just make it home and then Henry will take care of you."

This monologue hardly encouraged the horse, who slackened his pace and limped worse than before. Elsa pulled to the side of the road and dismounted. "Oh, no wonder you are limping," she exclaimed. "Your shoe is about to come clear off. It is barely hanging on by this one little nail."

Elsa stared up at the ever darkening sky, her brow creased in indecision. She was practically right outside the blacksmith's shop, and it would be easy enough to bring Sparrow in and have her shoe replaced. But a smithy was a distinctly masculine environment. She'd never gone there before. Well, that wasn't quite true. As a girl, back on the farm in Kentucky, she had gone practically everywhere with her father, blacksmith shops included.

But her father was dead now, and she was in Virginia living with her aunt, the great Madame Chesterfield. And refined, elegant young women did not go to the blacksmith. They had slaves to take care of such coarse matters. However, Elsa had privately wanted to meet the blacksmith for some time now, and if she didn't take this opportunity, she probably wouldn't get another. So with her heart beating at a ridiculously fast rate, she led Sparrow the short distance and entered the hot, dirty shop.

The smith's attention was occupied by two soldiers and their horses, so she stepped as much out of the way as possible and nervously waited for him to be done. Perhaps this was a mistake. She didn't belong here. Since the smith was busy anyway, she was almost ready to just exit as quietly as she had entered and lead Sparrow the rest of the way home, but before she had a chance to turn around, her thoughts were shattered by a loud crash of thunder. She glanced over her shoulder and saw a veritable river of rain streaking down. Well, that settled it; she had to stay.

She turned to study the smith as he worked. He was one of very, very few free black men in the state of Virginia, and although she had never met him and was sure he wouldn't know her from Eve, she looked at him as if he were a distant relative she had not yet met.

Elsa's mother had died from childbirth, leaving Elsa to be nursed and cared for by a black woman named Clara. Since Elsa's father was an abolitionist, who did not own slaves but rather had servants whom he treated as part of the family, she had never viewed Clara as anything but her mother. But now her father was gone, and the things which had happened to Clara were too dreadful to even think about. Haughty Aunt Ingrid, who was her closest blood relation, felt like anything but family, but Clara had a sister, Martha. They had kept in touch somewhat before—before *it* happened. A paralyzing fear slowly crept up Elsa's spine at the merest suggestion of *it*.

But she blinked hard and focused her thoughts. Several times, years ago, when business had brought her father to Virginia, she and Clara had accompanied him and managed to visit Martha, who was at the time a slave on the Winchester plantation. More recently she had tried to look Martha up, but she wasn't there anymore. Elsa wasn't quite sure why she wanted to find Martha so badly. Perhaps it was guilt, then again perhaps it was because she hoped if she could find Martha, it would somehow restore part of Clara to her. At any rate, if the rumors she heard were true, the man she was studying so intently was Martha's son. If anyone would know where Martha was, it would be he.

Everett Trenton was his name. He received his share of attention when it came to town gossip. The men of the town tolerated his presence much as they tolerated bitter medicine when sick or a scratchy scarf when the north wind blew. For while Elsa had heard nearly every other aspect of his personality and person discussed, she had never heard his ability as a smith to be in the least disputed.

It was said that no one in the state, perhaps in the whole Confederacy even, could swing a stronger or swifter blow. There was no other smith in their town and no one wanted to haul their broken implements to the half-drunken smith in the next village. Besides, they could pay Everett a fraction of what they would pay a white man, and he had no choice but to take it.

At present she could see only a profile of his face, but she could still find the resemblance to Clara that she was searching for. His skin wasn't nearly as dark as Clara's had been, but the nose was the same. Clara had not been a petite woman, and she decided that must also be a family trait. He was probably the largest man she had ever seen, about 6' 4", very broad shoulders and highly developed muscles. His hair was black and curly but not as wooly as most Africans she had seen. It had some gloss to it, or was it just the sweat which was glistening over his entire body?

Watching him work, it was easy to believe the stories she had heard about him—like the one about the traveling fair that came to town. Among the other spectacles provided for the onlookers entertainment, was a champion wrestler with an open invitation to any who dared challenge him. Some of the men had convinced Everrett to come and wrestler this huge brute of a man, hoping to win the bets they placed on him. They were not disappointed. Everrett soundly beat his opponent in no more than three minutes.

The professional was so chagrined that he wanted to challenge Everrett again and again until he won, however, Everrett had firmly refused to fight anymore unless he was paid handsomely. Knowing that the amount they stood to win with their bets on him and the fun they would derive from watching it, was significant, they had given him what he asked. Everyone went away very happy that day, except of course for the fair's champion, for he did not win once, and by evening no one would put their money on him.

Elsa didn't realize how intently she was staring at Everrett until she smelled a foul breath, reeking with whiskey, offensively close to her neck. She pulled back and found herself staring into the grizzled beard of one of the Confederate soldiers who had entered the shop prior to her. She gave a small gasp, and soon the eyes of all three men in the shop were turned towards her. She felt her face growing hot and no doubt very pink.

"Come on, leave the lady alone. You think she's got any interest in a soot bag like you?" the other soldier scolded his companion, but Elsa could see the same greedy leer in both their eyes. Instinctively she turned away, and her eyes met those of the blacksmith's. He was also staring at her, but she couldn't interpret his look. Both his face and eyes remained deeply expressionless. His stare was intense, but it said nothing—at least nothing she could understand.

The intoxicated soldier next to her reached out and touched her cheek. "You sure do got the prettiest eyes," he drooled.

Elsa shuddered.

"Here, here now." Everrett grasped the man's shoulders and roughly pulled him back. "You's think a dirty scoundrel like youhself can go touchin' any lady he wants? I's finished with youh damn horses. Pay up and git on youh way."

Elsa had never before heard an African use such a commanding tone with a white man, and there was something exciting about watching someone with such obvious disregard for etiquette, not to mention the fact that he had sworn in front of a woman.

The drunken man seemed equally impressed, whether by Everrett's tone or the strength of his sinewy brown arm, she couldn't tell. As the soldiers left and Everrett turned his attention to her, she felt suddenly embarrassed for having been the cause of such a scene. After all, she didn't belong here. But the smith didn't seem to care as he blandly said, "What kin I's do foh you today, Madame?"

"It is only a small matter. My horse's shoe has come off, and I knew I could not hope to make it home before the storm broke."

"De rain will bey oveh ifen you's wait ten minutes," he answered as he bent to examine the hoof.

Elsa stood to the side, keeping out of the way as he worked. Repeatedly she had words on the tip of her tongue, but her mouth stuck shut and she couldn't begin. Soon Everrett was finished and she was paying him. If she wanted to talk to him, it was now or never.

"May-may I ask you something?" she asked nervously.

Everrett made a sort of a nod-shrug combination gesture.

"Well, it is about your mother, Martha." At the mention of his mother, his expression became more attentive but not more approachable. "She-she had a sister named Clara, did she not?" Elsa went on.

He merely nodded. Elsa was already nervous, and he certainly wasn't making it any easier. But she had started and might as well continue. "Well, Clara was my mammy," she said quickly.

"Clara was youh mammy? I's don't think so." Elsa wasn't sure if the look he was giving her was incredulity or amusement.

"Well, that is what I called her. I don't mean that she was my actual mother, but we were very close, and now she is gone, and I knew Martha used to live in this town. So I have been—been looking for her. And I thought perhaps you might know where she is."

"Shey lives with me," he said slowly.

"Does she really? Might I come and visit her?" Elsa looked down. Why did Everrett Trenton persist in giving her that look which made her feel like an idiot for asking such a thing?

"Shey is ailing much."

"If she is unwell, that is all the more reason why I would like to see her. Perhaps I can help make her more comfortable. Clara and I used to visit her together, years ago, and I feel certain she would be glad to see me again."

"I's still don't see why, but mammy likes folks." The way he said it made it clear that Martha was the only member of the household who "liked folks." "Ifen it makes you's happy to do charity work foh us poor Negroes, I's reckon we should bey obliged."

His tone was so cold. Unless her memory failed her, Martha had been one of the warmest, sweetest women ever. Elsa didn't know quite what she had expected her son to be like, but not like this. "Where do you and Martha live?" she asked hesitantly.

"Yeah, I's reckon you's kinda need to know dat ifen you wants to visit heh," the blacksmith consented. "But I's don't like to tell folks where I's live."

"I won't tell anyone. I promise." He looked at her without answering, and Elsa decided that approaching him had been the worst idea she had in a long time. "It is alright. I—I should not have presumed to ask you. I will leave you alone." Elsa turned towards Sparrow.

"Wait," he stopped her, "Mammy would like a visitor." And he proceeded to give her rather vague directions to his cabin.

"Thank you," Elsa said when he was finished. She took Sparrow's reins, as he handed them to her, and tried to think of something nice and generally friendly to say in parting. "I am glad that I had the opportunity to meet you. I have heard a lot about you," she said at last.

13

"I's heard a lot about you too, Miss Elsa Grey."

She turned to look at him in surprise. She hadn't really introduced herself, yet he knew her name and apparently a good deal more. "What have you heard?" she asked curiously.

"Mostly how pretty you was. Dere's plenty of men in dis town as would like to s-court you." He almost said, "sleep with you", for he certainly had heard enough men make jests to that effect, but caught himself just in time.

Elsa blushed. "Well, if that is true, I think my reputation exceeds me by far."

When Elsa reached home, Henry was waiting for her at the gate.

"Der you is, Miss Elsa. De Madame is waitin' foh you. Shey ain't none to happy about it neither."

"Aunt Ingrid is waiting for me? I did not realize she had plans for the evening. Do you know what it is all about, Henry?"

"De Missus is in mournin' foh heh dead," he replied gravely. "And de way shey's been actin', de rest ob us ahe wishin' we was dead too."

"Oh, dear." Elsa put her hand over her eyes for a second. "I forget. It has been one year today since Uncle Albert died. I must go."

"I's suhe don't envy you," Henry said under his breath as he watched her rush towards the house.

Elsa entered the drawing room quietly. Her aunt was dressed in black silk and seated upon one of the elegant settees facing the doorway.

"Good evening, Aunt Ingrid," Elsa ventured somewhat cautiously.

"Good evening, Elsa," Ingrid replied with the cold politeness characteristic of their relationship. "You are late. I had so wanted you to accompany me as I laid flowers on the memorial to our honored dead." Ingrid wiped her eyes with the corner of her black handkerchief. "I expected you home from the Wilson's nearly an hour ago."

"I beg your pardon, Aunt. I was detained by the rain, but certainly I will go with you now. I know the pain of losing one very dear," she added softly.

"You can not know my pain," Ingrid objected. "Your father's death, lamentable though it was, was merely retribution for a life disgracefully squandered. Your only duty is to forget, and by filling your life and heart with people of a higher nature, you may find happiness. But I can never cease to mourn for my husband who gave his life so honorably for the cause we cherished. My grief and my duty are one."

Elsa's only response was the hurt which shone in her eyes as she lowered them to the floor. By now she had grown used to her aunt's caustic remarks, but they never ceased to hurt. It had been well over three years since her father's tragic death, but the wound had not even begun to heal as it was continually opened afresh by Ingrid's harsh censure.

Ingrid Chesterfield was the picture of propriety and elegance, but even in her younger days she had never been a handsome or charming woman, so when in her early forties her hand had been asked for by the refined Sir Albert, she accepted with the greatest pleasure her rigid rules of conduct allowed. After only several years of matrimony, he had dutifully given his life for the cause of the Confederacy. The grief had a most embittering effect upon Ingrid, and she found refuge from her own pain by scorning Elsa's. Elsa, the daughter of an envied and shunned younger sister, seemed at times the symbol of all she stood against.

"Well, do not just stand there like a statue," Ingrid snapped. "Go change your dress into something befitting this solemn occasion, and we will go to the garden together as an aunt and a niece ought to."

Elsa obediently turned and headed up the stairs.

The Worlds Meet

Early on the morning of May 7th, John set out with his group of thirty-one men, consisting of Sergeant Connly, Corporal Higgins and 29 cavalry dragoons. Taking the responsibility of his new authority seriously, he moved his men with perhaps more than necessary caution, keeping to narrow, seldom used country roads and sending out scouts frequently to check the safety of the region.

As they set up camp in a secluded clearing in the woods at the end of their first day, Connly remarked, "If every day be like this, we'll go home with no scars yet. I mean, talk about a boring day. Could things have been any duller?"

John smiled as he shook his head. "Suits me, Connly. I can be grateful all my men aren't wishing ill luck upon us, or we might not get home at all."

The next day passed with the same liturgical quality until late afternoon, after they had been following a winding, trail through the woods for such a long time that John began to grow uncertain of their position. He called his men to a halt and was about to send out some more scouts, when Higgins stopped him with a hand on his arm.

"Excuse me, sir, but I think someone is coming down the trail towards us."

John held up his hand to silence his men and listened intently. He nodded at Higgins. "It's only one horse. We don't have time to hide, so if it's an enemy we'll just have to shoot him," John said slowly, drawing his pistol as he spoke. Connly and the corporal followed suit.

"What if it's a woman?" Connly whispered.

"Let's hope it isn't," John whispered back, annoyed at the all too real possibility of such an uncomfortable situation.

"Or a child?" Higgins added.

John put his finger to his lips as a tall, powerfully built, black man on a black horse rounded the bend in the path and reined in quickly at the sight of three pistols menacingly aimed in his direction. Higgins sighed with relief that it was not a foe, John sighed with relief that it was not a woman or child, and Connly merely sighed as he somewhat reluctantly lowered his pistol.

"Greetings. Can you give us some directions?" John asked as he rode forward to meet the intruder.

"Greetin's? Dis suhe is some strange way of greetin', with three pistols pointin' at me jest like you was havin' a shootin' match and I's de target."

"My apologies," John said. "We're on our way to Sheridan's camp and, I'm afraid, completely boggled by the labyrinth of trails running through this woods."

"Good thing foh you dat you's met me jest now. Less dan one mohe mile de way you is goin' and you's gonna come right up alongside de Chesterfield plantation. And dis is a mighty poor night foh dat, on account ob dere's a big, old troop of rebels campin' dere tonight."

John's look did nothing to hide how startled he was. "Well, that's the first I heard of them."

"Oh, they's jest passin' through, undeh de command of a Captain Aldridge. But wheneveh dere's a rebel officer so much as in sight, Madame Chesterfield has to have dem up to heh great house and treat dem like kings," the black man explained.

John was thinking fast as he listened. This might be just the opportunity to prove himself a valuable officer. "We are obliged to you for the warning," he said. "But now that you've informed us, it might not be such a bad thing at all. Do they have many supply wagons with them?"

"Suhe thing."

"And how familiar are you with the area?" John continued. "Do you have any idea where Sheridan's camp is in relation to here?"

The black man nodded. "I's keep up on things. I's could take you dere myself ifen you's wanted."

"Oh, that is a generous offer and would save us a good deal of time, but I can't let you risk the trouble you might get into with your master."

"I's Everrett Trenton, and I's ain't got no master but myself," he said firmly.

John wasn't sure if he believed Everrett or not, but he didn't have time to worry about that now. Turning to Sergeant Connly, John asked, "What do you say we pay a little visit to the rebel camp? We can tear through, setting fire to the supply wagons, while Everett Trenton here can wait at some set spot, assuming he's willing, and then with him as our guide, we'll all set out at top speed and arrive at Sheridan's camp yet tonight."

"Yes, sir!" Connly's eyes flashed with tense excitement.

Fifteen minutes passed as the men discussed the idea and came up with a working plan. At the conclusion of their rendezvous, the soldiers broke into several small groups and retired into the woods to wait until nightfall.

It was during the afternoon of this same day, that Elsa paid her intended visit to Martha. She followed Everrett's imprecise directions with considerable difficulty, but finally arrived at a small two room cabin deep in the middle of the woods just north of town.

As she knocked hesitantly, a voice inside immediately beckoned her to enter. She stepped into the dim room and saw a bed in the corner, with a woman eagerly motioning her forward.

"Everrett said you was gonna come, but I's didn't know you's really would. Come oveh, Miss Elsa, and let me see ifen you's real or just my tired mind playin' tricks on me again. You's would bey surprised all de folks dat come visit me, but dere all up here." She tapped her wrinkled forehead with one finger.

Elsa stepped over to the bed, smiling at the enthusiastic welcome. But as she regarded the withered form before her, she saw Everrett had been correct with his diagnosis that she was "ailing much", her body aged far beyond her years from the hard toil and meager diet of a slave. Martha reached out and Elsa took her bony hand. "You remember me then? You remember Clara and I visiting you?"

"Of course, I's remember. A beautiful face like yours, I's would neveh fohget. And dose dresses you and Clara gave me, I's still habe dem. I's worn dem all dese years."

"I have looked for you ever since I moved down here, shortly after the war began, but I couldn't find you until now. I am so glad to see you have your freedom. Tell me, how did it happen?"

"Sit down." Martha patted the edge of the bed. "Everrett bought me." There was pride in her voice. "He's sech a fine son. What a big, strappin' man he's grown into."

Elsa smiled slightly. "He is that alright."

"So he fights dese men at de fair." Martha's voice betrayed how eager she was to tell the story. "And dey pays ifen he wins, and he made so much money dat he comes oveh to de plantation and says, 'I's come to buy my mammy,' jest like dat."

"I'm glad to hear you have such a devoted son."

"Hey is at dat." Martha's eyes were glistening. "You's know he's well nigh seven and twenty and got no wife? I's told him to buy hisself a young woman he's could marry, but hey wouldn't buy no one but me."

"Well, you deserved it. I am quite curious though, how did Everrett come to be free?"

"Clara didn't tell you's about dat?" Martha looked startled. "Where is Clara anyhows? I's suhe would like to see heh again."

"Me too." Elsa said sadly. "But she is gone. The consumption took her." Elsa's face grew hot and her heart heavy as she said the words, but there was no way she could tell Martha the truth. She tried to not even say it to herself.

"Oh, I's so sad to hear it." Martha was quiet for a minute but then brightened up. "Youh fatheh, is he well?"

Elsa shook her head. "The consumption took him too. That is why I had to move down here and live with my aunt." If Martha had not been almost blind, there was no way she could have missed the horrible remorse in Elsa's eyes, for if Elsa was anything, it was a bad liar.

When Elsa had first come, Ingrid had concocted the tale that everyone from Elsa's household had died in a fire and insisted that Elsa give that as an explanation to all who asked. But Elsa thought that if someone was to devise an imaginary fate for their loved ones, it should at least be slightly less horrifying than burning to death, so she had decided upon consumption. Ingrid had agreed, and from that day to this neither of them had so much as breathed a word otherwise. The lie got easier with the telling, but it didn't make the truth any less painful.

Eager to change the subject, Elsa asked, "So what about your son? How did he get his freedom?"

"Do you's know who his fatheh is?" Martha asked.

Elsa shook her head.

"His fatheh is de owneh of de Winchester plantation," the older woman stated matter-of-factly.

"Your former master?" Elsa asked, and then as the truth dawned on her went on, "Oh, I am so sorry. I would not have brought up the subject if I had known."

"For heaven's sake, child, you's act like you's neveh heard of sech a thing afore. It happens well nigh every plantation. Only dis time was different. Somebody convinced him it weren't seemly to be havin' his own son foh a slave, even though dat's common 'nough too. So he indentured Everrett to a man over on de otheh side of town, and he had to serve same as everybody else, till he was one and twenty, but den he's worked off his indentures and goes free, jest like dat."

Elsa wasn't sure whether the situation Martha had just described called for sadness or happiness, so she made no comment, but she could tell the frail woman was getting worn out from all the excitement. "Just relax a minute and catch your breath," she said, patting Martha's hand.

Martha closed her eyes for a second. "I's so glad you came to see me. I's happy with my life now, but I's do get powehful lonely."

"I know how that is. I have been terribly lonely myself since I lost Clara and my father. I'll come often if you like."

Elsa jumped as the door banged open. She turned just in time to see Everrett enter.

Everrett had been on his way home from the forge when he ran into the dragoons in the woods. As he rode the rest of the way, his mind had been whirling with thoughts. Perhaps for once the color of his skin was not a complete curse. As a blacksmith, he crossed paths with enough men each day to keep himself well informed on the current news, but as a dark man he also knew the secret trails and woodland paths frequented by the people of his race—something none of the other townsmen did. He was uniquely suited to assist John in his mission, and it made an invigorating, but very unfamiliar, thrill tingle up his spine.

Life had not been easy for Everrett. He certainly didn't fit in with any of his peers, if he even dare call them that, and even as a slave he had never belonged. There was always the knowledge that he would someday be free, and despite the hope this gave him, it had caused the others to look on him with a covetous admiration. Only once had he had a brief respite from the continual turmoil surrounding him. Shortly after he was freed, he had been taken in and spent a year with the Quakers. Their beliefs in equality had caused them to treat him with great kindness, and it was one of their number who had apprenticed him as a blacksmith.

Yet even there he had not fit in. He was not at all cut out for their quiet way of life, and too proud to leech off their generosity, he had left as suddenly as he had come. The next years had been ones of hard work, trying to make a home, first for himself and then his mother. His naturally stalwart personality had been made more so by the incessant struggle. He had always had to work twice as hard as a white man to accomplish half as much, but it had made him the best. He was stronger, faster, and tougher than any two of them put together, and they knew it. This was one of the very few things in his life which brought him any pleasure.

As he approached his cabin, he noticed the solid brown horse tied in the yard and immediately recognized it as the one Elsa had brought to him several days earlier. So she had come as she said. Although he knew his mother was glad of whatever company she could get, he felt annoyed. After all, it was her aunt's plantation where their raid was to take place tonight, and it was quite awkward to have her around. All he wanted to do was relax a little and prepare for his evening's adventures.

gracious, it must be later than I thought," Elsa exclaimed 'Martha dear, I must go."

"... ... you's come again?" Martha relinquished her hand reluctantly.

"Yes, of course, just like I said."

Everett stepped back outside and brought Sparrow over to the door.

"Thank you. It is very considerate for you to get my horse for me, although you needn't have bothered. I do not wish to cause you any inconvenience," Elsa said as she mounted.

"So why is you in sech a rush to leave?" Everett asked. Although he wanted her gone, he figured that as long as she was going to invade his privacy, he might as well ask her a few nosy questions of his own. Besides, he didn't trust her. Elsa might appear guileless, but no doubt there was some sinister ulterior motive for her pretended concern for his mother.

"I just did not realize how late it was until you came," she answered. "My aunt is having soldiers up to the house tonight, and she is probably quite vexed by now that I am late from work."

"You work?" This was something he had not expected.

"My aunt has allowed me to tutor the Wilson children. I like to feel as if I am doing something at least slightly useful with myself. Although if I do not hurry home, she probably will not allow me to do so much longer."

"You's sound as if you's afraid of youh aunt."

"She is a rather intimidating woman, and I seem to have an uncanny ability to displease her."

"Why does youh aunt care if you's are late?"

"Aunt Ingrid likes very much to be in charge of things, and I fear that is what I am to her—a thing to be in charge of."

The answers Elsa was giving to his questions were not at all what he had anticipated, but the surprise did not register on his face. Everett was staring at her the same way he had in the forge, and it was beginning to make her nervous—that intent gaze which said absolutely nothing, yet seemed to be reading her thoughts.

"I really must go. I trust you will have a pleasant evening." With a click to Sparrow, Elsa sped off.

Everett watched her disappear and whispered to himself, "I's will have a pleasant evenin', just you's wait and see."

*   *   *   *   *

John's heart pounded as he rode from under the cover of the thicket. A quick glance to his left assured him Conlly and his men were in readiness. He turned to his right but could see nothing in the darkness. Then the bulky outline of a horse emerged from the trees. Good, Higgins and his men were there; everyone was on time. The lieutenant drew a deep breath and set his lips. As long as their dark assistant proved reliable, he was confident of success. No fear was necessary on that account, for Everrett had been there well ahead of them, and from his hiding place in the bushes was watching their every move.

John hastily lit the torch in his hand. The most hazardous part of the venture was a small field that must be crossed before reaching their desired objective. Lighting their torches before crossing more than doubled the risk, but the horses made stealth impossible anyway, while the thought of a score of men all trying to light their torches while on the very brink of the enemy camp, was so impractical that it had decided all of them in favor of the afore said method. But once the torches were lit, there was not a moment to be lost. As soon as the two men behind John had lit their torches off his, he spurred his horse hard and tore off across the field. He did not need to look to know that Connly and Higgins were following suit.

As Everrett caught the flicker from the first torch, he crawled from his hiding place and ran to fetch his horse, Charcoal, knowing that their lightening style raid may be accomplished in a matter of minutes. As the soldiers reached the camp, they began to hurl their torches at anything flammable, especially targeting the conspicuous supply wagons.

When the dragoons had started to cross the field, a picket had cried an alarm, and now while the lieutenant's men galloped through dispersing their lurid destruction, complete bedlam reigned as sleepy men scrambled from their tents and tried to grasp the situation. Amidst the havoc shots rang wildly through the air.

John took a particular interest in several large wagons on the far side of the camp and rushed towards them. Suddenly a sharp pain shot through his left arm as his pistol fell from his grasp. If he had looked down, he would have seen the dark red stain seeping through his coat, but he did not look, and the adrenaline surging though him overwhelmed the pain. Undeterred, he continued to race for the wagons, his speed hampered by his disabled arm, for it was with difficulty that he controlled his horse. Many of his men, who had already spent their torches, were collecting on the west side of the camp. In just another moment they would be tearing down the road after their guide.

Reaching the wagons, John raised his right arm high in the air and hurled his flaming brand into the opening of the largest wagon. A terrible explosion ensued. John never knew just what happened, but he saw a mountain of flames, felt a violent pain in his chest right below the left shoulder, his horse bucked, and he flew through the air. When he landed, it was in the midst of a large pile of bushes. For a moment he was aware of nothing but intense pain and awful noise. Then even that began to fade as John slipped into unconsciousness.

A Troubled Night

"Niece, must you be so everlastingly late?" Ingrid greeted Elsa in a low tone as she hesitantly entered the drawing room where Ingrid was entertaining a half dozen officers.

"The fault is mine, Aunt," Elsa responded meekly, without attempting an explanation. "I beg your indulgence."

"We will discuss this later," Ingrid said curtly as she swept her glance up and down over Elsa. "I am glad to see you have dressed well for the occasion," Ingrid went on in a somewhat more affable tone. "I will assume that you did so realizing just who is here tonight—Captain Aldridge." Elsa flushed in response to Ingrid's meaningful smile.

As she glanced about the room, Elsa saw that Ingrid did consider this evening to be of more than ordinary significance. Besides the officers, several prominent members of society had also been invited—Judge Livingston and his more than plump wife, haughty Mrs. Deveraux with her bright red dress, long skinny arms, and thin pursed lips, and the Reverend and Mrs. Buchanan. Ingrid loved to maintain her reputation for stunning hospitality.

Roland, a handsome young slave, stood finely dressed behind a cart loaded with an array of expensive wines and liquors, which he was serving from cut crystal glasses while two maids in starched black dresses offered the guests dainty hors d'oeuvres from silver trays.

"Come," Ingrid took Elsa's arm as she led her into the middle of the room. "Gentlemen, allow me to present my niece, Miss Elsa Grey." Ingrid's voice was spiced with a piquant sort of exhibiting pride.

For some reason Elsa couldn't really understand, Ingrid had laid claim to Elsa's beauty to make up for what was lacking in her own, and it was very important to her that people take notice and talk about it. Ingrid even went so far as to make a point of not inviting other young women to most of her dinners and parties, so jealous was she that the attention of her guests be undivided. To this end, she also insisted that Elsa wear the most modern and revealing styles of the day.

Tonight Elsa had put on a dress she knew Ingrid particularly approved of: flowing emerald green satin, cut low enough to reveal all of her snowy white shoulders and just enough cleavage to pique the onlookers curiosity for what lay beneath. Although the way Ingrid exhibited her was embarrassing at times, Elsa was glad that at least she was good for something in her aunt's eyes.

She politely greeted the men as Ingrid introduced them. A light touch on her elbow, drew her attention and she turned to look up into the deep blue eyes of Captain Aldridge. "You look lovely tonight, Miss Grey."

Ingrid smiled in satisfaction while Elsa tried not to blush as she demurely gave him her hand to kiss, for she knew Ingrid's pride in her was not unfounded. Elsa was lovely. She was slender and petite, yet with a full supply of womanly curves. She had small, delicate hands and shiny, soft brunette hair. Her teeth where uncommonly straight, her lashes long and dark, but the most remarkable aspect of Elsa's features, was her eyes. They truly were the windows into her soul, for nearly every emotion she felt was written in them as their color and brightness changed with her moods, sometimes pale blue, soft gray, or flecked with green sparkles.

Aldridge kissed her gloved hand but did not release it afterwards. "Come, will you not honor me with your presence and sit with me by the window?"

Elsa knew the question was rhetorical, so she quietly let him lead her to a seat. Ingrid watched them go and remarked to the lieutenant standing next to her, "They make a perfect pair, do they not?"

The lieutenant, having had the unfortunate honor of serving under Aldridge, knew his character well enough to think him an unsuitable match for any delicate woman, but he assented that aesthetically they formed a pleasing picture, for Aldridge was a man not without beauty of his own. His features were formed with great precision and perfectly proportioned, as if he had been the work of a master carver. His hair was of such quality that from a distance it literally looked like waves of gold, and his neatly trimmed mustache was of the same sparkling blond. His eyes, very dark and very blue, made the perfect contrast to his fair features. He was the ideal specimen of the Arian race. And he knew it. Did he ever know it!

"I trust you are well this evening, Miss Grey, or might I take the liberty of calling you Elsa?"

"You may call me whatever you wish," she stated blandly. There really wasn't any need for him to bother to ask. She knew he would do as he pleased in any case.

"Well, now this is quite an offer. I must think on it while I fetch you a drink. What do you care for, my dear?"

"I am quite content with just water. It is the best for the constitution."

"Your constitution hardly needs any improvement. Allow me to bring you something more relaxing, perhaps some sherry."

"Well, a glass of sweet white wine might be nice."

"White wine it is."

Elsa watched him as he crossed the room to the beverage cart. Judging by the expression on Roland's face, he did not appreciate whatever Aldridge was saying to him. She knew better than to drink when with the captain, but what did it really matter?

Aldridge returned with the drinks and Elsa took a sip of hers. She was hungry and thirsty; Ingrid had not had time to plan a dinner for her guests, so had simply invited them for cocktails after dinner, and coming in as late as she had, Elsa had not had a chance to eat. The wine was cool and sweet, and she certainly would like a little relief from the stress she was presently feeling. She held the glass up to watch the light reflect off the beautiful crystal, and was tempted to drain it down as if it were a glass of water, but she restrained herself. Elsa was good at that, restraining herself. People generally thought her passionless, a flat paper doll in lovely dresses, but if they only knew what she restrained.

Aldridge's voice broke into her thoughts. He was leaning over her, arm resting on the back of the sofa, whiskey in hand. "I believe I have decided what name I shall a call you—my darling. Or sweetheart if you prefer," he continued since his first suggestion failed to elicit a response.

"Saying it would not make it true," she replied quietly.

"Oh, it might. Never underestimate the power of the spoken word."

"So if I were to call you a Negro, would that make it true?"

"My dear," he exclaimed. "What have I done to provoke such cruel words from so beautiful a mouth?"

"I meant you no offense, Captain. I am merely saying that one thing is not another."

"Why so cold, my darling? You know I would do anything for you?" He seated himself next to her, preparatory for a lengthy discussion.

"How does camp life agree with you? Having you been traveling much of late?" she asked to change the subject. At that moment several of the other officers came up, and not wanting to appear clumsy in the presence of his inferiors, or worse yet be the object of jesting on account of his inability to captivate the young lady, Aldridge immediately launched into an animated narrative on some insignificant aspects of camp life.

At the conclusion of his speech the other officers began to relate various pieces of trivia as they happened to come to mind, while Elsa politely smiled, nodded, and laughed just she knew her aunt would wish her too. Meanwhile, she entertained herself by trying to determine how much of what each man was saying was true by watching the faces of the other men as he spoke. Their was only one officer, an older gentleman, who she believed was being completely veracious, because no one in their right mind would contrives stories as boring as his.

After awhile someone suggested it would be nice to have some music, perhaps sing some of the popular patriotic songs of the day. Ingrid volunteered Elsa's talents at playing the violin, while Mrs. Reverend Buchanan accompanied her on the piano. Elsa eagerly welcomed the opportunity; she loved music. Songs were emotions come to life, and when she played songs of loss, such as *Lorena*, she found an outlet to pour all the forlorn, pent up longings of her soul into its plaintive melody. And heaven knew she had few enough such outlets.

Time flew by when she was playing, and soon the soldiers were thanking the ladies for a delightful evening and retiring to their tents. Finally everyone was gone except for Captain Aldridge, who was engaged in a deep conversation with Ingrid. Elsa picked up her still full glass of wine, for Aldridge had made sure that it was replenished throughout the evening, and stepped out onto the porch for a moment of silence and a breath of fresh air before the harangue which she felt sure Ingrid would deliver as soon as they were alone.

She leaned against one of the grand white pillars supporting the balcony overhead, and took in a deep breath of the cool air. After draining half the glass in her hand, she began to feel refreshed. Elsa gazed up admiringly into the sea of stars swimming in the clear sky and relaxed under the gentle touch of the night breeze playing with the curls around her face. Suddenly the tranquility of the moment was shattered by the light pressure of a hand on her shoulder.

She could tell by the scent of the heavy cologne, that is was Lester Aldridge.

"Are you trying to escape me?" he asked.

"Oh, I thought you had retired to camp with the rest of the officers."

"What, without saying goodnight? Darling, you have no idea how I look forward to the occasions when I get to see you, and they are so seldom. Yet now you treat me with such indifference—coldness even."

"As I said earlier, I mean you no offense, Captain."

"And as I said earlier, don't you know I would do anything for you?" The captain was evidently intent on picking up their conversation right where they left it, and Elsa knew it was useless to try to evade him. "Elsa, look at me," Aldridge slid an arm around her waist as he spoke. "With all my traveling I have met a lot of beautiful women. You are not the only beauty of the South."

"I labor under no such delusion."

"But darling, when I am alone, it is you who pervades my thoughts and haunts my dreams, your eyes I long to look into, your voice I yearn to hear, your smile I delight to see." He searched her face for some sign that his words were having their desired effect, and although it was dim, there was enough light to tell that the color was mounting in her cheeks. "Your touch I long, oh so passionately, to feel," he went on and smiled as he felt her stiffen.

How he loved playing with people's emotions, making them think and feel things they didn't want to. He might not at present have the power to make Elsa like him, but he could keep her from being indifferent, and in time the rest would come. He would make her so giddy and confused at the very sight of him, that soon she wouldn't know herself whether the emotions she felt were aversion or desire.

"And do you say the same to all of those beautiful women?"

He could hear an edge of anger in her tone, and his smile broadened at the thought of the conquest which would soon be his. "Of course not," he said innocently.

Elsa studied his face for a moment before responding, "I think you try to deceive me. I think you are a great ladies' man, and you love to flatter all of them."

"Darling, you might as well stab a bayonet into my heart, for so do your words cut me." He dropped the arm which was around her waist and turned away to grip onto the porch railing.

"Oh, Captain, I am sorry. I did not mean to hurt you." Elsa touched his arm lightly and he could hear the remorse in her voice. He felt a delicious little thrill of victory. He had not expected her to be this easy. Was he good or was he good?

"Then you do not hate me?" he asked, turning halfway to look at her, but not yet dropping his air of being offended.

"I do not hate you, Captain, I just fear we do not have much in common. In fact, I am certain we do not. I am sorry if that pains you, but I am powerless to change it. But as you yourself pointed out, there are many delightful women with whom you might find great accord. Do not trouble yourself over me."

Captain Aldridge stroked the back of his hand lightly over her cheek as he said quietly, "Oh, my dear beauty with the heart of ice, if only I could make you understand, a man may have an entire garden of flowers, but only one calls to him."

He bent forward to kiss her, but before their lips met Elsa jumped back with a scream, "Captain, look!" She was pointing frantically towards the camp.

Aldridge whirled around. "What the hell?!" he exclaimed. "There's a fire in the camp!"

"What has happened?" Elsa gasped.

"Confound it, how would I know? Go tell the others. We need water immediately," he commanded. Then springing nimbly over the porch rail, he dashed off.

Elsa ran breathlessly into the house, where her aunt was placidly waiting for her. "The camp is on water! Aldridge says they need fire," she cried.

"Whatever are you talking about? Fire for what?"

"There is a fire in the camp," Elsa said with forceful slowness as she collected herself.

"Mercy me! Awaken the Negroes," Ingrid shrieked.

Elsa dashed off to perform her aunt's bidding. The next several hours were a flurry of motion as the fires were extinguished and Aldridge tried, rather unsuccessfully, to restore order to his ravaged camp. Of course the perpetrators of the destructive deed were foremost in everyone's mind. The fact that a band of Union cavalry bore the blame was undisputed, since two caps were found to substantiate that supposition. However, the riders had swept through and left all in a matter of minutes, and due to the utter confusion of the moment, pursuit was impossible until it was too late.

A Daunting Discovery

Not anxious for any more discussions with the captain, Elsa remained upstairs the next morning, until certain the men had broken camp and moved out. Ingrid, also very fatigued from the night's excitement, woke with a headache which kept her in bed all the morning, so it was not until Elsa returned from the Wilson's in the early afternoon that she had occasion to speak with her. Prepared for a severe berating for her tardiness of the evening before, Elsa was quite surprised when Ingrid greeted her cordially and suggested they walk together in the garden.

"It was an evil shame that such a lovely evening should have been ruined by so inglorious an ending," Ingrid said with a dramatic sigh.

"Destruction and havoc are always a shame," Elsa said.

"But let us speak of more pleasant things. Before the evening was ruined, did you have a nice time with Captain Aldridge? He seems to delight in seeking your company."

"I regret to say I did not," Elsa answered laconically.

"That is cause for regret. Really, Elsa, you must learn better social graces in your relations with gentlemen if you do not wish to end up an old maid. Perhaps I can advise you. What went wrong?"

"He professes to care for me a great deal and to be pained when I do not return those sentiments. But if I encourage him in these fanciful notions, I only do him wrong, for if he were to come to truly know me, he would not only be bitterly disappointed, but no doubt quite angry as well."

"You ought not to talk so. He tells me you are the fairest blossom in the garden to him. But if you think there is aught in you which would displease him, why do you not fairly state the matter openly? What is there in you for which you fear his disapproval?"

"Of all people, I would think you would be the one to know, Aunt."

"Then why prevaricate? Just say it."

"Because I am not a Confederate," Elsa whispered. "If I were to say that to him, not only would it be very offensive, I would incur his anger upon myself, which I desperately wish to avoid."

"And his anger would be more than understandable. He is giving his all for our country, as are so many of us. How could he be anything but angry, were you to pour such contempt on him?"

"That is why I can not tell him. We both know that he is possessed of a temper which exceeds most in its hotness. The last thing in the world I want to do is to provoke it."

"You are being most unfair to him," Ingrid said severely. "He loves you, and yet you are too selfish to remove the one obstacle which stands in the way of your bringing him happiness. You would rather hurt him than give up your pride."

Elsa stared sadly down at the ground. She really did not mean to be a horrible person, yet no matter how hard she tried, she spent most of her days feeling like one.

"So why were you so late coming in last evening anyway?" Ingrid asked sharply.

"I do beg your pardon. The fault is all mine. I was visiting and became so engaged as to forget the hour. It was most thoughtless of me."

"Whom were you visiting?"

"Martha," Elsa replied in a low voice.

"I do not believe I am acquainted with her. Has she newly come into society?"

"She is Clara's sister."

"Clara?" Ingrid raised her stiff eyebrows in feigned confusion.

"You know whom I refer to—Clara, my nurse, the one who died

of…" Elsa paused and her voice was unusually sarcastic as she said the last word, "who died of—consumption."

"A Negress!" Ingrid exclaimed. "You are neglecting your obligations here because you are too busy making social calls to a Negress?"

Elsa's imploring eyes begged for understanding. "I consider her a friend."

"But why seek friends amongst her class? It is positively disgraceful. When your father died, I hoped it was not too late for you to mature beyond him and grow into a refined woman of dignity and grace. Have I not given you every opportunity to better yourself? But instead you cling to these sentimental attachments of your childhood with an almost distracted absurdity."

"She is a sick, dying old woman. Is there any harm in bringing a bit of comfort to her last days? Somehow I hope I can make up for—for what I couldn't do for…" Elsa's voice trailed off and she turned away.

"Oh, Elsa, not that again. Clara is gone. You can not bring her back anymore than you can bring your father back."

"You don't know that!" Elsa exclaimed. "We know my father is in his grave. We do not know that of Clara. She may be out there somewhere, waiting, wondering why I don't come to her."

"Elsa, be silent!" Ingrid's voice was harsh. "Clara is dead. She died of consumption as did your father."

"You know that's a lie," Elsa began, but Ingrid silenced her with a stinging slap across the face.

"Hold your tongue. I will never have you speak to me of this again."

Elsa turned away with tears in her eyes, and for a long moment there was no sound but the gentle hum of a bee nuzzling the sweet peas beside them. Finally Ingrid placed her hand on Elsa's shoulder and turned her around.

"I did not mean to strike you, niece, but you know how it incites me when you speak of such things. However, if it brings you peace of mind to help this wretched old woman, I will not forbid you. But see to it that it does not interfere with your duties here. I only hope that when she is gone, you will be free from this childish fancy with the past, which so consumes your life. If only you could see that it does not have to be this way. Get involved in social life; be bright and gay; make friends in the higher classes. Improve your self; improve your life; cultivate your talents. Then this gloom will pass. Are you listening to me, Elsa?"

"I am listening. And all those things I have tried to do, but I fear I am too hopelessly sad and lonely to ever be bright and gay."

Ingrid sighed. "And that is why you need a strong, determined man like the Captain. I have tried to help you, Elsa, but you refuse my help. Perhaps he will succeed where I have failed. Believe me, Elsa, if you would just relinquish these horrible conjectures you allow to dominate you and give him, or someone like him, half a chance into your ice-enclosed heart, you would be so much happier. I will leave you now to think about what I have said. I am having some ladies over for tea at four. Try not to be late."

As her aunt departed, Elsa sat down on the grass beneath one of the large maples beside her and allowed herself to be mesmerized as her eyes followed the ever changing patterns of shade and light filtering through the leaves. This was now twice in twenty-four hours she had been judged to have a heart of ice. If only that were true, she would not feel this pain. Ingrid was right about one thing though, she was dominated by the past. But was there any power in the world, human or otherwise, that could free her from that? She doubted it.

Finally her tired mind began to clear, and she stood up and wandered aimlessly. Coming to the field where the soldiers had camped the previous night, her listlessness lifted a little as she examined the marks of destruction left behind: large circles of black grass, the charred remains of several great wagons, and a wide array of burnt and broken paraphernalia scattered everywhere.

Her attention was drawn by dark streaks of dried blood, staining the leaves on a clump of vine-covered bushes. She slowly pulled aside one of the branches to see how far down the blood had run, and drew back quickly as she thought she saw the outline of a face below her. She stood frozen for a minute, but she must know. Elsa ran to the other side of the shrubs, where they grew less dense, and getting down on her hands and knees, scrabbled her way through the poky branches.

And there he was, a navy blue clad man, lying on his back, his limbs strangely bent around the branches containing him. Elsa stared in petrified consternation, her wide eyes transfixed on the bloody form before her. As she watched, there was a slight heave of his chest. She gasped, as she quickly began to break away the branches between them. She had not stumbled onto a corpse as she first thought. This dreadful, gray-faced man, looking like death itself, was still alive.

She examined him as carefully as she could without touching him. The source of the blood seemed to be from but two wounds, one in the left arm and the other just below the left shoulder. There was no fresh blood, only a sticky, half-dried mess, gluing his uniform to him. She carefully broke away some of the branches holding him in his awkward position until he was laid out more normally.

Her first thought was to obtain assistance from some of the slaves. But should it ever be discovered, they, not her, would bear the punishment. She knew she could never forgive herself were she to bring down Ingrid's wrath upon them. It was too much of a risk. If anyone was to help this man it must be she, and she alone. Elsa shuddered at the thought of such an overwhelming responsibility. For a moment she wished she had not found him. He would most likely die in any case, and now she would feel responsible for having not been able to prevent it. But she had to try.

Creeping out of the bushes, she looked warily around. No one was in sight. She ran to the house but stopped at the door and entered sedately. All was quiet inside. She headed up to her room, pausing outside Ingrid's door just long enough to hear her scolding the maid inside. She collected scissors, soap, and clean cloths as hastily as she could, placing the items inside her empty wash basin. She peeked into the hall to ensure it was still deserted and hurried down and out a side door, clutching her wash basin of supplies and empty pitcher.

Once clear of the house, she ran out to the old well behind the stables. Her hands were trembling so badly it was all she could do to haul up the full bucket of water. When she arrived back at the bushes, she found the man just as she had left him. She knelt in front of him for a few minutes, unsure how to proceed. Her heart was beating so hard, she thought it was about to take wings and fly from her chest. Her medical knowledge was limited, but she knew that his wounds must be cleansed and snuggly

36

bandaged, so after several long, deep breaths, she gritted her teeth and set to the task before her.

Her guess was that the wound on his arm had been caused by a bullet flying past and ripping open a wide gash. But the bone remained untouched, and there was definitely not a bullet lodged in the flesh. As far as she knew, this was all good news.

Next, she moved on to his chest. As she slowly pulled back the front of his jacket, her stomach wrenched, and she turned away and vomited into the bushes as far away from his head as she could manage. Almost his entire chest was bruised, while a large area on the left side had been deeply torn into jagged, little strips like a frayed rug. His raw, swollen flesh was pierced with many slivers of wood, and now that she had removed the front of his jacket, began to ooze with fresh blood. For a full fifteen minutes she hovered over him, painstakingly removing as many splinters as she could. Gingerly she began to wash the raw flesh, but the fresh well water was cold, and the man began to wake under the icy touch.

His eyes came open and stared up at her. Despite the state of near panic she was in, Elsa managed a smile. He tried to stir but seemed unable to.

"It's alright. Don't try to move. You have been hurt, but I'm washing and bandaging your wounds right now. I'm sorry if I am hurting you. I'm almost done."

He just kept staring at her without showing any sign of comprehension. The vacant look alarmed her more than his unconsciousness had. After all, it was typical for wounded men to be unconscious, but it wasn't typical for awake men to be unresponsive. "Can't you hear me?" she asked.

"Water," he mumbled faintly.

"Oh, yes, of course. I should have thought to bring you something to drink." Elsa finished with the bandages as quickly as she could and scrambled out of the bushes. She ran back towards the small well behind the stables. Just as she tossed the bucket over the edge, she caught sight of Henry approaching, a large pail in either hand.

"Henry, I need a drinking gourd. Fetch me one quickly," she called to him and then before he had a chance to respond, "Don't just stand there. Hurry!"

Henry had never before seen Elsa this impatient about anything. Even during the fire the night before, she had not yelled at him. Dropping his buckets, he dashed off and returned almost instantly with the desired drinking vessel.

"Thank you, thank you." She snatched it from him, and clutching her now full pitcher of water, turned back towards the field.

Henry gasped as she moved away from the well. "Missus, you's bleedin'!"

Elsa glanced down at her skirt and for the first time noticed it was significantly spattered with blood.

"What's happened?" Henry was by her side now.

She looked up at him with trembling lips and blankly shook her head. "I'm not hurt. Now go into the stables and stay there."

"But you's not well," he objected.

"Henry, I mean it. Go into the stables and don't ever mention this to anyone—never as long as you live."

With an incredulous stare, he turned and did as she said, but she knew there was no way he was going to disregard the matter.

Upon her return Elsa found the man lying motionless, his eyes once again closed. She raised his head a little and put the full gourd to his lips. He sputtered and shook his head as the water splashed onto his face. Opening his eyes, he stared blindly at her again.

"I have brought you water," Elsa said softly. In response to the familiar word, his lips parted and he swallowed several times.

As Elsa set the gourd aside, she glanced quickly at her watch. It was only several minutes until four o'clock—Aunt Ingrid's tea! She dare not be late again. Leaving her things where they were, she fought her way out of the shrubbery and dashed for the house as fast as she could.

Elsa slipped in the side door, just as the grandfather clock in the hall struck four.

"It is gratifying to see you well again, Matilda." It was Ingrid's punctilious voice.

"Mary White and Elsa will be joining us, will they not?"

Elsa recognized Mrs. Deveraux's shrill tone, and stepped behind the door just as the women entered the room.

"Yes, my niece ought to be here by now. Her procrastination is one of the daily trials I must bear. Some young women have no regard for the encumbrance they cause others."

"Being raised for so many years apart from a mother's refining influence has no doubt had an ill effect upon her character," Mrs. Deveraux replied condescendingly.

"If she had come under my care from infancy, I can assure you her temperament would be different," Ingrid responded.

"You would hardly have wanted her then," stated Matilda.

"My sister acted most irresponsibly in bringing her into the world as she did. But let it never be said Ingrid Chesterfield failed in her duty," she replied with stiff haughtiness.

Elsa felt unutterably dejected and worthless, hiding behind the door and listening to her aunt discuss her in such disparaging terms. She had never tried to displease Ingrid, yet it seemed she could do nothing else. And right at the moment she wanted more than anything to help this unknown soldier lying in the bushes, but an all too familiar, gnawing fear whispered that this would be but another addition to her list of failures.

In another moment Mary White arrived, and the ladies withdrew to the parlor. Elsa darted from her hiding place and towards her room just as she heard Ingrid saying to the maid, "Go and summon my niece. Perhaps she is in her room."

Elsa practically flew up the steps. She jerked a black silk apron, which she had embroidered with a dainty ivy design, from her bureau and was tying it on as Anna approached.

"Youh aunt is most anxious foh you to come."

"Thank you, Anna. I will be there momentarily," Elsa answered as calmly as she could, but her hands shook with the apron strings. Glancing up at the mirror, she was surprised by the pale, large-eyed reflection staring back at her. On an impulse, she seized the talc off her bureau and powdered her face well. She then walked primly down the stairs into the parlor.

"Come and sit with us, Elsa," was all Ingrid said upon her entry, but her look clearly telegraphed the message: "Late again!"

"My dear, what a color you have," exclaimed Mrs. Deveruax, forgetting for a moment to be formal.

"Are you not feeling well?" queered Matilda, eyeing Elsa's livid features with concern.

Elsa shook her head. "I fear I am feeling quite discommoded, thank you."

Ingrid laid her hand on Elsa's. "You do not seem very well, niece," she said as she felt her cool, clammy skin.

"Perhaps last night's commotion has been too much for her," suggested Mrs. Deveraux.

"The excitement has been entirely too much," Elsa agreed readily.

"Have you heard about that?" Ingrid leaned towards her guests.

"Only a fragment. We would be so gratified if you would tell us the whole story," Mrs. White said eagerly.

"Elsa, my dear, why don't you go rest a bit," suggested Matilda.

"If you ladies would be so kind as to excuse me." Elsa tried to keep from sounding too eager.

"Of course, go lie down for awhile," said Mary White.

Elsa looked questioningly at Ingrid, who frowned a little but dismissed her with a nod.

"I am truly regretful to be a disturbance. I do hope you ladies will have a lovely tea," Elsa said as she stood up and then made for the door as fast as she dared.

The Man in the Bushes

Night had not yet withdrawn her dark veil from the quiet landscape when Everett brought his horse to a stop in front of his cabin.

"We've done it, Chawcoal." He spoke in a low voice to his steed. "Yes, sir, we've done it." He swung himself off and took Charcoal's bridle. "We jest leads dose soldiers right through de fohest and drops dem off on de general's doohstep, jest as nice and fine as you please—only not de poor lieutenant. One of his men says he saw de lieutenant plumb blown to bits when he ignites de powder magazine. I's 'most hope foh his sake he be all blown up. Betteh dan being de prisoner of does bloody Rebels. But what was I to do? We's couldn't stay and look foh him, no, sir. We's jest had to git befohe all ouh heads be blown off." He finished his soliloquy with a resigned shake of his head, thus putting a conclusion to an immutable fact of life.

After putting Charcoal up in the lean-to, Everett lay down in the house and slept for an hour. He then arose at his usual time and began his morning's activities, as if the last night's drama had been nothing more than a dream. While at work in the forge that day, he listened expressionlessly to the animated townsfolk recounting various descriptions of the fire, which ranged in intensity from a horrible, destructive, appalling, pernicious conflagration that laid waste the camp, to, "A bit of a blaze our men took care of in no time."

Ample discussion was also given to the hasty and complete

41

disappearance of the "villains who committed such an atrocity". Many favored sending out the home guard to scour the woods in search of the culprits. Everrett finally interjected the remark, "You's do as well to search Sheridan's camp as to go on some wild goose chase in de woods."

Not seeing the relevance of such a statement, Farmer Hodkins denounced him as "a dullard who had not the brain to comprehend such matters." Everrett merely smiled to himself and thought what a town full of idiots he lived in.

He grew increasingly groggy as the day progressed and was more than ready to return home by the time evening came, so it was with some irritation that upon his arrival he found a bay horse grazing on the tender ferns before his cabin. He automatically assumed that it must belong to Elsa, since he had never told the whereabouts of his home to anyone else that owned a horse.

"Why's shey so anxious to see mammy?" he muttered to himself. "Jest maybe de kind folk of ouh fair town hired her to see if I's be makin' any plans against ouh dear Confederacy."

However, when he entered the cabin, he saw no one but Martha, quietly reposing on her bed, a dreamy look in her eyes. "Did shey leave heh horse behind?" he asked by way of greeting.

"What? Who? What horse?" Martha asked, startled from her reverie.

"Miss Grey's horse."

"What about heh horse?"

"Why did shey leave him in front of de cabin?"

"Did shey?"

"Well, dere is a horse out dere as plain as day."

"Miss Elsa ain't been here. Shey's only come dat one time."

"Den whose horse is it?" Everrett demanded.

"How's I's gwinna know whose horse it is, ifen I's didn't even know dere were a horse?"

"So no one has been here?" Everrett questioned.

"Nary a soul."

Everrett shook his head in confusion. "Well, dere is a horse out dere, and I's too tired to cahe whose it is, so it can jest stay until it's good and ready to leave."

But the next morning, the horse was still there and obviously taking great delight in Charcoal's company. Now that his faculties were rejuvenated by a night's sound sleep, Everrett took a much more lively interest in the animal and was intrigued to find that it bore the brand of the Federal cavalry. He toyed with the idea of returning it to the army, but that was far too much trouble, and he wasn't willing to take the risk of making himself look suspicious for something so trivial. On the other hand, he did not have the resources to care for it himself, nor did he have use for a second horse. The only thing he could think to do was wait a few days to see if the animal would leave of its own accord.

*   *   *   *   *

After Elsa succeeded in making her escape from Ingrid's tea, she hurriedly changed her soiled dress and then flopped down onto her back on the bed and tried to think. She had no idea how serious the man's condition was. Perhaps with a few days of rest he would be strong enough to leave, then again, for all she knew he might not live the night. Should she try to rouse him from his half comatose state, or let him rest? What about food? How was she to procure that for him? And what was it best to try to feed him anyway?

Then there was the matter of his location. The bushes afforded fine concealment, but not any comfort, or much protection from the elements. The weather had been mild of late, but what if it was to rain? Then again, was there any way she would be able to move him if she tried?

And then there was Henry to be considered. She knew that once his curiosity was aroused it was not easily quelled. She would love to be able to confide her secret to him and knew he would be most willing to help her with this overwhelming task, but she couldn't tell him. It would be most selfish to do so. But he would probably snoop around until he found out anyway.

Elsa was unbelievably nervous, fidgety and sick to her stomach all afternoon. She wanted to rush back outside and check on her man, but she knew she dare not risk returning before nightfall. Ingrid stopped by her room just before dinnertime and after looking at Elsa for several moments, did not object when Elsa asked to be excused from coming down.

Finally, after what seemed like a week and a day, darkness came. Just before the last servants retired for the night, Elsa requested a mug of hot milk be brought to her room. She then waited a bit longer, and when complete quietness rested over all, she made her silent way out of the house, carrying the warm milk and with a thick quilt folded over her arm.

It was so dark beneath the bushes. She waited several minutes for her eyes to adjust before she tried to do anything. It was a clear night with a bright moon and plenty of stars, but very little of that light was finding its way through the leaves. She reached out and gently touched his bandages. They were dry. Evidently she had done an adept enough job that he wasn't bleeding through. She slowly moved her fingers upwards, groping over the side of his face, since she still could not see much more than a dim outline.

In response to her touch, he began to mumble. She could make out some of what he was saying. "Connly, Connly, you take charge. I reckon I'm done for. Keep the horses quite. Connly,...if-if we can trust him. Everrett Trenton knows the way."

Elsa's ears perked up at the sound of a familiar name, and she bent closer to catch his faint words. "He knows the way...if we can trust...he'll come...Connly...Elizabeth...I don't know if I can..." His voice faded out. Elsa stroked her hand over the side of his face again, and he began once more to mumble, repeating the same things over and over and other jumbled words she could not understand.

She broke away a few more twigs to allow her to kneel next to him more comfortably, and began the challenging task of trying to help him to drink the milk. After sloshing several mouthfuls onto his chin, he seemed to get the idea and drank the rest of the cup quite well. When it was gone he mumbled, "Milk."

"That's right," Elsa exclaimed softly, excited that he was actually aware of something. She covered him with the quilt and began a steady stream of conversation. After awhile, she started stroking his hair away from his forehead. His eyes suddenly shot open.

"Where am I?" he demanded, and although his voice was weak, she could tell by the alarm in it that he was well aware of what he was saying.

"You finally woke," she said happily. "As to where you are, you are outside in the middle of a clump of bushes."

"What?"

"That is right, you really are inside the bushes."

"Who, who are you? Where are you?" He was growing more perturbed by the minute.

"It's alright. Don't be upset." She laid her soft hand over his cold one. "I am Elsa, and you are?"

"John, John Fairfield."

"You are a lieutenant, aren't you? I could tell that by your uniform."

At the mention of his uniform, John reached up with his right hand and groped the heavy quilt over his chest. Elsa quickly caught his hand before he could disturb his bandages. "I am afraid I had to cut off your jacket. It was the only way I could dress your wounds."

"Wounds? Is that what hurts so bad?"

"Yes, you were injured. You don't remember?"

"I don't know." John shook his head, trying to jump start his memory.

"Let me help. You are in the Union Cavalry, and you some other men came here and set fire to a Confederate camp."

"Oh," And then as the events prior to his injury slowly came back into focus, he asked apprehensively, "Where are my men?"

"I don't know. They left very quickly. Most likely they thought you were dead. I did when I first saw you."

"So what's going on now? Why am I in the bushes? How long have I been here?" John tried to raise himself up only to find that he lacked the strength to stir more than a few inches.

"Don't try to move," Elsa cried. "I bandaged your wounds the best I could, but I have never done that sort of thing before. You must be very careful not to start yourself bleeding again. Now, you have only been here since last evening when you did your raid. I found you here this afternoon, but I have not moved you, partly because I couldn't and partly because I have no safe place to move you to. I am the only person who knows you are here."

"And who are you?"

"I live up at the great house. I am the niece of Madame Chesterfield, who owns this plantation. Now I am going to keep your presence a secret and help you as best I can. I do not want you captured." Elsa shuddered as she thought of the stories of horror she had heard of Confederate prison camps. Even if her sympathies did not lie with the Union, she did not think she would have the heart to condemn him to such a hell on earth.

"You are very kind," John murmured.

Elsa just smiled at him in the darkness and continued to gently stroke his hair. She usually felt quite nervous when close to a man, yet now, as she knelt here talking with him, she felt calmer than she had all day. She was already beginning to think of him as her soldier. After all, she had found him. When he had been merely an unresponsive injured body, the responsibility had been more than daunting. But now that he was a man with a name and a voice, she felt very glad that she, and only she, had found him. He was hers to care for, and it gave her strange thrill.

She stayed with him all night. He slept most of the time, occasionally rambling out some incoherent phrases. She stole back into the house once to fetch her shawl and brought back bread and water. He woke just as the sun was starting to come up. She knew Ingrid was not an early riser and so figured she safely had another hour. Elsa helped him to eat and drink, and in the faint light of dawn, they both took the opportunity to really look at each other.

John had a full head of sandy brown hair with long sideburns and gentle gray eyes. He had no facial hair, except for one day's stubbly growth. He was tall, well, perhaps long was more the appropriate word considering his current posture, and although he was not broad, he had the filled out figure of a man rather than the gangly limbs of a tall youth. At present his complexion was a pallid grey, but Elsa thought him quite handsome, nonetheless.

John wanted to know about his wounds. Elsa hadn't known what to make of the strangely torn flesh on his chest, but John said that when he threw his torch, there had been a great explosion. Most likely, a piece of the wagon had been hurled into him, explaining the splinters and heavy bruising.

"It is getting light; I must go," she said reluctantly. "But I have filled your canteen. That should last you most of the day, and when I come back tonight, I will bring you some clean clothes and see what I can do about food."

Elsa squeezed his hand and then slipped out of the shrubs. It felt good to stretch her stiff legs. She paused for a moment to adjust the leaves on the bushes, to hide somewhat the gaps caused by the branches she had broken away. Elsa turned towards the house, and there was Henry standing beside the old well, watching her.

As she walked up, he came to meet her. "Missus, what's wrong?" he asked.

Elsa could not help but be touched by the concern written on his wrinkled face. She wanted so badly to tell him all about it and had to bite her lower lip to keep it from quivering. She was exhausted and overwhelmed, and the past 48 hours had been incredibly stressful. His heartfelt solicitude was almost too much to resist.

"Miss Elsa, tell old Henry what's happened. You's look like you's want to cry."

Why did he have to say that? Now she really was starting to cry. As he gently put his arm around her and patted her back, she let her aching head drop onto his shoulder and stopped trying to fight the tears. She had once taken care of Henry during an illness, and ever since, he had watched out for her with a grandfatherly sort of concern. He adored Elsa and hated to see her unhappy.

"Miss Elsa, you's don't have a secret loveh do you?" he asked, trying to guess the reason for her strange actions.

Now that was an explanation Elsa hadn't thought of. It didn't make a lot of sense, but she liked it. She straightened up and nodded at him. "He is very poor, and if Aunt Ingrid where to find out she would never let me see him again. He works on a farm, and yesterday he cut his arm badly. That is why I had so much blood on my skirt. You see, he came over from Ireland and the only way he could pay for his passage, was to indenture himself." Elsa couldn't believe how fast this story was coming to her. She almost wished it were true.

The worry on Henry's face wasn't decreasing much as he listened to her explanation. His young mistress was only setting herself up for heartbreak. He had been separated from his love when Ingrid had bought him years ago, and he would rather be flogged twenty times over than to live through that again. "Is dere anything I's can do foh you?" he wondered.

"Yes, there is," Elsa said eagerly. "You see the man he works for doesn't feed him well at all, and poor Erin is half starved. Now, if you could get Minerva to set aside a little tin of food each day and tell me where to find it, I would appreciate that ever so much."

"I's will. But be caheful, Miss Elsa. Is it really worth it? Dere comes a time when we's all jest got to accept ouh place in dis world, as unfair as it is. But dere, dere now, don't cry no mohe."

"I had better hurry back to the house now before Aunt Ingrid gets up. But thank you, Henry. You are a true friend."

Henry shook his head sadly as he watched her go. He had big ears, particularly when it came to Elsa's well-being, and he knew that Ingrid fully intended that before the year was out, her niece would be primly married to a Confederate officer. He had hoped, for Elsa's sake, that she might fall in love with one of an amiable disposition and have a life which was happy, even if not a dream come true.

But if Elsa was preoccupied with a futile romance, she would not fall in love with anyone else, and then Ingrid would force her into a marriage with Captain Aldridge. Although he did not know the man well, he had heard terrible stories of torture and brutality which Aldridge had inflicted on prisoners of war, or even employed in the discipline of his own men. Even Ingrid would be repulsed by the man, could she but see his true disposition. The fact that he was expert at hiding his evil character behind polite manners and flattering words, only made his venom all the more deadly. Henry shuddered as he thought of Elsa in the clutches of such a refined brute.

Elsa's Soldier

The next evening, when Elsa returned, she found John awake and watching for her. That morning, she had managed to sneak back into her room without Ingrid seeing her, had dispatched a message to the Wilson's that she could not come for several days on account of poor health, and then slept fitfully half the day. She still felt rather worn out, but was delighted to find John both awake and alert.

"Do you feel strong enough to move?" she asked.

"I would like to," responded John.

"Well, how about you try and leave these bushes. I want to change your bandages, and it is way too dark in here. I have a lantern in an empty stall in the stables, and I thought we could go in there if you are able."

John grunted his consent and very slowly and painfully managed to scoot his way out. "Oh, it feels so good to be out those poky branches. I feel like I just got out of prison."

Elsa laughed softly and helped him to his feet. John was still weak from all the blood he had lost and in a good deal of pain, but his injuries were not completely disabling. He leaned on Elsa for balance, but did not have as hard a time walking as she had feared. However, by the time they reached the stables, he was already worn out and collapsed gratefully onto the clean straw Elsa had spread out for him. After a moment of fumbling, she succeeded in lighting a small lantern.

"Well now, that's better. How are you feeling, a little faint?"
John nodded.

"I have some food. Henry said he would leave it over here with the saddles. Here it is." Elsa pried the lid off the old tin, and came back to sit beside John.

"Let's see what we have. Oh, sugar peas. These are fresh from the garden. You are ravenous, aren't you?" she exclaimed at the way he began to munch them down at an amazingly rapid rate. "Well, that is a good sign if you have a hearty appetite. I also have a nice big chunk of cheese, soda crackers, and…" She paused to unwrap something folded in a napkin. "Oh, pound cake. This is left over from dinner. It is delicious. But do not eat it so fast or you will miss the flavor and give yourself a stomachache."

"Yes, mother," John replied between mouthfuls of peas.

"Mother? You think I look old enough to be your mother?" Elsa tried to look offended. "I dare say I am younger than you, my child. How old are you, anyway? My memory begins to fail me."

"Twenty-four."

"I knew it. I am younger. I will have you to know, I have not quite reached my twentieth birthday."

"An odd conundrum," John agreed. "But the world is full puzzling things these days, such as, why are you helping me?"

"And what kind of a mother would I be, were I not to help my own son?" she exclaimed and then growing serious, went on, "I suppose you want to know the real reason."

John nodded, his mouth full of cheese.

Elsa was silent for a moment, staring off into space as she saw visions of people and places far removed from a Virginia plantation. She looked back at John, and although she smiled, he could see a deep sadness in her eyes as she said, "Since you have so much time to lie here and wonder about such things, I suppose I will tell you. My father was a comfortable, although not wealthy, horse breeder. He had a lovely little farm in a small town on the foothills of the smoky mountains, nothing at all like this dreadful, great establishment. He was an abolitionist. He had a few servants, but they were just part of the family. We never thought of them or treated them as anything else.

"Now, my mother was a Montgomery and grew up on a plantation much like this one. The summer she was eighteen, she spent visiting friends in Knoxville. Around Independence Day, my father came down to deliver horses to a very important client. He met mother at the town festivities, and it was love at first sight. Father was a good deal older than her. He must have been at least thirty at the time."

"I'm assuming the Montgomery's weren't too thrilled," John said.

"To say the least. I can just imagine what Aunt Ingrid must have had to say. Even now that he is gone, she still will not stop berating my father as the scum of the earth."

"I'm sorry," John said softly. "That must be dreadful for you."

Elsa drew a deep breath. "Well, my mother was a very strong woman, and she would not be dissuaded. She said she would die if she couldn't have her Louis."

"So they ran off and got married despite what anyone had to say," John finished for her.

Elsa did not seem to hear him, but finally she asked very quietly, "Do you think someone could actually die from being in love?"

"Oh no, not if they didn't want to," John said decidedly. "So your parents, did things work out for them?"

"Until I came along and cost my mother her life," Elsa said, with both her tone and expression combining to show how great she felt her personal responsibility be.

"What?"

"She died in childbirth," Elsa stated morosely.

"That is very sad, but not exactly your fault."

"It is more mine than anyone else's. I am also more than a little responsible for my father's death," she added.

John had never before met anyone with such a self-condemning attitude. He felt like asking if she was also going to take the blame for the war between the states, but instead he just raised his heavy eyebrows at her and changed the subject. "Am I putting you in danger?"

Elsa shook her head. "Not really. You are the one in danger. And I am trying very hard to keep any of the slaves from finding out, because if they do, they will want to help, and if Aunt Ingrid were to discover it…well, I do not even want to think about it."

"What will happen if she finds out about you helping me?" John asked anxiously. Elsa looked at him hard for a minute, reluctant to answer. "It's alright. I've been a soldier for over three years now, I think I can take the truth," he assured her.

"You will find yourself in a Confederate prison camp or possibly…" Elsa put her hand to her neck in an expressive gesture.

"I understand," John said. "And what about you?"

Elsa gave a small shrug. "I don't know, but it is not like my aunt is going to send me down to the county jail and have me flogged as she would with them. But she will not find out," Elsa added quickly. "Which is why I can not let you stay here in the stables during the day, although I would love to. It is simply too dangerous."

"That is alright. You have already been more than kind, and I will be forever in your debt."

Elsa smiled, and much to John's surprise, began to run her fingers through his hair. "Now I am going to change your bandages, and then when you feel rested enough, you can put on these clean clothes I brought."

The outfit Elsa provided for him had formerly belonged to her uncle, the late Sir Albert, who was to say the least, a little heavier and of a decidedly shorter stature than John. Elsa had not realized how much so until she saw John in the clothes. She broke into soft giggles.

"Well, at least if someone sees you, they will never guess you are a lieutenant in the Union army."

"I know, I will probably be arrested as a thief and a vagabond, but not as a soldier." John laid back on the straw, and they smiled at one another in the flickering lantern light, and laughed as hard as they dared.

*   *   *   *   *

"Look, Mammy, de buttercup is in bloom." Everrett handed her a small cluster of the shiny yellow blossoms.

"Dese here flowehs is so purtty."

"I's know you's like dem." Everrett stretched his rugged frame out on the braided rag rug, adorning the rough floor of his cabin—his favorite position for a Sunday afternoon. He knew the days he had with his mother where numbered, so he tried to stay near her as much as possible when he was not at the forge. It meant so much to her to have him there, but whenever she had the strength, she talked non-stop. And being a man of few words himself, he was beginning to get a little weary of it.

"Did I's tell you dat Miss Elsa visited me yesterday?"

"Yes, you's told me dat at least five times. And shey brought you's a new nightdress, and a pillow with goose feathehs in it, and it is very kind of heh, and we's ahe much obliged."

"Did I tell you's shey got hehself a soldier?"

"Well, good foh her. I reckon Madame Chesterfield is pleased," he said drowsily.

"I's reckon not. I's de only livin' soul shey's told 'bout her soldier." When Everrett made no reply, Martha went on, "Ain't you's gwinna ask me to tell you's about it?"

Everrett sat up listlessly. "Mammy, why would I's cahe if Miss Grey got hehself a soldier? Dat don't even make no sense. Can't you's jest talk 'bout something' else foh a couple minutes. I's plumb tired ob hearin' 'bout Miss Grey."

"Everrett Trenton, ain't anyone eveh learned you no mannehs?" she chided. "If you jest pay attention to what I's sayin' foh half a minute, you's would find out why dis interests you."

With a resigned wave of his hand, he resumed his former posture.

"So as I's was tryin' to say, dere were some Union soldiers lightin' fires oveh at heh aunt's plantation de otheh night. And de next day, shey finds dere lieutenant smack dab inside a bush."

"What?" Now this was starting to get a little interesting.

"Dat's right, he were inside de bush all knocked out cold."

"So what did shey do with him?"

"Shey don't know what to do. Shey's havin' a heck of a time tryin' to take cahe of him and hide him from dat awful aunt of hers. Shey were plenty upset 'bout it too. Said dere weren't a soul in de world shey could tell, but den shey reckoned as how I was safe 'nough to talk too. I's told heh to come back agin today ifen she's could and tell me what was goin' on."

"Well, what do you' s make of dat? Do you's believe heh?" he asked.

"I's do. What call would shey have to make up sech a story?"

Everett could think of a few reasons and laid down again to ruminate on them. From what he had seen of Elsa, she did not seem in the least wily, and he was usually a good judge of character. But he had certainly heard of female spies working with great effect on unsuspecting men. For instance, there was that notorious Antonia Ford who had recently come to light. Her father had run a bordering house near Washington, where she had beguiled many a lonely Union soldier with her womanly charms, only to hand over every scrap of information she gleaned to her cohort J.E.B. Stuart. She had even betrayed her lover, Brigadier-General Edwin Stoughton, into the hands of his enemies. Just because someone was sweet, innocent and a woman, was not sufficient reason to trust them.

But what were Miss Grey's intentions? Up till now, he had thought she was simply a pious do-gooder come to earn a few stars for her crown. Oh yes, there was that whole thing about Elsa's nurse being Martha's sister, but so what? Elsa was now a grown woman. She had no need of a nurse and certainly no need of Martha.

He was well aware that the citizens of the town bore him no love, and there was a very real possibility that they had sent her over to keep an eye on him and make sure he wasn't collaborating with the Union army, or aiding the underground railroad, or anything of that nature. Perhaps someone had found a reason to suspect him in the raid of several nights past.

On the other hand, if everything she said was true, then she was a different breed of woman then he had ever met. It would be nice to think, like Martha, that she was telling the truth. But what were the chances of that?

As he was contemplating all this, there was a gentle rap on the door. He opened it to find, as he had suspected, Elsa. Why had he ever told this witch where he lived in the first place? He was not usually that foolish. She nodded to him without making eye contact. She was a little intimidated of him. That was good. He would make sure it stayed that way.

"How are you this afternoon, Mr. Trenton?"

"Fair tolerable," he replied. What was up with the way she always called him Mr. Trenton? No one else called him that. If she thought that by being overly polite she would get him to let his guard down, well, that just proved how foolish she was.

"And how is your mother? Well I trust."

"I's think shey's sleepin'. You's might want to come another time."

"Alright." She turned to leave, but Martha's voice stopped her.

"I's ain't sleepin'," she said with a dark look at Everrett. "I's so glad you's came."

Everrett stood aside to let Elsa in. She stepped over to the bed, and he stood by silently against the wall, listening as they made small talk. He could tell his shadow looming over her was making her nervous because she kept fidgeting with her hands and glancing at him out of the corner of her eye.

After a minute Martha said, "So tell me's about your soldier. How is he?"

Elsa's face lit up at the mention of John. "Oh, he's doing a bit better. The poor man is hungry nearly all the time. I cannot seem to manage enough food for him. And it is really quite miserable for him to have to hide in those bushes all day, but I cannot think of any other place to hide him. But I will have to think of something, because I do not know how much more of that he can take. He is becoming anxious to leave, partly because his current situation is so uncomfortable, and partly because he feels badly to be an imposition. But I really do not think he is strong enough to leave yet. Yesterday I was trying to thoroughly clean his wounds because it seemed like they were getting some nasty puss, and I kept asking him if I was hurting him, and he said, 'Oh, no. Just clean them well.' Then he passed out, just like that."

"Ohhh," Martha exclaimed in sympathy.

"I know, isn't that horrible? I must have been hurting him terribly, and he did not utter so much as a groan but then fainted dead away.

Everrett was watching Elsa's face intently as he listened. Her concern for her soldier appeared genuine enough, and she was talking rapidly with no pauses to plan out her next sentence as he had anticipated. She was telling Martha now about how little sleep she was getting because she wanted to stay with him as much as possible during the night. That was believable; there were dark circles under her eyes. If he didn't know better, he would say she was practically lovesick over the man.

"What's his name?" Everrett asked suddenly.

Elsa must have forgotten for a moment that he was there because she jumped at the sound of his deep voice.

"John Fairfield," she answered without hesitation. "And he knows you," she added, "or at least someone with the same name, because when he was delirious that first night, he kept talking about Connly and Everrett Trenton. He said you knew the way."

So this was the part where she tried to trip him up. But he was certain of one thing now, she really had found John alive. There was no other way she could know all this. However, that didn't mean that she was caring for John as she said. She could have handed him over to the Confederates as most young women in her position would.

"So dis soldier of youhs, are his wounds severe?" Everrett asked.

Elsa immediately launched into a graphic description of John's major and minor injuries. Everrett was almost beginning to believe her. He racked his brain for some question which would definitively prove her veracity, but Elsa broke into his thoughts.

"I saw you got another horse."

Everrett shook his head. "Dat's jest some stray dats been hangin' 'round. Seems to have taken a hankerin' afteh my stallion, and I's haven't yet gone to de trouble of chasin' it away."

"Really? A stray?" Elsa asked with sudden interest shining in her eyes. Everrett nodded.

"Have you looked at her brand? That might help reveal the owner."

"I's don't know nothing 'bout brands. I's jest a dumb blacksmith."

Elsa gave him a funny look. "I would have thought that being a blacksmith you would know about such things, but what do I know? I am just a dumb woman. But if no one claims the horse, will you keep it?"

"I's don't got no use foh it."

"Well, in that case, can I have it? Not for myself, for John," she hastened to explain. "In order to leave he needs a horse. I would be happy enough to give him one out of the stables, but there is no way I could keep that from Aunt Ingrid."

Everrett shrugged. "I's told you it ain't my hohse. Ifen you wants it, I's not goin' to stop you. I's don't give a damn."

"Everrett," Martha exclaimed, "why's you talkin' like dat to Miss Elsa? Is it too much to bey civil foh one aftehnoon?"

"It is quite alright. Don't be upset on my account." Elsa laid her hand overtop of Martha's. "It is not as if I have never heard a man swear before."

Why did Elsa keep doing and saying the opposite of what he expected? He had thought she would get angry at his rudeness and begin to show her true colors.

Elsa looked back at Everrett. He was so dark and forbidding, towering over as he was. She truly did not want to speak another word to him, but a stray horse wandering around? It was too good to be true. It would solve a huge problem for John, and if she let this chance slip by, she might not get another.

"You do not understand," she said. "I cannot simply take the horse. Where would I put it? John needs a couple more days to get stronger before he can even try to leave. But if you would be so kind as to keep it here until he is has need of it, well, that would be ever so helpful."

"You's right. I's don't understand," Everrett said, shaking his head in feigned bewilderment.

My goodness, this man was dense. How much clearer could she be? She looked at Martha as if for an explanation.

"He don't trust you," Martha said.

"He doesn't trust me?" Elsa repeated in confusion, then drew in her breath sharply as the truth dawned on her. Of course Everrett didn't trust her. How could she not have realized that? "My word, you think I am concocting some elaborate scheme to trap you?" She looked up at him. "I can see now how it would look that way. You probably think that even that horse in your yard is all part of some conspiracy. But I am not what you think. I am not a Confederate. I thought you knew that. 'All men are created equal and endowed by their creator with certain inalienable rights, among these life, liberty and the pursuit of happiness.' I believe that, and

I have never felt otherwise. No one in my entire life has ever been the least intimidated by me, so it never occurred to me that I appeared that way to you. What can I do? How can I prove to you that what I am saying is true?"

Everrett shrugged.

"He's ain't gwinna believe you unless he sees John and hears it from his own lips," Martha said.

"I cannot blame you for thinking as you do," Elsa said with a sigh. "It is a dreadful shame that things in the world today are so bad that you can't trust anyone, but I will prove it to you. I will. And please don't let the horse wander off. John really needs it."

Everrett made no response, just gave her that intent stare. But he was starting to believe her, and it was a wonderful thought to think that she actually was as sweet and unaffected as she seemed—a wonderful thought, but was it too good to be true? He knew now how he would find out for sure.

What to Do?

That evening Elsa told John all about Martha and Everrett and the mystery horse, about Everrett's suspicions and her inability to allay them. "What should I do?" she asked when she was finished. "I hate having him think falsehoods about me, but how can I prove myself?"

John thought hard for a minute. "I guess, if we want the horse, the only thing to do is go over there together once I am strong enough, which will be very soon," he added.

"But that is not as easy as it sounds either. We cannot go during the day. Aunt Ingrid is far too attentive. But it would be more than awkward to show up in the middle of the night. Everrett Trenton is not the sort of man to see any humor in such a thing. I just don't know." Elsa sank her head into her hands. "Wouldn't it be lovely if just for a week or so, life could be easy and uncomplicated?"

"It will happen, I am certain, at least once in your life," John said reassuringly. "After the war is over things will start to get better, you'll see."

"So what about you, Lieutenant? What will you do once the war is over? Will you stay in the cavalry?"

"No. I want to go back home to Maryland. I like my home town. I lived there most of my life, and it is where I want to live the rest of it."

"Tell me about it. You have not told me much about yourself."

"There really isn't much to tell. My parents have a small dairy farm, as do the next-door neighbors. There is a strong sense of community. Everyone always gets all fired up and makes a fool out of themselves during elections." John smiled as scenes of home and happy days began to float before him. "I have two young brothers. They will be fine men some day. I guess that is about all. I am not a very fascinating man."

"I think you are," Elsa said dreamily. "So are, well, that is, do you have a-a fiancée?" she asked with a futile attempt at sounding nonchalant.

"No, not yet," John answered slowly.

"But you do want to get married after you get home?" she wondered hesitantly.

John nodded, and then because he felt uncomfortable with all the attention she was directing at him, he asked, "And what of yourself? Do you have a fiancé?"

Elsa shook her head and sighed. "My aunt has been becoming a little insistent of late that I am now of the age when I should get engaged."

"But you don't want to?" John queered in surprise. Most young women he had met were rather anxious for their engagements.

"Oh, I want to," she said quickly, "only not to a Confederate, and nearly all the men I know are."

"Speaking of Confederates, what news do you hear of the war?" John asked.

Elsa's eyes clouded. "I have not mentioned it because I wanted you to just rest."

"Is it bad then?"

"Well, it is not exactly cheery," she said with weak smile. "On May 11th there was a cavalry clash at Yellow Taverns—J.E.B. Stuart and Sheridan."

"And," John prodded as she paused.

"The Yankees lost, but they did kill Stuart.

"I guess Connly finally got his battle," John said thoughtfully.

"It is a shame," Elsa said. "You know J.E.B. Stuart really was fine a man. I think war is just horrible."

"You knew Stuart?" John asked with interest.

"I met him. Aunt Ingrid is determined to have every officer in the Confederate army over for tea at least once. She even managed to have

General Lee over once, and she saved the wine glass he drank from. She will not allow it to be washed. She has it sitting on her bureau, and threatened all the maids with a flogging should they so much as breath on it."

John laughed. "What is your aunt like? Is she ugly?"

"Lieutenant Fairfield, what an indelicate question," Elsa exclaimed, trying not to look amused. "I cannot believe you asked me that."

John gave her a crooked smile. "I am just trying to picture someone as beautiful as you having such a disagreeable disposition as your aunt seems to have."

Elsa blushed. "I have never heard anyone say that Aunt Ingrid and I look alike." Then she added shyly, "Do you actually think I am good-looking?"

"It is not a matter of personal opinion," John said casually. "It is simply an obvious fact that you are beautiful. I am sure everyone who sees you knows it."

Elsa flushed some more and looked away. Neither she nor John noticed a dark form slip in through the stable door, which they had left ajar, and creep silently forward through the deep shadows.

"Is there any more news of the war?" John asked.

"Yes, on the 12th there was a battle at some place called Spotsylvania. I really do not know who won, but I heard one estimate say that 12,000 men were killed."

"12,000." John shook his head. "Elsa, I cannot stay here any longer. I need to go back to the army."

"I know. I'm just afraid for you. If you could simply get on a train and ride to some place safe, it would be alright. But you will have to go by horseback, and you are still so weak and catching a cold. Do not try to deny it; I know you are. And traveling around here is anything but safe." Elsa reached over and gently touched his arm. "It is silly, but ever since I found you in the bushes, I have felt as if it were my job to care for you."

John took her hand. "That is very sweet of you, Elsa, and you have been wonderful. I will be eternally grateful, but every day I stay here is a danger to both of us."

"Which is why you's comin' with me tonight." John and Elsa both jumped at the sound of the deep voice, and glanced up, looking as if they had been caught in the act of stealing sheep.

"Henry?" Elsa whispered. The speaker was far enough back in the shadows that they could see only an indistinct figure.

"I's ain't Henry." Everrett stepped into the small patch of light their lantern was creating.

"Mr. Trenton," she gasped. "What are you doing here?"

"I's come to find out if you's was tellin' me true or not. And I's see you's was."

"But how did you know to come here to the stables?"

Everrett grinned a little at her astonishment. "You's fohget, everything you's tell Mammy, shey repeats to me four times oveh. And," he said, looking at John, "I's got youh horse. Dat stray dat come to my place is a bay mare with de brand of de Union cavalry. I's reckon it ahe de same horse you was ridin' dat night you's got wounded."

Elsa jumped to her feet. "Now which one of us is the liar? You told me you knew absolutely nothing about brands. How do I know I can trust John to your care?"

Everrett just grinned at her some more while John said, "I am sure he is trustworthy. He helped us with the raid the other night, speaking of which, are my men alright, Everrett?"

"Every last one of dem arrived safe and sound."

John smiled, but Elsa was giving Everrett the most evil look she could muster, which truth be told, was not very menacing. "Mr. Trenton, ever since the day I first spoke to you, you have been nothing but cold, intimidating and unfriendly. Even this very afternoon while I was trying to visit your mother, you were insufferably rude and refused to bestow even so much as one ounce of trust in me, and now you come skulking along through the dark, frighten me almost to distraction and assume that just like that I am going to entrust John to you."

The men exchanged amused glances while John reached up and took Elsa's hand, saying sweetly, "Mother, all little boys must grow up some day. I want to go see the big, dangerous city." Elsa smiled in spite of herself.

"He's will be safeh at my cabin den he is here," Everrett assured her.

"And in a few mohe days, when we's suhe he's well 'nough, he's can take de horse and go. And in de mean time you's can come and visit him and Mammy as much as you's please, and ifen I's around, I's promise I's won't swear at you."

"Have you been swearing at Elsa?" John questioned, bristling a little. "You ought to be ashamed of yourself."

Everrett nodded, although he didn't look terribly contrite. After an awkward moment he turned to Elsa. "Well?"

"You are right," Elsa consented grudgingly. "John will be safer and much more comfortable at your cabin. It will be ever so much better than having to hide in those bushes all day, and Martha will be pleased."

Everrett nodded with a slight smile at John. "I's hope you's like listenin' to an old woman prattle on, 'cause shey will talk to you's non-stop."

"I am sure I will find it a pleasant diversion," John said contentedly.

Elsa hadn't quite yet forgiven Everrett for usurping her position as John's guardian, but she did get a sound night's sleep for the first time since she had found John. It showed on her face when she came down to breakfast, and Ingrid greeted her with an approving smile.

"I am glad to see that you are finally feeling better. Had you remained unwell any longer, I was ready to a call physician," she said.

"I do feel better." Elsa smiled back. "There would have been little a physician could have done for me though. I fear it was my nerves that were the cause of all the trouble."

Ingrid nodded wisely. "I thought as much. That frightful night of the fire seemed to be the beginning of your indisposition." Ingrid took a dainty bite of her egg as she gave Elsa a scrutinizing look. "I have not been able to help but wonder if the captain was not the cause of this agitation."

Elsa hid her mouth behind her teacup so Ingrid could not see her smile. Ingrid thought she was so clever, when in truth she didn't know so much as the first think about her niece, and she was just going to let her aunt think whatever she pleased. Elsa was in fine spirits and no one, not grumpy Everrett, or condescending Aunt Ingrid, or egotistical Captain

Aldridge, was going to ruin that. Her soldier was safe and well, and that was enough for today.

Ingrid took Elsa's lack of response to be an affirmative answer. "I cannot say that I know much about lovesickness from my own experience, having always been of a stronger nature than to succumb to such feminine debility. However, it is most common among young woman and not inconsistent with good taste. I am glad to see that despite your premonitions you still have enough womanly instincts to realize a meritorious man when you see one."

"Yes, Aunt, I think that despite my horrible upbringing I have somehow managed to retain at least a few womanly instincts," Elsa replied in mock seriousness.

Ingrid gave herself a little smile; perhaps she was finally getting somewhere in the transformation of her niece. It had been most intelligent of her to devise bringing Lester Aldridge into Elsa's life. He was just what Elsa needed to repress all those ridiculous notions she had learned from that disgraceful father of hers.

"Seeing as you feel that way, my dear, I think I have some information which will make you very happy," Ingrid said. "I happen to know that Captain Aldridge is in Richmond at the moment and will be remaining there for at least another week. If you were to write him a letter today, you could rest assured that he would receive it. This will give you the opportunity to set straight some things from his last visit where things did not go terribly well between you. I am sure once you have written, it will be a tremendous weight off your mind."

Elsa, who had been staring off into space, suddenly realized Ingrid was speaking to her. "I am sorry, Aunt Ingrid, I was being absent minded. Whom did you say you wished me to write to?"

To her surprise, Ingrid laughed. "You are lovesick, aren't you, my dear? I was telling you, Aldridge is in Richmond at present so you have the opportunity to write to him. Give me your letter by 3:00 this afternoon, and I will see that it makes it to the post on time."

Later that morning, at the Wilson's, Elsa had just set the children to work writing letters to their grandmother and now sat down with her own paper in front of her. If she didn't write the Captain, Ingrid would be most aggravated, and Elsa did so want things to continue to go well as they had this morning. But what was she to write? She dipped her pen in the inkwell and held it for a minute, only to set it back down again with sigh.

This was her opportunity to say anything which she was too timid to say in person. Perhaps she should be very rude. He would be furious, but then he might never speak to her again, and she could pretend to Ingrid that she loved him desperately, but it was he who wanted nothing to do with her.

But more likely, if she wrote him a rude letter he would want to confront her about it, and that was the last thing she wanted. She had to think about the possibility that she would end up married to him someday. She should try to be on the best terms with him that she could. But if she wrote him a sweet letter, he would take it to mean she wanted a relationship with him, and then how would she get out of it?

But she must write something, so finally she picked up her pen and began.

Dear Captain,

I trust this finds you well and in good health. Aunt Ingrid and myself still cannot help but speak of the frightening events during the evening of your last visit. As my aunt will most likely inform you, I have not been myself since that fateful night. I am weighed down by a strange premonition that somehow my presence brings you ill luck.

I assume you remain unaware of the events surrounding my father's untimely decease, but this only confirms my fears that the hand of destiny is morbidly turned against me and all who venture within the sphere of what seems my ruinous predestination.

My heart is heavy as I pen these words, but I am compelled to write them, to warn you of impending doom. You reproached me for coldness during our recent encounter, but there was no way I could bear to speak these evil words. The very writing of them is a task almost beyond my fortitude, but please take this as a token of my regard for you. I have thought these things often enough but never before have I revealed them to another living soul.

If you have any regard for my feelings at all, or even for self preservation, do not dismiss this warning, but rather think of the pain it has cost me to write it and the far worse misery which will be mine should I be, however unwittingly, the cause of your demise.

With deepest concern I remain yours truly,
Miss Elsa Marie Grey

Elsa read over her letter with some satisfaction. This was better than what she thought she could do. The only thing about it that troubled her was that in part she believed it. She had never before had these thoughts in regard to Captain Aldridge, but they occurred to her often enough in relation to other matters. At times she did feel strangely surrounded by an aura of bad luck which seemed to extend not only to herself but even more so to those she cared about.

Her premonitions were not without grounds either. Her life experiences thus far were what had given birth to these fears. Had she but had someone understanding she could speak with on the matter, no doubt her view of life's woes would be significantly altered. But for a good three years now she had no such person, and so the voices in her head spoke on, uncontradicted.

The children were also done with their letters by now, and Elsa showed them how to seal them with hot wax, placing two seals on her own instead of one, as she knew Ingrid would try to read the letter if she thought there was any way she could get away with it.

Farewell

Slowly Elsa closed the door of the mahogany gun case, where all the family's expensive or rare firearms where kept, and turned the key in the lock. This place was pratically a shrine to her late Uncle Albert. Here rested in pristine display, his long hunting rifles, his gleaming pair of twin pistols, the revolver that he was carrying when he fell. Only one spot in the case was now vacant. The bright May sunshine, pouring in through the long windows of the library, gleamed off the barrel of the finely crafted firearm Elsa held in front of her.

It was the only gun she had ever seen which she thought truly fit the description of beautiful. Her mother had, had it specially crafted by the best gunsmith she could find as a gift for her father. Every detail was perfect, from the silver eagle inlaid in its handle, to his name finely etched on the barrel. Her father had always said it was a truer shot than any other gun he had fired.

Elsa had thought that she would never part with this. It was a family heirloom, meant to be passed down from generation to generation, but today she would give it away, for today was the day of John's departure. He had lost his pistol at the time of his injury, and she must not let him leave unarmed. Besides, she could think of no one she would rather bestow it upon. If anyone was worthy of such a gun, it was John.

Today she would get to see him one last time. Aunt Ingrid was gone for two days, visiting her late husband's brother in the next town, and she had been in such a wonderful frame of mind ever since Elsa had written Aldridge that she had excused Elsa from making the tedious visit with her. Elsa couldn't believe her good fortune. She would find some reason for leaving the Wilson's early, and then she could spend the rest of the day with her soldier. She sighed as she thought of the fact that after today he wouldn't be her soldier anymore, but for one more day she could pretend.

Elsa arrived at the cabin about 1:30. She checked John over apprehensively as he came to meet her. He laughed at her scrupulous gaze. "Do I pass inspection?"

"Don't laugh at me, John," she scolded as she slid down from Sparrow's back. "I believe I have earned the right to worry about you if I please."

"That I will not contest, but I should hate to be the cause of adding wrinkles to so fair a brow," John said with a hint of tenderness in his voice.

Elsa stood gazing at him for a moment before asking with a slight catch to her voice, "How far do you have to travel to meet up with the nearest body of Union troops?"

"Everrett says about seventeen miles. You know, Everrett seems to know almost everything. People don't expect much of him because he is so quiet and glum most of the time, but all day at the forge he listens and remembers everything he hears. He is so observant; I don't think so much as an acorn can fall from a tree without him noticing."

Elsa nodded. "I do not find that too hard to believe. How is Martha today?"

"Come in and see for yourself. You know what Martha calls me when she is speaking to Everrett? She always refers to me as 'that soldier', or 'Miss Elsa's soldier'."

Elsa flushed. "And which do you prefer to be called?" she asked. When John didn't respond immediately, she hurried to say, "That was a foolish question. Do not feel compelled to answer it."

Elsa turned back towards Sparrow. "I brought something for Martha," she said as she took a tin of gingerbread from of her saddle bag.

"And something for you too," she added shyly, drawing out the pistol, sheathed in its black leather holster, and handing it to him.

"Elsa, this is a magnificent pistol!" John exclaimed as he examined it.

Elsa smiled at his pleasure. "I trust it will serve you well."

"I am certain it will, and when I use it, I will remember the lovely woman who gave it to me," he said looking at her fondly.

The afternoon passed all too quickly. John and Elsa sat beside Martha and talked to her until she was worn out. Then they went down to the stream where Elsa changed John's bandages again. She was not terribly happy with what she saw. His wounds were not healing as fast as she had hoped, and judging by the way he gritted his teeth when she washed them, they still pained him terribly. By the time she was done, he was completely white. But he seemed energetic enough, and no doubt when he returned to the army, he could see a doctor, and his injuries would receive better treatment then what she was able to give.

After John's color had returned, he asked if she wanted to walk with him a bit. He then proceeded to lead her through a very dense part of the woods, where every two steps their feet got tangled in vines, and Elsa soon found herself fearing for the safety of her vision, as it seemed that sharp tree branches were continually materializing out of thin air to thrust themselves at her eyes.

"Lieutenant, don't you think we could perhaps find a somewhat more amiable place to stroll?"

"I'm taking you somewhere particular," John replied, then added as an afterthought, "Everrett told me I should."

Elsa stopped for a second, a slight voice of fear whispering that she should not continue.

"It's not much further," John reassured her.

The sound of his voice silenced Elsa's anxiety. If there was anyone she trusted, it was John. A few more minutes, and the trees suddenly parted to usher her into a chamber of beauty beyond anything she had ever seen. Before her lay a forest bower of such exquisite, yet gentle, charm that it swept her breath away.

Tender new ferns grew between patches of plush emerald moss and soft young grasses sprinkled with buttercups, sweet clover, and tiny daisies. Brilliant spring sunshine flooded over the verdant growth gilding it in liquid gold. Everywhere she looked in the small clearing Elsa was confronted with a scene of loveliness surpassing the last. Myriad shades of green blended together to form the walls of the garden, and as she stepped out into the center, she felt the sanctuary enclosing her within its tranquility.

"Lieutenant, it is so beautiful here," Elsa breathed, kneeling to gently touch the pale pink blossom of a primrose just coming into bloom. "This is the sort of place I always imagine fairies living."

John smiled at her enchantment while he sat down in the fragrence of some sprawling honeysuckle, to bask in the warm sunlight. Elsa came to sit beside him.

After a few silent minutes of drinking in the beauty of the place, she said, "You are making that up about Everrett telling you to bring me here, aren't you?"

John shook his head. "This is his garden. He said you would be sad today since I am leaving, and that I should bring you here to cheer you up, that all the flowers would make you smile. Why do you look so shocked?"

"It just amazes me that Everrett would say such a thing. It does not sound like him at all. He is probably the most sullen man I have ever met, and I can scarcely believe that he cares in the least whether or not I smile." Elsa plucked a daisy and began to slowly pull off its petals one by one as she spoke.

"Oh, but you're mistaken. Everrett thinks a good deal of you. I believe he is actually a little worried that you will be upset about my leaving. You won't be, will you?"

Elsa became very intent on smoothing the wrinkles out of her full lavender skirt as she quietly answered, "I want you to go. It is all for the best."

As John watched the zeal with which she was adjusting the folds of her skirt, while keeping her eyes carefully diverted from his, he realized Everrett was much more correct in his observations of Elsa's feelings than he wanted to admit.

"Elsa," John said softly as he took her hand, "everything will be alright."

She nodded without answering, but John could see two drops hovering on the lashes of her lowered eyelids.

"Don't cry," he said as he dropped her hand, and instead placed his own on the side of her face and gently turned her head towards him.

"I'm sorry. It is completely ridiculous of me; I feel such a dreadful idiot."

John flicked a tear from her cheek. "It will be alright," he repeated.

"I am sure you are right," she said with a vain attempt at looking cheerful. "But will-will…"

"Will what?" he asked.

"Will I ever—will I ever see you again?" She finally got the words out.

"Oh, Elsa." Why did she have to ask him that? It was so similar to what Elizabeth had asked him, and he hadn't been able to give her an answer either. Even if he had any certainty about the future, there was no way he could give both of them an answer they wanted to hear. So he merely caressed her face with his hand as he said again, "Everything will be fine." And then because he could tell she did not believe him, he leaned forward and kissed her forehead, then her cheek, and then her lips.

His touch was so gentle and reassuring. Elsa closed her eyes and let it transport her into a realm where there was nothing but warm light, the balmy perfume of flowers, and the softness of his lips. She kissed him back several times, very slowly and lightly, not wanting to break the moment, willing it not to end. But it did, and when she opened her eyes, she could see his own were troubled.

"I will not ever see you again, will I?" she whispered, afraid to hear the words.

He shook his head ever so slightly. "I don't know, Elsa, but I cannot promise you that you will."

Elsa put her arms around his neck and laid her head on his good shoulder. She was very still for a moment, absorbing his warmth and taking in the smell of him till she knew she would never forget it. She lifted her head, and they gave each other one last long kiss.

Elsa stood up quickly. "I am going to pick some flowers for Martha," she said as brightly as she could.

"She will like that," John murmured and wistfully watched Elsa's tiny

71

form as she glided through the field. He half closed his eyes, and she floated before him, almost angel-like, while the light zephyrs flitting through the grass, whispered, that like an angel she was but a dream to him in this world, a passing phantom of grace.

*   *   *   *   *

Everrett and Elsa stood silently watching as John disappeared into the blackness, and the clop-clop of his horse slowly grew inaudible.

"Do you think he will be alright?" Elsa was the first to break the silence.

"I's reckon so," Everrett answered, but his tone was not terribly reassuring.

"Well, I had best hurry home. It is quite late."

Everrett watched her mount Sparrow and then said suddenly, "You's afraid to ride home in de dark."

"How did you know?" she exclaimed. "Really, Mr. Trenton, I feel like you are divining my thoughts sometimes."

Everrett smiled slightly. "I's don't got to do no divining to be knowin' dat you's scared of ridin' in de dark. It's written all oveh your face."

"I am that obvious, am I?" Elsa asked dryly. "John did tell me that you noticed everything."

"You's want me to ride with you till you's gets close to de plantation?" Everrett asked.

Elsa hesitated a moment. "No, you needn't trouble yourself. I would hate to be the cause of occasioning you inconvenience."

But without waiting to listen to her answer, Everrett led Charcoal out of the lean-to. Jumping on, he set off in the direction of the Chesterfield plantation. With a little shrug, Elsa followed.

Ever since her father's death, Elsa had been plagued by frequent nightmares and a wide array of phobias. She tried not to let them affect her actions, but she was quite relieved to not be riding alone, even if the company was Everrett's. She did, however, trail along behind even when they reached the part in the path where it was wide enough for two horses to easily ride abreast

After several minutes, Everrett slackened Charcoal's pace and waited for her to catch up. He looked back over his shoulder as he said, "I's not always ill-tempered and abrupt. Not to say dat I's known foh my fine mannehs, but believe it or not, I's actually do know how to be civil."

As Elsa rode up along side him, she said, "John took me to this pretty little field of flowers this afternoon, and he said it was because you told him he ought to."

"Did you's like it?" Everrett turned towards her.

"I did," she said with a sweet sigh of remembrance, but it was John's kisses she was recalling even more than the flowers. "John said that it was your garden."

"No, it ain't." Everrett shook his head. "Dat place belongs to de forest; shey made it. All I's do is tend it a bit now and then."

There was a pause in their conversation before Elsa finally said in a quiet voice, "I did find it hard to believe that you had any interest in whether or not I smiled."

"Well, you's gotten de wrong impression of me. I's not sayin' I's sorry foh mistrustin' you. I's don't got no choice but to watch out. But I's believe you now, and I's reckon you's don't got dat easy of a life either. And I's know you's really not gonna believe dis, but I's sad foh you to have to lose John. I's know you liked him mohe dan a little."

Elsa's mouth dropped halfway open. He was right about her not being able to believe this. Had another man taken possesion of Everrett Trenton's body?

"So do you's reckon John will come back?" he asked.

"I cannot help but hope, but deep down I do not really believe that he will. When the war is over he wants to go back home to Maryland. It is easy enough for me to feel fondness for John, not just because I found him and claimed him as 'my soldier', but because nearly every other man I know is a Confederate, and I have no desire to spend the rest of my life pretending to be one. But for John it is different, he can go back home and be surrounded by women who think and believe just as he does. There is no reason for him to come back. These few days I have known him seem significant to me, and yet in the scheme of life they are probably no more than a drop in the bucket."

Everett nodded. "So what do you's want when de war is oveh?" he asked with curiosity.

Elsa sighed, "The more I see of life, the more I think that what I want is of little relevance. Fate seems to determine my course, with no regard for my desires."

"Dat is de first time I's have heard a white person say such a thing," Everett exclaimed, "although I's think every black folk in de whole south knows as much."

"And at present, what fate seems to have in store for me," Elsa went on, "is that I shall become Mrs. Captain Aldridge, although I have tried my best to dissuade him with my letter, and have yet to see what effect that will have."

"What did you's write to turn him away?" Everett queeried. He was finding Elsa increasingly fascinating. She was not a bit what he had expected, and in fact, not like any woman he had met before.

Elsa gave a soft laugh. "I told him I was surrounded by an aura of ill luck, and that I could not bear to see him fall victim to it."

Everett laughed too, but then grew serious. "Youh aunt can't really force you's to marry someone you's don't want, can shey? I mean, you's free. Don't you's got no say in de matteh?"

"I truly don't know," Elsa answered slowly. "If it comes right down to it, I probably won't oppose her too strenuously. Marrying Aldridge is not what I want, but it might not be that bad. He seems fond of me. Time will tell."

"Youh aunt is quite a rebel, ain't shey? Does shey know you's ain't?"

"She knows how I feel, but I pretend when I'm with her. You know, I go to sewing circles and stitch gold braid onto pants and knit gray socks. I know you probably think I am a coward, but I have nowhere else to go. I really cannot afford to antagonize her.

"Last Christmas we had several women staying at our house. They were the wives of some Confederate officers near Knoxville. Their town was of very divided loyalties, but for most of the war the Confederates had the supremacy. They arrested scores of people for no other reason than that their sympathies lay with the Union. Then last September when General Burnside took possession of Knoxville, everything was reversed in the blink of an eye. These women were asked to leave their homes in no uncertain terms. Just because I am the niece of a Chesterfield is no guarantee that the same would not happen to me if I were to show any opposition to the Confederacy."

Everrett nodded. "Same here. I's have to be doubly caheful. All it would take is one wrong word and I's would be driven from town or lynched. De only reason dey put up with me at all is cause dey needs me. Ifen anotheh smith would come to town, dat would be de end of me."

Elsa looked at him in sympathy. "I do not like this world we live in. It is such a cruel, unjust place," she said sadly.

"Dat it is," Everrett said in heartfelt agreement.

Two Young Confederates

John's trip proceeded neither as smoothly, nor as quickly, as he had hoped for. His shoulder, which he had judged sufficiently strong for the journey, began to throb under the stress of managing the reins, faintly at first, but with a growing intensity for each mile he traversed until his head swam dizzily. As the gray morning light displaced the darkness, it revealed a very bedraggled man, the left side of his shirt stained with fresh blood, and still six miles from his objective.

Everrett had warned him that ever since their raid, the home guard had been most active in patrolling the countryside and harassing anyone looking in the least suspicious, or even unusual for that matter. So as dawn broke John reluctantly guided his horse off the road and down a faint path bordered by a field on one side and a dense vine entangled woods on the other. He dismounted and slowly led his horse into the forest, wedging his way through the thick undergrowth.

Now that he was off the road, he was fast realizing how exhausted he was. Too weary to go any further, he tied his mount to a tree and sought out a refuge in the underbrush. He lay down, and as the hollow rhythm of a woodpecker, the lilting trill of a songbird, the mourning dove's coo, and the low whir of insects swirled together into one confusing murmur, he dozed off.

The following night he continued his journey, drawing near his desired destination a little after midnight. As he approached, he anxiously waited to be apprehended by the sentries and began to consider how he was going to prove his identity to them. But strangely, no one stopped him. Riding to the top of the last rill, he saw in the shallow vale before him, only an open field and matted grass where tents had once stood. He was too late; the camp had broken.

John sat staring dismally down at the dark, empty valley for only a moment before turning his thoughts to logical contemplation of the dilemma before him. Everrett had mentioned a larger body of troops, eight or ten miles distant. He was unsure of the way, but he had no choice other than to look for them, so turning his mount to the east, he rode on.

Morning light once again overtook the sojourner on the road, but unwilling to arrive too late a second time, John pressed on as long as he dared. Finally the sound of approaching hoof beats forced him to turn hastily aside into a rundown orchard. He picketed his horse to a gnarled pear tree and settled down to spend another day of restive waiting.

Yesterday he had eaten the food Everrett had sent with him, and his canteen was nearly empty. But as he searched around, he did find enough wild strawberries to take the edge off his appetite. The day passed uneventfully until mid-afternoon, when he was startled by the rustling of grass and the merry chatter of voices. He barely had time to lie down in the tall weeds encircling the base of an old cherry tree, before the speakers came so close he could clearly distinguish their conversation.

"Careful, Robbie, you'll spill the berries."

"No, I ain't, but you gotta stop eating them all."

"I ain't eaten no more than you."

"Here's a nice little patch, Paul." A moment of silence followed, and then Robbie's voice said, "That's funny; there aren't any berries here."

"Maybe they aren't ripe yet," suggested Paul.

"But they have to be. The other patches all had ripe berries, didn't they? 'Sides, there are little stems the berries were taken off of. See."

"Wonder if the birds could have done it," Paul said.

"I don't know. Look closer to that cherry tree. They grew good there last year," Robbie directed.

Paul hastened to obey. "Robbie!" he exclaimed an instant later. "There's a man here! I think he's dead. His shirt's got blood on it."

"What!?" Robbie bolted to the side of his younger brother.

John opened his eyes and gave a friendly smile to his incredulous audience.

"He ain't dead neither!" Robbie stated the obvious as if it were the headlines of the news. "Maybe he's a tramp," he added after a reflective pause.

"No, he's not; he ain't got no satchel. You ever heard of a tramp who didn't carry a carpet bag?" Paul stepped closer, staring inquisitively into the friendly gray eyes which returned his gaze.

"I'm not a tramp. I'm a soldier," John said.

"But he ain't got a uniform." Robbie continued to speak of John in the third person.

"He has soldier boots," Paul pointed out.

"You boys want me to tell you what happened to my uniform?" John asked in a confidential tone.

"Yes," chorused the boys.

"Well, if you are certain no one else is around…" John looked searchingly about, as if preparing to divulge the deepest secret known to man. "You see, it happened like this," he began in a low voice. "I'm in the cavalry. My horse is tied over there by that old pear tree."

"Ooohh," Paul crooned in admiration.

"And I'm not no private neither, no sir, I'm a lieutenant."

"Whew," whistled Robbie.

"And I've seen plenty of hard of fighting too, but the other night this man meets me in the dark and says, 'Give me your uniform!' Of course I say, 'No way! Who are you?' Then faster than you can blink an eye, he whips out a pistol and shoots me, right here." John motioned to his shoulder with a fearful grimace.

Paul blinked his big brown eyes, full of wonder and sympathy.

"What did you do?" Robbie breathed.

"Well, I reached for my pistol, but no sooner had I got it in my hand, then he shoots me again, right here." John held out his bandaged left arm. "Do you want to see it?"

The boys nodded wordlessly. John slowly unwrapped the bandage and presented his wound for their inspection.

"Ohh, that's terrible," Robbie exclaimed while Paul simply stared in awful wonder.

John nodded grimly as he tenderly rewrapped his arm. "But I'm going back to the army this very night. I just need to rest a mite."

"What about the man who stole your uniform?" asked Robbie.

"That is a good question. This is important for you to know. He was a Yankee spy," John said impressively. "He gives me these bad clothes and leaves me here to die. So you lads be careful. If you see someone walking around in my uniform, don't so much as speak to him. He's a spy, and dangerous."

"Yes, sir. You should come to the house and let Mom take care of you," Paul offered generously.

"No, I couldn't do that. If that spy finds out I'm still alive, he'll come back and kill me for real."

"Sure thing, but we'll help you," Robbie assured him courageously.

"Now you boys mustn't go telling anyone about me. You see, I don't feel too good about having my clothes stolen, and I don't want anyone seeing me this way—my being a lieutenant and all."

"I can see why," Robbie said seriously as his eyes traveled up and down John's pants, which reached only to the tops of his boots and were bunched around his waist, held up only by a belt.

John had to look away to keep from laughing as Paul said with less tact, "You look like the man doing tricks at the fair, only his face was painted funny colors too."

When John felt capable of once again maintaining his manner of over-dramatized solemnity which appealed so greatly to the gallant fancy of his impressionable young audience, he said, "Can I trust you to be keeping a secret? I sure don't want that spy to come back and kill me while I'm wounded."

"What a coward he must be," Robbie said, shaking his head.

"That he is," John agreed. "But if you loyal little Confederates want to help me, I could sure use a nice big drink of water."

The boy's were off with startling alacrity, returning in record time with a great draught of water which John received with profound thanks. As he gulped it down, they plied him with little boys questions about his war time experiences. John answered truthfully enough, except for portraying himself in gray rather than blue. After about half an hour had slipped by, during which the three consumed most of the berries in the lad's pail, John advised his young friends to return to the house, with a somber reminder to keep his presence in strict secrecy.

"Can't we ever tell anyone about how we helped you, Lieutenant?" queried Paul, his dimpled face puckered in concern.

"Of course, when the war is all over, just not now," John reassured him.

"Good." The boys exchanged a smile, their eyes sparkling with the thought of the commendation which would be theirs when their noble deed was manifested.

"I'll tell you what. If you keep my secret real good, I'll appoint you honorary members of the Confederate army."

"You mean we're soldiers now too?" Paul looked as if he was about to burst with excitement.

"We will guard your honor as if it were our own," Robbie said grandly.

"When I say my prayers tonight, I will remember you," said Paul with such sweet innocence that John felt a lump rising in his throat. With one last look of adoring awe, that so reminded John of two other lads on a Maryland farm, the boys scampered for home.

To Love or Not to Love

Twenty-four hours later found John lying exhausted but safe in a Union hospital tent, his shoulder still throbbing from the vigorous washing and dressing administered by the none too gentle doctor and his staff. After leaving the orchard, John had traveled all night, and shortly before dawn, located the Federal camp he was searching for.

The sentry, being of a less trustful nature than the two boys John had met, gave him considerable difficulty, and even accused him of stealing the horse he was riding on, when he tried to use its Union cavalry brand as evidence of his truthfulness. But fortunately for John, Arthur Connly was in the camp and gave him both a hearty welcome and vouched for his identity. John had now received the proper care, and for the first time in over two weeks, could rest easily.

As relieved as he was for his adventure to be over, reflecting back on the last several weeks, he knew he would not have avoided them if he could. There was something exceptional about them, which left him with no doubt that of all his war time experiences, this would be the one most remembered and talked about. A light touch on his shoulder brought him out of his reverie, and he looked up into Connly's smiling eyes.

"Lieutenant, you have no idea how glad I am to see you safe and sound. We thought you were a goner for sure." His voice was exuberant.

John smiled back at him. "So, you've had your first real battle now?"

Connly pressed his lips together and nodded grimly. "Corporal Higgins didn't make it. But let's not talk about that. I want to hear all about your adventures."

Connly listened with rapt attention as John began his narrative, but he had not even gotten as far as Elsa finding him in the bushes, when the medic's businesslike voice broke into their conversation. "I'm sorry, Sergeant, you better move on and let the Lieutenant rest now. I won't have my space cluttered with miscellaneous persons."

Connly directed a scowl in the departing medic's direction. "Well, he's a fine fellow. I'll get out of his way—for now. But be assured, your miscellaneous person shall return, impatient to hear the rest of your story."

"And I will make my miscellaneous person productive, by cajoling him to write down everything I tell him in a letter to my folks," John said laughing.

Connly returned late that afternoon, and true to his word, John set him to work writing a letter, although not without grumbling on the younger man's part, for Connly assured him that however dexterous his hands might prove in managing the reins or however great his patience display itself while breaking a wild colt, he had not equal aptitude for spelling.

"Then it will be good practice for you," countered John with the provoking air of an elder brother.

"Hmph," snorted Connly, who had only little sisters, and so knew nothing as yet of the joys of fraternal patronizing. "I'm writing this for you only because I want to hear your story," he reminded John.

"Really, Connie, sometimes I think you don't treat me at all like a lieutenant, but since I'm in bed, I guess I'll put up with it."

"Fire away. Once I dip the pen, I've got to write fast or I'll smudge it." Connly was holding the pen tensely poised over the ink well, as if waiting for a gunshot to signal him into flurried action.

"Here goes: Dear Father, Mother and boys, I am doing well. However, I was injured in a raid shortly after I last saw you. My horse threw me into some bushes, where I lay unconscious until I was found by a young Southern woman. She lived in the nearby manse, but surprisingly enough, her sympathies lay wholeheartedly with the Union, and she treated me with more than a little kindness."

"Hold on a minute. Give me time to get this down." After a long pause, Connly said, "All right. Go on."

"Then Elsa…"

"Who's Elsa?"

"Oh, that's the young woman's name."

"So we call her by her first name, do we?" Connly said with a sly grin.

"Under the circumstances, there was nothing extraordinary about that," protested John, coloring slightly.

"Of course not," Connly said expressively. "You know, this really is incredible. I mean, how many Virginia plantations just happen to have a beautiful young belle, with wholehearted Union sympathies, living on them? (Assuming she was beautiful.) From what Everrett Trenton told us, I got the impression the folks living there were pretty staunch rebels."

"I know. I've thought a lot about that. It seems too remarkable to be a coincidence. She only lives there at all because her father died a few years ago."

"Well, John," Connly said with a meaningful look. "So is she beautiful?"

"Oh—yes," John replied hesitantly.

Connly stared at him cross-eyed. "An abolitionist living in the South— I bet there aren't many eligible suitors around. What did you think of her?"

"She was very thoughtful, and rather devoted to caring for me," John said coloring a little darker. "A little too devoted maybe."

"And were you smitten?" Connly asked impishly.

"To be honest, I feel rather sorry for her. She wasn't the least happy with her life, thought she was responsible for her parent's death, and more than a little scared of that aunt of hers. The woman sounds like a real Medusa."

"So look her up when the war is over. You can be her knight in shining armor, and save her from the gorgon," Connly said dramatically.

"And what would Elizabeth think of that?" John murmured to himself.

"Elizabeth? Oh, you already have a girl back home? Skip it; I was half joking anyhow."

"But it's not so simple as that," John said, raising himself up a bit. "We're soldiers, aren't we?"

"Sure thing."

"And a soldier has to think of duty before everything else, right?"

"I guess."

"And our lives are uncertain. Any day we could get blown to bits, right?"

"Alright. So what of it?"

"Well, back home there is this girl, Elizabeth. Our families have been neighbors for as long as I can remember. It's like everyone just expects that we'll get married someday. I've kind of taken it for granted myself, and on my last visit home I was going to ask her. I even have a ring, see." John fished in his pocket and drew out the silver band. "But then I started thinking, 'Wait a minute—I could get engaged today and tomorrow be lying dead on a battlefield.' That just isn't right. Why do women always want promises? I'm not going to make a promise I can't keep. I am practically married to our country, and any woman, regardless of what I feel for her, has to be second to that. I don't want to be in love. Why can't they understand that?"

Connly's expression had grown increasingly skeptical during this speech. "I don't know what to make of all that, but if it makes you feel good to think that way, alright."

"But that's were the problem lies; it doesn't make me, or for that matter anyone else, feel good. But the very real possibility of getting killed is bad enough, without having to worry that you are going to break someone's heart in the process."

Connly knit his brow. "Now let me get this straight. Your noble theory held good on Elizabeth because you weren't really in love with her anyhow, but now when you try to apply your theory to Elsa, you are starting to like it less and less."

"I don't exactly like your way of oversimplifying things, but I guess it is a little like that," John admitted.

"If you want my advice, scrap your silly theory. Romance is supposed to be fun. If you got killed in battle, no sensible girl would hold it against you."

"Like I said, it isn't that simple. I didn't want to make any commitments, or have any feelings, that would be a burden to me or anyone else, and instead I managed to get myself neatly tangled up between two women—and probably both sitting at home worrying about me right now." John shook his head.

"You are in a bit of a dither," Connly smothered a chuckle, but a bright twinkle was shining in his eyes.

"Arthur Connly," John said sharply. "You actually think this funny, don't you? Just wait until your day comes, then you'll see how funny it is."

"If my day ever comes, I'll sit down and have a good laugh before I do anything. No good comes from being so serious."

John shook his head again, but more light-heartedly this time. "You are just airing your ignorance on how little you know about women. While you're laughing, she'll be off some place crying her eyes out, and there won't be any hilarity in the situation."

"What do you mean, I don't know anything about women? I have sisters," Connly defended himself, "which is more than you have. Now let's say we finish this letter before dark, huh?"

"Good plan. Where were we?"

"You just said how helpful Elsa was."

"Well, after several days, a most capable black man offered Elsa his aid in my concealment, and I spent several days with him. Almost miraculously, he had recovered my horse, and so I was prepared to leave when they deemed me sufficiently well. (Although I thought them both rather overly cautious in the matter.)"

"Is the black man you are referencing, Everrett Trenton?" Connly wondered.

"Yes. I was quite impressed with him. He comes off a little dull at first, but he is actually a very intelligent and well-informed person. He seemed to know everything about everyone. If it wasn't for his ailing mother he would join the army, and its our loss not to have him. But back to the letter. 'A fine friend, Arthur Connly, is writing this for me, as my left arm still has vigorous objections when I try to employ it in such a task.' I have to explain to them that I'm not writing it myself, so they won't be appalled by the spelling," John added with a naughty smile.

"Hey, do you want this letter written or not?"

And so between much talking and jibing, the men completed the letter, which when finished, read as follows:

> *Dear Famlie!*
>
> *I am fine. got hurt during a rayed. I was out cold in the bushes til a beautyful, kind young Lady found me she lived in the manse nearby but hain't no rebel. She and a black Man took care of me. finally let me go when they thought best. my Friend is righting cause my arm still hurts too bad. Hurry up and write. be Well. Curtis—hug Mom for Me. Lawrence—be a good boy! I will right soon ass I can.*
>
> *Love your good Sun John!*

John's eyebrows popped up as he read the letter. "This isn't exactly how I dictated it."

"It says the same things," Connly said unconcernedly. "I didn't know how to spell all those big words your were using—concealment, miraculously, sympathies. Besides, I would have filled half a book if I'd written all that."

"But what about this part about Elsa—'*beautiful, kind, young lady*'? You didn't have to put all that."

"It's true, isn't it? And mothers love to hear that kind of stuff."

John gave his grudging consent, but then went on, "What about this? '*Finally let me go when they thought best.*' It sounds as if they were holding me hostage. And you said my arm still hurts too bad to write. That doesn't sound good. They'll worry."

"Oh, your arm doesn't hurt too bad to write?" Connly snatched the letter away. "Well then, I will happily dispose of this inferior work, penned by the lowly hand of a miscellaneous person, and allow you to write them your own masterpiece. Perhaps you would care to include illustrations. A picture does say a thousand words. That could cut down significantly on your writing time. Oh, and would you like me to search the camp for some red ink so you can highlight the important passages?"

"No, no." John grabbed for the letter, but Connly held it teasingly out of reach. "It is a lovely letter. Never before have I read anything quite so inspirational." John clasped his hands in over-dramatized supplication. "I cannot bear to think of my parents going to their graves without having the chance to read it. Their lives would have been in vain should they be denied this. Okay, have I said enough?"

Connly screwed his mouth in contemplation and then shook his head. "It will take more than those puny words to melt such a heart as mine."

John rolled his eyes. "Noble sir, if you have no regard for my poor parents, will you not at least look with compassion on my two young brothers. Would you have them to go through their lives, denied so fundamental an element of life? You might as well deny them water or air itself, rather than deny them this letter."

"Alright, Alright," Connly sat down laughing. "You win. Your entreaties have not fallen on deaf ears."

*   *   *   *   *

The month of June passed with comparative calmness for John. There were several moves as the camp was relocated, divided, or merged with another. John's vitality returned quickly, and by the time spring had given way to a sultry summer, he was ready and anxious for action, so it was with a good deal of excitement that he received the news he had been chosen, along with several other junior officers, to lead small groups of thirty men. Their objective was to hound the enemy by making as many raids and engaging them in as many skirmishes as possible, and by any and all means, make themselves an unbearable nuisance.

Their main target was to be General Early's troops, spread throughout the Shenandoah valley. Early had failed in his campaign to take Washington, and Grant had given Sheridan orders to follow him to the death. Sheridan intended to wear his enemy down with unrelenting harassment.

Along with his new command, John was promoted to 1st lieutenant, and he requested Connly as his aid. Their first assignment was to confront a small body of infantry stationed near Thortons Gap. Early on the morning of June 28th, they set off, eager and ready for the new adventures awaiting them.

As the Captain Wishes

At first after John's departure, life seemed to come to a standstill for Elsa. She did not want to go forward, and she couldn't go back. She was afraid to do or say anything, for fear it would send her hurtling down some path she did not want to take. She accepted she could not have what she wanted, but what did her future hold? Although she didn't want to find out, she could hardly stand not knowing.

She became increasingly despondent and listless. Even the sunny days of summer, which usually brightened her melancholy nature, seemed to have lost their power to charm. She felt like a flower, snapped from its stem and left to slowly wither, denied any source of refreshment.

The one luminous point in her life, were her frequent visits to Martha. But even this joy grew dim, as each successive visit revealed a woman growing closer to the end of her sojourn in a world, which for her had been fraught with sorrows, yet had never overcome the bright spirit which leapt above them.

About two weeks after John left, Elsa received a reply to the letter she had written Aldridge. Ingrid handed it to her and stood by impatiently waiting for her to open it.

"Aunt, if you do not mind, I would like to retire to my room before I read it," Elsa said nervously.

"Look at you, your hands are practically trembling," Ingrid exclaimed.

"I never expected to see you this agitated over the captain. I did not think you had it in you." She sounded pleased, or was it triumphant?

"I know," Elsa said gloomily. "You thought I had a heart of ice."

"Well, I give myself some credit for facilitating its melting."

Elsa bit her tongue and ran up the stairs to her room. Locking the door, she sat down on the stool in front of her vanity. She stared at herself in the mirror for a minute, then down at the letter, then back at the mirror, feeling as if opening this letter was going to significantly alter her life, seal her fate in one way or another.

"Come on and stop being silly," she said to herself. "It is merely a piece of paper with ink on it, nothing more." And slowly she broke the seal.

When Aldridge had received Elsa's letter, he had been quite pleased. He had not thought he had made enough progress during his last visit for her to write to him. He didn't particularly care what the content of the letter was. Just to know that he was occupying her thoughts, was enough for now.

In most areas of his life, dominance by brute force was Aldridge's idea of success. However, when it came to women, that was not enough. He wanted from them the same things any domineering man does, complete obedience and sexual gratification, but he did not find any satisfaction in their obedience if it came out of fear, rather he wanted to be obeyed because he was worshipped. And no sexual act could satiate his passions unless he saw adoring submission in their eyes. Any fool could force a woman, but only the best could be the object of their constant devotion and desire.

This is why when he first met Elsa, he knew she was meant for him. Most women beautiful enough to be deserving, were well enough aware of their own charms, not to be so completely controlled. But physically Elsa was more than desirable, while her personality was sweet, easily manipulated, and eager to please.

She was just the woman who would make the sort of wife he was looking for, one who would be his constant devotee, admiring, adoring, and willing to give herself to him any time he wanted. Her hunger for approval was a handle by which she could always be turned to meet his needs.

He was not in the least daunted by the fact that she had responded to him with initial coldness. The challenge only increased the value of the prize. He would have her, and no one else would. With these thoughts in mind, he had written his reply.

> *My Darling Elsa,*
>
> *It is perfectly adorable of you to concern yourself so on my account, but allow me to assure you in the strongest possible terms that your fears are needless. Someone as beautiful as yourself could never be surrounded by so sinister an aura. But even if that were the case, I am much stronger than to be brought under the power of some evil accident of fate.*
>
> *The misadventure which befell us during my last visit is but part of the normal course of war. I have lived through things a hundred times worse and am but the stronger for it.*
>
> *As for your father's decease, to which you alluded as grounds for your apprehensions, perhaps destiny so willed it that you might be fully mine, for I am sure I am willing to share you with no other.*
>
> *It pleases me well to learn that your coldness stemmed only from so easily vanquished a fear. If as you read these words, you find yourself still in doubt, believe me, when I make love to you for the first time, all your forebodings will take wings and fly away, and from that day forward you will be blissfully unaware of any fortune beyond what I choose for you.*
>
> *I promise it will not be much longer before I hold you in my arms and kiss away all such troubling nonsense from that sweet head of yours. Even were all the powers of fate pitted against us, I would never relinquish you.*
>
> > *I remain your unyielding lover,*
> > *Captain Lester Raphael Aldridge*

Elsa read the letter and blushed, then read it again and thought it was rather sweet, then read it again, thinking it was shamelessly forward and presuming, and finally reading it one last time, she decided that although he was quite overbearing and obviously had no respect for her, he was no doubt going to be her future husband, and she should be grateful for the fact that at least he was romantic and handsome. That was more than some women got. And what was so bad about overbearing? She was used to it.

And then Elsa lay down on the bed and cried, because John was the only man she had ever felt truly attracted to, and the time they had spent together had been so short, and his kisses so sweet, and she would never get to see him again, but he would always be a dream in the back of her head, making her long for what she could not have.

Mid June, the tedious routine of existence at Madame Chesterfield's plantation was shattered by a Union raiding party, whose objective was not a Confederate regiment bivouacking in the adjacent field, but the mansion itself and its valuables. The incursion fell as a complete surprise, and it was not possible to even make an attempt at hiding any of the treasures. The soldiers, however, where interested mainly in the horses, silver, and money, and being limited on room to carry provisions, about half the stores of food and many of the more personal items remained unmolested.

Elsa regarded the raid with the somewhat detachèd view of a depressed person. She was not happy to see her aunt's beautiful old house looted and showed as much sympathy as Ingrid would receive, yet at the same time she was not exactly sad to see the proud wealth diffused to a good cause. Being no Robin Hood, the moral justification behind raids was dark to her, but by comparison it seemed one of the lesser evils with which the world was overflowing. She was truly sad to see Sparrow taken, but accepted it with the quiet resignation of one who expects little from life.

The financial blow to Ingrid was a heavy one, considering she had already nearly depleted herself with her unstinting generosity to the cause she loved. Because she was reluctant to discuss such things with Elsa, the younger woman had only surmised until now what their monetary situation actually was.

Ever since her aunt had grudgingly consented to her taking a paying job as a tutor, she had suspected that Ingrid's funds were less than her pride permitted her to admit. Shortly after, Ingrid had recommended that Elsa donate her earnings to help maintain the household's standard of living. This Elsa had willingly done, and the fact that her aunt had dismissed her arrogance enough to make such a request, seemed sufficient proof that Ingrid's pocket book was not bulging.

Now the true situation was manifested. Ingrid finally devised a plan whereby the almost wrecked ship of her finances, after being stripped of all its trimmings, was again made fit for sailing. Several old investments were disposed of, while the household was reduced to a minimum by selling many of the slaves. With a good deal of persuasion, Elsa was able to convince Ingrid to keep Henry, but beyond that one concession, she stood by silent and helpless as the plans were made.

The rain of troubles had not yet finished its deluge, however, for Elsa returned home from work the next day with the information that the Wilsons, finding themselves in similar straits, were no longer able to employ a tutor. She was surprised by the quiet steadiness with which her aunt received the news.

"Alright, so my fortune is gone," she said stiffly. "But I am still a Chesterfield, and my head is held high. I have given all I could, and I am willing to give more. I will give the very last penny I have if the occasion demands it. I have given my husband. What is everything else in comparison? I have staked my all on the Confederacy, and in her triumph I will prosper. Until then I will bide my time and wait. I have managed to scrape together enough recourses for us to get by, and our dignity need not be lost. So do not suggest running off and becoming a servant or some other such foolish notion. I will not permit even the mention of anything so scandalous."

"Then I will continue to tutor the Wilson children even though they can not pay. I must do something, and I have grown quite fond of the children."

"Very well. And now it is high time we secured your future."

"What do you have reference to?" Elsa asked, startled.

"The captain of course. We must not allow things to go hanging about in uncertainty any longer."

"But Captain Aldridge is busy. He is completely occupied with his duties as a soldier," Elsa objected. "I did not anticipate anything materializing until after the war."

"Nonsense," Ingrid said with a dismissive wave of her fan. "Aldridge has certainly given me reason to believe that he is quite anxious for his relations with you to progress."

Remembering the letter she had recently received, Elsa knew she couldn't argue with that.

"Besides, Elsa, if, God forbid, something were to happen to him, it would be much better for you to be Mrs. Captain Aldridge. His family is extremely wealthy, and you could insure that both of us were provided for. This marriage is not only about you."

"You want me to marry him because he is very wealthy?" Elsa wasn't sure why she was so surprised, but she was.

"Don't look so affronted. Any reasonable girl in your position would be delighted at such an opportunity. But do not think about the money if you do not wish. I thought you had feelings for the captain."

"Well, I really do not know him all that well," Elsa said hesitantly. "I do not think we ought to rush."

"I knew it was too good to be true that you were actually in love with him," Ingrid said with a humorless laugh. "But he loves you, is that not enough?"

"Love? What is love?"

"What kind of a question is that?"

"An honest one. You say Aldridge loves me, but what does that mean? Love has so many confusing synonyms. Romance is a feeling, lust a passion, amity an action, charity an attitude."

Ingrid was nonplussed for only a minute before she said, "Well, love alone is a poor foundation for a marriage. There are many other reasons one marries."

"Such as money," Elsa said with a sigh.

"Just so."

"I agree with you that love is not necessary for marriage," Elsa said slowly, "but trust." She lingered tenderly over the word. "I could marry a man I had no love for, if I trusted him."

"What are you trying to say? That you do not trust Aldridge?"

"I am rather-rather afraid of him." Elsa's voice was barely even a whisper.

"For pity's sake, niece, tell me something you are not afraid of. You are afraid of your own shadow. But I really did not expect you to be so selfish about this."

Elsa hung her head, Ingrid's words stinging like a hornet. Why could she never please Ingrid? Why was it always wrong for her to consider her own happiness for even an instant? When she looked up her face was pale but rigid. "Very well, if you both insist, I will be Mrs. Captain Aldridge. But I beg you, Aunt Ingrid, do not try to rush this. I have only just turned twenty. If he wants me, then let the timing be of his choosing, and do not pressure him. He may change his mind, and the only consolation I will have in this marriage is that at least *he* is getting what he wants."

Twilight Ends in Darkness

For Everrett, the days passed with undesirable rapidity, and all to soon the dark time had come when he must say goodbye to his elderly mother. The heat of summer was too much for her frail body, and just before the thirty days of June were spent, she made a plunge for the worse. The next morning the forge stood empty on a weekday for the first time in years.

The day dawned a glorious bright and clear summer morning. The birds sang their sweetest, the buttercups outside the cabin door bloomed more gaily and resplendent in their yellow satin gowns than ever before, and the squirrels chattered sociably as they scampered among the oaks. Martha's spirit seemed to reflect the sunshine of the verdant country around her. Only Everrett's countenance was dimmed behind clouds of sadness.

All that morning Martha's breathing was barely audible, and her pulse so faint Everrett could not feel it. She fell asleep for a time and about mid-afternoon, woke with a start.

"Everrett."

"I's here." He came to stand by her head to catch her faint words.

"Did Miss Elsa say shey was comin'?"

"Yes, shey said shey would come dis aftehnoon."

"Dat-dat is good. I's will not live till mornin'."

Everett stared moodily out the window and attempted no response.

"It's alright, son." She touched his hand. "I's not afeared to die. I's glad to go and hear dose blest angels singin'. Can't you's 'most here dem already?"

Everett stroked her thin hair back from her forehead. The singing of angels was so far from what he was hearing that he couldn't even imagine it. "I's jest wish you's had a betteh life to leave," he said morosely.

"Son, I's die—I's die a free woman. Dat is good."

"Yes, Mammy, but youh life has been vehy hard and bitteh."

"I's used to think dat way, only not no more. We's neveh talk about it 'cause it ain't nice, but even de worst wrong I's suffehed, brought me you, my only son. And you's grown into sech a strong man, and you's given me my freedom. So how's kin I judge what is bitteh and what—what is sweet?"

Martha's voice was slow and weary, but now she raised herself up just a bit, and a radiance shone in her eyes. "I's know you hate youh fatheh, and I's don't beah him no love myself. But, son, when I's gone, remembeh what I's jest said. And remembeh dat story in de Good Book about Joseph and his evil brothehs, but de Lord meant if foh good. I's reckon as how you's jest can't tell when somedin' is meant foh good until you's get to de end and sees it all backwards like. My dear Everett, remembeh dat." Martha sank back on the pillow, exhausted by her short exhortation.

"I's will remembeh," he said gruffly.

After a minute Martha went on, "Do you know why I's named you Everrett?"

"No. Why's did you?" Everett asked curiously.

"Two reasons. First, because the sound of it always makes me think of an evehgreen tree, standing dere all dark and alive when de otheh trees are dyin'. And second, 'cause it means 'strong as a wild hog'."

Everrett gave a choked laugh which came out more like grunt.

"Every motheh wants heh son's life to be full of happiness, but I's knew dat weren't what you was born to." A tear slid out of the corner of Martha's eye. "Youh life is like de wild boar's; free but neveh safe. He's got to spend his life roamin' and scroungin' just to survive, with men huntin' him down. But dey don't neveh catch him, 'cause he's too fierce for dem. I's always wanted dat strength foh you, and you's have it, Everrett. I's know you's gonna be alright." Martha squeezed his hand weakly and smiled into his dark eyes. "But der is one thing dat you needs."

"What's dat?" he asked when she didn't continue.

"You needs to take a wife. Some men ahen't meant to sleep alone, and you's one of dem."

Everrett looked a little startled but said calmly enough, "I's know where to find women ifen I's need dem."

"I's didn't say women, now did I?" Martha retorted as harshly as her weakened state would allow. "You's need a woman as you can always come home to."

"I's wouldn't know what to do with one."

"Dat's nonsense. You's know what do with a woman."

"But Mammy, a woman would want to be loved, wouldn't shey?" Everrett asked softly.

"Of course shey would."

"Like I's said, I's know well enough what do with women, but a woman…" Everrett ended his thought with a moody shake of his head.

Martha was quiet for several minutes, too tired to speak, but finally she said, "Find a woman who ain't nothin' like youhself, one as is gentle, and sweet, and shy, and she'll love you foh bein' everything shey ain't. And I's promise you, son, one day you's will find you love her foh bein' everything you ain't."

Everrett looked dismally dubious, but not wanting her to wear herself out anymore, he patted her hand as he replied, "Alright, I's will take youh word foh it."

A rap sounded on the door. Trudging across the floor, Everrett let Elsa in. She hurried over to Martha's side.

"Martha, dear Martha."

The ill woman slowly opened her eyes with a smile. "You's came."

"Of course I came. You think I would let you go without saying goodbye. Oh, Martha, you have been such a dear friend. At times you even made me forget how much I missed Clara, and now I will miss you just as much."

"I's can't wait to see Clara again. It won't bey long now," Martha said happily.

Elsa bit her tongue before she could say, "But Clara isn't dead yet." Martha would know the truth soon enough.

"You's been so kind to me, Miss Elsa. Now you's won't need to botheh anymohe."

"Oh, Martha, you have never been a bother." Elsa wanted to say more, but the lump in her throat prevented it. She was not going to cry—not in front of Everrett.

Martha reached out towards Everrett, and he grasped her hand. Her eyes rested on him lovingly for a moment, while a smile flickered across her face which looked to Everrett like the last blaze of a candle before it is snuffed out, and to Elsa was reminiscent of the final rays of sunset as twilight falls. Then her hand grew limp in Everrett's grasp.

The room was absolutely still. They both stood, absorbed in their own memories, as they gazed at the lifeless form before them. At length Everrett laid down her hand and turned towards the window.

"I's only wished shey might have known true liberty afohe shey died," he burst out in bitter passion.

Elsa's eyes darted up as his voice jerked her from her trance. "Didn't she, Mr. Trenton?"

"Not anymohe dan I eveh have. We might have been loosed from ouh mastehs, but we're still bound by de chains of prejudice and hate. We's neveh get half de chance of a white man. Look at me. I's as good as any otheh two smiths put togetheh, and see how I's live—poor as dirt. It doesn't matteh what we do or how good wey ahe; we can neveh have what de white man does or bey what he can be, and it's much mohe dan money I's talkin' 'bout. How's can you call what we's have liberty?"

Elsa nodded and finally said, "Martha was content and happy. That is something, isn't it?"

"Maybe if I's was an old woman on my death bed I could bey content with dat, but I's not, and I's tihed of a life of abuse. I's can't even bury heh where otheh men bury dere mothehs," he went on vehemently. "Oh, no, I's must use a little spot outside de walls of de churchyahd, as if I's less good in de eyes of de Almighty!"

Elsa looked up at him, empathy shining in her soft blue eyes. "I am sorry," she said as she lightly touched his arm. "I wish too that your life could be all you dream of and all you deserve." Something in her tone was so wistful that it made Everett really notice her for the first time that day.

"Do you's know what I's talkin' 'bout?" he asked quietly.

She nodded her head the slightest bit. "You say you are chained in you freedom, and I a fugitive in mine. Always seeking, never finding. Always wanting, never getting. Always trying, never succeeding. I know all too well. Having to bite your tongue and say only what people want to hear. Having to swallow your heart and give yourself over to suit their pleasure."

Everett nodded, and for a moment they both lapsed into silence again. Finally Elsa asked, "Do you want to bury her yet today?"

"Yes, I's will dig de grave."

"If you will allow me, I will prepare her body."

"Mammy would bey honored."

The Captain's Camp

"Lieutenant! Lieutenant!" Scroggins reined in his horse abruptly, panting, "I've found them."

"Good work. How far?" John asked.

"Only a little over a mile from here. I would say about fifty or so."

John and his group of thirty men had set out as the first tinges of dawn began to paint the eastern horizon. The morning star still hung in the sky while the dew lay thick on the grass. The crisp air was invigorating, the horses lively, and the men in high spirits as they journeyed rapidly towards Thortons Gap and the conflict awaiting them there.

It was now nearly six o'clock in the evening, and after some difficulty, one of his men had located the position of their foe.

"They seemed pretty comfortable camping there. I'm sure they didn't detect me," Scroggins continued.

"Good, as soon as the other scouts get back we'll set out. Now you go and have a bite to eat and tell Sergeant Connly I want to see him."

Connly cantered his horse alongside John's. "Sir."

"Scroggins just returned from viewing the rebel camp. Now this is what I'm thinking: we're outnumbered fairly significantly, but we do have the advantage of surprise, and we need to make the most of it. So we'll all go a little closer, and then I will leave you and half the men to hide in the trees beside the road. I'll continue on with the rest of the men and launch an attack. Of course, we'll be a mighty small group and retreat almost as soon as we start, but we will lead them back right in front of you. Then you guys come charging out. This way we'll have them on two sides, and chances are, when they are chasing us from their camp, they will not bring enough ammunition with them. Make sure you stay between them and their camp so they can't return to reload."

"Good plan. I like it," Connly answered. "What about Jenkins? You're taking him with you? I hope."

"Jenkins? Aww, no Connie, I think I better leave him behind with you. I don't know what to make of him, but he's nothing but trouble. That's for sure."

"He's in a bad way—poor chap." Connly shook his head.

"He's quite young, isn't he?" John asked.

"Seventeen."

"Must have seen too much for his age."

"Too much for any age!" Connly said fiercely. "Some of the men were telling me that back at Yellow Taverns, he saw his brother's chest ripped open and his brains blown in his face. They say he's been crazy ever since."

John's face turned gray. "I've seen some pretty nasty sights myself, but I guess we can be thankful we don't got any brother's fighting with us. It's not good to get too attached to your comrades."

Connly didn't answer that, but after a pause he said, "He's mean though, John."

"I reckon we all are sometimes." John's cool gray eyes had a steely sheen.

"Not like him. He's insane. I just about had to take his gun away from him earlier today keep him from plugging his fellow in the back. Every single man in the group has told me he won't share a tent with him."

John shook his head. "Why do they send a man like that with us? Never mind though; it can't be helped. I guess he'll make a good fighter when the time comes."

Connly raised his eyebrows and was about to say something when

John went on, "Look, there come the other two scouts. Call the men to order, and I'll tell them the plan."

*   *   *   *   *

Captain Aldridge strolled to the entrance of his tent and placidly surveyed the scene before him. Men were just finishing dinner. Some lolled leisurely in front of their tents. Off to the side he heard loud brawling as a verbal argument between three of his soldiers erupted into blows. He threw them a casual glance but did not attempt to interfere. The men were restless. Well, why shouldn't they fight? It would keep them in shape and their passions up for battle.

After taking a slow draught from the wine bottle he held in his hand, he jammed the cork in and punched it down with a firm whack. He tossed the bottle in the air and caught it again while he screwed his brow in contemplation. "Sergeant!"

"Yes, sir," A short, bald man hurried around the side of the tent.

"I'm thinking on leaving for a spell."

"All of us, sir."

"No. It would not be such a bad idea though. I haven't the faintest notion why I was left with this blasted company to keep watch after that skirmish with the damn Yankees. Nothing to do and all these wounded men; we can't possibly move till at least the beginning of next week. I'd like to know what damn son of bitch gave those orders. Sitting me out her to keep watch over nothing. Insult to my abilities!"

"Yes, sir," replied the sergeant with as much feeling as a scarecrow.

"What I was saying though. I'm going to visit a friend less than fifteen miles from here. I'll be back by the end of the week and I hope you have enough sense in that confounded head of yours not to let the camp fall apart while I'm gone. But I am just that damn sure nothing will happen, that I am leaving you in charge for a few days."

Ever since Aldridge had received Elsa's letter, he had not been able to get her out of his mind. He was tired of waiting. It was high time their relationship progressed. "I'm leaving tonight. Have one of the men saddle my horse and bring it around front for me. Any questions?"

"What if something should happen and we have to pull out before your return?"

"I'll assume you were killed and eaten by cannibals," Captain Aldridge returned dryly. "Don't be ridiculous. I said there is no way we can move before the beginning of the week. I will be back before you miss me."

"Yes, sir," replied the sergeant, and this time he meant it.

After giving a few more orders and attending to some other details regarding his absence, Aldridge handed his packed saddle bags to the corporal. Running a hand airily through his golden hair, he donned his hat with a flourish. He swung himself easily into the saddle, wheeled his horse around grandly, and was off.

The sergeant watched with a gratified little smile as his captain disappeared among the trees, while the corporals clapped one another on the back. They had fast grown accustomed to the impulsiveness of their over-bearing leader, but if they felt a little insecurity in his absence, they certainly felt no grief.

*   *   *   *   *

"Alright boys, this is the spot the lieutenant wants us to wait. Let's spread out a little. You men over there," Connly motioned to six of the men John had left in his charge, "you go hide behind that thicket and the rest of us will get behind the trees on this side of the trail. Remember absolute silence until after the enemy passes us. We need to get between them and their camp."

As the men scattered and began to search out suitable hiding places, Connly glanced over towards Jenkins. His hands were fidgeting rapidly with the reins as he leaned unsteadily back and forth in the saddle. Connly brought his own horse alongside him. "How ya doing?" Connly's manner was easy and relaxed.

"I'll be doin' great as soon as I can feel warm, slippery rebel blood on my hands." Jenkins' deep-set eyes, shadowed with a dark glint, darted restively through space.

"You understand how important it is that you stay completely hidden until I give the signal?"

"Aww, I should have gone with the lieutenant. An ambush is no place for me." The younger man was not listening. His breath was coming in fast unnatural jerks. "I can't wait to hear them shriek in agony when I get my hands…"

"Jenkins!" Connly interrupted, slapping him on the cheek to get his attention. "Listen to me. You have orders to stay here, quiet and still until I give the signal. Do you hear me?"

"I ain't stupid, but when my bloods up I got to kill," he sputtered shrilly. "I can't rest be—be quiet t-till I see everyone one of those confounded rebs sent to the damnation that's waitin' for them."

"You can do all the killing you want, but not until I give the signal. That is an order, sir. Now get behind those trees."

With an angry jerk on his reins, Jenkins followed Connly into the woods. Several minutes later all was quiet along the path. Nothing seemed amiss to the young Confederate captain as he sped down the trail. However, from the undergrowth along the road, a dozen pairs of eyes were following his every move.

Connly was puzzled. This was not at all what he had expected. He raised his pistol uncertainly. He did not want to take the chance of foiling John's plan. Perhaps it was best to just let this man pass and wait for the others to come. They were close enough to the rebel camp that the sound of even one gun shot could put the enemy on the alert. On the other hand it might be very helpful to remove this officer now.

Connly's finger tightened on the trigger of his pistol. He must be sure of his aim; he couldn't have this man shoot back and throw his men into confusion. Just then, Jenkins gave a wild whoop as dashed out from their cover and into the middle of the path, shooting recklessly as he went.

A bullet whizzed within inches of the captain's blond hair, however he proved himself more than a match for his crazed assailant. Whipping out his revolver with an oath, he downed his opponent with one swift shot. Jenkins fell with a blood-chilling shriek.

Connly would have shot back, but the captain spurred his horse and rushed on, delivering the young man his coup de grace as he passed. The sergeant froze his finger just in time. If he shot, his men would take it as a signal and rush out in pursuit. Then when John came, their ambush would not be ready and the day might be lost.

Captain Aldridge glanced over his shoulder and seeing he was not being chased, halted. He blinked for a minute as he considered the baffling situation. Was this man he had just downed, alone? If he was part of a group, where were they? Perhaps he should return to his camp. On the other hand, he doubted there were others or else they would have come out after him. But if he was being secretly followed, it was just as well that he was heading away from his camp. His men were in no danger. So satisfying himself that there was no reason he should return, and because he really didn't want to, he rode on.

"Farris, come help me move his body out of the road," Connly said grimly to the man nearest him. "Jones, fetch his horse and tie it a little ways back in the trees."

The men barely had time to complete their tasks before the sound of an approaching tumult assured them the lieutenant's strategy was going as planned. Connly saw with pleasure that there were only about twenty men chasing John. Evidently they thought this a task not worthy of their whole force. He gave the signal, and his men rushed out, shooting.

The enemy, although weak and disordered in the absence of their aggressive captain, did manage to put up a valiant defense under the their sergeant's direction, but as John had hoped, once cut off from their camp, they soon ran low on ammunition and were forced to surrender.

A number did manage to escape, but John made no attempt at pursuit since he already had almost an equal number of prisoners to dragoons, for when they took possession of the camp, he realized why their pursuers had been so few. The camp was practically a hospital, where a small number of able bodied soldiers had been left to watch over the wounded until they were well enough to be moved.

John had never before been in charge of a significant number of prisoners, and being the conscientious man he was, he found a myriad of things to attend to concerning the security of his captives and the welfare of his men, so it was well after midnight before he and Connly entered their tent.

"Twenty-four prisoners, twenty-one wounded," John thought out loud. "And now only twenty-nine of us. Well, I suppose wounded men can't cause too much trouble. At least I'm glad the medic didn't escape."

Connly removed his shirt and lay down without comment. (He always got quiet when tired, and John the opposite.)

"You know, something that puzzles me is I have not seen a single officer all night."

"Oh, I saw one," Connly said and proceeded to explain the situation surrounding Jenkins' death.

"Poor Jenkins," John said. "So young. I wonder what that captain was up to? I bet you we haven't seen the last of him. Where do you suppose he was going?"

"Don't know," Connly said with a yawn.

"It really bothers me not to know," John went on. (He would have been even more bothered if he had known.) He couldn't have been going for supplies; there are plenty here. Besides, he would have sent one of his men."

"Excuse me, sir," Connly interjected, suddenly raising his head, "don't you hear something?"

Insurmountable Obstacles

Elsa returned home after Martha's burial with a heavy heart. She had spent most of the afternoon assuring Everrett that Martha had gone to a far better world where she was now enjoying every blessing she had been denied in this one. While Elsa believed her own words, they brought little solace. She was tired, unbearably tired, and entertained herself with the fanciful notion that perhaps she would languish, and waste away, and die before her 21st birthday. But sixteen years spent romping on a Kentucky farm had not fitted Elsa with a particularly frail constitution, so there seemed no escape for her.

On the morning of only the second day after Martha's death, Elsa woke from a night of disturbed and restless dreams just as the first lights of dawn were brightening the horizon. She lay for ten whole minutes, staring at her slender wrists in the gloomy semidarkness and thinking of butcher knives in the kitchen. With a guilty little start, she threw off the sheet and crossed to the window.

A stark line separated the deep black of the landscape from the pale light of the sky. Elsa watched as color seeped up almost imperceptibly from the horizon—orange, tangerine, yellow, soft blue. In the middle of the gentle beauty hovered a lumpy little gray cloud, so stolid that no light could bounce from its murky surface or illumine its dark edges. There it sat, stern and unresponsive, amid the softening tones of color. For a moment Elsa almost hated the ugly little cloud so marring the gentle dawn. But in an instant her anger melted into pity, and she felt her eyes growing moist as she watched it hang there alone and forlorn, unable to reflect the beauty around it.

Slowly she turned her gaze away and up above to where stretched a long fluffy bank of light clouds. The bottom edge was a glowing apricot and the feathery top a gentle pink. Lighter and lighter it grew, till it seemed but a gauzy veil to shimmer over the glories of the golden sun.

As the colors began to diffuse, Elsa glanced back to see what had become of the dirty gray cloud, but found only a thin streak, it had so dwindled in the morning warmth. She felt an indefinable empathy for the little cloud. It was so out of place, and it couldn't conform. All it could do was cease to exist. Elsa wondered if ceasing to exist was as painless as it seemed.

Elsa jumped and dropped the curtains as a rap on the door brought an end to her reflections. She opened it to find, Ingrid, her austere face wreathed in smiles.

"Niece, we have a guest. Just guess who has come to visit us." Not waiting for Elsa to reply, Ingrid rushed on. "He came especially to see you."

The questioning look of interest on Elsa's face flickered out to one of dismay while the picture flashed through her mind that her life was like a whirlpool, hurling her ever closer to the frightful and menacing void at its center. Ingrid was quick to catch her change of countenance but chose to ignore it.

"This is your opportunity to secure your future. Now do not let it scare you. Leave it to me, and everything will work out beautifully."

"To secure my future is the only thing that can make it worse," Elsa thought frantically, but she merely shook her head in weary discouragement.

"Now, Elsa," Ingrid chided. "He is our guest, an honored guest, and your future husband. You must treat him accordingly."

Elsa swallowed hard and nodded.

Ingrid patted Elsa's cheek as she said brightly, "We will see you at breakfast, my dear—on time."

Elsa stood frozen for a moment as she watched Ingrid mince exultantly down the hall. Her pulse quickened as a line from Aldridge's letter flashed through her mind. "*I promise it will not be long before I hold you in my arms and kiss away all such troubling nonsense from that sweet head of yours.*"

Elsa sat down on the bed, feeling weak. Why was she so perturbed? She thought she had reconciled herself to the fact that she was to be Mrs. Lester Aldridge. But she had accepted it as something to happen eventually. She wasn't ready yet. Somehow she had hoped that if she waited long enough the situation would change. But there wasn't anything to be done. The time was now.

She dressed very carefully and slowly. But finally, running out of excuses to dawdle, Elsa headed down to breakfast and whatever awaited her there. As she reached the top of the stairs, she saw Captain Aldridge at the foot, smiling up at her. She gave him a curtsey and began to descend very slowly. Aldridge bounded up to meet her halfway.

My darling, Elsa, allow me." He took her arm. "You have no idea how happy I am to see you. You look absolutely ravishing." He raised her hand to his lips and kissed it.

Aldridge was in very high spirits and did seem genuinely delighted by her presence. Elsa found herself smiling in response to his enthusiasm despite the promises she had just made to herself not to show him any encouragement.

"Did my aunt tell you about the raid?" she asked to make conversation. "They stole all the horses and most of the silver. I think war is so sad. I can hardly wait for it to be over."

"It won't be too much longer now, my dear."

"I do so hope you are right."

"I am. You will see." And then to Elsa's amazement, the captain leaned over and gave her a long, hungry kiss on the lips. He smiled at her astonishment. "I'm sorry, my dear, I just couldn't wait any longer," he said, without the least hint of apology in his voice.

She wanted to reprimand him for his impudence, but the words stuck in her throat and all she could do was give him an embarrassed smile. Out of the corner of her eye, Elsa saw Ingrid at the foot of the stairs watching them. She looked pleased. Elsa turned a deep pink as she gently pulled the captain down the stairs, for he was still holding her arm. "We must hurry to breakfast. Aunt Ingrid does not like people to be tardy," she said to him.

Now if Elsa had been a strong tempered woman, she would have firmly told Ingrid and Aldridge and anyone else concerned that she would not be coerced into matrimony, and held her ground. But Elsa was not a strong tempered woman. If she had been cunning, she would have donned her least becoming dress, made her hair look a fright, broken her violin string, and spilled her tea on him. But Elsa was not cunning, and there was an aspect of her personality which liked very much to be petted and admired.

Nearly every woman has felt the tug of these longings at least once, and Elsa may have had more than her share of this weakness. So despite her dread at the thought of marrying the captain, she could not still the butterflies in her stomach or the flutter in her heart every time he went into raptures over her hair or she caught the flirtatious leer in his dark blue eyes. All in all, the stage was set for a sad tragedy of which Elsa would be at the center. It seemed she could not escape walking defenselessly into a marriage which would only break her heart and forever sap the vitality from her delicate young life as it bound her ever tighter in its clutches.

All throughout breakfast, she kept looking up to find Aldridge's eyes fastened on her in the most unnerving manner, and she was bracing herself with the thought that she could soon retreat to the safety of the Wilsons, for this was one of her usual days to tutor, when Ingrid broke into her thoughts.

"Niece, I am sure you need not concern yourself with the children today. The Wilsons would not expect you to come when you have other social obligations."

"Perhaps not, Aunt, but I have been entertaining the children with the reading of a novel. They have become unduly engaged in the story, and I promised them I would finish it today. Should I fail to appear I am afraid they will be cruelly disappointed."

Before Ingrid could object, Aldridge broke in. "Then go, by all means.

If this diversion brings happiness to you and the children, why shouldn't you pursue it? But how do you travel there? I was under the impression that all your horses had fallen prey to our enemies."

"I walk," Elsa responded. "It is but a short distance, and the weather has been very amiable of late. I find the fresh air most invigorating to my constitution."

"Indeed so," Aldridge agreed. "I will be most happy to escort you this morning. It is hardly safe anymore for a young maiden to be out walking alone," he added.

"So I tell her nearly everyday," Ingrid broke in imperiously. "But Elsa seems to put little stock in what I have to say anymore. She seems to have inherited a degree of her mother's obstinacy."

Aldridge looked amused as he said drolly, "Indeed, Ingrid? I would have thought you flattered yourself in that trait much more than our gentle dove, Elsa."

Ingrid coughed and eyed him severely, but ignoring her displeasure, the captain turned back towards Elsa. "When will you be ready to depart, my darling? It looks a most glorious morning for a walk."

Several minutes later, Elsa found herself walking down the porch steps, side by side with the captain. It was indeed a glorious morning, and Elsa tried to keep the conversation light by discussing the trees and birdsongs. They took the back way through the fields as it was much pleasanter walking than the dusty road.

At first Aldridge said little, watching Elsa walk and talk, much as one would watch a cute puppy doing tricks. She was so small and feminine and fun to watch, especially now because he kept creating a picture in his mind of how she was going to look without her clothes on. He wasn't going to wait much longer.

"Look at the honeysuckle here. Just breathe in its perfume. Isn't it delicious?" Elsa paused by an immense clump of bushes to take in a deep breathe of the sweet fragrance.

"Not half so delicious as you, my darling," he returned, catching both her hands in his. "My own darling Elsa, you are perfect for me. Do you know that?"

"I am not so perfect to hear Aunt Ingrid talk."

Aldridge just grinned at her. "And what does she know about it?"

"I thought you held my aunt in high regard," Elsa said in surprise.

"Good heavens, no," the captain laughed out loud. "Ingrid is a most pretentious and overbearing woman. And that is why I like you so well, my darling, because you are not a bit like her."

Elsa wouldn't admit to agreeing with the captain's remarks about Ingrid, but hearing him say them elevated him a little in her esteem. And he was well aware of this.

"Your aunt is jealous of you. You know that, don't you?" he said next.

"Aunt Ingrid jealous of me?" Elsa exclaimed in amazement. "I hardly think so."

"Oh, yes, she is practically sick with envy. Why look at you. You are beautiful and charming and men desire you. When was Ingrid ever those things?"

Elsa giggled nervously. "You are just trying to flatter me."

"But you know I speak the truth," Aldridge whispered as he leaned over and began to very sensuously kiss her neck. He felt her jerk as a little tingling shiver ran up her spine, and then she tried to pull away. He gave a light laugh. "Am I too much for you, sweetheart?"

She nodded, and the serious look on her face amused him even more. "You never had a man kiss you like that before, have you? I have so many things to teach you," he whispered into her wide eyes.

"We had best keep going if we want to reach the Wilsons," Elsa said as she tried to turn, but Aldridge was still clasping both her hands and didn't cooperate.

"Not before we talk," he said.

"Talk about what?" Elsa asked, rapidly turning pale.

"Well, to start with, your letter. Why do you fancy yourself to be cursed by fate? What in the world has filled you with such amazing fears?" Elsa looked away without answering, so he went on. "You said something about your father's death. Ingrid tells me he died of consumption nearly four years ago. My father is also dead, and I do not allow it to torment me." He could tell by the stony look on Elsa's face that she had no intention of explaining herself. "Alright, Elsa, that's enough. Stop ignoring me. What is it you don't want me to know?"

Elsa looked up in answer to the cold authority in his voice. "If Aunt

Ingrid already told you all about it, what do you want to hear from me?" she said softly.

"Do not take me for a fool. There is something both of you are trying to hide from me. You do not write a letter like that because your father died of tuberculosis. I deserve an explanation."

"You said you were much too strong to be influenced by bad luck in any case, so it really does not matter what I meant."

"He probably died of something shameful you don't want me to know about. Let me guess. Syphilis?" Aldridge only said it to see how much of a rise he would get out of her.

Elsa felt her cheeks growing hot, and her head ached from the rush of blood pounding through it. She wanted to scream the truth at him, but her lips felt glued together. Not once in her life had Elsa ever yelled at anyone, never had she stood up in the face of opposition and asserted herself. When she was a child there had been no occasion for aggressiveness. Her father had been such a gentle person. She couldn't recall him ever raising his voice more than a few decibels.

Then on that cursed night when she lost him, she had been too stunned with horror to even breath, and it was as if the paralysis had stayed with her ever after. Elsa was staring hard at the shiny toes of Aldridge's boots, trying to block out the borage of thoughts and memories assaulting her. She didn't realize how tightly she was clenching her jaw until she began to feel dizzy from the tension, and small blue shadows began to dance in front of her eyes.

"Elsa, answer me." The captain's annoyed voice was loud in her ear.

Elsa's eyes darted up as she tried once more to pull her hands from his grasp, but he tightened his grip.

"Oh no, I'm not going to let you escape," he said grimly.

"Let go of me," Elsa cried, and pulling with more strength than he thought she had, she jerked one of her hands free and reflexively sent it up as if to hit him.

Captain Aldridge caught her wrist easily before her hand reached his face. His dark blue eyes snapped at her, as he said in slow, measured tones of warning, "Don't ever even think about trying to do that to me again." And then he slapped her face, not hard, but very deliberately.

He let go of her, and Elsa stepped back, scared and eager to appease him. "I'm sorry—I shouldn't have..." she stammered and then, as he had expected, started to cry.

Aldridge watched her cry for a minute. He didn't know why some men were so unnerved in the presence of a crying woman. Such a display of vulnerability was actually rather bracing. Tears generally softened a woman, making her much more pliable to mold.

Aldridge came up and very tenderly took her in his arms. He felt her stiffen in response to his touch, but he pressed her head against his shoulder, caressing the side of her face with his hand and gently rubbing her back, and dropping warm nuzzling kisses onto her forehead, until he felt her give up and let him hold her. It wasn't as if she had much choice. He smiled a little. Now they were getting somewhere.

Finally Elsa said, "I am sorry I tried to hit you. It was very unladylike and ill-mannered, but you were scaring me."

"How was I scaring you, sweetheart? Because I was holding your hands? Or because I asked you a simple question about your father?" he asked, with a very good impersonation of offended innocence.

Elsa had already been feeling stupid, but now she felt like a complete idiot. She had known well enough at the time why she was upset, but in the face of his gentleness, she was suddenly left defenseless. So for lack of anything better, she laid her head against his shoulder again and kept crying.

"You should not be afraid of me touching you, darling," he said reproachfully. "After all, I am going to be your husband."

"Captain," she said looking up at him and brushing the tears from her face. "Just please do one thing for me. Please, do not ever, ever, ever speak to me of my father again." She tried to sound calm, but he could see the tremble in her jaw.

"As you wish, dove," Aldridge said kissing her. And Elsa was so relieved that she kissed him back.

Aldridge really didn't give a hoot what had happened to her father. He had only pressed the issue as a way of getting to her, and it had proved most effective. He would remember that. Oh, he loved her. She was so easy to control, and she didn't have a clue how he was doing it. He was going to be everything to her, her danger and her protection, her terror and her comfort. Soon she would have no world beyond what lay in his shadow.

And so, alternating harsh words and looks with gentle caresses and endearing names, he wore her down, each minute making her more unsure of herself. By the time they reached the Wilsons, Elsa was thoroughly flustered, her mind and body sending her such contradicting signals. At that moment she was entirely unable to say whether she wanted the captain desperately or despised him deeply. There was only one thing she knew for certain, and that was that Aldridge held a terrible sway over her which she felt powerless to break.

Captain Aldridge had told her that he would come for her at half past two, and she was so eager to avoid another walk with him, that she left the Wilsons about one forty-five. Now that she finally had a chance to listen to her own thoughts, she decided that although she didn't know how he did it, the captain's tendency to make her miserable was quite intentional. What was being his wife going to be like? But after they were married he would have nothing to prove, so perhaps things would be better.

Another line from Aldridge's letter popped into Elsa's mind. *"After I make love to you for the first time, all your misgivings will take wings and fly away."* She desperately hoped that was true. There was something rather intoxicating about his kisses, so presumably he was equally accomplished in the more intimate aspects of love making. Elsa was sure he had no lack of experience.

Experience—that was a disturbing thought. Would Aldridge be faithful to her? For how long could a man, who was used to a whole garden of flowers, be content with just one? To share one's bed with a less than ideal man was one thing, but to also have to share it with only God knows how many other women, was a thought too dreadful to contemplate. Perhaps she should address the issue, but what was the point? Elsa had no trouble imagining just how he would respond. His face would go slack with shock, and then he would say in tones of deep distress, "How can you even insinuate such a thing, darling? You have no idea how much I love you."

Elsa shook her head. Well, at least Aldridge had enough pride that she could trust him to be discreet. He wouldn't want himself or his wife to be the subject of gossip.

But on the topic of marriage, Aldridge always talked as if they were engaged, and Elsa had told Ingrid she would consent, but he hadn't officially asked her yet. No doubt he was waiting until he had her in a situation where she couldn't say no. Elsa didn't know how, but she was certain he would be able to contrive such a situation.

By the time she reached the house, Elsa was feeling rather sick to the stomach and determined to slip up to her room, for at least a few moments, to compose herself before facing him again. However, Ingrid saw her come in and drew her into the library. The captain rose politely as Elsa entered.

"Have you been having a pleasant day?" she glanced uncomfortably from one to the other.

"Yes, most assuredly," Ingrid responded. "The captain has been assisting me in taking care of some most troublesome business affairs. He has such shrewd business sense."

Aldridge smiled, self-satisfied, but then looking at Elsa he said, "It is a pleasure to see you so soon, darling, but I had rather wished you had waited for me. I will not have you putting yourself into unnecessary danger by walking about alone. It is most unwise of you to so disregard my instructions." There was something of a veiled threat in his voice. "From now on you will at the very least have one of the slaves accompany you when you leave the house. As you do not seem to have an appreciation for the current state of danger our country is in, I will take it upon myself to see you are protected. You are far too precious to me, to let you assume any risks."

Elsa sighed inwardly. Already he was beginning to treat her as his personal property. She might as well get used to it. She remembered what Henry had said about there coming a time when they each must accept their own lot in life, regardless of how unfair. Evidently this was her time, so she gave the captain a small nod, saying meekly, "I beg your pardon. In the future I will show more regard for your wishes."

Aldridge smiled. She was learning fast.

"But the Captain and I have not been discussing business all day,"

Ingrid said. "We have also been making plans much more to your personal interest."

"No, no, not yet. Give me more time," Elsa's mind was screaming.

"I do believe the Captain wants to be alone with you now," Ingrid said, standing up.

"Do not be in such a rush, Aunt." Elsa stopped her. "I would love to hear all about your day first."

"That reminds me," Ingrid said. "There was something I wished to ask you. Earlier, I brought the Captain up here to show him that magnificent pistol from your late father. But it is not in the case. See, the spot is vacant. I thought perhaps you took it out for something."

Elsa immediately turned an ashen white, and they both stared at her in surprise. This day was going from bad to worse.

"You know where it is?" Ingrid asked.

"I did take it out of the case a few weeks ago."

"So where did you put it?" Ingrid pursued somewhat impatiently now.

"I don't know exactly where it is at this precise moment," Elsa replied with a nervous attempt at a laugh.

"Come on, what's the big mystery?" Aldridge asked.

"I can not imagine you would take the gun out of the case for no reason and then lose it," Ingrid went on. "That does not sound like you, Elsa."

"Well, it's—it's..." Elsa stopped in confusion.

As Aldridge watched her obvious discomfiture, he came to the conclusion that she probably had misplaced it through some carelessness, and he didn't want Ingrid heckling her about it. It was high time Ingrid learned that if he was to be Elsa's husband, he also carried the exclusive right to domineer her. Besides, if he stood up for Elsa against Ingrid, it would go a long way towards endearing himself to her. So he said, "It was likely carried off by the soldiers during the recent raid."

Ingrid shook her head. "They did not have access to the key, and as you can clearly see, the case remains undamaged. And if they had found a way into the case, they would not have stopped at stealing that one firearm."

"Then it remains an unsolved conundrum," he said lightly. "But do not allow it to trouble you, Madame. I have come here to gaze upon something far more wondrous than a fine gun."

"But there must be an explanation," Ingrid insisted. "Elsa, tell us when and why you took the pistol from the case." Elsa stared at the hem of Ingrid's skirt and opened her mouth, but no answer was forthcoming. "I know what happened," Ingrid exclaimed. "One of the slaves took it, and you are trying to cover for them. Just wait till I get my hands on that culprit."

"Oh, no, they didn't. You see I gave it away myself," Elsa blurted out with more goodwill than common sense.

"Whatever for?" Ingrid demanded.

"Well, I gave it to a lieutenant. He had lost his, and he desperately needed another." Elsa's shaking hands belied the nonchalant manner she tried to assume.

"That was very sweet of you," Aldridge said.

But Ingrid, who knew how strongly Elsa's sympathies lay with the Union, didn't believe a word of it. "But Elsa, I thought that pistol was very dear to you, not to mention its value Why did you not give him one of the other guns? You know I would not have objected to them going to so worthy a cause as the support of our troops."

Elsa stood like a statue, staring at the ornate rug beneath her feet. Where was good lie when she needed one? She hadn't had any trouble coming up with the story about a secret lover to satisfy Henry's curiosity. But here she stood before the two people who intimidated her the most, and nothing, absolutely nothing, was coming to mind.

"What is wrong with you, Elsa? Just tell us where the gun is," Ingrid was irritated now.

"Stop pestering her," Captain Aldridge said severely as he turned towards Ingrid. "It is a matter of little significance."

Ingrid's back fairly bristled. "This is a matter between me and my niece, and I would thank you to stay out of it, Captain," she replied haughtily. "You are not Elsa's husband yet, and until such time, I am still her guardian, and as such, have every right to ask her whatever I please."

"No, you don't. I will not stand by and watch you harass her over something so trivial. It was her pistol in any case, and she is under no obligation to divulge her personal secrets to you unless I so direct, which I do not."

Elsa did not like the way that sounded at all. At first she had been glad Aldridge was standing up for her, but this was getting dreadful. They were squabbling over her like two children pulling on opposite ends of a rag doll, and she felt herself tearing apart down the middle. The only thing they agreed upon was that she was an object to be possessed, and it made her want to be sick.

The air in the room was heavy enough to be felt as Ingrid and Aldridge stared daggers at one another. Elsa's mind whirled. Her eyes wouldn't focus. She felt like a caged animal trapped between the two of them. She hated her life, she dreaded her future, and she saw no escape, so what did it matter anymore what she did? And then, for one glorious instant, she felt the courage which flows from desperation. Rising up on its wings, she lifted her head and came to life.

"You wish to know the truth? Then I will tell you," she addressed her aunt. "The last time Captain Aldridge was here and that Union raiding party came and lit fires in the camp, you remember?" She raced on recklessly without waiting for a reply. "When they went, they left their lieutenant behind in a clump of bushes, badly wounded. I found him unconscious, and I cared for him until he was well enough to leave and gave him Papa's pistol when he left." Elsa's courage spent, it dropped her as swiftly as it had swept her up. Her eyes once again sought the floor as she stood there gray and trembling in the deep silence which filled the room.

Ingrid's ire had already been provoked by Captain Aldridge, and now her face was livid with rage. Elsa stole a glance towards the captain, but he was staring out the window, and she could not see his face, only that his knuckles were white. When Ingrid at last found her voice, even Elsa, who had expected the worst, was not prepared for the outburst.

"I once said you were as obstinate and foolish as your mother. Now I know better! You are as dull-witted, pernicious, and contemptible as your odious father, and I beg that you mark well his repulsive fate, for you may expect none better to befall you. All wandering children of darkness, who weave for themselves only crooked paths of deceit while ungratefully casting aside all restraints of duty, will find their steps arrested in the same miry pit of desolation. The unmitigated truth of the matter is you are worse than he, you—you traitor!" For a moment Ingrid's voice was choked in an angry sob.

"Oh, to think that after all the wealth of training and time I have poured into you, I could not redeem you from the dreadful curses of blood and lineage which passed onto your infant head. From the day that your father seduced my sister in his crafty iniquity, I dreaded to see what frightful effects should come, but you have surpassed my most terrifying premonitions.

"In dishonor you were conceived, and in death you were born, but I thought I could bring you out from it all. You spurned my every effort, yet out of duty I have kept you, tried to reform you, but my patience is at an end. I cannot endure the sight of your malignant presence under this grand old roof another moment! You are no kin of mine, only of him whose seed I despise. I am through with you—once and forever through with you! Leave this house today and do not return to my arms, for never again can they be open to you. The scourge of your disreputable shadow is more than I can bear."

Ingrid practically shrieked as she ended her harangue. The vials of her wrath not yet spent, she strode across the room and shook Elsa firmly by the shoulders. "Do you hear me? That you should repay my kindness with treachery is too much to endure. I have given everything, my husband, my wealth, everything to our country, and at the first opportunity you turn behind my back and try to undermine all I have done. Be gone—be gone today! You shall no longer disgrace the home of a Chesterfield. I wash my hands of you." With that she turned on her heel and swept out of the library.

After a minute of stunned silence, Elsa walked to the doorway. All at once the brunt of the past several days came crashing down on her. Once again the little blue shadows came fluttering before her eyes, and then everything began to turn dark and close in. She reached out to grab onto the doorframe, but it wasn't there. Nothing was there, only a dark cocoon closing around her. Elsa tried to scream, but all she heard was a small strangled sound which seemed to be coming from very far away.

When she revived, Elsa found herself lying on the pale gray recamier by the window, Captain Aldridge leaning over her. She did not look at him but simply waited for a similar denunciation to what she had just received from her aunt, and fearing it even more. But he was silent for so long that finally she ventured a glance at his face and was arrested by the expression written there. So acute was it, frightening because she could not interpret it, and it vibrated no mental cord to bring back familiar experiences by which it might be judged.

At last he spoke. "You have been very foolish, my dear." She was startled by the quiet, controlled manner of his speech. "So what now?" he continued after a pause.

"I think my aunt made it rather clear what I must do."

"But where will you go? What will you do?" he pressed.

"I must work," Elsa said slowly.

"You won't find decent employment, not with the war. People can no longer afford to employ tutors or governesses and such. What do you have left? You go out from here practically a pauper to scrounge around dismally amid the scum of society and find what scraps of subsistence you might."

Encouraged by the wide-eyed attention of his audience, he went on in a gush of colorful phrases, "In time, when your strength has failed and your health is gone, you will crave your aunt's protection, but she placed her curse upon you—or rather you have placed it upon yourself—and you are barred from her house forever. And not without reason. You have behaved horribly towards her. Why, if you had merely dressed the wounds of this soldier, it could be excused as feminine emotion, for you are soft-hearted, my dove, and Ingrid knows nothing of that. But to hide your enemy and send him away armed is entirely beyond comprehension."

Elsa turned her head away from the blue condemnation of his eyes.

"Yes, I'm sure you see that now." He waited to let his words sink in. "Before this fiasco of a situation developed, Ingrid said I had wished to be alone with you. I had hoped to do so under much pleasanter circumstances, and I had intended to ask you for your hand properly, and that we should make arrangements to married as soon as possible."

"But now you realize what scum I am, not even worthy of your disdain," Elsa said. Her tone was lifeless, in sharp contrast to her over-dramatized words.

Aldridge took one of her hands gently between both his own. Elsa thought she saw a flicker of amusement around the corners of his mouth, but his tone was serious as he said, "I cannot tell you how much you have disappointed me, but unlike Ingrid, I know you are capable of much better things. So if you will swear never, and I mean absolutely never, to do such a thing again, you will still find my arms open although all other's are closed." He smiled, pleased with his own magnanimity.

Elsa's heart thumped hard as she sat up and tried to stand. She saw dark spots and reached for his shoulder to steady herself. Aldridge slid an arm around her waist and drew her close. She wanted to turn and run. It was only because of Ingrid's coercion that she had planned to marry him in the first place. That didn't matter anymore. She didn't have to listen to him, and yet she found she clung to him in the absence of all other support.

Where was she to go? How was she to support herself? Perhaps it would be better to face life with him than to face it alone? Her timid nature shrank from the sordid picture he had painted of the degradation to which she would sink, while her revulsion to being alone ran deep into the roots of her past and held her now with an icy grip. She craved protection and felt powerless to break from the spell he held over her in that one word.

Aldridge kept one arm snuggly around her waist while he ran his other hand slowly up the side of her tight bodice and over the smooth curve of her breast. At first he had been angry when he heard her confession, but it was all going to work out wonderfully in his favor. Now that she was left with nothing, she would need him and belong to him all the more fully. He pulled her tighter against himself and moving his hand up, gently tipped her head back so she could not turn her gaze from him. He brushed his lips lightly over hers and began to whisper to her.

"You're mine now, Elsa. There is no one now but you and me. Tell me you're sorry. Swear never to betray me again. I'll take care of you, my darling; just give yourself to me."

Elsa felt his eyes holding her. It was like a dream, where although her thoughts raced and her heart jumped, she was frozen, unable to move or speak. His body was so warm, his hands so strong; she felt herself melting into him.

Aldridge slid his hand on her back down lower and pressed his hips against hers, while at the same time he slowly lowered the hand which was holding her head, leaning her back. She felt so vulnerable, so exposed. Goose bumps were tingling across her body. She tried to turn her head, but he wouldn't let her, and he laughed, "You can't fight me, doll, not anymore. I am all you have."

It was something about his laugh, so cold, self-satisfied, arrogant. She was a game to him—a game he had won. He didn't care about her misery or her helplessness; it was funny to him. And once again her utter, hopeless despair lent her boldness. It no longer mattered what she did because she didn't think her life could get much worse, and in that moment she honestly didn't care.

Elsa closed her eyes for a moment, and forced her muscles to relax. As he felt her yielding to him, he loosened his hold and Elsa jerked away. She looked straight into his dreadful blue eyes and said, "So you would like that, would you? You would like me to come begging and eat out of your hand? But I won't—not today and not ever! You don't care about me. You just find me attractive because you want a woman too timid to ever oppose you. You do not even know what the word love means, only lustful passion. Why don't you just go out and find yourself a whore? You aren't kind; you only want to flaunt your pretended virtues before me, but you would be as happy to enslave me as you are to bind a whole race of innocent people."

Aldridge couldn't believe his ears. "How dare you speak to me like that?" he exploded. "You think your aunt will take you back? She won't. She didn't want you even before all this happened. She has practically been begging me to take you off her hands. The only hope you have to reconcile yourself to her or save yourself, is in me. Don't you know that?

Or are you simply too stupid to admit it? Like it or not, I am all you have now."

"Would you put yourself in the place of God to me?" she asked through lips which trembled violently.

"No. God is distant and far away; I am here." He reached for her, but she drew back.

"Since God is invisible, how would you know if He is here or not?"

"Arrogance ill becomes those who cannot afford it," he snapped.

"And it proves an unsightly crutch for those who cannot walk without it," she countered.

"You are an ungrateful wretch! Perhaps Ingrid was right about you. If I was merciful I would relieve any woman so beautiful from having to live with such scrambled brains. I would free you from yourself." His hand rested heavily on the handle of his pistol.

"Are you going to shoot me?" Elsa asked in a breathless whisper. Her bravado was leaving her quite quickly, and for a moment she almost thought he was going to.

But Aldridge shook his head and moved his hand away from his gun. "Since you say I know nothing of kindness, I will leave you to your misery. Of course, there are other ways of freeing a woman from herself," he said menacingly as he reached out, and since she was already backed up almost to the wall, she could not evade him.

He drew her too him one more time, gripping her shoulders with a force which left the imprint of his fingers for several weeks to come, and gave her a kiss so violent that she choked on his tongue. He pulled away in disgust. His whole body was pulsating with his desire for her, but this was giving him no fulfillment.

Aldridge envied those men who could find pleasure in rape. The one thing he wanted was the only thing he couldn't force. What was wrong with her? He was smarter and stronger. He had money and power. She needed him. Why, why, why wouldn't she give herself to him?

His frustration seethed over, and although he cursed himself for doing it, he slapped her hard across the face. Then he said, and his words were laced with an animosity which terrified her more than his blow, "If you find the prospect of sharing my bed distasteful, rest assured you will know far worse. You will live to regret this day with every fiber of your being. You may walk away from me today, but you will never be free of me. Wherever you go, I will be there, and whatever you do, I will know. Someday we will meet again to see who was right—you or I. Oh, Elsa!"

Aldridge grabbed her upper arms and held her firmly against the wall. He stared at her hard for a moment. When he began talking again, the anger was gone from his voice, but replaced with a despondent resentment. "Darling, why are you doing this to me? I love you—and yet I hate you for it. You will never be free from me because I will never be free from you. You've bewitched me. I see your smile in my dreams. I hear your voice in the wind. When I sit in silence I can feel the softness of your skin against mine. I want you more than I have ever wanted anything in my entire life, and I would make you happy. I know I would. All I ask is for you to be mine. Why? Tell me why?"

Elsa stared back at him blankly. Her mind was beginning to pass the stage of lucid thought. She was confused beyond words, but more than anything she was frightened.

"Come with me," Aldridge said softly.

"Just-just leave me alone," Elsa stammered.

"Damn you, woman," Aldridge said bitterly. He twisted his hands into her hair, until she had to bite her lip to keep from crying out. "You will be sorry. I swear to you, you will. You will never know happiness apart from me. I will see to that."

Aldridge lifted his hand again, and Elsa closed her eyes as she flinched. Very suddenly Aldridge let go of her.

"Get out of here before I kill you," he said in a choked voice, and then turned his attention to viciously smashing a chair.

Elsa fled from the house in a state of veritable terror. She wanted to run and run as far away as she possibly could. But as she reached the long magnolia bordered lane, her foot caught on a rock and she tripped. Hearing hurried footsteps behind her as she stood up, she wheeled around to find herself face to face with Henry. She heard his condolences and saw his grief only faintly through the bewildering fog which was swirling around her head. She hugged him and then stumbled on.

Her mind reeled, and she was dazed as if under the influence of some drug. No doubt her senses were trying to spare her some pain by refusing to feel. She passed familiar objects, yet nothing seemed real. She did not weep, nor did surges of anger sweep her breast. It was as if life had come to a state of suspended animation, and she was walking through a cloud.

Try as she might, Elsa could not grasp the import of what had just transpired and was unable to focus her thoughts on the future. All that she had known as real and true was gone. All that she might rest her hopes on was far away and uncertain. She walked on, rapidly at first, but gradually slowing down, taking no thought to her path beyond the next step.

The sun was dipping low on the western horizon, while the stark, chill tombstones cast long shadows on the damp grass as Elsa came to a standstill by the fresh mound of dirt just outside the churchyard wall. As she stood staring at the wilted buttercups lying on the center of Martha's grave, she realized to where she had come.

She gazed up over the low stone wall of the churchyard, past the cemetery and up to the beautiful white steeple, its cross lifted high for all the world to see, proclaiming love and righteousness. Of course, a church, a church was a haven of refuge and hope, she would go there. She scrabbled over the wall and ran to the church steps. She walked up them slowly, praying. Approaching the big white doors, she grasped the handle, and found them locked.

With dragging steps and heavy heart, she returned to Martha's grave. She sank down beside the rugged stone wall and leaned against it, hugging her knees and staring into the twilight. If Aldridge came searching for her, as she fully expected he would, he would not look in a cemetery.

Too exhausted to stay awake, and too upset to sleep, Elsa spent most of the night in a state of half consciousness, where one is aware of things around them but powerless to understand or change them. The night stretched on interminably, full of darkness and rain, prickly blades of grass, and eerie sounds. Then she felt a warm touch, and a man's voice was speaking to her.

Love or Horses

John grabbed his pistol and strained his ears to hear the faint shuffling sound behind the tent. "Perhaps it is one of the horses," he said doubtfully.

"Let's go have a look," Connly whispered as he loaded his gun.

Together the two men crept from the tent and edged slowly around to the back.

"There isn't anyone here," John yawned.

"But there was," Connly insisted.

"It's hard to say what we ought to do." John rubbed his head sleepily. "It might have just been a raccoon or something, but better safe than sorry. Let's go back inside and wait a spell to see what happens."

Connly nodded wordlessly.

"You go ahead and sleep. I'll stay up," John offered.

"That's alright, Lieutenant, I don't mind watching; you're sleepy," said Connly, who privately considered his hearing to be sharper than John's.

"And you aren't?" John laughed dryly. "Perhaps we had best keep each other awake."

And so the two men settled down for a sleepy vigil. The minutes crawled by on leaden feet. John's head nodded drowsily. Connly kept hiding tremendous yawns behind his hand. By the end of twenty minutes both men were ready to suggest they abandon their present enterprise in favor of sleep, when Connly jerked his head up to the sound of a snapping twig. They ducked out of the entrance and once again stole around back.

"Halt!" Connly shouted, finger poised on the trigger of his revolver.

Two white eyes stared back at them in the darkness.

"What have we here?" John asked sternly.

"I ain't doin' nofin', sir." The intruder knotted the grimy fingers of one gnarled hand in the long wisps of his scraggly beard.

"What's that in your hand," John demanded.

"Aww, nofin'," he growled as he thrust his hand into his pocket.

"Connly, see what he's got," John directed.

"Flint and steel," Connly reported after a quick investigation. "You aimin' to start a fire? Couldn't be our tent you wanted to burn, now could it?"

"No, no. Course it couldn't. Why, how's could some little fire burn down a whole big tent like that hickey you've got here?"

"I see," said John. "Now just what were you trying to do?"

"You just don't unde'stand," the old man whined. "I wouldn't be driven to sech things if my old woman weren't such a damn bitch. Nag and complain, nag and complain, dats all dat old hag is good for. Why she just drove me plumb to distraction. And I ask you, unde' sech circumstances, what's a God fearing man to do?"

A slight smile was twitching around the corners of John's mouth. "While you have my condolences concerning your domestic troubles, I fail to see the relevance to the matter at hand. Now kindly tell me, what were your intentions as you skulked about our tent in a state of such helpless distraction?"

"But that is jest my here point; I wasn't."

"Hmm," Connly snorted, "and I suppose you are going to tell us you aren't one of our prisoners either."

"Dat's right." The man nodded decidedly "I was jest out for a bit of a walk, tryin' to escape de missus and wandered plumb through dis here camp."

"You haven't gotten through yet," Connly reminded him.

"I'm as harmless as sweet clover in the spring. I was jest walkin' and tryin' to relieve my troubled soul." The man looked at John with what he no doubted intended to be sad puppy dog eyes, but looked so comical that John had to turn away to keep from laughing.

"It's rather an ungainly hour for a relaxing stroll, wouldn't you say?" John said when he had sufficiently recovered to speak solemnly again.

"No, sir. I reckon as how there ain't no better time to walk than in the dark."

"Well, sorry to say, my dear fellow, your story simply does not carry the ring of truth," John returned placidly. "And try as I might, I cannot find it in my heart to believe you."

"All the same, I ain't doin' nofin' 'cept takin' a little walk," replied the dauntless man.

"Alright. This is quite enough nonsense for one night," John said firmly. "I don't have time for such tomfoolery. You just walk with me back to where you belong."

After returning the miscreant to his proper place and giving instructions to the vidette to keep watch over the rover, they proceeded wearily back to their own tent and some much longed for repose.

The next day passed uneventfully, but early the following morning, John was startled by the sound of gunshots on the verge of the camp. Racing over, he found his sentry leaning dazed against a tree, a bloody hand pressed to his cheek.

"What happened? Are you alright?" John took him by the arm.

"I—think—so," stammered the youth. "Just a graze. I think I got him though. But he was on a horse and galloped off."

"Who was?"

"Some rebel captain. He comes riding up like he owns the place, so I challenged him and quick as you can bat an eye, he shot me. But I dodged, and he just got me a little on the side of my face," he responded, obviously enjoying the attention.

"So he came back? I wondered if we'd hear more from that captain," John mused. "What did he look like?"

"Yellow hair, 'bout this long." The soldier drew a line just under his chin. "I don't know what else."

"That sure sounds like the one that shot Jenkins," broke in one of the other men who had congregated around the commotion.

John nodded. "Scroggins, you take over sentry duty here. Come on, Tommy, we'll get a bandage on your face. The rest of you start breaking camp. We're moving out, wounded men or no wounded men."

Now that John knew this mysterious captain was aware of their presence, he feared a counter attack and knew his handful of men would hardly be able to resist, especially with so many prisoners to guard.

They were only able to make about seven miles that day before John decided they really couldn't move the wounded men any further without significant risk to their lives. The location he choose for setting up camp was a fairly large meadow, flanked by a woods on the south and a deep valley on the north. Connly objected to this choice of a site on the grounds that the valley turned into a jagged ravine a little ways to the west and posed a danger to the horses.

"I see your point, but the wounded can't travel any farther, and there is water here so we need to stay. Just make sure the men tether their mounts securely," John said.

They all retired soon after making camp since John was anxious to make as early a start as possible the next day. The responsibility of prisoners weighed heavily on him, and he couldn't wait to deliver them into someone else's hands.

Just as dawn was breaking the next morning, seven of John's men made their way to the back pasture where they fell silently to their task of caring for the horses. Suddenly the stillness was shattered by an exclamation from Tommy Reckels, the sentry who had been injured the previous day. "Hey men, the lieutenant's horse ain't here!"

"Why not?" called back a friend.

"Oh, he's got to be there. I tied him myself, good and tight," insisted another.

"He was tied alright. His rope's been cut," Tommy went on. Soon an excited knot of soldiers had formed around Tommy as he ruefully held up the severed rope for their inspection.

"Why didn't someone just untie the damn rope?"

"They couldn't see it in the dark."

"Skip the rope, boys. We'd best look for Red Lightning; he was a fine horse."

"You don't suppose he fell in the gorge, do you?"

"Hardly. Who's gonna cut a rope and not take the blasted horse with them?"

"We'd best tell the sergeant about this. He's gonna be mighty sore. Just the other day I heard him saying what a great animal Red Lightning was."

"Yeah, if someone had to steal a horse why couldn't they have taken the old nag I got stuck with?"

"You sure are getting your share of excitement out of this maneuver, Tommy."

"Aww, it will put hair on his chest."

The group headed for the ravine as they talked, while one of the men darted back to camp to inform the sergeant. Connly was in the act of attempting a shave when the excited dragoon dashed up, shouting.

"What's all the excitement?" Connly asked without looking, as he intently tried to stare at himself in the shiny blade of a knife.

"Red Lightning's gone! Some bastard cut his rope."

"They did?" Connly straightened up with a jerk. "Ehww, you shouldn't shout like that; now I cut myself."

"Connie, I don't know why you play with razors," said John, walking by at that instant. "You're too young to have anything stiff, and you always cut yourself. Didn't your mother teach you to stay away from sharp blades?"

"Good morning to you too, Lieutenant. Your horse is gone," Connly said a little peevishly.

"Red Lightning gone?"

"So I am told. I'm going to check it out right now. I sure hope she didn't fall in any ravine." Connly raised his eyebrows at John.

As Connly approached the valley, he heard voices ascending from the mist below. Clambering down the steep slope, he arrived, somewhat breathless, at the bottom.

"Did you find her?"

"Yes, sir, but her leg is broken."

"I say two of her legs are broken," corrected Tommy.

"No, the right leg is just a sprain; I saw her move it," disagreed his friend.

"It doesn't make a difference," Connly broke in. "If she's that bad off there is not much we can do for her. Let's have a look. There, there now girl." Connly gently, almost tenderly, stroked the mare's neck. "You poor little thing. What did someone do to you? Aww, you're real bad off," Connly sighed as the animal struggled violently, trying to rise. "Whatever damn fool's been messing with you deserves to break his own neck— treating a lady this way."

"Sergeant! Sergeant! Over here." A yell pierced through the mist.

Connly rushed over.

"Look." The man pointed to a gray clad corpse, lying crumpled against a rock.

Connly slowly shook his head. "He must have been trying to escape on Red Lightning and fell over this precipice." Connly laid out the body and made sure there was no sign of life left in the still figure. A scraggly tell-tale beard, and fingers, gnarled and grimy, informed him who the man was.

In the end, it was necessary to put Red Lightning down, and they buried them both in the same grave. When they returned to camp, Connly gave John a report of the affair with a look as much to say, "Didn't I tell you?"

If that gorge hadn't been there, he probably would have succeeded in escaping," John responded. "Isn't there a man in this camp who understands what sentry duty means?" John shook his head wearily. "I think I am going to have to teach a class on it," he added dryly. "And maybe hand out some spectacles. So the rope was cut, huh?"

"Here's the knife." Connly handed John a rusty dinner knife.

John gave an exasperated sigh. "I am going to personally see to it that a thorough search is conducted. We can't afford to have any more of this type of thing. It is pathetically hard to make good time with so many wounded men, especially without enough mounts, and now we are just one shorter."

"You don't like having to look after prisoners, do you?" Connly asked.

"Oh, I'm having the time of my life," John replied sarcastically.

"I've been thinking—now I wasn't going to mention anything, but seeing you feel the way you do about the prisoners and all, well, I've been thinking: we really need more horses, right?"

"That goes without being said."

"And you particularly need a new mount. It's not very glorious for a victorious cavalry officer to come walking back into headquarters. And it is some lunatic rebel who is responsible for Red Lightning's death, right?"

"Yes," John replied tentatively, wondering where Connly's fast reasoning was going to lead him.

"Then I put it to you that it is the rebels' responsibility to furnish us with more horses, seeing as we need them to transport their own men anyhow."

"I don't object; but I have this premonition that they would," said John, raising his heavy eyebrows.

"I wasn't planning to ask them pretty please," Connly rushed on. "Now I know it is a bit out of our way, but I've heard tell there is a gang of rebs near Rudes Hill. We could make camp several miles from there, and it wouldn't be too difficult for some of us to spirit away a few mounts."

"Connie, did I ever tell you that I think you are capricious?"

"What am I?"

"Never mind. Let me look at a map. So you really think," John murmured as he unfolded a worn map, "that I should relieve the rebels of a few horses?"

"Not you, sir," Connly corrected. "This would definitely be the sort of job for me. You know I'm good with horses, and I could hardly stay back and watch the prisoners. You're much better at that sort of thing."

John gave a wry smile. "You know, sometimes little raids can take much longer than anticipated," he said meaningfully.

"Maybe I'd meet a beautiful southern belle too," Connly grinned.

"Then I'd never hear from you again."

"Oh yes, you would, John. Because when she bats those beautiful dark lashes of hers and says, 'Which will you take, sir, love or horses,' I'll say, 'Tonight madam, I'll take the horses.'" Connly swept off his cap with a dramatically elegant bow.

John laughed. "Alright, you can take nine of the men and make a raid tonight, if you're sure you can handle it."

This last doubtful comment was all Connly needed. Squaring his slim shoulders and drawing himself up to his full 5' 6", he did everything but say, "You just see if I can't!"

*   *   *   *   *

A cool drizzle was falling as Connly and his men, approached the outskirts of the Confederate camp. They had come on foot in order to allow for a maximum number of horses on their return. John had not asked what method Connly intended to employ, and Connly had not volunteered any information, but as the men chatted throughout their long walk, Connly believed he had found a kindred spirit in Tommy Reckels.

"Now listen boys," he said, turning to the others. "They will most likely have their horses staked on the outskirts of the camp like us, but nine chances in ten, their sentries are better than ours, so stay together and all grab horses near each other. That way you shouldn't have to encounter more than one picket. And anyone you do encounter, jump him—and I mean fast. And be sure to get a tight hand over his mouth so he can't wake the whole damn camp, or we are screwed. Remember, we don't want to do any fighting, just quietly slip off with some horses. You all got knives handy, right?"

"Yes, sir."

"Good. Don't use any guns unless absolutely necessary. You can kill a man just as well with a knife, and it is a hell of a lot quieter. Also, cutting the horses' ropes will probably be easier in the dark than untying them. Any questions?"

"No, sir."

"Alright, let's go then."

The men quietly edged closer.

"Look, there's horses right over there," one of the men whispered.

Connly nodded. "Now go ahead and as soon as you've got your mount, high tail it out of here and head for camp. I'm going further in, but can find my way back alright. Are you all ready?"

The men murmured their consent.

"Good luck, men." Connly laid a hand on Tommy's shoulder and said softly, "You can come with me if you want, but it will be risky."

Tommy answered with a nod and a grin.

As the other eight men headed off into the darkness, Connly tossed Tommy a light bundle. "Put that on; we're Rebs tonight."

"What are you aiming to do?" Tommy whispered.

"Red Lightning was the best horse we had, and I ain't gonna replace her with some nag. I mean to get an officer's horse. Just follow me and do as I do."

The two men circled the camp until they came to a convenient laurel bush which they crouched behind, only feet away from the nearest tent. As the sentry turned his back and began to walk in the opposite direction, Connly jumped up, with a motion to his companion, and darted into camp. He strode purposefully through, followed quietly by Tommy.

After an investigatory round, Connly headed straight for several large tents with mounts tethered behind them. They approached a fine black steed, and Tommy began to untie it while Connly concealed his action with an intent inspection of the animal.

"What are you boys doing?" A grumpy, corpulent man coming out of the tent challenged them.

Connly hardly glanced up as he slowly drawled, "The officer asked me to inspect this horse. Said he seemed to be ailing a bit today."

"Really?" The man stepped closer. "I'd hate to see anything happen to him. You think he's alright?"

Connly shook his head dubiously. "I'd have to say this horse isn't none too well. You can see it in his eyes."

The corpulent man leaned his thick neck over and squinted into the animal's eye. "You're right. He isn't well. What do you think the problem is?"

"Don't rightly know," Connly said, scratching his head. "I think the lieutenant better have a look. He'll know what needs to be done. You take him, Tommy."

"Wait a minute, young fellow. If this horse needs attending to, we can do it right here!" The man gave a grunt which shook the ends of his long walrus mustache.

Tommy continued as if he hadn't heard, and Connly merely laid his hand consolingly on the stranger's arm as he said, "Don't worry. I'll bet you anything he will be as good as new in the morning. You had better get some rest. It's been a long day."

The man reentered the tent. Connly flicked out a sharp knife and sliced through the lead rope of the pinto which was standing next to where the black stallion had been tethered. Just then, the man reappeared, followed by two others, one man tall and wearing only his pants over his union suit, the other husky, with his face hidden in a full black beard. Connly made a quick wave to Tommy, who swung up onto his horse and galloped off.

"Who are you? I never said my horse was sick," barked the bearded man, while at the same time, the first man seized Connly's arm. Deeming this no time for words, Connly broke away with a sudden twist. He hopped onto the pinto's bare back and pressing his knees hard against the horse's sides, tore off, skillfully dodging between tents.

A gunshot, followed by angry shouting, sounded behind him, but he did not glance back. He tore out of the camp and disappeared into the dark shadows. Weaving a zigzag course to avoid being followed, Connly looped back around to the place where he had left the other dragoons. No one was to be seen. "Good, the others must be on their way back to camp already," he thought.

Just then his alert ears caught the sound of snapping twigs and voices in the trees behind him. Urging the pinto into a gallop, he took off for camp. Two miles before arriving back, he met up with Tommy, still mounted atop the sleek black stallion. As they rode into camp, he saw the others standing in a group near John and surrounded by a small swarm of nervous horses. He made a quick head count. Eight—all back.

"Where have you two been? I was getting concerned." John ran over and took the dangling lead ropes as they dismounted.

"Well, sir, I figured a fine horse should be replaced with a fine horse. I hope one of these beauties will suit," Connly replied with a stiff salute and a flash of his contagious smile.

The Calm After the Storm

The sun rose on the first Sunday in July into a clear blue sky with only occasional streaks of hazy clouds. The air was fresh from a short downpour during the night, and the dawn held promise of a beautiful day. It wouldn't be long before the wealthy plantation families would be riding to church in their plush, gilt carriages, admiring the nature around them as they reveled in the superiority of their state. They would sit down in in shiny wooden pews, graced with tasteful carving, and hear an inspiring oration on their rights as Virginians. Then they would ride home, complacent in their own goodness and oblivious to all the heartache and loss which mourned together outside the cold walls of their own churchyard.

Everrett was trudging down the road, shoulders as erect as ever, but his head bent forward and his hands jammed deep into his trouser pockets. Only once did he look up to silently curse the flourishing world around him as its vigor mocked his pain. Of all the blooming foliage, only the buttercups along the roadside seemed to share his mood as in sympathy they bowed their heads under the weight of raindrops lingering on them.

Everrett walked along beside the wall of the churchyard, pausing to return the distrustful glance of a beady-eyed squirrel perched atop an imposing marble cross. As the squirrel darted away chattering,

Everrett hurried past the polished and engraved slabs standing sentinel about the tombs of the rich. He slackened his pace as he reached the poor man's cemetery. Here, outside the wall and far enough away that the shadow of the church, however long, could never reach it, only plain stones and bits of wood bore witness to the loved one's buried beneath. A little set off from the others, behind a big oak, lay his mother's grave.

He slowly rounded the tree and leaning his back against its rough trunk, looked up. His eyes opened wide in surprise, for there in a heap by the side of the moist, brown mound lay a woman, her hair bedraggled, clothing wet, and a streak of dirt smudged across her bruised cheek.

He did not immediately recognize her, and when he did, there was a moment of delayed reaction before he responded. "Miss Grey!" he exclaimed softly.

She didn't stir. He stooped down and gently shook her shoulder. In response to his touch she let out a quiet scream as her eyes fluttered open. "How, how did you find me?" she asked in a panicked voice. "Oh, Mr. Trenton, it's you." Her tone changed to relief.

"What's happened to you?" he gasped, kneeling down on the wet grass beside her and placing his hands on her shoulders in concern. "You's look terrible." The previous day Captain Aldridge in the heat of the moment, had struck her much harder than he intended, and now with the combined effect of the spreading bruise, the rain and the dirt she had been lying on, Elsa looked her worst.

"I feel terrible," she said with a shiver.

"Who did dis to you? And why's you's hehe? You's needs to go home and get in bed," he said as he helped her to sit up.

"I don't have one," she said vaguely.

"What's you's talkin' about? Did you's fall off youh horse and hit youh head?"

"I didn't mean to come here. When Aunt Ingrid told me to leave her home, I just started walking and came here without thinking on it. Then I figured it was as good a place as any, and he wouldn't find me here."

"What?! Why youh aunt done kick you's out of de house?" he

139

exclaimed incredulously. "And who's you hidin' from. You's not makin' any sense. I's don't think you's alright at all."

"She found out about John."

"Oh," Everrett said gravely and then after a minute, "and shey did dis to you?"

Elsa put her hand quickly to her face. "Does it look very bad?"

Everrett nodded. "Awful." Judging by Elsa's expression, that was the wrong thing to say, so he hurried on. "Tell me what youh aunt did when shey found out?"

"She was horribly angry, said I was contemptible and ungrateful and that she couldn't stand the sight of my malignant presence under her grand old roof another moment."

"Hmmph," Everrett snorted. "Heh damned old roof don't deserve to have you's undeh it."

Elsa almost smiled at his vehemence. "All the same, it is nice to have a roof over one's head."

"Speakin' of which, we's should not stay out hehe. Next thing we's know, folks will bey comin' to de church, and I's reckon you's don't want to meet up with dem any mohe dan I's do."

Elsa shook her head. "I do not feel like speaking to another person in my entire life. People are too dangerous and mean and impossible to please." They looked at one another, and a silent communication passed between them as they each saw their grief and unhappiness mirrored on the other's face.

"Come on. You's can come to my cabin and get dry," Everrett said as he extended his hand to pull her up.

No sooner had Elsa risen to her feet, than her face turned grayer than it already was. "Oh, I do not feel so well." She leaned against the oak.

"You's wants to vomit, and you's see dark spots, and you's feel like you's got a freezin' mountain stream runnin' through youh veins instead of blood," Everrett said.

"How did you know?"

"A girl back at de plantation, Lucy, shey used to get dat way every time shey didn't get fed enough. Come on, you's will feel betteh afteh you's dry and ates something."

"Alright," Elsa said, although she didn't believe that all the food or dry clothes in the world would make her feel better in the least.

They made it about halfway to Everrett's cabin before Elsa rushed to the side of the forest trail, sank to her knees, and began to wrench and vomit. After several minutes she stood back up, holding weakly onto a tree. "I am so embarrassed. I go one day without eating much and spend one night in the rain, and you would think I had been starving and exposed to the elements for a month. I am probably the worst weakling you have ever met."

"Dat you's is," Everrett agreed as he came over to her, "and I's seen about as much of you staggerin' along as I's can take. Now let me." He put her arm around his neck and lifted her up.

Elsa felt too lousy to object so she just murmured, "Thank you," with a slight nod that ended with her head dropping onto his shoulder. Her mind was spinning with a merry-go-round of thoughts, ducking and bobbing and chasing each other round and round. She tried to shut them off and be aware of nothing but the rough texture of his shirt under her cheek and the cheery morning songs of the birds. There was a nice, steady rhythm to his stride, and the solid warmth of his shoulder was somehow reassuring. She didn't know why. He was after all the coldest, most morose man she had ever met, only it did not seem like that now.

The next thing she knew he was setting her down in the yard. Elsa walked slowly into the cabin and sank down on Martha's bed. "I wish so much that Martha was here now," she said sadly.

"Me too." His voice was soft.

"Do you think she is looking down, watching us right now?"

Everrett shrugged. "I's couldn't say."

Elsa buried her face in the soft goose feather pillow she had given Martha and listened to Everrett as he built a fire and made coffee. She tried to picture Martha strong and healthy, walking around in a glistening white robe, playing a golden harp, and looking benevolently down on them. But it was hard to imagine Martha anywhere but lying frail on this very bed.

Elsa sat up as Everrett offered her a cup of coffee. "Thank you. You are being very kind." She sipped at it, but her stomach was still upset and the strong, bitter coffee tasted horrible. She ate a little bread but it was dry, and her mouth was dry, and it made her feel like she was going to choke.

"You's need to get out of dose wet clothes," he said. "Mammy's things ahe in a chest oveh dere." He nodded towards the small bed chamber. "See ifen dere's anything you's can use."

Elsa gently fingered through the clothes. There were the dresses she and Clara had made for Martha so many years ago, now threadbare and beyond mending. It felt like they were part of a different lifetime. And there was the soft, white nightgown with the delicate lace that she had given Martha more recently. The only halfway decent dress Martha had, they had buried her in.

Finally Elsa put on the nightgown as it was the only untorn article of clothing in the chest, and knew how John had felt when she gave him Uncle Albert's clothes. Then because she felt embarrassed to be wearing a nightdress, she picked up a very large, worn indigo shawl and wrapped it around herself. She brought her dress out into the main room and carefully spread it before the fire, then sat back down on the bed.

"So how did youh aunt find out about John?" Everrett asked.

Elsa told him about the scandal of the missing pistol, how Aldridge and her aunt had started fighting over her, and how she lost her head in the stress of the moment. "You see, I am not only the worst weakling you ever met, but also the most scatter-brained," she finished.

"No, I's definitely met folks as was mohe scatter-brained."

Elsa wasn't sure whether that was supposed to make her feel better or not.

"So afteh dat, youh aunt tells you's to leave and does dat to you?" Everrett seemed to be staring at her neck so Elsa glanced down. The collar on the nightgown was loose, especially since it was too big for her, and had slid to one side, revealing a very distinct set of fingerprints on her shoulder.

"Oh no, Aunt Ingrid would not do that," she said, quickly adjusting the fabric to cover the marks. "After Aunt Ingrid left the room, Captain Aldridge was all insistent that I marry him, and I was going to, but then... I do not really remember what all I said to him, but obviously I should not have said it."

"Damn coward," Everrett scowled. "I's sure whateveh you's said to him it weren't even half what he deserved."

"I am so scared of him," Elsa whispered, turning pale at the memory. "He swore to me that he will make me regret not going with him. He said that no matter where I go or what I do, I will never be free from him. He said he loves me so much, he hates me for it. When he finally let me go, I just ran out and left as fast as I could. I wish so much now that I would have brought a few things with me. You know, some dresses, and if I had brought some of my jewelry, I could sell it. Now the only thing I have that I could sell is this watch, and no money at all. I don't know what to do. I wish I had not angered the captain. I should have just given him what he wanted. Now-now I will never be able to escape him."

Everrett looked grimly amused. "I's don't know what it is with some men; dey thinks dat just 'cause they've got white skin and a gun, dat makes dem God. But dey ain't no stronger dan anyone else."

"Oh, you don't know this man," Elsa objected. "If he said he is going to find me and make me regret it, he will. There really isn't anywhere I can be safe from him."

"You's really terrified of him, ain't you?" Everrett said slowly.

"Of course I am. Look at me. How can I protect myself from someone like him?"

"Stay hehe with me. He's won't find you." Everrett caught his breath. Had he really said that out loud?

Elsa looked as startled as he felt. "Do-do you mean that?" she whispered.

Everrett slowly nodded. At first when he met Elsa, it seemed they had nothing in common. But over the past month he had come to think he understood how she felt better than just about anyone else. And she always looked at him and spoke to him just as if he were white. Never once had she given him a condescending look, or had a scornful edge to her voice. And she was gorgeous and sweet. What man in his right mind wouldn't welcome her company? And he was now in a position to offer her more than what she had at present. If only—if only he was full white, if only he was not half black.

"But what-what if he did find me? Then I would have brought you into danger too," Elsa was saying.

"Then he would wish he hadn't. I would kill him." Everrett said very calmly.

Elsa sat in startled silence for a minute, then she asked softly, "Have you ever killed anyone before?"

Everrett didn't seem bothered by the question, but he paused, accessing how much information she really wanted to know. Finally he said, "I's know what to do."

Elsa nodded. "Why are you being so nice to me?" she asked. "After all, I am not one of your people."

"Does dat make a difference to you?" he replied defensively.

"No. But I thought it did to you."

"I's don't belong to any race. I's a half-breed bastard. Pardon my language. It's position not color dat mattehs to me. You's an outcast now too."

"I suppose I am," Elsa responded with a weak smile. "I wish I could stay here," she went on very quietly. "But if anyone ever found out…" Elsa shook her head.

"Den marry me. It will make it less scandalous." Now Everrett thought he was the one who had fallen off a horse and hit his head. Everything he was saying was completely ridiculous. But then life in general was ridiculous so he kept talking. "Now's don't get de wrong idea. I's wouldn't expect you's to share my bed ifen you's wasn't inclined, but I's would be happy of youh company, and you's would have a place to sleep and food to eat, and you's wouldn't have to eveh see youh aunt or dat infernal captain again."

"Alright," Elsa said.

"Alright what?"

"Alright, I would like to marry you."

Everrett was speechless for a moment and then said very carefully, "Perhaps I's have not told you enough. Ifen you's marry me, I dare say you's will regret it. You'll be lonely as heck. We's couldn't neveh go in public together. And look what a worthless shack you's have to live in."

"Well, I figured you did not really mean it. Things which seem too good to be true always are."

144

"Too good to be true?" Everrett almost choked. "You's don't have a clue what you is saying."

"Then I will say nothing more."

Everrett watched Elsa intently as she gazed into the fire. He could almost see the thoughts flickering across her face. "What about John?" he asked. "What ifen he comes back?"

"He won't," Elsa answered. "I asked him if I would ever see him again, and he said, 'I can't say that you will.' If he had any intention of coming, he would have said, 'I will try,' or at least, 'I hope.' But all he said was, 'I can't say that you will.' And why should he? He knew me not even two weeks out of his life."

Everrett was inclined to agree with her. John would never be more than a memory to either of them. "So it really doesn't botheh you's dat I's black?"

Elsa looked at him thoughtfully for a moment. "No. There are many things in life which bother me, but that is not one of them. Of the best people I have ever known, all but one were black."

Everrett smiled. She was unique. "Alright then," he said. "Let's get married."

"Perhaps no one will perform the ceremony," Elsa said, suddenly growing concerned.

"I's have already thought of dat. I's will ask de Quakers in de next town. I's think dey will do it."

"Quakers?" Elsa asked in surprise.

Everrett nodded. "I lived wid dem foh a time afteh I's came out of my indentures. Afteh a few days we's can go oveh to see de Quakers, ifen you's haven't changed youh mind by den, as I suspect you will."

Elsa shook her head. "I won't, unless you change yours."

*   *   *   *   *

After exchanging a slightly nervous glance with Elsa, Everrett drew a deep breath and knocked on the door of the trim white farm house. While they waited for an answer, Elsa's eyes took in the meticulous yard, bordered by a simple picket fence. Flowers bloomed in colorful and aromatic profusion from two small beds. In the background, several Jersey cows grazed contentedly in a bright green meadow. A worn footpath led from the house to a tidy barn. The very air here seemed drenched with a quiet serenity, whispered among the balmy breezes.

Had Everett really lived among these people once? It seemed to Elsa like a sort of utopia. Why had he left? Perhaps he would tell her someday, then again, perhaps not. There were plenty of memories she was certainly never going to share with him.

A tall, slender man with thin, white hair reaching to his shoulders, opened the door. "Everrett?" he exclaimed, as he warmly grasped his hand.

"Joshua," Everrett said softly.

"Young man, I did not think we would ever see thee again. Come in. Lydia, look who has come." The man beckoned his wife.

"Everrett, thee has returned." The woman's face broke into a joyous smile as she embraced him.

As she stepped inside, Elsa felt herself being transported into another world. How different this was from both Everrett's rude cabin and the ornate mansion of her aunt. Tranquility—that was it. It rested in the faces of the two people before her, just as it had outside in the perfect flower beds and simple buildings. Something about their gentleness was reminiscent of her father, but their faces bore none of the suppressed grief that had always characterized him. The elderly couple was radiating an aura of peace and goodwill. Elsa felt it flowing over her like sunlight. If only she knew the secret to such peace. But Elsa had no time to dwell on these thoughts; Everrett was introducing her.

"Elsa, this is Joshua Trenton, and his wife Lydia."

"Trenton?" Elsa said in surprise.

Everrett nodded. "I's took my name from them."

Now Elsa really wondered why Everrett had not stayed. The couple was obviously very pleased to see him again, and he must be fond of them to have taken their name.

"Miss Grey and I wish to be married," Everrett stated flatly.

Joshua Trenton's eyes got a little wide as he said with concern, "It is a big thing thee asks."

146

"I's do not take it lightly," Everrett replied.

"People will not understand, my son," continued the older gentleman.

"I's do not expect dem to."

The Quaker and his wife exchanged glances, first to Everrett, then Elsa, then one another.

"I forget to be hospitable," Lydia said softly. "Come and sit in the parlor. May I take thy wrap, dear?" She turned towards Elsa.

Elsa had found a black riding veil in the bottom of Martha's chest and had concealed her face with it on the way over. She removed it rather reluctantly. She could feel Joshua and Lydia's eyes turning in surprise at the large bruise on her face, but they graciously made no comment.

Once they were seated in the parlor, Joshua ended the awkward interlude in conversation by asking, "Does it not concern thee, the mixing of the races?"

"As you well know, my blood is already mixed, so if it were sin foh me to marry a white woman, it would be equally so foh me to be joined with a black."

Elsa was curious to see what Joshua's response would be to that, but he merely looked thoughtful and didn't reply.

"The Lord did allow Salmon the Israelite to marry Rahab, even though she was of the children of Canaan," Lydia reminded her husband. "And in Colossians does not the apostle Paul tell us that in Christ there exists neither Jew nor Greek, slave nor free?"

"And did not our Creator form every race in the world from but one man?" Elsa added.

"I cannot say it is wrong," Joshua consented. "All races are the same in the eyes of God, but unfortunately not so in the eyes of men. It may not be prudent. People will be resentful, cruel."

"When ahen't dey?" Everrett's voice was bitter.

"I know," Joshua said gently. "But if thee loves this woman, does thee want to bring that lot of pain upon her also?"

"Look at heh and see if you think shey does not already know de cruelty of man," Everrett replied coldly.

Joshua lapsed into contemplation as Lydia picked up the thread of conversation. "Elsa, my dear, I remember when I was a young bride." She reached over and laid a wrinkled hand on Elsa's cool one. "Everrett stayed with us for a time, years ago. He is a fine, strong man. I always thought thee needed a wife," Lydia said with a smile towards Everrett.

"So did my motheh," Everrett replied.

"But what if thee has children?" Lydia continued.

"I will hope and pray that the world they live in will be more kind and just than the one we have known until now. I do not think it could be worse," Elsa replied quietly.

"Does thee love this man enough to share his lot of hardship?"

"His lot is not worse than my own." The concern on Lydia's face was not allayed by that answer. But what was Elsa supposed to say? She and Everrett were not in love. She was marrying him because as Lydia said, he was a fine, strong man, and she did not want to be alone. In time she would love him, she felt fairly certain, but that didn't have to do with why they were marrying. And she really wasn't sure what his reasons were.

"Perhaps we should consult the other ministers," said Joshua Trenton, looking up.

"No." Everrett's face grew taut. "I's not a Quaker, and I's won't be examined by youh board. We's only wish to be quickly and privately married. I's came hehe because I's thought dat to you I's was de same as any otheh man, but perhaps it is not so." There was a cold challenge in his eyes.

Joshua nodded. "We do occasionally, under exceptional circumstances, act as witnesses for people who are not members of the order, but it is still customary to have a waiting period during which the couple's intention to enter into holy matrimony is announced and duly approved by the meeting."

"I's know," Everrett said calmly, "but Miss Grey has nowhehe else to live, so of necessity must stay with me. Do you's think it seemly we should continue so without being married."

The Trentons looked a little shocked. "Truly, it is an exceptional circumstance," said Lydia to her husband. "I fear we would fail in our duty to our fellow man should we refuse to immediately help this young couple to make their relationship pure in the Lord's eyes."

"Alright, if thy minds are made up, I will not stand in thy way," said

Joshua after a pause, during which he did not lose his poise. "Thee knows the manner of our weddings."

Elsa looked up questioningly.

"We sit in silent prayer and meditation," Lydia explained, "until such time as the couple is ready. Then they stand, hands clasped, and solemnly promise to be loving and faithful. After that we continue in silent prayer. Also, everyone present must sign a certificate, which is then read aloud. I believe I have several prepared." She crossed to the desk and took out three crisp pieces of parchment, covered with neat calligraphy. "There will be a copy for thee, one for the records of the Society, and one which we shall file with the proper authorities at the county seat."

"Don't we need a minister?" Elsa asked.

The Friends have multiple ministers," Everrett explained. "Joshua and Lydia are both ministers."

"But we do not marry thee," Lydia interjected. "Only the Lord can marry. We simply witness thee consent to marriage before Him."

Elsa gave Everrett a confused look. She had never heard of such a ceremony.

"It's very simple, just repeat what I's say to you," he said softly.

"Does thee wish to begin now?" asked Joshua uncertainly.

Everrett nodded. "We's kin not have a long ceremony as I's wish to get back befohe it is too dahk."

After that, everyone sat down, and no one said a word. Elsa peeked up and glanced about. Joshua sat as still and solemn as a statue. She wondered if he could have fallen asleep. Lydia's lips moved soundlessly, her face still sweetly radiating a silent peace. Before closing her eyes, Elsa peeped at Everrett. Little drops of perspiration were shining on his brow. Somehow it was comforting to know he was as nervous as she.

Ten minutes, which seemed like an eternity, slowly ticked by. "Until such time as the couple is ready"; the phrase kept running through Elsa's mind. What dreadful words, fraught with uncertainty. She had thought they were ready when they had arrived. If they waited much longer she was afraid she wouldn't be ready anymore. And what about Everrett; what doubts were plaguing his mind?

Just when Elsa thought she couldn't bear it another moment, he reached out and hesitantly took her hand. It was cool and clammy against his hot, sticky one. Together they stood up. Elsa wanted to look down, but forced herself to turn her eyes up to his. They were very honest eyes she thought. Sometimes hard and cold, but always big and truthful. They never narrowed, squinted, or leered like the captain's. She wondered what they saw in her.

Everett thought how frail and small her hand seemed in his, like a child's hand. He wondered whether or not she really cared for John more than she would admit. He almost wished John were there now. He seemed to have a gentlemanly suavity that would know what to do. Elsa was so lovely and fragile, like a blossom bruised and battered in a storm. And there was so much fear in her gentle eyes. Life was hard enough for a strong person like himself. How was someone so delicate supposed to survive it? He wanted to take her in his arms and shield her from it, and yet he wasn't sure if he could.

He cleared his throat, and said slowly, "Friends, in the fear of the Lord, I take this my friend, Elsa Marie Grey, to be my wife, promising, through divine assistance, to be unto heh a loving and faithful husband, so long as we's both on earth shall live." He nodded slightly to her.

Elsa took a deep breath and said in an embarrassingly tremulous voice, "Friends, in the fear of the Lord, I take this my friend, Everett Trenton, to be my husband, promising through divine assistance..." And then her mind went blank.

"To be unto him a loving and faithful wife," Everett whispered very quietly.

"To be unto him a loving and faithful wife, as long as we both on this earth shall live." She rushed through the last words before she had a chance to forget them.

With this simple exchange of vows, they quickly sat back down and waited once more in stifling silence. Eventually Lydia, and then Joshua, offered some words of encouragement and blessing, which were no doubt very wise, but neither Everett nor Elsa could recall them afterwards.

Then they all crossed to the table, and Everett took the grand quill in a brawny hand, much more suited to swinging a hammer than to the task he now assigned it, and roughly scratched his name on the three documents. In her elegant, flowing hand, Elsa signed, and then the Trentons added their names as witnesses.

They all sat back down, except for Joshua, who picked up one of the papers and began to read in his soft, tenor voice. *"Everett Trenton and Elsa Marie Grey, having made known their intention of taking each other in marriage, and public notice having been given...* Well, unfortunately that part is a lie. But I shall make public notice at our next meeting. Does thee think that will suffice, Lydia?"

Lydia Trenton nodded sweetly, and her husband resumed reading. *"The proceedings were allowed by the proper officers of Burea Monthly Meeting of the Religious Society of Friends. This is to certify that for the solemnization of their marriage, Everett Trenton and Elsa Marie Grey were present at a duly appointed public meeting for worship of the Society...* This is also a falsehood," Joshua said gravely, "and without this certificate I fear the marriage is not valid."

"Remember, my dear, exceptional circumstances," said Lydia coming to the rescue. "We will present the document to the Society at the next monthly meeting and will receive their signatures then."

"But they will not have been witnesses," Joshua said, feeling his integrity was being pushed to the limit.

"But we shall bear witness to them of what we seen and heard this day, and they will bear witness to our truthfulness, for they know we would not lie."

Joshua gave a helpless sort of look and tried to continue reading, *"at Burea, this 6*[th] *day of...* What date shall we use, the date the vows were spoken or the day on which we present the document to the Society?" Joshua was looking increasingly perplexed.

"Use today's date," Everrett said firmly.

"Ahh, but this document is not true as of today."

"It is alright," Lydia reassured him. "On the couple's copy of the certificate we shall put today's date, and on the other copies we shall but the date on which the certificate is verified by the Society."

"Then I will never know when my anniversary is," Elsa thought gloomily, but she said nothing.

Joshua drew a deep breath and with a look of trepidation, went back to reading. *"this 6ᵗʰ day of July, 1864. Taking each other by the hand, Everrett Trenton declared: 'Friend's, in the fear of the Lord, I take my friend, Elsa Marie Grey, to be my wife, promising, through divine assistance, to be unto her a loving and faithful husband so long as we both on earth shall live.' And Elsa Maria Grey declared:...* She declared in like manner. *In confirmation of these declarations they have in this meeting signed this certificate of marriage. And we, having been present at the above marriage, have subscribed our names as witnesses."*

Joshua laid down the document and said with a look of relief, "Everrett and Elsa, thy wedding is over."

They all stood around and stared at the floor, or the walls, or each other. Then Lydia drew Elsa into the kitchen. She opened the cupboard and took out a corked bottle.

"My dear," she said. "It is of great importance that thee is not seen with Everrett in thy current state. I have known colored men to be hung for sleeping with a white woman. The fact that thee has a certificate of marriage is certainly some protection, however, that will not necessarily be enough to protect him should he fall into the wrong hands."

Elsa blanched. "I have no intention of being seen with him in public."

"All the same, no doubt at sometime thee will have necessity to be seen together. And that is why I give thee this." She handed Elsa the bottle. "It is ink made from the hulls of chestnuts," she explained. "And when applied to skin it stains a lovely brown. If the occasion ever arises, thee can dye thy skin with this, and with thy dark hair, thee can pass for a quadroon."

When the women returned to the parlor, Lydia handed Everrett a rectangular object wrapped in brown paper. "A loaf of bread," she said. "When thee eats it together, think on the honest earth from which it came and of the faithfulness of the seasons which produced it, and may thy marriage grow in the light of such honesty, and such faithfulness, and such simplicity."

From This Day Forward

Although in most cases, such a hasty and anomalous beginning as the one Everrett and Elsa chose to begin their married life, could do naught but presage a regretful union, the new couple found the strain of adjustment greatly mitigated by certain similarities in their characters. Both were deeply lonely, industrious, and eager to improve their lives. Beyond these foundational traits, their personalities were sharply contrasted.

Everrett did not at first treat Elsa much as a wife. Respect, pity, admiration, and above all, masculine protectiveness all found their place in his feelings toward her, but not amorous affection. Cupid's arrows were as foreign to him as the ancient tongue in which such tales were recorded. Since his mother had gone and Elsa had come in almost the same breath, it was only natural that he would treat her much as he had Martha. Only Elsa's responses were nothing like Martha's, and it was a with a growing uneasiness that Everrett saw more and more each day, the dissimilarities between Martha and his new companion.

For instance, her passion for cleanliness amazed him. He couldn't so much as walk across the floor in his boots without her quietly sweeping up behind him. Martha had never cared if the floor was dirty, and if she had, would have told him to clean it himself. Elsa never told him to do anything. For that matter, she hardly ever told him anything at all. He could see she was still somewhat intimidated of him but couldn't imagine what she was waiting for. He had married her, hadn't he? If that couldn't break the ice what would? He worried that after she had time to reflect on her new life, she would regret her impulsive decision.

But his fears were needless. This was not the first time Elsa had needed to adapt, and she welcomed this change more than most of the previous ones. Having been raised on a farm, she was not as entirely unprepared as would appear from the last few years of her life. She had always tagged along after the servants back home and had an adequate grasp of what was involved in housekeeping. Of course knowledge and ability are far from synonymous.

If Everrett had not been such a poor cook himself he may have been unimpressed with Elsa's early culinary efforts, as she had never before cooked over an open fire. But fortunately anything was an improvement, so they managed satisfactorily along that score.

In her spare time, Elsa utilized her talents by knitting lace and stitching embroidery for which Everrett found a market in town. Elsa stayed mostly in the cabin and surrounding woods, avoiding town as if it were the plague. And although life was somewhat dull, she didn't care, because she felt safe, which was something she had not felt in a long time.

One evening, about two weeks after their marriage, as they ate supper in silence, (a bad habit Elsa didn't know how to break, and Everrett showed no initiative to), Elsa suddenly asked, "Have you ever attended church since you left the Quakers?"

"No, I's reckon I's had enough of silent prayeh and der ain't no otheh church as would want me." Then he added in a lower tone, "I's used to go to de meetin's de darkies held at night sometimes, but not since Mammy was so sick. Why's do you ask?"

"I don't know. I guess it is just something I have always done, and it seems strange not to. But there is nowhere around here where I would wish to go anymore."

Everrett nodded. "Der ain't no point in goin' where you's isn't wanted."

"That is the truth," Elsa agreed. "But do you believe in God, Mr. Trenton?"

"Of course. But how's come you's always calls me Misteh Trenton? Don't you's like de name Everrett?"

"No, no, it isn't that. I have always liked that name. It—well, it just seems so familiar," she stammered.

"Ands you's doesn't want to be familiar with me? Well, you doesn't have to, Miss Grey," he replied tersely.

Elsa's eyes opened wide, "But I do want to. I would like that very much, but I thought *you* wanted things to be more—more formal between us."

Now it was Everrett's turn to look surprised. He shook his head. "I's not a man foh formalities. What would give you's dat idea?"

What Elsa had reference to was the fact that since their marriage, Everrett had taken it for granted that she would not want to sleep with him, and had given her no indication that he would like it otherwise. So she said, "Well, you do not really think of me as your wife, do you?"

Everrett wasn't quite sure how to answer that. He had been with enough women before that he wasn't shy about it, but they had all been black, and more importantly they had all been pretty clear about what they wanted. When a woman opens her blouse and puts her breasts in your face, there isn't a whole lot of room for misgivings. But what Elsa wanted, he had not a clue. "How do you's want me to think of you?" he asked.

"I guess it does not matter. Just so long as it is a good way."

There she was again, telling him absolutely nothing. The truth of the matter was that Elsa was so used to deferring that she no longer knew what she really wanted.

"But at any rate," Elsa went on, "I will certainly call you Everrett if that is your preference. I really do like that name. Perhaps you will name a son that some day," she added bashfully. Everrett didn't say anything so she hurried to change the subject. "Do you have a middle name?"

"No, but I's like dem."

"I could give you one if you want," Elsa suggested.

"Alright." Everrett shrugged his broad shoulders, but he smiled, so Elsa knew he liked the idea.

"Let me think—something strong and not too common." Elsa considered for a minute. "I know. How does this sound? Everrett Jethro Trenton."

"It's a foul, dirty name," he exclaimed. "I's would neveh weah a name like dat!"

Elsa drew back in her chair. "I'm sorry. What is wrong with the name?" she asked tremulously.

"Jethro." Everrett's tone was absolutely dripping with disdain. "My damn fatheh had dat name. I's like him as much as you do dat bloody aunt of youhs. I *hate* him." Everrett hissed the word through closed teeth.

"That is a strong word to use for your own flesh and blood," Elsa said softly.

"And a strong meanin'. De fact dat he is my own flesh and blood, only makes him dat much de worse. His skin might bey white, but his heart's blackeh den a pail of swamp slime."

Elsa looked puzzled. "But he must have felt ashamed or sorry for what he did, or he would not have given you your freedom. I do not mean to trivialize anything you have had to endure, but everyday men are buying and selling mulattos and quadroons without a thought. Often they even pay much more for them then for a full-blooded African. Your situation is very unusual. You are really a lot better off than most."

"Dat's no credit to him," Everrett snorted. "Ifen he had his way, I'd still be out in de fields with de rest. But you's see, he had a heck of a pious wife. Mammy said shey were fittin' to be tied when I was born. Shey jest up and done told my fatheh dat he'd betteh free us both. He wouldn't hear nothin' of it at first. Said shey shouldn't cahe what hey did wid his slave women so long as he hid de evidence. But finally to make her stop a pesterin' him, he indentuhed me like you's been told, which weren't de same as given me my freedom. He made suhe he still got some money out of me. And even den, it is highly unlikely dat my new masteh would have let me go free when I was twenty-one, as was de agreement, except dat my fatheh's wife made suhe de man he indentuhed me to was halfway decent and took de papehs down to de courthouse herself so dat de matteh could neveh be contested."

"I see." Elsa stared into her mug of water.

156

"Shey took de scarlet fever and died a couple of yeahs lateh, and he ain't done nothin' halfway right eveh since."

"Do you have any siblings, Everrett?"

"Any what?"

"Brothers and sisters?"

"I's reckon I's got mohe half ones dan I's know to tell."

"Do you know where any of them are?"

"De boys are pickin' cotton on my fatheh's plantation, and de girls were sold mostly, 'cept foh de uncommonly pretty ones. My fatheh kept dose foh hisself."

"You don't mean…"

"Yes, I's do mean," he interrupted her. "Dat's what slavery is—ownin' a person's body, using dem foh whateveh is most handy; ownin' dere soul, makin' dem sin ifen it suits youh pleasuhe. Now you's see why I hates my fatheh. And he's only one of a breed ob sech men. Dere all as damned as de devil to me."

"I do see why." Elsa nodded, but after a pause went on hesitantly, "But I-I do not hate Aunt Ingrid. I wish dreadfully that she liked me, and I feel sorry for her because she is investing everything she has and is, in things which bring her no happiness. I feel just a little sorry for your father too. He must be a terribly wretched man. Cruelty can certainly bring no peace of mind. Sometimes I envy people who have so many opportunities to do good, and when I see them take those opportunities and use them for evil…Someday they will realize what they have done, but then it will be too late. You say they are damned. Well, perhaps they are, but for that very reason, don't you pity them?" Her voice was very quite.

"No! I hate my fatheh and youh aunt as well," he exclaimed adamantly. "And I's couldn't worship a God dat didn't bring punishment to such."

After a moment of strained silence, Elsa asked softly, "Is that why you didn't stay with the Quakers?"

"Dey is good people, and maybe lovin' everybody is good foh dem, and maybe it is foh you—though I's hardly thinks so—but it suhe ain't foh me."

Elsa stood up and placed water over the fire to heat for the dishes. She stirred the coals and added another stick. Straightening up, she gazed at the embers glowing among the black stubs of charred wood. She did not blame Everrett for his feelings, but neither did she understand the passion burning within him. She never felt fire surging through her own chest, only cold, slithering fear, tightening around her and weighing like lead in the pit of her stomach.

Although she kept staring into the fireplace, she could see Everrett in her mind's eye—tall, powerful, a dark mountain, rising out of the sea, firm and unmovable while storms raged about its peak. But what was the core of this mountain? Was it molten lava, awaiting its chance to spew? Or was there somewhere a cool, dark emptiness, waiting to be filled?

Suddenly she felt his hands, heavy and warm, on the sides of her waist. She was rather glad he was behind her, freeing her of the necessity of looking into his face. The back of her head touched his chest, and she closed her eyes for a second and let it rest against him.

"I's didn't mean to shut you's up," he said.

"I suppose this is almost the longest discussion we have ever had," Elsa said with a wry smile.

"I's often wonder why you's so quiet. You's seemed to talk fine with Mammy."

"That is because she did the talking. But we should talk more, Everrett. It seems very silly for us to be married and yet not even know one another."

He didn't say anything, but she could feel him nodding.

It was Saturday evening, now drawing close to three weeks that they had been together. Elsa stepped into the yard and peered down the path for the 6th time that evening. Everrett was not usually this late in coming back from work. She had not been unduly concerned at first. No doubt he had some project he wanted to finish before the new week. But it was 8 o'clock and still no sign of him.

She sat down on the low porch step and resumed knitting, but she kept hearing Lydia's words. "I have known colored men to be hung for sleeping with a white woman." Not that he was sleeping with her, but if anyone found out she was staying with him... Perhaps it had been a mistake. She stood back up to glance down the path again.

Unconsciously, she stared chewing on her fingernail. She could almost see Everrett with a rope around his neck, and it would be all her fault. So engrossed was she in conjuring up this horrible mental image that she didn't hear his approach until he was entering the yard.

"Oh, Everrett, I am so glad you are back." With a cry of relief she ran over to him.

He dismounted and then stopped in astonishment as he turned to look at her. "Elsa, youh face is wet. You's been crying? What's wrong?"

"Nothing. I am just glad you are home." She took his hand and pressed her cheek against it. "I was worried about you."

"You was?" He sounded quite surprised.

"Why is that so hard to imagine? You saw how silly I was worrying about John. Why can't I worry about you too?"

"Well, I's home now, and I's got somethin' foh you." He unfastened a burlap bag from his saddle and handed it to her. "Dis is why I's so late."

"What is it?"

"Come in de cabin and open it," he said taking her arm. "And give your husband some dinneh afore he starves."

"I can't imagine what it is. Something soft," she said as she gently squeezed the bag.

He smiled at her curiosity while he sat down to pull his boots off. "Jest open it."

Elsa reached slowly in and pulled out a dress. "Everrett, it's my clothes," she exclaimed in delight. "How did you ever…?"

"Henry," he answered. "He's came into de shop de otheh day, and was tellin' me all about how's youh aunt kicked you out. Said shey won't let any of dem so much as mention youh name in front of heh. He thinks it hurts heh conscience too much. But no one was around so I's tell him how's you been with me, and how's you wished you had brought some things with you. So he says he'd have de maid get some stuff out of youh room. Couldn't get you's anything valuable like youh jewelry, jest a few of youh older clothes dat Ingrid wouldn't cahe about enough to know dey was missin' even ifen shey looked. So he left dem in de woods foh me to pick up dis evenin'."

"That is so nice of both of you. You have no idea how glad I am to finally have more than the one dress." Elsa began to quickly empty the contents of the bag on her bed. There were two dresses, underclothes and stockings, and then at the bottom of the bag she felt something hard and heavy. "Oh, Everrett, look at this, my favorite book." She held up a small volume of poems by Elizabeth Barrett. "I feel so rich. Isn't it strange? I have had so many things my whole life, and I always appreciated what I had, but they didn't seem terrible significant. Then I go and lose everything, and now I feel rich just to own three dresses and one book."

"I's like dat about you. Most folks would bey so angry about all dey had lost, dey wouldn't bey able to appreciate gettin' a little back," Everrett replied as he splashed water over his face from the basin.

He found Elsa so fascinating. He had liked her ever since the day he sneaked up on her and John in the barn, and she had been so affronted that he would try to steal "her soldier". But he didn't understand her. He was good at placing people into categories, and he had thought that by this time he would have discovered hers.

On slow days at the forge as he pounded out his thoughts on red hot sticks of iron, he would puzzle over the wife he had taken. Her patience and meekness were a marvel to him, and always she responded with quick deference to his slightest spoken wish. He had to be careful what he said around her because she always took him so seriously. She was ridiculously sensitive, and yet at the same time, appeared strangely unperturbed by the things most people found irritating.

Sunday was the only day of the week Everrett did not go to the forge, and he relished the opportunity to sleep in. He awoke late to the aroma of something which smelled surprisingly good. He dressed and moved into the next room. Their sleeping arrangements consisted of Elsa occupying what had been Martha's bed in the main room of the cabin, while he continued to sleep in the small bed chamber he had added on when his mother came to live with him.

Elsa was fussing over the fire and had her back to him. He stood quietly in the doorway watching her. She was a beautiful woman, and so small—too thin actually. She hadn't been eating well lately. No doubt she was used to a better diet.

It was a very strange arrangement they had—married and yet not married—and one which would be difficult to maintain over any length of time. He wished he had a way off getting inside her head and seeing what went on there. What was she thinking about right now?

"Good mornin'."

"Oh, good morning, Everrett." Elsa spun around, her face flushed from the heat of the fire. She looked as if she had not gotten much sleep. "Your timing is good. Breakfast is almost ready—cornbread and salt pork. And better yet, I think my bread is actually looking like bread. Come see."

He came over to the fireplace to examine her bread, and agreed it was certainly her finest specimen to date. "I's would say you is gettin' de hang of it."

"Do you want coffee?"

"You's bet. It was de smell of it dat woke me."

"Did I awaken you too early?" Elsa asked anxiously as she handed him a steaming mug.

"No, I's was ready to get up. But even if you's had, I's don't cahe 'bout little things like dat."

"Most people do."

"Well, I's not most people, am I?" He took a big gulp of the hot liquid. Nice and strong—the way he liked it. Elsa must know that was what he liked because she always made it that way, although if she drank any, he had seen her dilute it with water. After they sat down to breakfast he said, "If I's ask you's somethin', will you give me an honest answer?"

Elsa looked a little startled. "It depends on what you ask me," she replied slowly.

"Is you's afraid of what I's would do ifen you's said or did somethin' I's didn't particularly like?"

She answered a noncommittal "perhaps", which he felt certain meant yes.

"So what do you's think would happen ifen you's made me upset?"

Elsa slowly swirled the coffee in her mug as she murmured, "What happened when I said something Aunt Ingrid didn't like? What happened when I said something Captain Aldridge didn't like?"

"Elsa, I's would never."

"It is no reflection on you," she hastened to assure him. "It is just that—well, remember when you first met me and could not help but be wary, just because that is how your life had trained you to think? Well, it is something like that for me."

Everrett nodded. He could see how the world had made her believe security was a nonexistent thing. He did not want her to be afraid of him, but how was he to change it? Being frightened was her default position, especially with men. She hadn't seemed that way with John, but that was no doubt due to his vulnerable situation. Everrett didn't say anything else until they were done eating and Elsa started to clear the table.

"Wait." He laid his hand on her arm. "Dese things won't go nowhere. Come walk with me."

"Oh, I would like that." She immediately set down the dishes in her hand and turned towards him.

"You's can bring youh book and read de poems to me ifen you's so inclined."

"I would like that even more."

He watched with a surprised smile as she hurried to get the book. It was beautiful out, bright and sunny, but not too hot yet. They walked in companionable silence, broken only by an occasional comment about a squirrel or a plant as they passed, until they reached the meadow, the one Everrett had told John to take Elsa to. He had secretly wanted to come here with her himself, and yet when he realized he had the opportunity, he had felt strangely hesitant to do so.

"It is even more beautiful than last time," Elsa breathed as she spread out her hands as if to catch the sunlight. The flowers were now in the peak of their bloom and the small clearing was a gay profusion of color and texture. "I am glad you wanted to come here. I just can't get over how lovely it is." She sank down into the knee-high grasses.

Everrett lowered his hefty frame beside her, and contentedly watched her obvious rapture.

"I don't know what it is about beautiful things. It is almost as if they speak to me," she murmured dreamily.

162

"Dat's not hard to believe," Everrett replied. "You's one of dem. It's only natural you's would undehstand their language."

After a little while Elsa began to read *Lady Geraldine's Courtship*, the story of a poor poet who fell in love with a countess. Everrett listened more to the softness of her voice and the cadence of the verses than the actual words, until she reached the part where Bertram, in a fit of desperate passion, began to rant against all the haughty aristocrats who judge a man worthless for lack of wealth and rank. Everrett smiled a little as he imagined himself raving against the world's injustice with such a plethora of lofty, rhythmic phrases.

Then Elsa read what she said was her favorite poem—*Cowper's Grave*. There didn't seem much to like about it. Everrett found it a rather morbid piece about a mentally distraught saint.

"What's you like about a poem like dat?" Everrett asked when she was done.

"Well, Cowper spent his whole life doing good, and yet he was so sad, thinking that no one, not even God, cared for him. But when he got to the end of his life, then he realized he had been wrong; his life wasn't a waste after all. I always hope that perhaps it will be like that for me," Elsa said very softly, "that when I reach the end of my life, I will discover that I actually did accomplish something good along the way."

"You's think youh life is a waste?"

"I often fear that it is."

"I's can't say I've eveh thought on it much. It ain't like we had no choice 'bout being born, so I's don't think we's need to justify ouh existence."

They were both quiet for a minute, Elsa watching Everrett as he lay on his back with his hands behind his head and eyes closed.

"Everrett," she said softly, "do you ever think it was not such a good idea for me to start living with you?"

He opened his eyes and saw her face was very solemn. "I's fine with it."

"Last night when you were late coming home," Elsa went on slowly, "I started remembering how Lydia Trenton told me that you could be hung for being with me. I thought about it all night. I think perhaps I should leave."

Everett propped himself up on one elbow. "Ifen you's want to go, dere is nothin' holdin' you, but don't leave on my account. I's well able to look out foh myself, and no one is going to find you's hehe. Durin' de five yeahs I's lived at dis cabin, no has been hehe except foh dose dat I's brought or told how to get hehe. And you's and John ahe de only white folks dat's so much as laid eyes on de place. I's didn't build out hehe in de middle of no place foh nothin'." He could see relief in her eyes. "Tell me honest, do you's want to go?"

Elsa shook her head. "No, but I really, really do not want anything bad to happen to you."

"It won't," he averred. "And I's would be very much annoyed with you ifen you's left."

"Would you?" Her voice was combination of surprise and concern.

Everett nodded grimly. "I's would be mohe den annoyed, I's would be furious." He felt a little bad when he sensed her alarm at this statement. He wasn't doing a very good job of keeping his resolution not to scare her, but he wasn't about to have her go running off alone and penniless to God knows where, just because she felt guilty to stay, so he went on a little fiercely, "And ifen anythin' bad happened to you on account of youh leavin', I's would neveh forgive you foh it."

"I did not realize you felt that way," Elsa said as she intently dissected the blade of grass in her hand.

"Ifen you's can worry about me, I's reckon I's got de right to worry about you ifen I's want."

Elsa smiled a little. "It has been a long time since anyone has cared enough to worry about me," she murmured.

"I know." Everett lightly ran the back of his hand down the side of her face. "Elsa, don't be scared of me," he said, looking steadily into her eyes. "You's can think any way you's want to. You's can say anythin' dat comes to mind. You's can ask me anythin' you wants to know. De world is full of dreadful people, and you's got to watch youhself every minute you's around dem, but not here. I's always liked my cabin in de woods vehy much cause here I's can jest be myself, and it's youh home now too, where you's can jest be youhself."

"That is probably the nicest thing anyone has ever said to me," Elsa whispered.

Everrett kept his hand against her face for a minute. Then he sat up and said, "De thought has occurred to me dat perhaps we's should try to go fatheh north. Virginia really ain't a good place foh eitheh of us. What do you's think?"

"It is a good idea. Did Martha ever tell you that I inherited my father's farm in Kentucky?" she asked.

"No. Would you's want to go dere?" Everrett responded with interest.

"No, never," Elsa answered very quickly. "But if we could sell it, we could use the money to go wherever we wanted. I do think it would be quite difficult to sell until the war is over, but someday…"

"Why is you's so suhe you's would neveh want to go back?" he questioned.

Elsa turned pale, and her voice was a little shaky as she said, "Please do not ask me that."

"Alright," he said amiably, but he stored the information away as one more piece of the puzzle to understanding Elsa. "You's want to walk some more?"

"I would like that," she answered as the color slowly came back into her face.

Desperate Nights

"Aaaooohhh!" The piercing sound jerked Everrett awake. He tossed over as he tried to drive the grogginess from his mind. What was that dreadful shriek? It sounded so close. Blinking open his eyes, he stumbled into the next room. Elsa was sitting stiffly erect on the bed. All was quite now except for her breath which was coming in short, unnatural gasps.

"What was dat awful loud noise?" he asked huskily.

"I'm sorry I woke you," she gulped.

"What happened?" he demanded as he sat down on the bed and laid his hand on her shoulder.

"I had a nightmare."

"Dat's no good. You's want to talk about it?"

"I don't think so." Elsa's voice was a tight, jerky whisper. Her eyes were dilated, and her face looked rigid and ghastly in the white moonlight fluttering through the small window. Everrett had never before lived with anyone predisposed to nightmares, and he wasn't quite sure what to make of it. They had always seemed rather irrational to him.

"It's just a dream, and dey ain't true," he began.

"But mine was," Elsa interjected.

"What did you's dream?"

Elsa shook her head. "You don't want to know."

Everrett rather thought he did want to know and was about to ask,

"Why not?" But before he could, Elsa disintegrated into choking sobs. She covered her face with trembling hands as her whole body shuddered with the force of her tears.

Instinctively he put his arms around her, and she turned hungrily, desperately, into his embrace. He had not expected that. He could feel her fingers digging hard into his upper arm, and her tears were hot against the bare skin of his chest as she buried her face in his shoulder. Everrett wrapped his arms snuggly around her. She was so small she was practically lost in them.

"Don't—don't cry," he muttered, although he knew it was a little too late for such advice. Of course he knew women had a tendency to shed a few tears now and then, but this was another thing entirely. After all, Elsa had not cried when Martha died or when he found her in the cemetery, yet now she was hysterical, completely beside herself, over a dream. A dream of all things—if only it was something concrete, something he could see and understand. But the very mystery of it stimulated him, and he was determined to solve it.

He held her a little tighter. It wasn't a very helpful thing to be thinking at such a time, but she actually felt quite good in his arms, all soft and warm and quivering. Little by little her sobs were subsiding, until at length she lay limply against him.

"Is you alright?" he asked quietly.

"I guess," she sniffled.

"You's want to tell me what's wrong now?"

"I can't. I can't," she wailed and seemed on the verge of resuming her former activity.

"Don't cry," he said quickly. "You's don't have to be scared; nothin' bad is gonna happen."

"How do you know?" she questioned doubtfully.

"Because I's won't let it." Even as he said the words, they sounded a little too good to be true. He just hoped that Elsa, in her current state of mind, would not think that through. And to distract her from contemplating it, he started to comb his fingers through her soft hair. He could feel her relaxing under his light touch. "You's will feel betteh in de mornin'."

"I am sorry to have woken you and made such a fuss," she said, sounding more natural.

"It's alright. You's want to lay back down?" he asked, releasing her.

She nodded and then took his hand as she said haltingly, "Everrett, would it...that is, if it's not too much trouble..." Her voice faded out.

"What do you's want?"

"To be with you," she whispered. "I hate to be alone, and I like you very much. You are one of the nicest men I've ever met."

"If dat's true, you's haven't met many nice men," he said with a slight smile. "But what is you's sayin'?"

"That—that—if you don't mind...I don't want to sleep by myself tonight," she finally blurted out.

Everrett caught his breath before he could make some silly exclamation. Once again, that was not what he was expecting her to say, but he must not read too much into it, so he said calmly, "Alright."

He lay down on his back and Elsa stretched out right next to him and was about to put her head on his chest. "Do you mind?" she asked timidly.

He shook his head and put his arm around her as she settled down. Everrett listened to her rapid but shallow breathing gradually grow softer. As she finally drifted off into the mystical world through which the sleeping mind journeys, he could feel her begin to tense and jerk as if in pain.

He gently began to massage her neck and shoulders. Elsa snuggled closer to him. Everrett was acutely aware of her supple warmth as she molded around him. He could feel her breasts distinctly through her thin nightgown which was hitched up far enough that the silky smooth skin of her leg was pressing against the firmness of his own. She stirred in her sleep, drawing still closer, and he felt his whole body tense as her sleek leg glided up along his.

He reached over and laid his hand on her thigh. It was smooth as satin beneath his touch, and he could not help but slide up it. And then he stopped, stifling a moan as he realized she was not wearing any undergarments. He did not know what he had expected.

Everrett had never before let himself think about it. He knew Elsa had married him out of sheer desperation, and under any other circumstances they would not be together. He had told her beforehand that he did not expect her to share his bed and had been quite determined not to put any pressure on her. But now it was she who had asked for his company. No doubt she had not had this in mind. But for pity's sake, he was man, and she was exquisite—not to mention that she was his wife. How was he supposed to lie with her and not grow hard and hot?

His hand continued to slowly grope over her body, exploring, and liking its discoveries very much. He was glad he had not touched her before now; it was indescribably wonderful and yet unpleasantly overwhelming. It had been a long time since he had slept with a woman, and never before with one so perfect. He was not appreciating the insistent signals his body was sending him. There was no way he was ever going to get to sleep at this rate.

He halted his hand on the smooth curve of her hip, afraid to go further and yet not wanting to go back. Elsa stirred again and started to wake up. He froze, expecting her to jerk away in alarm, but she didn't. Her hand was on his shoulder, and she tightened her grip. For a moment they both lay very still, afraid of breaking the spell of the moment.

Everrett felt a tiny wet drip on his chest and pulled away abruptly.

"I-I'm sorry, I's didn't mean to…" He broke off mid-sentence, not really knowing what he didn't mean to do.

"No, Everrett. Don't be sorry." Elsa lifted her head to look at him in the moonlight. Although her face was wet, she didn't seem upset. "Don't mind me if I cry. I just seem to want to cry about everything tonight," she said with a lame smile. "But you can touch me all you want to. I like very much to be close to you." She blushed and quickly lowered her face back down to his chest. "This is very embarrassing to talk about," she whispered. "Because, I've always been a little afraid to be with a man, and I don't know exactly how it is done, but—but if you want to show me…" Her voice trailed off, and she pressed her face into his chest as if trying to hide.

Everrett could feel the rapid pounding of her heart, but it couldn't equal his own. His veins were beginning to tingle with the liquid fire it was pumping. She had no idea how much he wanted to show her how it was done. But he was also very afraid of hurting her. He wrapped his arms around her protectively, and his whole body throbbed with desire.

He released her and moved away a little. "I's you suhe?" he asked huskily. "It's not like I's eveh been with a virgin befohe, but from what I's hear, women don't find it too pleasant de first couple times."

"I know," Elsa answered. "And I won't say I am not scared, but, Everrett, I think you are wonderful. You are so strong and sure. You're like a rock. No matter how much the rain beats on you, you can't be washed away. I love that about you. And you have no idea how glad I am that you asked me to stay. Everrett, I don't have anyone else in the world, and I want to be yours. I truly do, if-if you want me that is."

Even in the pale moonlight Everrett could see the deep blush on Elsa's cheeks, and she was fidgeting busily with her hands as she waited to see what his response would be.

"Elsa, you adorable woman, of course I's want you. Will you's let me look at you?" He tugged gently on the hem of her nightgown to convey the whole meaning of what looking at her meant.

Elsa very slowly undid the tiny buttons on the front and pulled it off over her head. Everrett caught his breath. She was even more beautiful than he had anticipated, and he couldn't stay away. His hands glided over her slender body as effortlessly as running water. She was smooth and perfect and unbelievably soft.

"Elsa, you's an angel, no, a goddess," he breathed.

More than anything, he was surprised by the eagerness with which she received his caresses. She seemed hungry, almost starving. He let go of her just long enough to remove his pants and she fell eagerly back into his arms, then suddenly grew rigid and perfectly still. Everrett froze himself, waiting to see what she would do. Finally he felt her fingertips moving slowly, very slowly, across his back, and then he knew what she was doing.

His first impulse was to pull her arm away, but he stopped himself. As much as he wanted to shield her from everything sordid, there was no point in trying to hide the truth from her. It would only be an exercise in futility. Elsa's fingers kept tracing the scars on his back, from his shoulders down to the end of his spine.

"Everrett, I'm sorry, I'm so sorry," she breathed and there were tears in her voice. "How many times?"

"Only three. My masteh didn't approve of such goings on. But foh a yeah or so, he had a foheman who hated me on account of de fact de I was meant to go free someday."

"When I think of all the people who have been cruel to you over the years, I wish—I wish…"

"What do you's wish?"

"I wish so much that there was someway I could take it away, someway I could make up for all the people who should have been good to you but weren't. But I know that's impossible. Everything which happens becomes a part of who you are, and no matter how much time passes or how many things happen after that, it can never be taken away."

Everrett nodded. "It turns you off, don't it? Makes you's want to bey sick."

"It does make me want to be sick, but not in the way you're thinking. But let's not speak of it anymore." Elsa took her hand off his back and wrapped her arms around his neck.

Everrett laid his hand very lightly on her hair. He wanted to embrace her, but held back. It seemed as if the chasm, which had been closing between them, was suddenly wide again. What was he doing with a woman like her? What was there in him which she could possibly be attracted to?

Elsa sensed his hesitation. "Are you angry with me? Did I say something wrong?" she asked anxiously.

"No, you's perfect, too perfect."

"I have made you angry," Elsa said sadly. "I'm sorry; I didn't mean to."

Everrett felt her drawing away, and before he realized he was doing it, wrapped his arms tight around her and pulled her snuggly against his chest. "I's not angry, not at all," he murmured.

"Then-then make love to me," she whispered.

Everrett took her face between his hands and kissed every inch of it. He worked his way down her neck and gently nuzzled each of her breasts, then slowly laid her back.

He could tell she was nervous by her unnatural breathing and the way she trembled each time he touched her in some new place, but he didn't see the fear which so often floated in her eyes, more like excitement. Why she could trust him about this and seemingly nothing else, he couldn't imagine. He wasn't sure if he trusted himself.

He placed his hand on her ankle and ran it up the inside of her leg and into her crotch. It was very slippery. He moved his fingers back and forth, causing her to moan with unexpected pleasure. He climbed on top of her and bent his mouth down to hers, kissing her softly several times. Then unable wait any longer, he sank into the moist, tight depths of her body.

Elsa screamed with the sudden burning pain and dug her fingers into his back. He held still for a minute and wrapped his arms around her, lifting her shoulders and holding her close to himself. And then she said the absolute last thing he expected. He thought that right about now she was probably having some serious second thoughts, but she gasped, "Everrett, I love you."

He clutched her tighter and began to move, urgently, ever deeper into her soft warmth. Her fingers pressing relentlessly into his back only heightening his intensity until his frame shook with a quivering spasm of pleasure as he released into her pressure.

Afterwards they lay together, the room quiet except for their hard breathing. Everrett tenderly ran his hand over Elsa's breasts. "How was it?" he asked.

"They say it gets better the more you do it," Elsa said slowly.

"So you's might bey willin' to try it again some time?" Everrett asked with a smile.

Elsa nodded. "Everrett, please, let me stay with you—always."

"Elsa, as long as you wants me, dere ain't no storm, no man, no demon dat can eveh take you's away. If anyone eveh tries to hurt you, I's will kill dem. And you's know I can too."

Everrett opened his arms to her, and she snuggled into them. The freshness of the pain was still too sharp to allow for sleep, but she was lulled by the slow rise and fall of his chest, and she soaked in the protective warmth of his embrace and was happy.

Everrett also lay awake for a long time, although the slow rhythm of his breathing made Elsa think he was asleep. He wondered why Elsa had said she loved him. He had not been prepared for that at all. Of course, this whole night was completely unanticipated. If she had said such a thing when he was fondling her, he would have dismissed it as merely a reaction to pleasant stimulus, but judging by the way she screamed, she was not exactly reveling in enjoyable physical sensation at that moment.

That thought brought up another disturbing one. Why had Elsa wanted to sleep with him in the first place? Was it her way of asking for affection? Perhaps she thought that because he had sex with her it automatically meant he loved her. Then again, knowing Elsa, he wouldn't put it past her to do it just because she thought a good wife ought to.

But what if Elsa really did love him? Everett supposed that love was something generally implied by marriage and physical intimacy. After all, it was called making love. He opened his eyes and looked at her for a moment, so lovely and soft. If anyone deserved to be loved, it was Elsa. But how was he supposed to know what she needed? And even if he knew, Everett doubted very much that he would be able to provide it.

What had Mammy said that last day? "Marry someone as is nothing like youhself, and shey will love you foh being everything shey ain't." Well, he had taken her advice alright. Martha had also said that someday he would find he loved her back, but Mammy didn't know him all that well if she believed that. Everett had seen people passionately in love before, and as far as he could tell, it was just a synonym for vulnerability— not something he was ever going to get mixed up in.

But perhaps it didn't really matter so much if he couldn't love her. It wasn't as if Elsa had much of a frame of reference. He wasn't going to take advantage of her timid disposition to control her like Ingrid. He wasn't going to vanish from her life like John. And he certainly wasn't going to abuse her like Aldridge. Everett's arms tightened reflexively around her. How a male could so forget his manhood as to strike something so delicate and fragile was beyond him.

Everett looked at her again. Her body was so perfect. It would never again bear the marks of a man's rage; he was certain of that. Yes, maybe he couldn't give her love, but he could protect her, which was better.

*   *   *   *   *

The next several weeks passed quickly as Everrett and Elsa successfully tested the theory that it does get better the more you do it. For a brief time the humdrum troubles of living receded into the background against the dazzle of their new found interest in one another.

August began with a hot, dry spell, each day determined to outdo the last in oppressive heat. One particular afternoon grew especially hot, while all the little breezes playing among the tops of the oaks grew still. A stifling, eerie calm hung thick in the air. The hens did not lay a single egg that day. As Elsa took down the clothes from the morning's washing, she kept giving anxious little glances towards the motionless trees, missing the usual songs of the birds and chatter of squirrels which kept her company.

Everrett arrived home from work a little early. "Nobody wants to come to de forge dis aftehnoon. Dey's all at home boarding' up dere barns. Dere's gonna be a storm tonight. I'd best see if Charcoal's lean-to is in good 'nough shape."

Darkness fell early as thick, black clouds moved in from the west and the sun set behind a murky veil. Sleep was hard to find in the dense heat, but Everrett finally dozed off. Elsa lay awake for a long time, listening to the deep stillness, broken only by Everrett tossing fitfully beside her.

Around midnight, a strong wind swept out of nowhere and flew angrily over the sleeping countryside, moaning as it ripped past the corners of the little house. The tiny panes of glass rattled in their frames, shuddering in its wake. Overhead, the wind tore through the treetops in great rushing breaths.

Elsa jumped out of bed and over to the window. The sky was pitch black. Little thuds sounded above her as twigs, acorns, and broken tree branches bounced on the roof.

Elsa hated storms—Nature's fury unleashed. They seemed a living thing, like some huge, mindless brute flailing its arms and indiscriminately destroying all that lay within its reach. Or sometimes they seemed more intentional, like this one. The elements had been provoked and were preparing to pour forth retribution.

First there was the wind, screaming its displeasure as it haughtily brushed aside everything in its route, knocking its head ferociously on anything with the temerity to block the way. And now the lightning was starting, tremendous bolts zigzagging across the sky. They looked to Elsa like fiery darts thrown from the hand of some pagan deity. The thunder was beginning its constant roll, like the fierce roar of cannons—a giant shaking the earth with bellows of his wrath.

In the distance there was the crash of a falling tree. Elsa could feel the thunder reverberating right through her. She pressed against the wall, seeking reassurance from the solidness of it. There was no rain. Perhaps when the elements held their council of war, water had refused to participate. But whatever the reason, she felt a weird sense of the earth having lost its equilibrium.

Elsa was just telling herself how ridiculous such a thought was, when the room was dazzled by a terrifically close lightning bolt, followed instantaneously by a loud crash, while the whole cabin reverberated beneath a dreadful impact.

Elsa's hands flew to her throat, while Everrett, rudely awakened from his restless slumber, leapt from the bed. "Elsa!"

"I'm here by the window," Elsa answered while another lightning streak splashed white light across their faces, then left the room in inky blackness.

"What was dat?" Everrett demanded as he stumbled over to her.

"I don't know, but I think a tree might have fallen on the cabin. Everrett, do I smell smoke? Ooh, this door doesn't want to open."

Groping his way over, Everrett moved the stubborn door with a kick. The room beyond was already beginning to glow with a ghastly orange light, and there was an ominous hiss and crackle of flames. They darted outside, where the sporadic illumination of lightning forks showed them what had happened. The old maple near the corner of the cabin had been struck, crashed over on the house, and ignited the dry wood into a hissing blaze.

"The cabin is going to burn down," Elsa gasped. "We must get a few things out."

"You stay here," Everrett ordered as he disappeared back inside.

Elsa darted over to the lean-to, jerked open the door, and let out Charcoal and the chickens. Everrett appeared in the doorway, his arms loaded. In an instant he vanished again.

"Water," Elsa thought frantically, but the stream was a good twenty yards away and the bucket still inside the burning house. The cabin was dry as a box of kindling, and the fire was growing by leaps and bounds. There was no way they could possibly bring water fast enough to make a difference.

Where was Everrett? It seemed like an eternity that he had been inside. Elsa turned Charcoal's face away from the flames and pressed her cheek against the horse's smooth neck, her lips moving silently in hurried prayers.

The ghastly flames danced weirdly in the uneven wind whipping between the trees, blazing to ever new heights as they merged. Gyrating like a ring of druids preparing a human sacrifice, they contorted themselves into glowing whirls of horror—ruthless, unfeeling, unfettered tongues of destruction.

Elsa let out her breath as Everrett finally reemerged and ran over to her, coughing. For several minutes they both stood mesmerized by the hideous inferno.

"If only it would rain," Elsa breathed.

Her voice was drowned by a booming crash of thunder, and as if in answer to her request, big drops of rain began to spatter through the leaves. Within minutes, the drops turned to a downpour, gushing down over the burning house. Hissing a smoky protest, the flames began to die. Elsa hugged herself and shivered as she gratefully watched the rain extinguish the cruel fire. Everrett came to stand behind her and wrapped her in his warm arms.

With steady insistence the rain poured down for a good half hour. It made rivers through their hair and little rivulets streaming down their noses, and soaked their clothes through until they could feel the rain cascading over their bodies like a waterfall.

Although the air was not cold, the rain was gelid enough that Elsa soon felt chilled to the bone despite Everrett's arms around her. Her teeth started to chatter, and the chattering started to turn to laughter, at first an idiotic little giggle, but fast turning into incapacitating, hysterical laughter. Her legs got weak, and she collapsed on the sodden earth, breathless and helpless to do anything but give in to the waves of hysterics shaking her as her tears mingled with the rain flowing down her face.

At first Everrett seriously wondered if she had altogether taken leave of her senses, but a slow smile crept across his face as he watched her complete discomposure, and he couldn't help a chuckle or two at the sight of her. "What's you doin'?" he laughed.

"Everrett, look—look at us. We are like a couple—a couple of fish in the middle of the sea, trying—trying to dry off. That is what our—our entire lives are like. Why do we even bother?" Unable to say anything more, she continued to simultaneously cry and laugh very hard and choked several times in the process.

Everrett felt like joining her, but he didn't. If she was going to be emotional enough for the two of them, it was up to him to be the strong one. Finally the ran subsided, and with it, Elsa's hysteria.

After that there seemed very little to say. Elsa viciously wrung the water from her hair and nightgown while Everrett stroked Charcoal's wet face. They both stared at the demolished, sodden wreck before them.

"It is completely ruined, isn't it?" Elsa said at last.

"I's reckon it is. Jest ouh luck. Is you alright?"

Elsa shrugged. "I don't know, and I don't particularly care."

"It will be a site of trouble to rebuild it."

Elsa came to stand beside him. "At least Charcoal and the hens are safe."

Everrett nodded.

"Do we have the money to rebuild it?" Elsa wondered.

"I's jest been figurin' on it. Not hardly. I's couldn't get as much work done at de forge while I's building', and we's got to live somewhere in de mean time. I jest don't see how…"

There was a long pause, and then Elsa said hesitantly, "I suppose we could go to my farm."

"Would you's like to?" he asked.

"No." Elsa shivered and hugged herself tightly. "But it might be the only thing to do. You were talking about moving anyway, and now it seems as if we don't have much choice. It will be hard to make a go of farming though. We're not exactly a couple of old farm hands," she ended dryly.

"Don't you's think I could work as a smith dere? Is it a friendly community?"

"A divided community—the very good and the very bad." Elsa stared off into the darkness as she spoke. "There are some who would not tolerate a free black holding a public job like a smith, but if you didn't charge too much I am sure you could get some private work with old friends of my father's." Elsa was quiet for a moment and then said, "I am frightened to go back there."

"Why?"

"Memories, only memories, always memories. I shouldn't let them hold me back. I know that. You are always so strong. Are you never afraid?"

"I's ain't one to give up."

"There is nothing left here. At least there is something in Kentucky. But it takes so much courage to start again. Oh, I wish we could just fly away like a couple of birds to a distant island and hide there for the rest of our lives. I've liked this past month—just being here alone in the middle of the forest with you. I wish I never had to venture out."

"What is it you feah?" he asked.

"Hate," she whispered after a pause.

"Elsa, I's hate dose who hates me. Dat is why I's not afraid. Hate is something you's can't eveh escape; it's everywhehe. But if my hate is stronger dan theirs, I's don't fear dem."

"If I bore a hate that strong, I think the very weight of it would kill me."

"And do you's find feah any easier to live with?"

Elsa didn't have an answer for that.

After a bit, Everrett said, "I's reckon dere ain't anything we's can do until mornin'. Let's sit down and try to rest." Suiting actions to words, he proceeded to find a seat on the wet earth and lean back against a tree trunk.

"Rest?" Elsa raised her eyebrows. "We are soaked to the skin and have nowhere dry to go. How is a rest even a possibility?"

"Come on." He held his arm out to her. "Dere ain't a blasted thing we's can do. Dat damn tree ruined everything, and de fire burnt de ruins, and de rain killed de fire. Now all we's have is a soggy, burnt mess, and it's de middle of de night, foh pity's sake."

Elsa sighed resignedly and snuggled up to him. "What about your mother?" she asked.

"What about heh?"

"Did she hate people? I mean she never seemed afraid, and she was so happy. Was she always happy?"

"Afteh shey had heh freedom, shey was always vehy content."

"I wish I could be like her." Elsa's voice was wistful.

"You aren't ever going to be like her," Everrett thought, but he didn't say so. He merely patted her shoulder and said consolingly, "Well, you's betteh company. I's can think of some things I's like vehy much to do with you dat I's suhe neveh could have done with heh."

Elsa smiled a little. They sat in silence for a time, staring at the desolation before them, each absorbed in their own thoughts. Elsa shivered and Everrett pulled her closer. She listened to his heart beat, slow and powerful.

Finally Elsa asked, "Do you think there is such a thing as a love so strong that it would be stronger than hate?"

"No, there isn't," he answered without hesitation. Then he wrapped her fast in both his arms, but when he spoke, his tone was cold and unemotional. "Elsa, I's always took cahe of myself, and when I was able I's took cahe of Mammy, and I's gonna take cahe of you. And dat doesn't have to do with love. My hate is a shield, and it will protect us both."

Matters of Conscience

"Come on, boys. Let's get going," John called as he wheeled his horse around and led his men out of the front yard of one of the numerous plantations they had despoiled. Several wagons piled with provisions and valuables jostled along behind them.

"This has been a good day, Lieutenant," Connly said exultantly, cantering his pinto alongside John's jet black mount. "There was a heap of provisions at that old manse, and we've got a total of ten horses so far today."

"You've proved to my satisfaction that you know your business in that department." John patted his horse's shoulder as he smiled at Connly.

"I'm truly glad I was assigned to your group," Connly went on enthusiastically. "Raiding like this is great—better than a battle any day. I guess this is more what I had in mind when I joined up."

"I couldn't have asked for a better detail," John replied. "We do our job well and efficiently. I have heard that from more than one superior."

It was now autumn of 1864. General Philip Sheridan was succeeding in driving the Confederates from the Shenandoah valley, while simultaneously carrying out a campaign to devastate the crops and food supplies of the region—a campaign so successful that he was able to boast, "A crow flying through would have to carry provisions on its back." He knew that by laying waste the fertile valley, he was destroying the Confederates' bread basket, and with it, their hopes.

John Fairfield and Arthur Connly were at the heart of this project from the outset. After safely delivering their prisoners into the care of others, they had been commissioned on a number of small missions and were now busily engaged in a series of sweeping raids. The danger was comparatively minimal, and even on their worst days they had more to show for their efforts than scars. Yes, this conformed much closer with Connly's picture of a dragoon's life—dashing, full of excitement, and always the sweet taste of a job well done, a mission accomplished.

It was now drawing towards twilight on a sunny late September day. Something about the area they were riding through held a vague familiarity to John. He had been puzzling over it all day, and now it came to him in a flash. The last time he had seen this checkerboard landscape, dotted with sylvan acres amid grain fields and open meadows, all had been dark, and he had been more the fugitive than the threat.

"Commander, are we going to make camp soon?" John recognized Tommy's voice behind him.

"Are you hungry again, Tommy? We'll stop yet at the farm over there—the one you can just see the top of the barn. After that we will call it a day."

Ten minutes later saw the soldiers galloping up a dusty dirt lane leading to an old farm house. The boards were a weathered gray, but the yard was neatly kept, and the windows gleamed gold in the evening sun. The door opened and a tall, gaunt-faced woman stepped onto the porch. Her dark brunette hair, pulled into an ample bun at the back of her neck, was flecked with gray. The soft lines at the corners of her eyes bore a motherly expression, although at present her features were tense and drawn as she silently surveyed the group.

The soldiers quickly scattered to their assigned tasks, for John never allowed his men to fulfill the stereotype of a raucous gang. John paid little more than a glance to their observer on the porch, until the front door slammed and two familiar voices drew his attention.

"Mama, who is it? Soldiers!"

"Yankees! Are they gonna kill us?"

"Look, they're taking the meat from the smokehouse."

"Hush, hush, boys. They are not going to kill us. Soldiers only shoot other soldiers," replied the woman consolingly. "Perhaps you had better go back in the house."

"I'm going to stay with you, Mama. I'm the man of the house now that Papa and Fenton are away," piped up the elder of the two youngsters.

"But Robbie, they might shoot us. Remember, we're soldiers now too," exclaimed his little brother in distraught tones.

"Then we will die with honor," Robbie said solemnly.

As John overheard this exchange, it struck him like an arrow just whose farm he had happened upon. Reigning in his horse in front of the porch, he prepared to speak, only to realize he had no clue what to say. However, if John was at a loss for words, his young acquaintances certainly were not.

"He looks 'most the same as the man we helped," whispered Paul in unsuppressed excitement and dread.

"Paul, be quiet," Robbie ordered. "What do you want, soldier?" he demanded of John.

"Robert, what are you doing? Don't bother the soldiers," broke in his mother.

"I guess at least one of you recognizes me," John said quietly, looking at Paul.

Paul tugged at his brother's shirt sleeve. "I told you. He's the man we gave water and strawberries to. I knew he was."

"What are you talking about?" queried the woman as she looked from one to the other in confusion.

"One time when I was wounded, ma'am, your sons helped me by bringing me water."

"And strawberries," piped up Paul.

"And strawberries." John smiled as he nodded to him.

"Boys, you never told me about this," said their mother.

"I told them not to, ma'am."

Robbie was staring hard at John. "But we helped a Confederate soldier. Do you mean that tale you told us in the orchard was a fib, and you were a Yankee the whole time?" His small hands were clenched into fists.

"Yes," John answered simply.

Paul blinked at him incredulously, but Robbie shot back with a scornful reply. "You're a traitor! You've disgraced your word of honor and your army, and now you will steal all we have as well."

"Robert!" exclaimed his mother. "What has come over you? The excitement has become too much for him, sir." She turned apologetically towards John.

"It's alright, ma'am."

John sprang from the saddle and bounded up the steps. He knelt on one knee to look into the two sets of brown eyes fixed accusingly on him.

"No, boys," he said gently. "I'm not that low. I may not have partaken of your salt, but I ate your strawberries and drank your water, and I can see you have guarded my secret. I will not harm anything of yours now." He gravely extended his hand, which after only a brief hesitation, Paul took trustingly. John then proffered it to Robbie, who folded his arms across his chest and gazed reproachfully at him.

Standing up, John shifted his weight from one foot to the other and cleared his throat before asking, "Do you have a gun, Robert?"

"No." Robbie flushed and drew back a little, but did not take his eyes off John.

"If you are the man of the house, you will need one." Avoiding the gun Elsa gave had given him, John slipped a small pistol from his belt and offered it to Robbie.

The young boy eyed it for a moment, obviously struggling between his desire to take it and his unwillingness to show any sign of friendship to John. Finally, unable to restrain his eagerness any longer, he unfolded his arms and snatched it.

"Now, if we can make an agreement that you won't shoot me, and I won't filch from you, and shake on it like men, I will give you two shells," John said with as much gravity as if he were laying out the terms for an armistice.

Robbie bit his lower lip and turned over the pistol, scrutinizing it. At last he extended his hand. John shook it firmly and handed over the promised shells.

"But I still don't trust you," Robbie said.

"I am sorry I have not proved more worthy," John replied, and he meant it. The look of betrayal in Robbie's eyes made John feel as if he had committed one of the seven deadly sins. Turning to the boys' mother, John said, "It is two fine young gentlemen you have for sons. I will tell you honestly, if they weren't, your farm would be as devastated as a good many others around here. But now I will tell my men to return your things, and we will be on our way." John tipped his hat to her and leapt onto his waiting horse.

"God bless you," she called after him, still in bewilderment about what had taken place.

"Come on, men. We're moving on and not taking anything from here," John shouted to his men as he sped away from the house. "Stanford, don't torch the barn. Reckels, release the chickens. Return the meat to the smokehouse, Pickford.

"What's up?" demanded Connly, who had been watching John speak with the boys.

"I'll explain later."

After they stopped to make camp, John gave the men a brief explanation for his sudden change of plans. Most of them were in sympathetic agreement, but much to his surprise, Connly set his lips in a tight line and looked away with an obvious expression of disapproval. Later that night, when they were alone in their tent, John waited for Connly to broach the subject. Although John was the commander, their relationship was such that Connly was usually very frank about sharing his opinions. But tonight Connly remained stolidly silent and merely gave John dark looks when he tried to make cheerful small talk.

Finally John's patience wore thin. "What's wrong with you, Connie? Do you have a toothache or is your nose out of joint?"

"My hair is out of joint," Connly said without humor.

John raised his eyebrows. "What's that supposed to mean?"

"It doesn't mean a damn thing." Connly gave John a very withering look, intended to squelch all further attempts at conversation.

However, John was much more intrigued by Connly's sullen mood than intimidated by it. "Arthur Connly, what is your problem?"

"Why did you do what you did today?" Connly burst out with unprecedented foul temper.

"I told you why. What's eating you?"

"Every single farm and plantation we go to has real people on it with sad stories of their own. If we follow your philosophy, we should leave everyone alone. We might as well give up being soldiers all together," Connly replied petulantly.

"I told you, I knew those boys personally. It was just a small farm anyway. I don't get it. Why does this matter to you?"

"So it's alright for you to spare your feelings, but when it comes to the rest of us, we might as well not have a conscience. Is that how it works?"

"I don't have a clue what you are talking about. Don't tell me it bothers your conscience to burn barns. You certainly never acted like it."

"It doesn't." Connly's tone, which had started out angry, was fast turning sad. "Forget it. Let's go to sleep."

"No, Connie, something is eating the hell out of you." John sat down on his blanket and eyed the younger man closely.

"There ain't nothing to talk about," Connly replied tersely, but John could tell by his eyes that there was a lot which needed to be said.

"Stop acting like a woman and just tell me your bloody problem," John sighed.

"Damn." Connly kicked his boot across the tent and hurled his gauntlets viciously into the corner. Finally he turned to face John. "Have you ever killed a man?"

"Well, I've done my share of shooting."

"I don't mean that. Have you ever killed a man point blank. Where you looked him in the eye, then spilled his blood and took his life away, and you knew that you, and you alone, killed him?" Connly sat down on his blanket, facing John.

"Well, I've certainly seen men go down, but I guess I never stayed around long enough to know if they died." When Connly didn't respond, John said, "I take it you have?"

"It was horrible, John. I ran my bayonet clear through him—awful bloody mess. At first I felt like lying down and dying right there with him, but then I said to myself, 'This is war. We are fighting for a cause, a just, righteous cause, and whatever we have to do to promote it is right.' It has to be. It isn't about individual people or personal feelings. Honestly, John, I can't fight if I look out across the field and see individual people and their lives. All I let myself see is our cause, what we are fighting for. We are crushing evil and bringing freedom, and that is right and something to be proud of."

"It is, Connie."

"How can you sit there and say that to me? You thought it was wrong to take chickens from a couple of boys because you knew they were innocent and trusting. How can that be wrong for you, and yet it be right for me to look a man in the eyes and send him to hell?" Connly's voice was strained, and John could see the moistness in his eyes. "Life is such a wonderful thing; I love it. There is nothing better than to see people live, and laugh, and fall in love, and—and live everyday to its fullest. I've never wanted to take that away from anyone, but I believed that we were following a calling that was worthy enough to justify whatever we had to do in the pursuit of that calling. But obviously you don't think so." Connly turned away from John and put his hand over his eyes for a second.

John reached over and clasped his shoulder. "Why haven't you told me about this before?"

"Oh, you know how much I like discussing dismal things," Connly answered dryly. "It happened about a month ago. I didn't think it would bother me like it did, and I haven't let myself think about it. I just figured this was something we all face, and we all just have to put our personal feelings aside and do our job. And that was that. John, you're my commander. I follow you. I admire your strength, your confidence. If you can't handle something like this, how do you expect the rest of us to?"

John rested his chin on his hand. He could think of many different reasons to vindicate his actions, but realized that wasn't the issue. At length he said, "I'm sorry I let you down, Connie. I believe that in this particular situation my decision was the right one, but I agree with what you say. You are the best man I've ever fought with. I mean that. I admire your strength, your spirit, your vitality. It's hard to be a soldier, and still treasure the beauty of life. To have what you have, to have such strength of purpose, and yet care so much—it's more than most men will ever know. It's what draws people to you, Connie; don't ever lose it."

*　　　　　*　　　　　*　　　　　*　　　　　*

As the autumn advanced, Sheridan and his Army of the Shenandoah were engaged in a deathly tussle with General Jubal Early, an uncouth infantry general creating a fierce menace in the Shenandoah valley. Such was the unbridled violence of this general, that even Lee referred to him as "my old bad boy".

On account of their preoccupation with raiding, John and his band missed many of the battles as Sheridan relentlessly hounded his opponent. By the middle of October, Early's army had been weakened by so many defeats that Sheridan no longer considered him much more than a nuisance. But then disturbing rumors began to spread, rumors that General Longstreet was bringing his Corps up to reinforce Early. Not wanting to take the chance of being caught off guard and losing all he had spent the summer fighting for, Sheridan began to call all his raiding parties back to the main body of the army.

John and his men joined up with the 1st Cavalry Division under the command of General Merritt. The rest of the Army of the Shenandoah consisted of three large infantry Corps camped to the south of them in a line along Cedar Creek, while slightly to their west was the 3rd Cavalry Division, commanded by General Custer.

Since merging with the rest of the division, John's platoon no longer functioned as a unit with him as their sole leader. They were part of General Kidds' Reserve Brigade, whose function in battles was to be an emergency backup for the other two brigades. They also carried out the majority of the raid and reconnaissance missions.

As John's group was not large enough to form their own company, his men had been distributed among several companies who were dwindling due to casualties. John himself was assigned to serve under Captain Lipton as part of the 5th US Cavalry Regiment, a regiment which seemed to be permanently attached to headquarters, doing he wasn't sure what.

Already John was beginning to itch from the inactivity and miss the close comradery he had enjoyed with his men. He had not yet found his place among the other officers, and suddenly found an abundance of time to reflect on burdensome thoughts which he had been able to all but crowd out of his mind during the past hectic months—primarily, Elsa, Elizabeth, and what he would do after the war.

On October 17th, Sheridan was gone on a brief trip to Washington to attend a war conference, leaving his men with no major responsibility other than to rest while keeping a casual eye on the enemy's movements.

"Lieutenant Fairfield."

John started at the sound of a familiar voice. Hurrying to the tent opening, he saw Connly standing in front of him, saluting.

"At ease. How have you been?" John's face broke into a smile.

"Delivering the mail, sir."

"Thanks. Do you have time to stay and talk?" John asked as he eagerly took the letters Connly extended.

"I wouldn't have brought the post myself if I didn't." Connly's warm grin was like a sunbeam brightening everything around John.

"Then get yourself in here."

"Fancy," Connly whistled as he entered. "Better than the tent we shared, huh? You even got yourself a table."

"Go ahead and have a seat."

"Would the other officers care that I'm sitting in here?"

"They better not. They're not around anyway," John mumbled absently as he scanned the two envelopes in his hand. He recognized the handwriting on both.

"Go on; read your letters. Don't torture yourself on my account." Connly smiled at John's eagerness.

John opened the one from home first. He read slowly, savoring each line of motherly endearment, each morsel of fatherly encouragement. As he finished reading, he looked over at Connly and was pleased to see his friend was absorbed in mail of his own, and judging by the smirk on his face, was enjoying himself quite a bit.

"What's so funny over there?" John asked.

"My little sisters sure do write the silliest letters. Listen to this."

Greetings Soldier,

    The days I spend without you are long and dreary from the pain which weighs down my heart. Muriel read that to me from a book. I simply couldn't think of anything more delicious to say. Can you?

    I tell Mama nearly everyday that when I grow up, I am going to be a soldier just like you. But she won't believe me. I would consider it a great favor if you would write to her and set her straight, Papa too. He won't even let me go horseback riding alone. I keep telling them I must train for my career. They will listen to you I am sure.

    I could think of no one else to turn to during such desperate times. But you my brother in arms will understand the importance of this. My country needs me.

    Kitty, at school, says soldiers are awful dirty men and swear all the time. You aren't dirty, are you? I know you never swear. If I was in the army I would take anyone that swore and wash out their mouth with soap. That would teach them.

Heaps and heaps of Love,
Anna

"How old is your sister?" John laughed.

"Anna is eight, but this is written in Muriel's hand. She's twelve."

"I never had a sister," John said. "But I always had Elizabeth to harass just like a sister, until she got to be thirteen and didn't want anything to do with me. Then a couple more years and she wanted everything to do with me," he added ruefully.

"Do you miss her?"

John nodded. "I should write her. We've just so been so busy these past couple months."

"That's for sure," Connly agreed. "So is she the only one you miss?"

John made a sound halfway between a laugh and a sigh. "If you mean Elsa, yes, lately I've been thinking about her a lot too."

"Which one is the prettiest?" Connly prodded.

"Elsa," John said wistfully. "I sure wouldn't mind sleeping with her. Damn, did I just say that out loud?"

Connly burst out laughing as John's face turned beet red. "Don't worry; I won't tell on you. You've never said anything like that about Elizabeth though," he continued. "I think you find Elsa more attractive because she is the damsel in distress."

"Well, I do feel some sense of obligation to her. She did save my life." John's tone was serious now. "And I was never quite sure, but Everett said Elsa was in love with me, and I think he may have been right. She was so sad all the time. You know, even when she laughed, you'd see it in her eyes. I would like to be the one to change that.

"But then what about Elizabeth? I really thought I was in love with her. The only reason I didn't put a ring on her finger the last time I saw her, was because I know my life as a soldier is too uncertain to ask anyone to share it with me. I think you know what I mean, because for all your talk about women in the abstract, I never see you with one in the flesh. But back to what I was saying—Elizabeth is like me. I understand her. She is reasonable, intelligent, straightforward. When she talks to you, her thoughts follow a logical progression."

"And Elsa's don't?" Connly asked.

"Oh, Connie, I wish you could meet her. Then you would know what I mean. When she talks to you, you keep getting the feeling that there is something on the tip of her tongue that she wants to say, but she never does. It annoys the hell out of a man."

"John, did I hear you swear? Lucky for you Anna's not here, or you'd have a mouth full of soap."

John laughed. "I guess I had better shut my dirty mouth and see what Elizabeth has to say. She always writes interesting letters."

Dear Lieutenant Fairfield, (John frowned; she had never addressed him as that before.)

You have not written me in a long time. Your mother always shows me the letters you send home, so I am informed how you are getting on. I have read all about the wonderful service performed you by this charming southern belle, Elsa. I can tell you hold her in high regard. No doubt the desperate circumstances under which fate threw you together, could only form a bond between you.

This, combined with the fact that your silence has led me to the conclusion that you no longer hold an attachment to me—if indeed you ever did—causes me to say with reluctance but the utmost sincerity, that in accordance with what I believe to be your wishes, I will consider any relationship between us to be terminated.

Cordially,
Elizabeth

John let the letter drift from his hands to the ground. If he had known the mental anguish it had cost her to sign, "Cordially, Elizabeth" rather than, "Yours, Elizabeth", he may not have come to the conclusion he did. But how could he have known?

When Connly finished with his mail and looked up, he was surprised to see John standing, face to the open tent entrance, absorbed in a small, shiny object he held between his thumb and forefinger. He did not turn around while Connly retrieved the fallen letter and scanned its contents. But even this did not prepare Connly for when John revolved and said solemnly, "Sometime soon, perhaps a week, perhaps longer, there will be a fierce decisive battle— necessary, but the type in which we always lose so many good men and officers. I am going to die in that battle."

"That's a lot of nonsense; you don't know that. Why do you want to die? Did that letter really depress you?" Connly exclaimed.

"This is not a sudden decision, Connly." The color mounted a little in John's tan cheek. "I have thought for a long time that if someone has to die—which unfortunately they do—it might as well be me. I grow more certain of it all the time."

Connly shook his head. "A man should always go into battle with the realization that he might die, but the determination that he won't. Being killed in battle because you fight your hardest might be heroic, but premeditated suicide is nothing but cowardly. How unworthy a man of your stature!"

"But someone has to take the most dangerous jobs. Someone has to lead reckless charges. Someone has to run messages under heavy fire. Someone has to be at the front of the line. It's only my duty to our country to be the one to do it."

"Oh, that sounds terribly noble," said Connly scornfully. "But you can't buy me with a bunch of horse crap. You wouldn't talk like this if you weren't upset on account of your gals. So now you decide to get yourself killed because it is easier than facing up to the problems in life you don't know how to face. If that isn't cowardice, I'd like to know what is."

"Arthur Connly, I won't listen to talk like that! A man's duty…"

"You and your silly duties!" Connly interrupted. "As an officer your duty is to not lose your head. Honestly, John," he continued, his dark eyes flashing with intensity, "responsibility, honor, duty, all that is great so long as it helps you to be a better soldier and a better man, but when it incapacitates you for life, because your mind is so befuddled with duties, you can't even recognize your own balls when you see them, things have come to a pretty pass. Now listen." He stepped closer to John. "Get engaged to whatever girl you love the best, or none at all if that suits you. Don't worry about it, and for goodness sake, stop acting like a damn fool."

"I don't have any women!" John exclaimed hotly. "And if I did, they wouldn't have anything to do with something like this."

"They have everything to do with it," Connly muttered, turning away, and as he did, something inside him changed. Connly had once had an older brother, who died when Connly was only six. Although his memories of Michael were few, he had grown up with a slight feeling of deprivation, knowing that he was missing a blessing others took for granted, while his affectionate nature had silently searched for a leader whom he could follow. When he had come to know John as both friend and commander, he had unconsciously enthroned him upon that vacant seat in his heart, and the family had been complete. He had loved John as a brother, looked to him as a chief, and admired him almost to adoration.

Now John came crashing down from the seat of honor to which he had exalted him.

Although John would not admit it, Connly could see that John believed the entire meaning to his existence was based upon his strict adherence to duty, and that should he ever be negligent in his conscientiousness towards anyone, his life would be a failure. Now that he had unwillingly entangled himself in the intricacies of romance, and not seeing a way to discharge what seemed his duties to everyone, he saw an honorable death as the only way to retain the untarnished merit he had strove to cultivate his whole life.

John was not depressed or suicidal, nor was he responding out of rash emotion. Rather, the course he was charting for himself was a considered decision, entirely in keeping with the career he had chosen and the desperate times in which he lived, and which was also the most expedient way to preserve his legacy in stellar condition.

Had Connly not loved John, he would not have been unduly upset, for John's approach was one of commendable sacrifice. But as it was, John's attitude both frightened and disgusted him, and his fear found an expression in anger.

John was talking again. He stood in the center of the tent with his hands clasped behind his back, feet apart, and eyes on the ground. His voice was slow and steady. "Perhaps, I shouldn't have told you, Connie, but when the battle comes, I will die. Take this for me."

Connly turned back around hesitantly, and John dropped a plain silver ring, inscribed on the inside with the words "semper fidelis", into his hand. "What am I supposed to do with this?" Connly demanded.

"Whatever you wish. I don't want it anymore."

"Well, I don't want it either," Connly protested, trying to hand the ring back to John, who returned his hands behind his back as he stepped away from his companion.

"Perhaps someday you'll find a nice finger it will fit," John said.

"If I do, I certainly won't put this ring onto it. Lot of good the bloody thing's done you." Connly extended the ring farther towards John.

"I'm not going to take it back. Do what you want with it. I don't care."

For a minute the men stared at each other in silence. Connly's face was flushed a deep brown, while John's looked abnormally pale against the navy blue of his uniform. Suddenly Connly thrust the ring deep into his pocket, turned on his heel, and strode from the tent.

"Where are you going?" John called after him.

Connly glanced back only momentarily. "To get drunk!"

Where Darkness Dwells

It was a warm day for the middle of October, but in Kentucky the summertime is long—a fact which Everrett and Elsa found due reason to appreciate. For although their unanticipated move came late into the season, they still had time to plant peas, cabbage, beans and a few other crops requiring only short growing seasons. Clearing and planting the garden plot was the first task they set into upon arriving at the old homestead.

Their journey there had been long and exhausting. The morning after the fire, Elsa had rummaged through the ruins and attempted to salvage and clean whatever she could. Meanwhile, Everrett went to the forge to collect his tools and try to find a buyer for what he could not take with him. It took several days for him to dispose of as much as he could and find a horse cheap enough to afford. A cantankerous nag it turned out to be too. She and Charcoal found a mutual revulsion between them and tried to bite each other the entire way to Kentucky.

Elsa thought she should ride the new mount since Charcoal had been Everrett's companion for the past several years, but Everrett insisted she ride Charcoal because he strongly doubted her ability to control the horse, whom Elsa christened with the name of Rose. Everrett laughed at her when she sprinkled several drops of water on the animal's head and solemnly pronounced that from this day forward she would bear the Christian name of Rose Trenton.

"What's you give a pretty name like dat to sech an ugly horse for?" he asked.

"Because," Elsa laughed with him, "she is beautiful to us on account of the fact that we need her so much, and she is also a thorn in the side."

It seemed like they would never reach Kentucky, as day after day they trotted on, and night after night they camped out under the stars. Whenever they went through a town, Everrett rode behind Elsa and acted as if he was accompanying her as her servant. Elsa hated it and never felt safe until they were alone. But finally, after what seemed like years on the road, they reached their journey's end.

There was a patch of woods blocking the farm from view of the road, and Elsa felt her heart double its pace as they turned onto the lane leading through the trees. When the white farm house came into view, she felt as if time had turned back four years, and she was once again sixteen years old, sobbing as she sat in the carriage beside Aunt Ingrid and said goodbye to the only life she had ever known. She jerked Charcoal to an abrupt halt as tears sprang to her eyes.

"Elsa," Everrett exclaimed as he turned to stare at her. "We're here. We's finally made it. Isn't you's happy?"

"Of course I am," she responded. But Everrett thought it was the most obvious lie he had ever heard. "Everrett," she went on as she regained her composure, "I don't have a key. I had one, but of course I didn't take anything with me when I left Aunt Ingrid."

"Well, I's reckon I can take dose boards off de windows and pry one ob dem open."

After the death of Elsa's father, the estate had never been disposed of. Elsa being too far gone with grief and Ingrid being slightly superstitious, everything had simply been boarded up and left as it was. As Elsa entered the musty house, the dejavu was overwhelming. Aside from a thick layer of dust having been added, everything was just as it had been when she left.

Everrett found himself equally entranced, howbeit for different reasons.

"You's never told me how rich you was," he said a little incredulously. "I's would of thought you's would have wanted to come here right away."

Although the house wasn't elaborate by the standards Elsa was used to, compared to a sparsely furnished two room cabin, it was rather impressive.

"Really, Elsa," Everrett went on, "all dese rooms, and dere's furniture, and carpet on de floor, and a big old woodstove in de kitchen. Why's did you eveh want to live in dat shack with me, ifen you's owned all dis?"

"I liked living in the forest with you," she replied wistfully.

Everrett put his arms around her waist and looked into her eyes with a bemused smile. "You's is different dan anyone else I's eveh met. Any otheh woman as young, and beautiful, and well bred as you, would want to improve heh life as much as shey could, and instead you's want to marry a black man and live dirt poor in a hut in de woods. And I's always thought you's only married me 'cause you's was havin' sech an awful day."

"Perhaps I did, but I don't regret it."

"Don't you's eveh wish you was with John?" he asked a little hesitantly.

"No. You care about me more than he ever did, even though you don't love me," Elsa said, hoping he would contradict her.

But instead Everrett nodded. "Dat's true. I's do care about you mohe."

Elsa laid her head against Everrett's shoulder and hugged him tightly. "Oh, Everrett, I hate this place. There are no words to tell how much I hate it."

"What?" Everrett exclaimed, quite startled by the intensity of her outburst.

"I wish this place had burned to the ground instead of your cabin," Elsa went on.

"Why's do you say sech a thing?"

"Everrett, this place is haunted. It is. I hoped that after these years it would be better, but it's not. It's so much worse than I feared."

Everrett could feel her heart pounding against his chest, and her voice was so strained it hardly sounded like her. "No, Elsa, it ain't haunted," he said firmly. "Such things ahe all in folk's heads."

Elsa didn't respond, but continued to cling onto him and breath very rapidly.

"How did youh fatheh die?" Everrett asked suddenly.

Elsa made a small squeaking sound. "He—he died of con-consumption." She could barely get the words out.

"Darling, you's don't know how to tell a falsehood, so you's really shouldn't even attempt it," he replied softly.

"I can't tell you anything else," she said in a pained voice, and then took several very deep breaths. "You are right though, it is foolish of me to believe that a house could be haunted. Come, I will show you around."

*   *   *   *   *

As the days passed and the couple buried themselves in cleaning, repairing, and preparing for the future, Elsa repeated to herself over and over again that this was once more her home, and she must find the strength to make it a happy one. She did try hard, but all too often she would come upon some familiar object or sight pregnant with haunting memories, and from some deep place within would arise an awful terror, tightening around her like a boa constrictor.

An overwhelming urge to run would surge through her veins, and yet the very fear which compelled her to flee would paralyze her ability to do so. Sometimes she would seek out a hiding place and eventually wash off this unnatural dread in a torrent of tears, but usually she held herself in check and silently continued on with her daily tasks, as the terror ate at her heart. She must persevere; she had no choice.

Not being as dense as Elsa imagined him, Everrett was well aware of the change in her mood. He had thought things had been going quite well between them. During the strangeness and excitement of their journey there, Elsa had been quite talkative, and presumably because of the hardness of the ground they were using for a bed, had always slept in his arms. But no sooner had they arrived, than she became extremely withdrawn.

Sometimes she was tense and would start at the slightest sound, other times he would have to repeat himself three times before she even noticed him. But the worst part was her nightmares. More often than not, he would wake in the night to find her moaning or thrashing in her sleep.

At first she said it was because they were sleeping in the wrong room. That seemed a dubious explanation to him, but he did not disagree with her until they had tried sleeping in each of the four bedrooms without success.

He figured she would tell him what was bothering her when she was good and ready, but after about two weeks, and he woke once again to find her whimpering and mumbling frantically in her sleep, Everrett decided he could wait no longer for an explanation.

He shook her by the shoulder. "Elsa, Elsa, wake up."

"Stop it, please just leave." She tried to push him away and scratched his arm rather hard in the process.

"Elsa, it's me. Wake up."

"What's going on?" Her eyes flew open in alarm.

"I's think you's betteh tell me what's goin' on," he said a little irritably as he rubbed his arm.

"Oh, I was having another one of those dreams," she answered with a small shudder.

"I's know dat. But what was you dreamin'?" he demanded.

Elsa didn't answer his question, but after a moment she said, "I am waking you up practically all the time, aren't I?"

"Yes, you's is, and it's vehy annoyin'. Most ob de time you's try to hit me or scratch me too. It's high time you's told me why."

"Everrett, I'm sorry," Elsa said, and he could tell by her tone that she sincerely was.

"I's not mad at you. I's just want to know why."

"It doesn't make a difference why. The point is, I can't help it. This house does it to me," she said solemnly. "I told you it was haunted. I am just going to sleep in a different room so you can actually get a good night's rest." Elsa got out of bed as she said this.

Everrett sighed. "Come here." He held out his arm to her.

"I told you I can't help it, and the last thing I want is to constantly annoy you," she said as she turned to go.

"Don't go nowhere." Everrett grabbed her wrist and jerked her back down onto the bed. She lay there woodenly, staring at the ceiling.

"I's hate to see you's upset," he said, "and I's annoyed cause you's don't trust me enough to tell me why. When I's try to talk to you, all you's do is cry. So I's just got to watch you's be miserable and scared, and dere ain't a damn thing I's can about it. And dat makes me angry."

"I do trust you, Everrett, and I want to tell you, but—but..." Elsa's voice choked up, and she bit hard on her lower lip to keep from crying.

Everrett had been determined not to let her evade him this time. But she looked so pathetic and so lovely at the same time, while the pain in her eyes was so sharp he could almost feel it cutting him, and he couldn't bear to be hard on her.

He pulled her into his arms and kissed her forehead. "Alright den, cry ifen you wants to. I's know you's can't help it," he said tenderly. "Elsa, I's don't know what you's scared of, and I's suhe can't help as long as you's ain't talkin' to me. But you know you's safe with me, don't you? And you's don't got to answer dat because I's know you'll jest say whateveh you's think I want to hear," he added quickly. "But you is safe with me."

He put a hand on each side of her wet face and gave her a very intent look. "Darling, I's not goin' to let anyone hurt you. And even if you's wake me up every night, I's won't let you go sleep by youhself, 'cause when you wakes up from dose nightmares, I's want you to look at me, and get close to me, and know you's is safe."

"You are nicer to me than I deserve," she said softly.

Everrett kissed her and thought what a shame it was that she really believed that.

After that night, Elsa tried doubly hard to appear bright and cheerful. While Everrett was rather impressed with her effort, he was not in the least deluded. But he said nothing more, merely watched with a growing uneasiness as she continued to fall under the spell of some evil power he could not see or feel. And although he was fast becoming a sounder sleeper, Elsa's increasing reluctance to go to bed and the dark circles which were so often under her eyes, left him no doubt that sleep was a pastime in which she took no pleasure. But for the most part, he was too preoccupied with stress and difficulties of his own to devote much time to figuring his wife out.

Despite the fact that they now had a lovely, furnished home, they had virtually no money. Everrett realized that the possibility of modest prosperity was within their grasp and plunged vigorously into the work before him, sweating out his anxieties at the end of a hammer.

For the past several days he had been cutting hay in the west pasture. Now on this warm October morning, Elsa had come out to help him rake it. All forenoon they worked on steadily. Finally Everrett paused to squint at the sun.

"I reckon it's jest past noon. Let's take a break and ate."

"That's a good idea; my stomach has been complaining to me for the past hour," Elsa agreed. "Do you want to sit by those trees over there?" She pointed towards the timber covered hillside halfway encircling the field. "The shade looks really inviting right now."

"You's know, dis reminds me," Everrett said as they reached the tree line.

"What is that?"

"Afteh we ate, dere is something in dis here woods I's want to show you."

Elsa swallowed hard and said quickly, "Here, have some bread."

In a short time they had disposed of their simple lunch of bread and apples. Everrett stood up and stretched his long arms behind his neck.

"Well, I suppose we ought to rake some more," Elsa said.

"First I's want to show you dat thing I's mentioned."

"Oh, there is not much to surprise me on this farm," Elsa stalled.

"I's doubt if you's eveh seen dis before. Leastwise you's neveh mentioned it. Here, it is jest a little way in dese trees."

Elsa followed as he led her through the tangled underbrush and vines. Only sporadic patches of sunlight managed to dart furtively between the thick foliage, leaving the woods in a dense shadow. Elsa shivered and hugged her arms around herself.

"Nice and cool in here, isn't it?" Everrett said. "I's jest stumbled onto dis place one day when I was workin' and needed a little break from de heat. I's though it was kinda interestin'. See what you's make ob dis."

He held aside some branches to let her through, and Elsa found herself standing before a low, rocky orifice. She did not need to look to know that it opened into a small cave. She was afraid this was what he wanted to show her.

Nothing had changed. Elsa thought she recognized every rock strewn on the ground, and as the trees towering above rustled their leafy boughs, they spoke like so many specters of the past. Instinctively she shut her eyes, but with them closed, the scene seemed to be burning into her retinas, just as after looking at an object against a bright light, the image blazes sharply in the eye.

"A place like dis would make a good root cellah," Everrett was saying. "It's jest too far away from de house. I's always liked caves. When I was jest a little guy, I's used to dream dat someday I's gonna live in a cave. And I's said I'd be all by myself and neveh let..." Everrett stopped mid-sentence as he followed Elsa's eyes to where her gaze was transfixed on the yawning little mouth of the cavern and the black depths beyond.

Elsa stood motionless, one of her hands on her breast and the other clenched in the folds of her skirt. In the shadowy light her features looked as if they had been chiseled in marble. She did not seem alive, merely another one of the stones deposited outside the cave, rigid and paralyzed.

Everrett realized he had come across something very significant and made up his mind right then, neither of them were going to leave the woods until he got a straight answer out of her. For a minute he hesitated to speak. It seemed somehow wrong to intrude into the inert hush enfolding her. At last he said, "You's seen dis befohe?"

Elsa's head nodded like a marionette.

Everrett stepped in front of her to read her eyes. Elsa could never keep her true emotions out of them. They were gray now, much darker than normal, and in their lifeless depths he saw only a frozen horror. "What happened here?" he questioned.

"Evil," she said slowly.

"Go on," he prodded.

"This is were they raped them, on—on this ground. And that," Elsa turned her head towards the drooping boughs of a large hemlock, "that is where I stood."

"What is you talkin' about? Who are 'they'?"

Elsa blinked very quickly several times, as if trying to clear her eyes,

202

and shook herself out of her trance. "I am not going to talk about this," she said breathlessly as she turned away from the cave.

Everrett caught her arm. "Tell me," he said firmly.

"No!" she cried with more vehemence than he had ever heard from her before and threw his hand off her arm. "Don't talk to me, and don't touch me. Just leave me alone."

Everrett shook his head vigorously. "It's too late foh dat."

Elsa backed away from him and into the trunk of a tree. She flattened her back against it, pressing the palms of her hands hard into its rough bark to keep them steady.

Everrett stepped squarely in front of her, but resisted the urge to put his hands on her shoulders. "Ifen you's wanted me to leave you's alone, you's should have said so in July, and I's would have, but not now. You's think youh demons ahe only youh own? Well, dey ain't. I's have to live with dem now too, and I's won't let you evade me anymohe. It's high time I's knew what dey were."

"No, no, don't ask me." She tried to step to the side, but he put out his arm to stop her.

"If I's didn't cahe about you, I wouldn't. But damn it, I's do cahe."

Elsa shut her eyes as if to escape him, and he could almost see her withdrawing like a turtle into its shell. "Everrett, just leave me alone," she said with a choked sob.

"Why do you's want me to leave you alone?" he asked slowly.

"I did not marry you so you could get inside my head. No one, no one is allowed there. Ask anything of me and if I can do it, I will, but don't try to get inside my head."

Everrett made an exasperated grunt. "Believe me, right about now I's would like vehy much to leave you alone, but I can't. I's can't jest stand by and watch you's die inside a little mohe everyday. Dere aren't many things I's can give you. Suhe as hell I can't give you's half what you deserve, but dere is one thing I figure I's can give you. I can protect you. And dat's why you's married me, because you's knew I could give you dat, and you's wanted it vehy much. Something is eatin' de life right out of you, and ifen you's think I's jest gonna stand by and watch it, you's dead wrong."

"If—if I tell you, it will make you dreadfully angry," she said haltingly.

"I's will bey mohe angry ifen you's don't tell me," he said quietly.

"Alright, I-I will try," she said after a moment's pause. "But—but, Everrett, I don't have anyone but you, and if—if…" Elsa's jaw was trembling so she could barely speak, and she clenched her teeth for a moment to steady it. "If you start to despise me as well as everyone else, I—I can't bear it."

Everrett wasn't sure where to begin to refute the flawed logic in that statement, not to mention the fact that a she had just told him to leave her alone. So finally he just said, "Dat's not gonna happen." Putting his hands on her waist, he gently pried her away from the tree. "Now jest sit down," he went on as he guided her to a seat on a large rock, "and calm down, and talk to me."

"Alright." Elsa took off her sunbonnet, drew a long breath, and nervously twisted the strings around her fingers as she began her story. "I guess it all started when I was fourteen. It was then that I realized the sad plight so many of your people are in. For some reason it especially bothered me that so many cannot read. I taught Clara how to read, and it made her so happy. She said that not being able read was like having poor eyesight and no spectacles. In a way you know what is going on, and yet you're always missing out on things that are obvious to everyone else.

"I think most people know deep down that the color of a person's skin does not really have anything to do with their intelligence. But as long as your people are kept in ignorance, it is so much easier to manipulate them and treat them as if they were stupid. So after teaching Clara, Simon and Rueben to read (Simon and Rueben were the two men my father employed on the farm) I got the bright idea that my father and I should teach all the blacks in the community to read. It sounded like such a nice plan; I couldn't see why anyone wouldn't like it."

"It sounds like you," Everrett assented.

"It also sounds completely stupid and dangerous," Elsa said bitterly, "but I couldn't see that, so we used to go together secretly to the neighboring farms and give reading lessons to the slaves. Everything was fine for awhile, but then someone found out. Some people were very angry. There was one group of radical secessionists who were really enraged. If we had stopped right then perhaps-perhaps things would have been alright.

"If only I had known then what I know now—how cruel people can be. I think my father knew, but he adored me, and he did not really care that much about his life after my mother died, except to make me happy. Everrett, you have no idea how many times I wish that I had never been born. Then my mother would not have died in childbirth, and she and Papa could have had a lovely life together. But I was born, and Mama did die, and then my father…" Elsa's voice faded out and she stared darkly into the depths of the cavern.

"What happened den?" Everrett pressed.

Elsa opened her mouth and closed it again several times, then abruptly turned towards Everrett. "I can't—I can't tell you. Please don't ask me," she implored. "Let's just go back and rake."

Everrett felt like shaking her by the shoulders and yelling, "Stop torturing yourself and just tell me what the damn problem is." But instead he said, "I's know how hard you's try to act like nothing's wrong, but ever since we's came here, you's a different person."

Elsa nodded. "If only we had never come to this cursed farm. I would be alright if we were back at your cabin in Virginia."

"If dere were somewhere else I's could take you, I's would," Everrett said sadly. "But dere isn't. And you's can't keep living like dis—never bein' able to sleep—constantly afraid. Tell me, how is I's supposed to help you, if I's don't even know what it is dat torments you?"

"But, Everrett, you can't help me," Elsa said desolately. "There is not a single person in this world who can. And I do not want you to hate me. Knowing that at least you like me a little, is the only thing that makes my life bearable."

Everrett shook his head and laid his hand on her thigh. "Remember back in Virginia, dat first time I's made love to you, and you's said you wanted to be mine?"

"I remember, but I am surprised that you do."

"Of course I's remember. You made me vehy happy. No one had eveh said dat to me befohe and most likely dey neveh will again, and dere hasn't been a time from dat day to this, dat I's haven't wanted you every minute of every day. And dat's not gonna change."

"Do you really mean that?" Elsa's expression was one of amazement.

"Yes!" he exclaimed. "Why is dat so hard foh you to believe? What pleasure do you's think I would get out ob tellin' you lies? Foh pity's sake, darling, talk to me."

"Well, like I said, some people were very angry," Elsa started again after a long pause. "Then the war began, and it was like a powder keg was ignited in this community. Some for, some against—everyone at each other's throats. My father was well known as an abolitionist by that time and started to get some threats. I was a little scared, but I did not realize how bad the threats were until one night a group of night riders called on us. I guess they were part of one of these white supremacy groups that have been getting so popular. They were horrible, cruel men, and everyone of them as drunk as could be. They were terrible; even Captain Aldridge couldn't compare with them. They were in such a frenzy they didn't even seem human. They looked like demons, standing in the dark with the firelight on their faces."

Elsa's bonnet tumbled to the ground as she jumped up from the rock. "We hid Clara, Simon, and Rueben right here in this cave. I have tried a thousand times to block the memory of that cursed night from my mind, and yet I can still see every detail as if it were today!" Now that Elsa had started talking it was like a leak had been sprung in a dam, and she rushed on in an animated torrent of words. Everrett stood stock still with his brawny hands knotted into fists at his sides as he listened silently.

"They hung my father up by his thumbs and-and burned his feet with hot coals. I can only imagine how horribly that must have hurt." Elsa shuddered violently. "He was so brave, but it was useless. He told them where the money was, but he wouldn't tell them where the servants were until-until they threatened me. Oh, Everrett, why can I remember it so well? One of the men stood behind me, and he clutched the back of my neck hard, so I couldn't turn my head." Elsa reflexively rubbed the back of her neck, trying to erase the feel of his fingers. "And he pressed his other hand under my breasts, like this. In my dreams I can still feel him and smell him. He smelled like brandy and some feminine sort of cologne. Even then I remember thinking how strange it was for a man to be wearing such a scent.

"They said they were going to rape me and throw me into the fire if he didn't tell them where the blacks were. I think they would have to, but I just stood there like a rag doll and didn't try to do or say anything. I was so afraid, and there were so many things I wanted to do, but I couldn't move. I was frozen, so I just stood there like an idiot, thinking my heart was going to stop. And they kept going on about all the horrid things they would do, so of course Papa told them. Then they came back here and made us go with them. They tied my father to that black locust tree over there, and I was here by the hemlock. They didn't tie me, but one of the men kept his hand digging into the back of my neck the whole time, so I couldn't look away.

"The looks on Clara and Simon and Rueben's faces—that was the worst part of all—they couldn't believe we betrayed them. And if I could do it over, I wouldn't let my father tell. I would rather they had raped and killed me than leave me to live with this. But I stood there and did absolutely nothing while my father told. Those devils who called themselves men, they-they raped them, but not Clara. They said she was too old and ugly. I never knew before then, that a man could rape another man.

"I screamed, so the man holding me put his hand over my mouth, and then I just stood there like a rag doll again, until finally I got sick on him. Oh, he didn't like that. He started to hit me in the head, and then thankfully he knocked me out. When I woke up they were gone, and they had taken the blacks with them. There was only my father tied to the tree. I went to untie him, and-and there was a knife right through his stomach." He was still alive, but barely. He was crying and talking to my mother. He saw me and said, 'My poor Elsa, I love you.' He only lived a few more minutes before he passed on."

Elsa ran over to the tree and started running her fingers over the bark, searching. "Here, here it is. The knife was stuck deep into the tree so I couldn't get it out." Her voice faded to a whisper. "So I just knelt down and wrapped my arms around his legs, his blood running all over me."

Elsa started to shake uncontrollably, her hand quivering over the scar on the tree. "I only wanted to help," she moaned, "and accomplished nothing but bring about disaster! My birth took my mother's life, and my dull-witted stupidity cost Clara her freedom and sent my father to his grave. I have been nothing but a curse to all the people I loved the most. I have tried—I have tried so hard to forget, and I have tried to somehow atone, but I can't."

Elsa's dropped to her knees, and wrapping her arms around the trunk, wept bitter tears, not cleansing tears of sorrow or fear which may in time bring relief, but acrid tears of inconsolable desperation. As the torment of a prisoner reminded of a life sentence, closed in on her, she almost hated Everrett for having forced her to relive this agony. It was always there, a festering wound she had learned to live with, but now it lay open and streaming, her spirit draining from it. The chains of self condemnation and guilt, forged from the anguish of her soul, bound ever tighter around her, constricting her breath, killing all hope, squeezing even the desire of life from her breast.

She knew Everrett's arms were lifting her, pulling her away from the tree, but she could not feel their warmth or strength. Had he been on the far side of the ocean, she couldn't have felt anymore distant or alone. There was the low rumble of his voice, but she wasn't aware of what he was saying.

"Elsa, Elsa, listen to me." He held her out at arms length and gently shook her. "Why is you's actin' like dis was youh fault? Evil men did horrible things. De world is full of dat, but you's had nothin' to do with it."

"Aren't you dreadfully angry?" she sobbed.

"Indeed I is. I's would like vehy much to kill someone about now. But I's not angry at you. Why would I's be? You didn't do nothin'."

"But don't you realize I could have prevented everything that happened?" Elsa asked in amazement. "Not a day goes by that I don't curse myself for having gotten my father involved in giving those ridiculous reading lessons. If only I hadn't done that, those men would not have been antagonized, and they would never have come, and-and..." Her voice was lost in a fresh outpouring of tears.

"Has you taken complete leave of youh scenes?" he exclaimed. "You's couldn't be more wrong. I's always wondered how you's could be so forgivin' of everybody—youh aunt and all, and now I's see. You jest blame youhself foh everything bad dat happens. No wonder you's miserable."

"But it is my fault, because I could have prevented it."

"You poor thing, you's really believe dat." Everrett shook his head incredulously as he enfolded her in his long arms, pressing her snug against his chest. He could feel every muscle in her body throbbing with distress. "It isn't so. It isn't so," he murmured softly. "First off, youh fatheh was a grown man, completely responsible foh his own decisions. Even if you's had suggested he become a highwayman, it would be his own fault ifen he did it. Second, teaching someone to read isn't wrong in de least. You's was only tryin' to be nice. Third, you's don't really know why dose damn bastards did what dey did. But even if you's had provoked dem on purpose, dey would still be entirely to blame foh committing such villainy. Oh, I could go on and on givin' you reasons why it wasn't youh fault, and I bet you's wouldn't believe any of dem."

"Then-then you don't hold it against me?" she asked tremulously.

"No, no, no! If I's have to say dat everyday foh de rest of our lives, I will."

Elsa gulped several times and made an attempt to stop sobbing.

"You's actually thought, all dese years, dat what happened was youh fault?" Everrett asked.

Elsa nodded.

"No wonder you's didn't want to talk to me about it. Darling, what is I's supposed to do with you?" He tightened his grip on her and felt at a complete loss for words.

She was beginning to feel some comfort from his embrace and a strong sense of relief.

"What did youh aunt have to say about what happened?" Everrett asked, trying to imagine how she could have become so firmly convinced she was to blame for the whole dreadful affair.

"Aunt Ingrid wouldn't let me talk about it. All she had to say was what a dreadful man my father was, and how bad things happened to bad people. That I should be so grateful to be getting a chance to improve my life. She hated Papa so much, even said he deserved what happened to him. But I never told her how they killed him."

"And you's knew it wasn't youh fatheh's fault, so you figured it must be youhs?" Everrett said, still shaking his head in disbelief. "Darling, as soon as de war's oveh, we'll sell dis place and move far north—someplace you's will feel safe. We'll have a new life, and all of dis will be in de past."

"I would like that," Elsa said softly. "But there is one thing that has been bothering me a terrible lot lately. Even if you say that what happened was not my fault, and I hope with all my heart that it wasn't, even so, you can't deny that dreadful things have a way of happening to the people I love. Oh, Everrett," she squeezed him tightly, "I am so afraid that I will bring a curse to you. I love you, Everrett, and I would rather die than bring you suffering. If I had stopped to think about what was best for you, I would have left you alone." She felt a fresh shower of tears coming on and pressed her head gratefully against the firmness of his shoulder.

"A curse to me?" Everrett smiled a little. "My whole existence has been a curse to me, except foh you."

"But is was pure selfishness that made me marry you," Elsa insisted. "I need you. You don't need me."

Everrett didn't say anything, only shook his head. Taking her hand, he led her away from the cave, stopping when they reached a patch of sunlight pouring down between the trees. Elsa found her handkerchief and wiped her nose and eyes. Everrett took her face between his hands and regarded her with an expression halfway between perplexity and wonder.

Slowly he began to pull the hairpins from her bun until her hair cascaded down over her shoulders in soft waves. He knotted his big calloused hands into its silky smoothness and pulled back just enough so that she was looking up at him.

"I's don't need you? I's don't need you, do I?" he questioned her. "How—tell me, how I's supposed to show you how much I needs you?" He began to cover her face with kisses. At first very lightly, but gradually growing more passionate.

"Then you really are not angry with me?" Elsa said, still sounding unconvinced.

"Oh, darling, why can't you's see youhself de way I's see you? You's de kindest, most cahing, beautiful, desirable woman I's eveh met. I's met plenty of devils who thought dey was angels, but you's de first angel who thought shey was a devil." He filled her mouth with his own before she could answer him.

It was a long time before he finally pulled back, and when he did, he dropped to his knees in front of her. He ran his hands lightly up her legs, making her shiver. When he reached her waist, he loosened her pantalets till they dropped to the ground. His head came to about the level of her breasts, and he rested it against them, gently, slowly feeling his way around under her skirt.

"Everrett," she objected with an embarrassed giggle. "What are you doing? We're outside in the woods. This isn't very appropriate."

"No, no it isn't," he agreed as he pulled her down onto his lap, her legs spread on either side of him, his hands still busy beneath her skirt. "I's bet several squirrels ahe mighty scandalized about now. But I's neveh said I's was appropriate, did I? I's neveh said I was a gentleman. But I's saying I needs you, and I's won't eveh listen to anyone, not even you, say othehwise."

"Everrett!" Elsa clutched his back and sank her head into his shoulder with a small moan of pleasure. "It is terribly nice of you to say so," she said breathlessly. "But you don't need me; you are so strong and capable. How could you possibly need me?"

Everrett hugged her as he gave tickling little kisses from the base of her neck up to her temple. He ran his hands up her back and under her hair, feeling the smooth curve of her scalp. "Why can't you's see how perfect you's is?" he said quietly.

"How can you say I'm perfect? Look at me. I am scared of practically everyone and everything. I cry all the time. I am always waking you up with my nightmares. I…"

"Stop." Everrett put a finger to her lips. "Not one of dose things makes you's a bad person. Dey jest show how cruel de world has been to you." He gave her a long kiss. "I's not a man of words. I couldn't give you's an answer you'd accept." He laid her back onto the plush moss beneath them.

Elsa gasped as he entered her suddenly, almost roughly. "But, Elsa, I do needs you. I need you. I need you." He spoke in rhythm to his movements. Placing one hand under her shoulders and the other behind her hips, he pulled her to him hard.

"It's too much," she objected, making a slight effort to squirm away, but Everrett thrust himself into her harder than before.

"I's know it is," he answered. "I's know it's too much. But dis is how much I needs you. I's neveh wanted to need anyone, but I do, and you's can't change it. You's can say all day long dat it isn't so, but you's can't change it."

"But Everrett…"

"Oh, stop arguing with me," he interrupted, and then pressing his lips against hers, pulled her to him again and again until her felt her surrender to it and melt around him like hot wax.

Afterwards they lay together on the moss for a long time, Elsa at first half fainting, with her head pillowed on his chest. He stroked her hair away from her hot face and dropped light kisses on her forehead. When she was completely peaceful, almost asleep, he whispered to her, "Now, now you are mine."

"And I always will be," she murmured back.

*　　　　*　　　　*　　　　*　　　　*

The days that followed were the happiest Elsa had known since she was little girl. Deep wounds always leave their scars, and chains formed over long years are not easily severed, but no longer was she in the midnight of her life. The sun's rays had begun to make the horizon glow, and for the first time in four long years she could feel its warmth slowly seeping into her as she watched with an ever increasing assurance for the dawning of a new day.

Completely contrary to what she had imagined, Everrett also seemed more lighthearted and took her into his confidence more than ever before. He even began to tell her about her his childhood and the long struggle he faced as a young man, striving to establish a home for himself, alone in an unwelcoming world.

As to the new vicinity to which they had transplanted themselves, from the outset, they attempted to eliminate friction with the neighbors by avoiding contact with them. Gradually Elsa began to call on old family friends and cautiously revealed their secret to a few who she deemed trustworthy and found some side work for Everrett among these acquaintances. But the majority of the town remained unaware that the farm was once again inhabited, much less by an inter-racial couple.

Invariably such a life was lonely, but this mattered little to them. They had both already tasted of a deeper and more complete loneliness, and now at least they had one another, in whose company they were each learning to find succor.

They talked frequently of moving to a safer region where they could live their lives without the need for such constant secrecy. The reports they heard of the war were continually more encouraging. Times would be easier after peace came. More and more they began to look hopefully ahead towards the future.

The Creek Runs Red

John was awakened a little after 5 o'clock, to a frantic rendition of reveille, accompanied by loud shouting. He jerked on his boots and dashed for division headquarters, buckling on his pistols as he went. By the time he reached it, headquarters was already swarming with yelling officers and clanging swords. Captain Lipton grabbed John's arm.

"Sir," John saluted. "Are we actually being attacked already? It's only the 19th. Sheridan is still returning from his war conference."

Lipton nodded grimly. "A dispatch has been sent for him. The enemy snuck up on the IIIV Corp and attacked them in the dark. They were completely shattered, lost most of their big guns, and only God knows how many men were captured. Now the XIX Corp is trying to hold them off, but their men are retreating back our way."

"That leaves only the IV Corp between us and the enemy," John exclaimed.

"Just so, and our videttes have been attacked. The 1st Brigade has already gone to help them, and General Lowell just gave orders for us to go stop those fool infantry from running off like a bunch of cowards."

Several minutes later John was galloping off across the field at the head of company E. The weather had been serene the last several days, and the night bright with moonlight, but as morning approached, a dense, eerie fog had descended, providing the perfect cover the for Confederates'

214

surprise attack. Now as John rode forward, he could hear plenty of noise, but all he could make out was shadowy forms scuttling through the motionless shroud of mist.

"Spread out. Form a line." John could hear Colonel Dunberry's voice bellowing through the fog. "Form a line. Don't let anyone through."

"He's right men," John turned in his saddle to address the disordered troop behind him. "We need to make a tight line and not let the XIX Corp run off on us."

"Like we can have a clue what's what in this blasted fog," mumbled one of the corporals.

"We don't have to know what's what. Stop anyone who's not on horseback. Like those fellows over there." John turned his horse sharply to the right, and sprinted several yards. "Halt! Just where do you think you're going?" he demanded.

"The Rebs are after us. Just came down out of the night—thousands of them. Run for your lives."

"This is as far as you run," John said firmly, thrusting out his to saber to block the path of the two shaking young soldiers.

"Can't you hear them guns?" wailed one of the privates.

John would have had to have been stone deaf not to hear the thunder of the guns. They were drawing close enough that he could feel the vibrations trembling through the ground, and his own heart was beginning to race, but he kept his voice calm as he said, "We've started a line, come join it."

"We're fr-from the IIIV," stammered his companion. "They cap-captured our guns and t-turned them r-round on us. T-took hundreds of prisoners."

"Then we'll just have to take them back, won't we?" John replied. "Today is a day for men, not for cowards. Get over there and join the line! That's an order."

The next hour was a blur of motion as the cavalry relentlessly blocked the path of the terror stricken infantry. Finally, John found a moment's pause to collect his thoughts. He recalled vividly his conversation with Connly of only two days past. He had meant every word he said, even written letters to his parents and Elizabeth in preparation for never seeing them again. All the same, the realization that the time was now, that he was on the very verge of what was most likely the last battle, the last day, of his life, sunk like a lead ball into the pit of his stomach.

Oh, yes, he had this dread before every battle, but ten times stronger today. He was riding into a holocaust from which he had no expectation of returning. There was something very surreal about everything around him, as if he already was no longer part of the same world. The sea of fog was beginning to shimmer in the gold of the rising sun, casting an unnatural glow around the phantom forms passing through it, while noise with no visible source swirled out of everywhere and nowhere. The solid warmth of the horse beneath him was the only thing which assured him he wasn't dreaming.

"Fairfield!" John started at the sound of Captain Lipton shouting to him. "Lowell just ordered us to go rejoin the rest of our brigade. The XIX Corps is making a stand on Red Hill. We need to support their left flank."

Shouting to the men to follow suit, John galloped along the base of the hill and around to the left. He felt his eardrums splitting as a shell exploded not more than five yards in front of him, hurtling fiery shards of shrapnel in all directions. The mist was somewhat lighter over here, and he could make out a swarm of Confederates moving in.

The earth shuddered from the report of a cannon. Lieutenant Taylor, from their Division, had just brought several large pieces to the front of the lines and was commencing firing. Aside from the two companies of cavalry assisting him, John couldn't hear a single piece of Union artillery. Well, one should know better than to count on the infantry.

The air was beginning to stream with fiery balls, hissing a sharp warning as they sailed towards their targets. As the fog gradually lightened, the angry gray line of the approaching enemy seemed to stretch on endlessly. Another shell exploded, and Captain Lipton fell from his horse, blood streaming from a hole through his skull.

Two horses glistening with sweat were charging up a small rise of ground about thirty yards to John's left. A wagon loaded with shells rattled behind them. The soldier perched atop kept cracking a long whip over the heads of his team while he shouted loud curses. Behind him several men were straining as they pulled against a heavy gun, dragging it slowly up the slope. A mounted lieutenant screamed unintelligible encouragement to a company of men swarming alongside the laborers.

John realized in alarm that once the rebel's gun was operating on the top of that slope, Lieutenant Taylor and his artillery would be right in their line of fire. "Sound the *charge as foragers*," John called to the bugler behind him. "Men, we're not letting the Rebels take that high ground." John waved his saber towards the Confederates hauling the Parrot Rifle. "Charge!"

John spurred his horse across the field, company E thundering along beside him. A ripple of falling men went through the mass of Confederates as the dragoons began to fire, but it only took a minute for them to collect themselves and blaze back with a molten stream of bullets. Screams and shouts of pain, rose above the crack of muskets, the thud of ramrods, the stamp of feet and hooves, and the clang of metal.

With loud shouts, John led his men up into the swarming mass of Confederates. The infantry began to scramble out of the way of stabbing hooves, but without an apparent let up in firing as John had hoped. A soldier jammed a bayonet into the side of the horse next to him. John's pistol cracked, and the man fell down howling below the hooves of the plunging animal.

John flashed a critical glance behind him. He saw one of his horses topple onto its side, the rider's foot caught in the stirrup and his leg pinned beneath the animal. Too many of his horses were falling. Up ahead he saw Confederate forces running to the aid of their comrades.

He ordered the bugler to sound a retreat, and the men hurried back down the rise. Fighting hand to hand from the saddle was too precarious. When skirmishing like this, the cavalry almost always dismounted, saving the horses for transportation or charges which required a long dash across open ground. John had hoped that with the added momentum of the horses, he could knock the rebels from the knoll in one quick sweep, but that was not to be.

After having most of his men dismount, leaving some to take the horses to the rear, he led the rest back up the slope. Back and forth the shots flew in frenzied succession as foot by foot his men pushed into the enemy ranks. John noted with relief that a Union captain was leading his company up to help. For every fallen rebel, another seemed to drop from the sky to take his place.

"Forward men! Show these confounded Rebels what Union dragoons are made of. Make them eat a little Yankee fire!" John had to shout at the top of his lungs to make himself heard above the hellish din exploding all around him.

Thankfully the fog had all but vanished, but the air was now hazy with a gritty mist of smoke and gunpowder. Just in time, John noticed the young man to his left, raising his bayonet for a lung. John caught him across the face with his saber, slitting a sharp gash from cheek bone to jaw. John's stomach started somersaulting, and he had to swallow hard against the bile rising in his throat as the young soldier staggered backwards, blood streaming profusely from his mouth.

The youth was slender, with dark curly hair that brought a sudden picture of Connly to John's mind. Where was his friend? John hadn't seen so much as a glimpse of Connly all day. John hoped to God that he was on some safer part of the field than this.

The men toiled up inch by inch, struggling into the burning gray wall. Sabers clanged against bayonets; revolvers answered rifles; blue and gray fell silent together while their flags of red, white and blue dipped and plunged in the thick, dirty air above. Clouds of bluish smoke swirled over and around the brilliant banners, now eclipsing their colors, now blowing aside to give the harassed soldiers a glimpse of their life.

The dragoons were reaching the top of the hummock. They had succeeded so far in keeping the Confederate artillery on that rise silent, but how long could the Yankees hold? It was the question foremost in everyone's mind. Could the disorganized Union army hold until Sheridan arrived? Would he make it in time?

The doubt thundered through John's mind even louder than the howling inferno around him. It reverberated with every roar of a distant cannon, every explosion of a mortar. Little by little the Union troops were being pushed back, yet the losses they were inflicting on the enemy were tremendous. Surely the Confederates couldn't continue to gain ground at such a high cost.

As another company of Yankees surged up the slope, the

Confederates began to relinquish their position, drawing back to the cover of the trees. They had no choice but to leave their heavy Parrot Rifle behind. John was very wary of Parrot Rifles as they had a most disconcerting tendency to explode while firing. All the same, a gun was a gun, so he quickly set some of his men to manning it. Shouting in indignation at having their own piece turned against them, the Rebels began to disappear behind trees and into ditches.

John took advantage of the momentary lull to help some of the fallen men bind up their wounds. The ground was already strewn with casualties as far as he could see in all directions, and it was only about 10 o'clock.

John looked up towards Red Hill where the infantry was distinctly wavering under heavy rebel fire. He wanted to bring his men over to help, but there was no way he could afford to weaken their position here and risk losing both the Parrot Rifle and the high ground. At least Lieutenant Taylor's men were still manning their guns. Without him, Red Hill would definitely have been lost by now.

"Lieutenant!" John turned in the direction of the husky voice to see a grimy young man with soot blackened face, calling to him.

"What is it?"

"Lowell got a message. Sheridan's only three miles away. He'll be here soon."

"Thank Heaven! Men, did you hear that? Sheridan's coming!"

The messenger was already galloping off to spread the news, but no sooner had he left the knoll and the protection of the booming Parrot Rifle, then Confederates began to sprout up from the ground, sending him and his horse down in a rain of musket fire.

John urgently sought out the 1st sergeant of his company. "Kenton," he shouted to him. "I'm going to relay the message to Red Hill. Maybe it will keep them from breaking. Hold our position here and give me cover."

Receiving a salute of recognition from Kenton, John lowered his head and tore off as fast as his powerful black stallion could carry him. The sound of the whistling balls was like a gale of wind, yet he remained unscathed. As he approached Red Hill, the air grew even denser, sickening with the bitter taste of powder and the stench of burning flesh.

John tried to swallow to quell the wrenching of his stomach, but his mouth was dry as paper. He ducked as a bullet hissed past his ear.

Without warning, his mount wobbled and lurched forward. John tightened the reins to steady him, but he began to tremble uncontrollably as he sank beneath John. Jumping off just in time to keep from having his leg pinned beneath the great horse, John stared wildly about. He tried to focus his eyes against the stinging smoke. There had to be a riderless horse around here someplace. He spun around, squinting to see through the smog enveloping him.

Another shell exploded, the sound of it nearly knocking him over. John pressed his hands against his ringing ears. No one but a veteran soldier could understand just how devastating the sounds of a battlefield could be—constant, hammering, volcanic noise, assaulting you, shaking the ground beneath your feet, shuddering up through your legs, till your very heart quivered with the pain of it. It hit against your head like an unrelenting borage of stones, until your thoughts shattered and flew away in a thousand fragments, leaving you a crazed brute, with no more sense of who you were or where you were, only that you must fight. And fight you did, swept up in the raging whirlwind of sound.

John instinctively turned towards the blood curdling shriek of agony. One of the shells had ignited a fire in the grass, and a wounded man was helplessly struggling to get out the flames. John grabbed the soldier under the arms and jerked him out of the fire as others ran up to stamp out the blaze. John looked at the man he had just rescued. His abdomen was torn open and his entrails scorched with the flames.

"Kill me! Kill me!" he howled at John. His eyes were two pleading orbs of terror, his face contorted in word-defying agony. John grabbed the man's rifle from the ground and whacked him firmly in the head, sending him into unconsciousness. John knew he would be in another world before he revived.

Looking up, John saw a horse running in frantic circles only a few yards away. He managed to catch hold of the trailing reins. "Steady there, old girl," he soothed as he stroked the pinto's face. She had obviously been well trained for battle and grew calm as soon as she felt a rider on her back.

With his saber high in the air, its steely grey glinting in the dull blue clouds of smoke, John galloped up Red Hill. "Sheridan's coming! He'll be here any minute," John yelled, trying to raise his voice above the din

A few of the soldiers around him began to perk up. John sucked on his tongue, trying to moisten his mouth. His throat felt like it was full of sand. He blinked against the perspiration dripping into his eyes. At the top of the hill, all was chaos, and not an officer to be seen. Just then he caught sight of a bugler, clutching his instrument tightly to his chest.

"Sound the rally!" John bellowed. The frightened youth's hand shook as he mechanically raised the bugle to his lips. "It's alright, boy." John placed a hot hand on his trembling shoulder. "Go ahead, sound the rally. Everyone's waiting on you."

The youth began to pipe out a thin stream of music, slowly growing louder with each note. John continued to roar encouragement to the bedraggled men. Twenty yards away another bugler took up the strain. Slowly the men began to draw together into a solid line while those on sides of the hill began to ascend.

Faintly, through the rush of horrific sound, John heard a cheer rising up from the cavalry to his extreme left. It began to swell along the lines in ever higher tones of triumph.

"Men, do you hear that? Sheridan's here! Three cheers for the General."

Weary heads turned to look. A second wind breathed through the men with these tidings. With rejuvenated vigor they began to form ranks and send out a furious burst of fire. John spurred his horse and bounded on down the bleary line, encouraging and rallying the men with the good news. It fell like cool drops of rain on a wilting plant.

After Sheridan's grand appearance on the field, everything changed, the tide of battle sweeping out instead of in, as the Union soldiers became the aggressors and the Confederates the defenders. All day they fought, across open fields, through dense trees, from behind stone fences, up and down hills, on foot and on horseback, with rifles and bayonets, with pistols and sabers, with mortars and cannons. As the Federal army grew ever more organized, the Confederate army gave way to confusion, and vast numbers of men surrendered themselves rather than face certain death as they found the Yankees closing in on them from all sides.

Only nightfall finally put an end to the fighting, and the exhausted warriors began to trudge from the field. Even as the taste of victory was sweet in their mouths, the hundreds of wounded men moaning as the last of their life trickled into the ground, were a grim testament to the brutal horror of war. As the sun set and the clouds of smoke slowly drifted away, the armies began to gather up their wounded.

John felt relieved to be alive, but also strangely troubled. Why must men die who wanted so desperately to live, while he, who had consented to death, was as alive and well as ever? Suddenly John stopped to stare at the horse he had just dismounted. He had seen this pinto before—he knew he had. His heart sunk as he realized the truth; this was Connly's mount. He dreaded to confirm it, but he forced himself.

As he had expected, the brand was Confederate. This was the lovely pinto mare Connly had stolen from the Rebel camp. The brown spot over the left eye, the black tipped ear, the sensitive mouth—John recognized it all. How Connly had loved this well-trained, spirited mount, and now...

Numbly John rubbed the horse's shoulder, as he closed his eyes in a vain attempt at shutting out all that his senses, intuition, and experience were telling him. He could almost see Connly, standing there in front of him, his dark eyes flashing and his white teeth showing in an eager grin.

John knew he should be looking after the men of company E and making reports, but he didn't care. He was going to find Connly, and nothing else mattered until he did. John headed out on foot, back towards the battlefield and the base of Red Hill.

It was almost full dark now, and the moon was rising, a luminous disk of cold light. Dew was softly dropping its chill kiss on the gray lips of the dead, and the quivering lips of the dying. The awful noise of battle was gone, but the field was far from silent. Everywhere, John could see little clusters of men, silhouetted black against the faint glow of the night sky, gathering up the wounded or stripping the dead.

"Will you help me over here?" John turned in the direction of the voice. "It's my brother. I can't carry him all the way back to the field hospital myself."

John nodded his consent and helped the stranger lift the barely conscious man. They set off for the field hospital, an interminable distance away. Thankfully they met an ambulance halfway, which had just enough room to squeeze in one more man.

John turned back towards the field, but every time he began his search, he was stopped by some desperate soul in need of assistance. He couldn't refuse anyone, so by midnight John was thoroughly exhausted and still no sign of Connly, but he had picked up a lantern along the way.

John stopped dead in his tracks. There were two corpses lying at his feet, both stripped stark naked, not so much as their union suits left to them. He felt a sudden burst of anger and turned away muttering a few very bad words under his breath. As he turned, his light fell across an unforgettable form, the man whom he had pulled shrieking from the fire. John felt a slight easing of the tension in his chest as he saw the sufferer's face had relaxed into peace.

He wondered what death was like. John believed in the afterlife, in God, in heaven, but what would it be like? Would he have to spend years of miserable boredom, waiting in purgatory? Or would it be like drifting off into a state of bright, warm rest? Or would it be a land of enchantment, where all his wildest dreams came true?

John shivered. It was turning out to be quite a cold night. He must find Connly soon.

"Lieutenant Fairfield, is that you?"

John glanced up, his lantern casting shadows across the dark ridges of Tommy Reckels' smudged face. A bloody cloth was tied around the young man's forehead, and his eyes were deeply circled, but he looked hail enough.

"Tommy," John said softly. "I'm glad to see you."

The young soldier nodded, but his expression bore nothing but dejection.

"I'm looking for Sergeant Connly," John said.

"They took him away already," Tommy answered.

"Is-is he…?" John was afraid to ask the question.

"He was still alive last I saw," Tommy said dismally. "But his-his…Oh, never mind. Go see for yourself."

"Where did they take him?"

"I think that ambulance was going to Belle Grove, but I'm not certain."

"Thank you." John patted the young man's shoulder and hurried off.

Every available building in the nearby hamlets of Middletown and Belle Grove, had been pressed into use as a hospital. The streets were alive with swinging lanterns, unhappy soldiers, stressed physicians, townsmen helping to carry in the wounded, and women eager to help with the nursing. John searched building after building, slowly walking down the rows of torn men, scanning the face of each one as he passed. They stretched on endlessly, one after another, all horribly the same, mangled men lying in their own blood and that of their comrades. He finally found Connly in the courtyard of the Belle Grove church.

There was a large slab stone of stone near Connly's head, and an awful chill ran up John's spine as he realized the courtyard was also a cemetery and Connly was lying directly over a grave. The flickering light of John's lantern showed a piece of the young man's boot clinging to the ragged edge of his gory pant leg, but his foot was completely gone. Only ripped flesh and the tip of a bone stuck out. John quickly set his lantern down on the headstone before he had a chance to get a better look.

"Connie, Connie," he called softly.

Connly blinked and slowly opened his eyes. "This is the last place I expected to see you, John, visiting the dying," he mumbled with an attempt at a smile.

"Maybe we got our orders mixed. Are you in much pain?" John knelt down beside him.

"Ooh, some pretty girl gave me a glass of whiskey awhile ago."

"Good."

"I thought you didn't drink."

"I never needed to," John responded as he gently laid his hand on Connly's shoulder.

"Didn't do much good anyhow. Does less good all the time." Connly shut his eyes again.

John didn't have a clue what to say, but he felt unbelievably horrible as he watched his best friend lie there in such torture. He never knew before what it meant to want so badly to take someone's suffering away, that if he could, he would have transferred it to himself. But now he knew. Connly's teeth were slightly chattering.

"I'm going to go find you a blanket," John said, quickly standing up. "I'll be back."

John practically ran out of the churchyard. He was suddenly very angry, angrier than he had ever been before, angry at the damn men and guns which had done this to his friend, angry at the self-serving politicians who had not prevented war, angry at the incompetent doctors who were leaving Connly there in the cold with untreated wounds, angry at the stupid commanders who had put Connly in a different company where he could not look out for him, angry at himself for caring so much, but most of all angry at God for letting such a thing happen.

As John walked swiftly down the street, his thoughts tumbled over each other in furious succession. How could this be happening to Connly? If God had wanted to take someone, why not him? Not that he wasn't grateful to be alive, but it would have been alright if this had been his time, but not Connly. Connly was so full of vitality and high spirits. He loved life so much.

John knew the statistics. Men who lost their whole legs had less then 20% chance of living. But Connly shouldn't have to lose his whole leg. If they took it off at the knee that gave him at least 40% chance, and if the surgeons cared enough to save his knee, he might have 60% chance of living. But what sort of a life—the life of a cripple?

John careened into a heavy woman, her arms so full of quilts she could barely see where she was going. "Pardon me, ma'am. Can I take one of these to my friend down at the church? Thank you so much."

The woman stared after John's departing figure and shrugged. At least she could see where she was going now.

John knew it wasn't much help, but at least it felt good to be doing something for his friend.

"I'm glad to see you're well, John," Connly murmured as John covered him with the thick blanket. "I just wish you would have told me you weren't going to die, so I could have gotten some sleep the past two nights."

"There was some truth in what you said to me the other day," John assented.

"Does me good to hear you admit it." Connly looked at John with a weak smile. With difficulty he reached into his pocket. "Here, John."

John took the ring from Connly's bloody hand. "I guess it is always easier to do anything else than accept life for what it is, and isn't. You've always been an inspiration to me in that way." Connly didn't respond, and John had to keep talking to keep from thinking. "I found your horse. She's fine, and I'll make sure she is waiting for you when you are ready to ride again."

"You had better just take her for me; I don't think I'll be riding again." Connly's voice was becoming faint and breathy.

"Of course you will. They won't take your leg off above the knee, and you'll get a wooden foot and be riding around as good as ever before you know it." John was trying very hard to sound convincing.

"What if I don't make it? John, listen. Hear that sound?"

John winced as a heart-stopping scream, followed by an unrelenting stream of curses, rose above the constant groans surrounding them. "I try not to."

"That's all I've heard for the past hour. If I don't die first, my turn will come."

"Aren't they giving chloroform?" John asked in alarm.

Connly shook his head a little. "Rumor is they're out, and I reckon as how we've already drunk up about every drop of whiskey there is in this damn town."

"I'll go find you some more." John started to stand up, glad to once again have something to do, but Connly grabbed hold of his pant leg.

"No, don't go. Just stay with me."

"Connie, you aren't scared, are you?" As John reached out to grasp his friend's hand, Connly clutched it with a frantic grip.

"How would you feel?" He tossed his head restlessly.

"Scared," John answered very slowly.

Just then Connly looked very young, and very frightened—Connly who had always been so optimistic and ready for anything. John had never before considered that Connly was only a teenager, and now far from home and family, he was about to face one of the worst ordeals dreaded by soldiers. John knelt back down by his side.

"I won't leave you," he said. "You'll make it alright. The doctors are very fast, and when it's all over, I'll find you enough liquor to put you to sleep for a week."

"The waiting might be the worst part. If I can make it through that..." Connly responded with another agitated toss of his head.

"You will make it." John said, as he gently pushed back the dark curls of hair sticking to Connly's sweaty forehead. "You will."

A Life Worth Living

Connly did live through that shadowy night, and the next, and the next. True to his word, John supplied him with a veritable deluge of alcoholic libations, enough to make Connly's fellow sufferers vie for the cot next to him. And finally with the wonderful resilience of youth, Connly began to recover his spirits and, little by little, his strength.

In order to provide for the quiet rest his recuperation required, John was able to arrange for him to return home to spend the winter with his family in Kentucky. Here, propped up by fluffy goose down pillows and eagerly waited on by mother and sisters, he came to fully enjoy his role as venerable hero. He soon learned, his was the power to raise the hair on a young boy's neck or the blood in a lass's cheek with no more than a word or wink.

But as his health returned, his impatience rose proportionately. As he was asked to tell and retell his anecdotes of colorful raids or fiery charges, the satisfaction of these memories gave way to the restlessness of unfulfilled ambition, while the phantom pains from his missing foot goaded him on to action. Soon he was strewing his mother's tidy floor with wood chips as he whittled a wooden foot and ankle, while the fact that the surgeon had been able to save his knee, grew ever more meaningful to him.

By the time the March rains had come, his wooden foot was finished.

Connly began to painfully practice his walking. He soon learned to mount a horse again, and after that, was uncontainable.

It was then that John managed to obtain several days leave, while the troop he was with was stationed only a short distance away. He made a trip to see Connly, who announced on the first evening of John's visit, as they all sat around the parlor, his intention of returning to the corps with John.

"You sure are looking chipper as a squirrel," John said, enthusiastic at the thought of having his friend with him again.

"Arthur, not yet," objected his mother, dropping her knitting and half rising from her rocking chair.

"Arthur!" exclaimed his sister, Muriel, mimicking her mother's tone as she impulsively threw her arms around his neck from her position behind his seat.

Connly reached around to gently tug at one of her braids. "You won't miss this will you?"

"Let me go with you! Let me go with you!" cried Anna as she bounced about the room in glee.

"It was hard enough to let you go the first time," Connly's mother, Rebecca, went on. "Then to have you so injured, and we thought we might lose you. And now that you're finally getting well again, I can't bear the thought of losing you a second time."

Suddenly sensing it was his duty to dissuade his friend, John began a different approach. "Don't feel badly about staying here and taking care of yourself. Things are really looking up. Sherman occupied Savannah in December, and now he's heading up to join Grant in Virginia. If that happens, the Rebels don't stand a chance. Soon we'll both be home to stay. You have done your part, Connie. No one would say otherwise."

"Hear that?" Connly said, looking at Anna. "Your country doesn't need you." But turning back towards John he went on. "That's why I've got to go back. If I've done my part to win this war, I don't want to be cheated out of sharing in the victory."

"But you will share in it, Arthur. You'll share in it here," argued his mother.

"Not really I can't." Connly looked at his father, who up to this point had remained silent in the conversation. "You understand what I mean, don't you, sir? I can't be licked just on account of this old foot. I got to finish this before I can go on with the rest of my life."

"I understand, son. You're a grown man, and you must make the decision which is right for you. It is just, you've been doing so well, and we don't want for anything to happen and you to get worse. It might be too soon."

"Thing's always happen. John will remember when I first lost my foot. I thought that was as good as the end for me. But now I've come to the conclusion that it is better to take chances and live with the results than to be safe and do nothing. If I let this stop me, then my life is over."

"You might lose both feet," piped up Muriel in doleful warning.

"Don't say such things, Muriel. Don't even think them," scolded her mother.

"If that happens, I suppose I will have to stay on horseback all the time." Connly grinned at her. "I'll even have to bring my horse right into the house and ride him up the stairs to bed."

Well, that settled it. Rebecca knew that the call claiming her son was stronger than she could ever suppress, so she left off trying and instead created an outlet for her motherly concerns by seeing how much food a young man could consume with pleasure in three days. And having two young men to cook for instead of one, made it that much more gratifying.

John had more fun during the three days he stayed with the Connlys, than he had, had in the past three years combined. While Rebecca busied herself in cooking up scrumptious feasts, twelve year old Muriel, who found John enormously attractive, spent her time continuously concocting some new way to make a fool out of herself in hopes of impressing him, much to John and Connly's amusement.

Meanwhile, Anna, seeing that her time was growing short, began with renewed zeal to try to convince Connly that he should take her with him. Finally, in desperation, he sat down and gave her a much too graphic description of having a limb amputated. She never again spoke of becoming a soldier. In fact, she was so depressed by Connly's dissertation that John had to make up no end of silly stories and ridiculous faces before she bounced back to being her radiant little self.

For the rest of John's stay, the two girls constantly vied for who would receive the most attention. In the evening, after the girls were in bed, he enjoyed long talks with Connly and his parents, sitting in the comfort of the parlor, watching the flickering firelight, and solving all the world's problems.

Somehow it seemed to all of them like only three hours, rather than three days, before Rebecca was cooking up her last breakfast of grits, fluffy baking powder biscuits drowning in creamy gravy, and sizzling homemade sausages for the men. She watched Connly as he ate, and while his grin was as spontaneous as ever, he ate only lightly and passed up seconds, so she knew he was sad to leave her too.

Dawn was just breaking as Connly hugged everyone goodbye, and then for good measure John hugged everyone too. Muriel turned bright pink and replayed the moment a thousand times in her mind.

The town was waking up as John and Connly rode through, breathing in deeply the cool, quiet promise of a new day. A groggy shopkeeper was opening his shutters. A little girl on a doorstep was giving her kitten a bowl of milk. In front of them a tavern door banged, and eight men rambled out.

John drew in his breath sharply. Their uniforms were gray—or was it just the early morning light deceiving him? He paused momentarily to glance at Connly, and in that split second their presence was observed.

There was an excited exchange between a few of the Confederates, and then without warning, a shot rang out. A wild and reckless shot to be sure, but it slammed the door on John's hopes for a peaceful passing. Drawing their own pistols, the two men returned the compliment, an act altogether unappreciated by the rebel leader, who perceiving his clear advantage by way of numbers, leapt onto his horse with an oath and an order to his men to follow suit.

John and Connly had already wheeled their horses around and were dashing off. "Follow me," Connly called as he whirled down a side street. He led the way as they galloped down alleys, around the churchyard, and between houses in attempt to baffle their provoked pursuers. Finally weaving their way to the edge of town, Connly turned down a narrow country lane.

"About a mile down this road is a deserted farm. We can turn in there and hide in the woods. When they don't see us anywhere, maybe they'll give up the chase," Connly said in a loud whisper. Without wasting time for an answer, John tore after him.

The road was winding and hilly for the first half mile. John thought he heard hoof beats behind them, but didn't turn to look. Rounding a curve, they came to an even straightaway. As they entered it, the men spurred their horses towards the break in the trees indicating the entrance to the farm. But they were not quite fast enough. The Confederate commander whirled out of the curve just in time to catch a glimpse of the rump of John's mount as he disappeared into the trees.

*   *   *   *   *

"Everrett, something unusual happened today," Elsa said as they concluded supper one wet evening in March.

"What's dat?" Everrett asked, leaning back in his chair and resting his feet on the table.

"When I went into town this afternoon, there was a letter for us—well, for me actually." Elsa's face was turning a gentle pink with the significance of the news she had to tell.

"Dat is a surprise. Who's even know dat we's live hehe, 'cept foh a couple ob folks as would jest stop by ifen dey wanted to say anything?"

Elsa nodded. "I think we have done quite well at concealing our identity. Mr. Thomas, at the store, thinks you are a hired hand. But someone guessed that I might be here."

"Yeah, since I got dat part time work with Aaron Flinders, some folks thinks I's hired help here too. But who's de letteh from?"

Elsa drew it from her pocket. "The date shows it was written a good three weeks ago." She took the paper from the envelope and slowly unfolded it. "Do you care for more coffee?" She reached for Everrett's mug.

"Dat bad is it? No, I's had enough coffee. Go 'head and read it."

"It's from Aunt Ingrid."

A scowl made Everrett's face turn a shade darker. Elsa turned away from his forbidding expression and began to read.

My dear niece Elsa,

I don't know where you are, but am writing just in case. Perhaps I was wrong to send you away.

In any case, I am a ruined woman. I have been stripped of everything. They have burned and broken everything they did not take—the food, the silver, my jewels, everything. I am left alone in this God-forsaken house of ashes. Even the slaves are gone. I have no more hope for the Confederacy. It is as ruined as this doleful place. Its doom spells my own.

My nerves are shattered with everything else. I can't even sleep anymore. I've never learned to care for myself. I know no occupation nor is there anyone that would employ me if I did, and I have absolutely nothing of value that I can sell. I realize now my cruelty in sending you out alone as I did.

I do not expect this letter will reach you, but I hope you have found a future, though I cannot. I am nothing now but a broken old woman. I do not expect I have many days left, and I hoped I could ease my conscience before I completely waste away in this castle of my pride, which will soon become my coffin.

I never had pity for the desperation of others because I never knew total desolation myself. I wish I had died rather than lived to see this day. My pride, which has been my support my whole life, has now become a demon to torment me.

Kind Regards,
Ingrid Chesterfield

"What does you think of a letteh like dat?" Everrett's legs came down with a thud as he sat up.

"Everrett, I feel terrible for her. The poor woman is wretched."

"Poor indeed! Dat is a selfish letteh if eveh I's heard one." Everrett's voice was dripping with disgust. "Shey didn't want to have nothin' to do with you's a few months ago, when de wind blew in heh favoh, but now when shey's in trouble…uuh! Is you's honestly gonna tell me you's don't think shey deserves to bey wretched?"

"But you don't understand. The Aunt Ingrid I knew would never have written such a letter. She must be horribly desperate. Haven't you been listening to this? *I never knew total desolation myself. I wish I had died rather than lived to see this day. My pride, which has been my support my whole life, has now become a demon to torment me.*" Elsa reread the end of the letter.

"Let it torment heh den."

"Why do you say such things?" Elsa implored. "Aunt Ingrid is finally ready to change. I am amazed that she wrote."

"I's not. It's like I said. She'll do anythin' ifen it will help *her*, but when did she eveh cahe about you?" Everrett asked.

"It isn't just like that. She gave me every opportunity to become just the type of woman she thought I ought to want to become."

"Suhe, shey tried to make you's as evil as hehself," Everrett said sarcastically. "I's don't think shey deserves no credit foh dat,"

"But to her, it seemed like the right thing," Elsa insisted. "She honestly didn't know any better."

"As far as I's can see, dere ain't anythin' honest about heh," Everrett replied with a disgusted shake of his head. "Youh Aunt is a smart, educated woman, and shey chose to bey selfish and spiteful. Don't tell me, shey didn't know no betteh."

"But you can't deny that is was my own fault that I fell out of her good graces."

"I's told you, you's got to stop thinkin' dat way," Everrett exclaimed as he stood up. "It was *her* fault, and shey ain't a woman ob good graces."

Elsa looked at the floor and sighed. "I am not saying Aunt Ingrid ever liked me much, but family duty was strong to her. She did what she thought was right by me, until she saw I was irreconcilable to the cause she loved. Her husband did die for the cause. It was only natural that she would resent anyone who tried to aid her enemies as I did, but for awhile she really did try to help me. She made sure I was well provided for, got a good education, and had lots of opportunities. Even when she tried to arrange a marriage for me with Captain Aldridge, she thought that would make me happy."

"Oh, yeah, shey tried to marry you's to a man would have abused you youh whole life. Don't tell me you's think shey had youh best interests at heart foh a moment. Uhh, I hate her mohe all de time."

"But, Everrett, now that she is really desperate and ready to change, you wouldn't want me to turn my back on her and be just like her, would you?"

"You's don't eveh have to fear you's will bey like her," Everrett said, almost smiling. "You's fah too innocent to even undehstand sech things, but dere are some people with whom evil is a part ob dere nature, and we ain't got no call to be doin' anythin' foh dem."

"Do you really believe that? I think we are all equally human and capable of the same mistakes, and we all need love and help sometimes."

Everrett was silent for a moment. He knew that if he said, "What about de men dat killed youh fatheh?", that Elsa would have to admit that perhaps her theory wasn't true for everyone. But he was too keenly aware of just how excruciating Elsa found the memory of her father's death, to be willing to bring it up merely for the sake of making a point. Besides, Everrett knew that in the end Elsa would always defer to his opinion, no matter how strongly she disagreed, making this whole conversation pointless and certainly not worth hurting her feelings over. The truth of the matter was that Elsa so rarely stated a strong viewpoint on anything, that had it been anything less important, he would have gone along with her, but this was ridiculous.

"I's don't want to argue with you, darling. Now listen," he said very patiently, as if explaining something to a small child. "Youh aunt is very selfish. Even heh so called love foh de Confederacy was selfish. As long as shey thought you's could be ob some use to heh, shey kept you, and when shey saw you's wouldn't, shey threw you away. I's know you's don't want to admit dat, but it's de truth. Now jest fohget her."

"But if we could help her, she might become a new woman," Elsa pleaded.

"Shey neveh asked us to help her."

235

"But shey wants us to, or she would not have written. If we were to invite her to come live with us…"

"Never!" If Everrett's face could have turned white with horror, it would have. This conversation was quite deteriorated, and it was high time it came to an end. "I's can't believe you's would even suggest sech a thing. I's done talkin' about it." His voice was commanding.

Elsa turned and began to silently clear the table, as he had known she would. Everrett stood watching her for a moment. It was extremely easy to control Elsa. He tried not to take advantage of the fact, but honestly, she was just so damn gullible. How could she not see what a snake Ingrid was? Everrett knew he was right, and he didn't want her disagreeing with him, yet at the same time it bothered him vastly how easy it was to silence her. Why did she shut up the moment he told her to?

Everrett suddenly realized that he had never felt that way about anyone before. He couldn't think that he had ever before cared much what anyone thought, especially if he knew they were wrong. Why did he care so much if she was upset about it? What did it matter if she was moody and distant? Elsa would always do as he said, and in time she would get over being irritated about it. But he did care. It mattered very much to him if she was happy or not, and it drove him nuts when she was silent and withdrawn.

"Oh, Elsa, what have you done to me?" Everrett thought. "You hold more power over me than any master I ever had, and you don't even know it."

He came up behind her and put his hands gently around her waist. "Darling, I's don't want you's to be taken advantage of. I's know you's betteh dan you's think, and so does youh aunt. Shey knows you have a kind heart, so shey writes you a sad letteh jest so shey kin get somethin' from you."

Elsa leaned back against him and closed her eyes. When she opened them again, she said, "What about Christ? He forgave people who were terribly cruel and merciless to Him, even though they never asked for it, and where would any of us be if He hadn't?"

"Dat has nothin' to do with this. Dis is de judgment ob God, jest like Noah and de flood."

"I thought you'd say something like that," said Elsa, drawing away. "You aren't one for interfering with divine retribution, are you?" she added dryly and set to washing the dishes in earnest.

Everett went out to the barn and hoped that it wouldn't take her too long to get over being upset. He would have liked to strangle Ingrid for having had the gall to send such a letter.

It was soon bedtime. Everett had just thrown his sweaty shirt over the back of a chair and sat down on the bed to pull off his boots, when Elsa suddenly spun around from where she was combing out the soft waves of her hair in front of the mirror, and announced, "I am going to keep it forever."

"What?" he asked, looking up as his boot thumped onto the floor.

"The letter," she said matter-of-factly, as if she couldn't possibly have been making reference to anything else.

"Is you still thinkin' about dat?"

"These are the kindest words my aunt ever said to me. I am going to place it right in this drawer and keep it for the rest of my life." Elsa picked up the envelope from the top of the bureau and knelt down to open the bottom drawer. She pressed the paper to her breast, then resolutely laid it in the drawer and shoved it closed.

Everett watched her silently, and when she was done, held out his arm to her. She came and sat down beside him. "I's am sorry dis is so upsettin' to you," he said softly. "I's don't blame you foh havin' a tender heart. Jest try and believe me; it is best dis way. I's only want to protect you. Heaven knows you's been hurt enough times already."

Elsa laid her head wearily on his shoulder and said nothing.

Everett was disappointed in his hopes that Elsa would soon forget about the letter. Although she did not mention another word about it, the letter was clearly still very much on her mind. The most annoying part was the way she was so extremely agreeable about everything, yet so withdrawn that he felt sometimes like he had the company of a rag doll rather than a woman.

Why, the one time Elsa made up her mind to want something, did it have to be something so absurd? He had the feeling there was more troubling her than just Ingrid's situation, but there was precious little he could do about it, so he pretended not to notice until one night about a week later, when he awoke to find the bed beside him empty.

With a grunt, Everrett rolled out of bed and stumbled down the dark stairs. He saw a faint light seeping from under the parlor door, and found Elsa sitting in the rocker in the corner, wrapped in her shawl, knitting industriously. She did not look up as Everrett entered.

"Darling, what's you doin'? It's de middle ob de night," Everrett mumbled, sleepily scratching his head.

"I know what time it is," she answered, still without looking up.

"Time to be in bed," he yawned.

"I went to bed," she stated blandly.

"And now you's sittin' in a cold room, straining youh eyes to knit by a little candle. Come back to bed."

"I will."

Everrett stood in the doorway for a minute, waiting, but Elsa made no move to get up. So he pulled up a chair and sat down directly in front of her.

"So is you goin' to tell me what's wrong?" he questioned.

"Nothing is wrong. Can't I knit if I want to?"

"Of course you's can, but I's don't think you's really wants to. Leastwise, you's don't seem to be enjoyin' youhself all dat much."

Elsa set the knitting aside, but continued to look down.

Everrett took both her hands in his. "Now is de part where you's tell me what's wrong."

"I just could not sleep," Elsa said with a little shrug.

"Den jest come back to bed and keep me company, alright?"

"Whatever you say." Elsa stood up, but she pulled her hands from his.

Everrett bent over to pick up the candle, and as he did so, noticed a folded piece of paper beside it. He reached for it, but Elsa snatched it first.

"What's dat?" he asked.

"Nothing you want to talk about," she replied coolly.

"Foh pity's sake, Elsa, it's dat damn letteh from youh aunt, ain't it? Let me see it."

Elsa obediently handed it over. Everrett hesitated a second. Elsa was going to be very upset with him, but this letter had done nothing but make her miserable, and there was only one thing to do with such a piece of refuse. He stepped over to the empty fireplace and passed the paper into the flame of the candle.

"Don't do that," Elsa cried, plucking it away and frantically blowing out the fire. She spun around and attempted to dash up the stairs, succeeding only in knocking her head soundly on the wall as she rounded the corner. "Ouch," she moaned, clutching her head between her hands.

"Darling, is you alright?" Everrett hurried over to her. "It's just a damn piece ob papeh, and it suhe ain't worth gettin' hurt oveh."

"Perhaps it's just a piece of paper to you, but it's a lot more than that to me," she snapped. "It was dreadful of you to try to burn it. You are not usually that mean." Elsa leaned back against the wall and took several deep breaths, then went on with forced calmness. "You said the other night you didn't want to talk about it anymore, and you are right, there is nothing more to talk about." She proceeded up the stairs, Everrett following close behind with the light.

"So ifen we's both agree dere ain't nothin' more to talk about, why's you been so upset eveh since you's got it?" he asked as he set the candle down in the bedroom.

Elsa sat down on the edge of the bed and drew her shawl more tightly around herself. "I am not upset about anything, except that you tried to burn it," she answered.

"I's glad to hear it." Everrett knew she wanted him to apologize, but he wasn't sorry in the least. He wished he had succeeded. Then perhaps she could actually think about something else. "Ifen you's not upset about anything but dat, let's go to sleep. Come on." Everrett pulled back the quilt and motioned for her to crawl in.

"I'm not sleepy, Mr. Trenton, but you go right ahead and sleep; no one is stopping you," Elsa responded quietly as she traced her finger over the scorched edge of the paper in her hands.

"Ifen you's want to yell at me, why's don't you?" Everrett asked calmly.

"I don't yell. Even when they were torturing my father, I did absolutely nothing. If I didn't yell at a time like that, do you think there is anything that would make me?"

"You's should try it sometime. Might make you's feel betteh."

"If I yelled at you, it would not make you change your mind about anything, now would it?"

"No, I's not changin' my mind about dis, but ifen it would make you's feel betteh to say how much you's disagree with me and what a awful, mean person I's is, den say it."

"It wouldn't make me feel better, not—not at all," Elsa said, choking on the last words.

"Elsa, don't cry." Everrett was standing in front of her, and he placed his hands on her shoulders. "I's really make you's miserable, don't I?"

"No, no, you don't."

"Den why? Foh goodness sake tell me, why is you so upset? Darling, de last thing I wants is to make you's unhappy. Why's can't you believe what I's tryin' to tell you's about youh aunt? Why is dis so important to you?"

I don't know why," Elsa burst out. "But I feel terrible, Everrett. I have spent my entire life feeling terrible. I feel terrible every time I think of Aunt Ingrid. I feel terrible every time I think of my father. I feel terrible every time I think of my mother. I feel terrible every time I think of Clara, or Simon and Rueben. I even feel terrible every time I think of Martha.

"But there is one difference. All of those people are gone, and there is not a single thing I can do for any of them, except Aunt Ingrid. She's alive, but maybe not for long. I know you are right when you say she is not that good of a woman, but I have always tried to help, to somehow make things better, to justify my existence. I want the world to be just a little bit better place because I lived in it.

"But I have never succeeded. My whole life has been one long string of futile efforts, trying to do something good, trying to make someone's life better, and I am the most miserable failure that ever walked the face of the earth. I wish I had died at birth, and my mother had lived instead of me."

As she finished speaking, Elsa drew her legs up onto the bed and sat hunched over, hugging her knees. She reminded Everrett of the morning he had found her in the cemetery—so sad, so hopeless. She seemed to have almost reached the point of giving up on trying. He sat down beside her and stroked her silky hair with one hand while he slowly shook his head.

For a few minutes Everrett couldn't think quite how to answer her, but finally he said, "What about Lieutenant Fairfield? I's dare say you's made his life betteh."

Elsa nodded a little. "I hope so. But we don't know what happened to him. For all we know, he might not have made it back. His wounds were still far from fully healed, and I'm fairly certain the one was getting infected. Or he could have been captured before he found the Federal camp. I would feel better if I knew that he was alright."

"And what about me?" Everrett continued. "How many times must I's tell you's I needs you, befohe you's believe me?"

"I do appreciate your saying that, but how am I supposed to believe it? When you first met me, you didn't like me much at all, and you certainly did not need me. You were so self-sufficient. I admire that about you, but why do you need me now, if you didn't then?" she asked glumly.

"Because—because…Because I's do," he stammered.

Elsa gave him a joyless little smile and looked away again.

"Oh, Elsa, why's can't you see it?" Everrett exclaimed. "You's like de best person I's eveh met. You's cahe so much, and you's try so hard. Den you sit here and is miserable 'cause you's think you ain't good enough. When de problem is, you's almost too good. You is kind, and gentle, and sweet, and I's love you foh it. But dis here world is cruel and harsh, and it will tear you's apart, jest because you's is so soft and gentle. And I's won't let it. I won't."

He put one arm snuggly around her and cupped her face in his free hand. "I's can't beah to see you's be hurt, and I's have to protect you, even you's don't want me too. I's won't let dis evil world or anyone in it hurt you anymohe!" Everrett's face was hot, and he had to pause for a moment to swallow the choking in his throat. Elsa was staring at him in surprise. "Because, I's love you, Elsa, dat's why I needs you, because I's love you."

He pulled her head against his chest so she couldn't see the moistness in his eyes. "I's won't let anything or anyone, not even youh aunt, hurt you again—not eveh." It seemed like he couldn't hold her tight enough. No matter how snuggly he wrapped her in his arms, he felt as if something evil were about to tear her away.

"You said you loved me. You never said that to me before," Elsa breathed.

"I's neveh said dat to anyone befohe. But, darling, I do. I's neveh in my life wanted to love anyone. When we was married I liked you fine, and afteh you's started sharing' my bed, I's liked you a heck of a lot, but I's neveh thought dat I would love you. I's didn't think I could. But I do. I's loves you like all hell broke loose, and I's can't help myself. I's know you thinks I's dreadful and unreasonable to feel about youh aunt like I's do and to burn youh letteh, but I's can't help it. Anything or anyone dat causes you pain, I's want to destroy.

"I's haven't told you befohe, 'cause it almost scares me sometimes. It's like a fire inside me, and sometimes when I's look at you, I's think it will burn me right up. I's don't think I's could let go of you, even if you's wanted me too. I's don't mean to feel dis way, but honestly, I can't help it."

He wanted to pull her closer. Elsa was already completely enveloped in his arms, yet even that somehow wasn't enough. "Darling," Everrett whispered, pressing his cheek against the smooth hair of her scalp. "Even if you's don't want me to protect you foh youh own sake, please, let me do it foh mine."

"Everrett," Elsa wrapped her arms around his neck. "You are marvelous. In a way I guess I knew you loved me, but I had no idea you felt like that." She kissed him soundly. "I don't deserve you, I really don't."

"You's deserve much betteh than me."

"Don't say that, Everrett. When we were married, I liked you. I admired you, so much, and felt grateful too you, but I didn't think you were the man of my dreams. But you are so much better than I ever dreamed of. I can not even imagine how you can see something in me that is worth loving that much, but I am so, so glad you do. Oh, Everrett." She eagerly sought his mouth, and he just as eagerly received hers.

Everrett began to rub his large hands over her, groping, caressing, with ever increasing fervor. Even through her nightgown, Elsa could feel the urgency flowing through his fingertips. Each one was a burning candle, igniting her, till she felt herself flaming all over.

"What are you doing to me?" she gasped. She placed her hands just below his shoulders, and he let her shove him down onto his back.

Elsa was glowing as she straddled him and slowly pulled her nightgown off over her head. Had a seraphim been hovering above him, Everrett could not have been more mesmerized. He gently glided his hand up her thigh. In that moment she truly did seem to him like a creature not of this earth. Her breasts floating before him were two lustrous pearls, her eyes sapphires, shimmering with her love for him. She smiled as she realized her gaze was holding him transfixed.

"Elsa," he breathed. "I'm all youhs. You's have no idea de spell you hold me in."

"I hold you in a spell, do I?" She spread her legs a little farther and gently shifted her weight back and forth, so he could feel the slipperiness between her legs moist against his stomach.

"Oh, darling, stop teasing me," he moaned.

"Well, why don't you do something about?" she said with a small smile.

"You's don't know what you is askin' foh," Everrett responded as he rolled over, bringing her with him.

"Oh, yes, I do. Everrett, I am yours every bit as much as you are mine, and I want you to take me, and fill me, and make me a part of yourself, and...ahh," she drew in her breath as he entered her.

Everrett placed his hands over hers, pinning them down above her head. His movements were slow, deliberate, as he rotated his hips from side to side, distinctly prodding every inch inside her with an intense tickling sensation. It was impossible not to squirm, but he had her pinned down so firmly she realized she couldn't move, so settled for a few very girlish squeals.

"Oh, don't stop, Everrett."

"Don't worry, I's not going to," he said, as he bent down to kiss her breasts.

They made love that night, slowly and tenderly, with lots of kisses and endearing words, not wanting it to ever end. Finally exhausted, they fell asleep in one another's embrace, their hearts still brimming over with a love for which there is no words and a passion too deep to ever be filled.

The Return of Evil

Everett and Elsa awoke early the next day to a damp and slightly misty morning. Everett went out to the barn while Elsa moved quietly about the kitchen. She had started a fire in the big iron stove, made coffee, and was putting on some water to heat for oatmeal, when she was startled by the sound of voices outside. She picked up her egg basket and hurried out onto the porch.

She gasped. "John!" Elsa flew down the porch steps and over to where Everett stood talking with two men on horseback.

John looked in consternation from one to the other. "Miss Elsa, I never imagined…"

"Elsa, dese men have to hide. Dere's Rebels chasing dem," Everett interrupted.

"Oh, Everett, the cave. Take them there!" she cried as her face blanched.

"You men dash for dose trees oveh dere," Everett pointed in the general direction of the cave. "I'll come and lead you to a hideout quicker dan you's can blink."

Spurring their horses, the two men were off in a flash for the refuge of the trees. Everett dashed into the barn with Elsa at his heels. With deft fingers, trembling slightly, she untied Charcoal, as Everett swung himself up.

"Hurry, Everrett!" her voice was frantic. "Confederates! They mustn't find you here." An icy shiver ran up and down her spine.

"You come too." He held out his hand to swing her up.

"No, Everrett, there is a fire in the stove and breakfast half made. If we all leave it will be terribly suspicious," she objected. "I'll just be very polite and send them on their way. Then I'll come and get you and the soldiers when it's safe."

He hesitated a second. "I's don't want to leave you."

"I will be just fine. They aren't interested in me. Only you and the soldiers are in danger. Oh, do hurry! I couldn't bear to see anything happen to you. Believe me; I can handle this."

Realizing he had no choice, Everrett kissed her quickly and sped across the field and into the protection of the forest. He soon caught sight of John and Connly through the trees and swiftly guided them back to the cavern behind the west pasture. All three men dismounted and tied their horses in the dense foliage a safe distance from their hideout. Connly laid his hand on John's shoulder for balance as Everrett hurried them along.

"Is you's hurt?" Everrett asked in alarm as he noticed Connly limp and saw the tight line his mouth was set in.

Connly shook his head. "But, sir, I really apologize for coming here and putting you in danger. I thought this place was vacant."

"It was, an it suits us foh folks to think it still is," Everrett replied. "Here we are." He stopped in front of the cave. "Jest stoop down, it's snug, but you's should be safe enough here."

"Sir, we are immensely obliged to you," John said as at last he let out his breath easily. "But I am more confused than I can tell you. How in the world did you and Miss Grey get here? This is the last place I expected to see either of you, and together."

"Mrs. Trenton," Everrett corrected. "We was married afteh heh aunt done kicked heh out of de house. Dis is her farm shey got from heh fatheh."

"Oh," said John.

"Yes, and I's worried enough about heh right now. I's have to go."

"I always seem to cross her path when I'm in a position to cause considerable inconvenience," said John uncomfortably.

"Ya'll jest sit tight. I's goin' back towards de house."

"I really think you ought to stay here," Connly objected. "Pardon my saying so, but these men are much more likely to be civil to a beautiful young woman than to you. If Elsa's half the woman John says she is, she'll manage alright."

Everrett didn't seem to hear him but scrambled out of the cave, pulled some vines down over the opening, and was gone

"So that was the girl I used to tease you about?" Connly said.

John nodded. "She was the one. It never crossed my mind that Everrett Trenton would marry her. He isn't right for her at all. But I guess he was there when she need someone and saw his opportunity."

"Well, now you don't have to worry about her anymore. You know she has someone and isn't living with that dreadful aunt of hers."

"But it just isn't right. He shouldn't have married her," John persisted. "They're two completely different types of people."

"You know, I think you're jealous, and I have no sympathy for you there. He's seems a very decent man. I just wish we hadn't come here and caused them all this trouble."

"I couldn't agree with you more about that," John said grimly.

The men lapsed into silence and waited tensely in the murky dimness, each minute its own mini torture of dread and uncertainty.

*　　　　　*　　　　　*　　　　　*　　　　　*

No sooner had Everrett disappeared into the woods, than the dull thud of hooves and the sound of irritated voices and whinnying horses, announced to Elsa the arrival of her dreaded callers. She reflexively drew back behind the barn doorway, where she could hear what was going on but not see or be seen. She clutched the handle of the egg basket and frantically rehearsed fragments of what she intended to say. "No, I haven't seen anyone around this morning. Yes, my husband is gone at the war. Perhaps you had best search farther down the road."

The men seemed to have paused in the yard, and Elsa could catch enough bits of their conversation to tell the general drift of their feelings.

"Where in hell did they go to?"

"We've lost them."

"I don't even believe those two confounded men turned in here at all."

"This is a wild goose chase…"

"Quiet!" The voice was authoritative and somehow familiar. "I saw those damn bastards turn this way. We'll search till we find them. Spencer, Kenderton, head…" He broke off abruptly as Elsa stepped out of the barn.

In a moment every remaining drop of color drained from her face as her eyes fell on the wavy, golden locks framing the determined face of the handsome, young captain who turned to look at her. Could it be? Could it possibly be? It was like a nightmare come to life.

"Madame, have you seen any Union renegades tearing through here?" he addressed her politely enough.

"No, I haven't seen anyone," Elsa answered, but her voice faltered just a little.

The officer wiped the back of his hand across his eyes, then jumped down from his horse as if unable to trust his vision at that vantage point. "Elsa Grey!" he exclaimed, momentarily distracted from his pursuit. "Well, what have we here?" His eyes were glinting like a cat's, eager to tease its prey.

"Captain Aldridge, what a surprise. I never expected to see you this morning," Elsa said weakly.

"Didn't I tell you, you could never escape me, that we would meet again to see who was right—you or I?"

"You were right; we've met."

"What are you doing here anyway?" He glanced about suspiciously.

"I live here now."

"Alone?" There was a suggestive hint in his voice.

"No," she answered quickly. "I live here with my husband and our servant."

"Oh, so you are married?"

"Yes." Elsa lingered over the word with a sweet pleasure, because she knew that they had met again to see that she had indeed been right. She did not need him in order to survive in the world as he had once so arrogantly tried to convince her.

"Where is he?" Aldridge demanded.

"Who?"

"Don't be an idiot—your man of course." Not waiting for her to reply, he turned towards his men. "Enough of this wasting time. Scatter and search for them." As his men headed off in various directions, Aldridge turned his attention back to Elsa. "So, this man of yours, where is he?"

"Oh, he's around," Elsa stammered.

Aldridge smiled cruelly and began to very slowly circle her. "*Around*, oh yes, I'm certain he's *around* just like you say. And these servants of yours, no doubt they are also *around*? Oh, and the Yankees are they *around* too?"

"There aren't any Yankees," Elsa stated as firmly as she could.

"There are, and you're hiding them from me."

"You give me too much credit, Captain," Elsa said with an attempt at a smile. "You know me better than that. When have I ever had the presence of mind to successfully conceal anything?"

Aldridge gave a short, humorless laugh. "Never, but that doesn't keep you from trying. Now stop lying to me. I saw them turn in here." Aldridge stepped closer until he was practically breathing down her neck, and Elsa felt sickened by the heavy scent of his cologne. "You can't escape me, so you might as well make up your mind to tell me before we have any *trouble*." He put a sinister emphasis on the last word.

Elsa shook her head ever so slightly.

Aldridge stood still and regarded her for a moment, trying to asses how far he would have to press her before she snapped. He had seen her break in front of Ingrid and in one hasty torrent of words tell her all about how she had hidden John, and he felt confident he could elicit another such response now. Elsa bent to set her egg basket on the ground. As she straightened up, he took hold of her arm. "Where!?" he bellowed at her.

"I'm not going to tell you anything." Her voice was barely above a whisper, and the frightened look in her eyes belied her words.

"I will make you tell me," he hissed.

"You can't."

"Oh, yes I can!" he shot back as he shoved her away and instinctively drew his pistol.

Elsa focused on his tense features, the lurid glare in his ominous, deep blue eyes—like the darkness of a stormy night—the taut muscles in his jaw, his lips set in a relentless line, the menacing barrel of his pistol pointed in her direction.

"Please, Aldridge," she said softly. "I am one the most insignificant people you could ever hope to meet, and I don't want any trouble as you say. All I ask is to live here in this quiet corner and cause no inconvenience to anyone. You once said that you would do anything for me. Could you not, just this once, let it pass?"

"What right do you have to remind me of that? When have you ever given me anything I asked of you? Or is that about to change?"

"I have nothing I can give you."

"I could think of something." Once again there was that suggestive hint in his voice, and Elsa knew his meaning.

She stared at him for a moment in indecision. All she wanted was to protect Everrett and the soldiers. If satisfying Aldridge's lust was what it took to make him leave, she felt she could endure it. How bad could it be? She would just close her eyes and think about something, anything, else. No one need ever know. It could be her secret.

Seeing her hesitation, Aldridge stepped closer and quickly slid an arm around her waist. "I always knew you would be mine someday," he whispered as he pressed his lips to hers.

Elsa tried to think about canning apricots, but every thought filling her mind was of Everrett, his passionate love for her and the glorious night they had just spent together. If she allowed Aldridge to use her now, would she ever again be able to experience that dazzling sense of oneness with him? And Everrett seemed to know her so well; she wouldn't be able to keep this from him. He would know, and he wouldn't understand.

Elsa gave a choked scream and tried to push Captain Aldridge away, but he only tightened his grip. Although she desperately wanted to avoid antagonizing him, Elsa responded to reflex and bit down hard on his lower lip. Aldridge yelped as he jumped back.

"Damn you, woman! How dare you?" The captain hooked his boot behind her ankle and very neatly pulled one of her feet out from under her. Elsa toppled to the ground as she lost her balance. "You find it amusing to trifle with me?" he snapped.

Elsa did not attempt to stand back up, but looked up at him, fixing her gaze straight in his eyes. "Captain," she said very softly, "if I could give you what you wanted, I would. But I've already given myself, body and soul, to another. I may not be able to stop you from doing as you please, but how can I give you what is no longer mine to give?"

Aldridge glared at her as licked the blood off his lip. "Then you will tell me where the men are!" he commanded.

"I can't. I truly can't." Elsa clenched her hands in the folds of her skirt so he could not see how they shook.

Lester Aldridge felt—felt not thought, for the rage taking possession of him rendered him beyond lucid thought—Lester Aldridge felt the impact of several years of frustration swelling around his throat with a strangling force. She was just a woman, like so many other women, but he wanted her more than he had ever wanted anything in his entire life. He knew she spoke the truth when she said she could not give him what was no longer hers to give, but the fact that another man now possessed what he wanted so desperately, filled him with a murderous fury.

Aldridge was a man of great abilities and prowess in war, and he adulated himself in diplomacy as well. On the battlefield, he attacked, he killed, he swore, he ranted, he raved, he forced his own way to whatever objective he set for himself. Off the battlefield, he had polished the art of flattery to a high gloss. He had succeeded in obtaining the rank of captain despite his poor leadership qualities and explosive temper.

He knew he had faults, yet he considered himself immune to failure. His ego was swelled to allow no room in his mind for any considerations unfavorable to himself. And now here was Elsa, once again shattering his smug satisfaction. By hook or crook he had been able to lay his hands on whatever he had wanted, except her.

What was she?—a young, timid, modest girl. But he had never mastered her, and the admission was more bitter to him than death. When she was prosperous, she would not swallow his flattery. When she had nothing, she refused his help. And now, when he definitely had her at his mercy, she would not yield. She was afraid of him—he could tell—very afraid, and yet she would not cave.

Aldridge knew so little of true love, loyalty, or devotion that he could not come close to understanding the inward strength bracing a heart kindled by these. He knew only what he felt, what he saw. He could intimidated her, but he could not coerce her. He could force her if he chose, but he could not own her. And it angered, no, it infuriated, incensed, enraged him.

"Tell me!" His voice was strained to a crimson tenor.

"I can't."

His finger trembled on the trigger of his pistol. Then it fired. Elsa screamed once and kept staring at him for a minute as she swayed. Then she fell backwards, her head hitting the earth with a dull thud.

Captain Aldridge's lips turned ashen as the heat of his passion faded to a cool chill in an instant. He hadn't meant to shoot her. Although he knew it could never be, Aldridge truly wanted Elsa to love him. He wanted her to be his, not dead. The pistol fell from his numb hand as he whispered, "Oh, my God, what have I done?"

But the Greatest
of These Is Love

When Aldridge fired, Everrett was in the pasture just behind the house, but shielded from view by a windbreak of gaunt poplars. Elsa's scream surged through his body like an electric current, and it took only an instant for him to gallop through the trees and into the yard.

Captain Aldridge was sufficiently shocked, as the weight of what he had just done settled upon him, that he was unaware of Everrett's approach. He knelt down beside Elsa, reaching out a hand to support her head, but she tried to push him away with a weak cry.

"Elsa, I didn't mean—this—I only, I only wanted you to—why wouldn't you just," he stammered on without realizing what he was saying.

This was the first sight to hit Everrett's eyes as he entered the yard, and he leapt from his horse like a panther springing onto its prey, strong, lithe, and with a deadly fire in his eyes. He grabbed the captain by the arm, jerked him to his feet, and threw him down on the ground as far away from Elsa as he could. Everrett didn't know what had transpired during his absence, but he saw Elsa lying bleeding on the ground with this scum bag hovering over her, and that was all he needed to know.

Everrett flew at the captain with all the unleashed rage of a husband's fury. Aldridge scrambled to his feet just in time for Everrett to meet him with a tremendous kick. He stumbled backwards and looked up into a deathly black face, all but spewing lightning. As Aldridge took in what he was up against, it suddenly became his turn to be afraid. Everrett was definitely larger and stronger, but Captain Aldridge was quick on his feet and a more experienced fighter.

He rolled out of Everrett's way and jumped to his feet in time to miss the next kick that Everrett had directed at him. He came at Everrett now with both arms up in a defensive position. He circled around him, trying to keep out of the way of Everrett's arms. But Everrett managed to grab hold of one of his wrists and punched him hard in the jaw. Aldridge struck back, hitting his opponent squarely below his right shoulder, but Everrett didn't seem terribly phased and kept a tight hold on the captain's wrist. Aldridge struggled and managed to free himself from his adversary's grasp, but only with a painful crack which broke the bone in his wrist.

He dove for Everrett's legs, hoping to trip his giant opponent. Everrett reeled but caught his balance before he fell. Aldridge collected himself and made another dive, but this time his foe was ready and met his attack with a hard kick which sent him sprawling. Before he could scramble to his feet, Everrett lunged at him again.

This was hopeless; he was outdone. Every black deed of his life rose before him, smeared over now with this atrocity. He no longer saw Everrett's fierce face, but the pleading fear in Elsa's eyes seemed to be piercing right through him. Captain Aldridge was too proud to beg for mercy, and he knew he could expect no quarter from his dark foe. But summoning all his strength, he turned his good hand into a claw and struck out for Everrett's face as he closed in on him.

"Everrett," Elsa moaned as she turned her head on the damp grass. Everrett glanced behind and suddenly was faced with the worst struggle of his twenty-eight years. Up to this point in the fight, he had been possessed by only one passionate yearning—to close his brawny hands around the neck of this villain. But why was he doing it? For her, of course. But Elsa was yet unconscious that he had even come. She lay bleeding to death on the ground. Would killing Aldridge really render her any service when she needed him desperately as she was painfully gasping her last breaths. If there was to be any hope of saving her, he must act now. Killing Aldridge required time, and he had no time.

Elsa moaned again. The deep crimson stain on the side of her pale blue dress was rapidly growing larger. Aldridge was on his feet again, but catching him by his disabled arm, Everrett gave him a tremendous kick in the groin which sent him down to the ground, cursing in agony. Everrett rushed over to Elsa and pressed his hand to her side. "Elsa, I'm hehe."

"Everrett," she whispered as she opened her eyes.

Seizing his opportunity, Aldridge scrabbled painfully over to his horse and dragged himself up. As he turned his horse, he cast one glance back and only then, as he saw Everrett wrapping his shirt tightly over Elsa's wound in an effort to staunch the blood, did he realize why he had not fought him to the death. His life had been indirectly saved by the very one who now lay suffering, perhaps dying, because of the unbridled violence of his passions—one he had once professed to love. With an inward groan too deep for vocal expression, Lester Aldridge turned and fled.

As he tore out the end of the lane, a black phantom of guilt rose out of the shadowy forest and swept after his trail. He kept casting nervous glances over his shoulder to see if it was still in pursuit. Crying out in pain, he spurred his horse harder, yet still it gained on him. Suddenly the brilliant rays of the morning sun turned gray as it settled over him. Terror gripped his soul. In a flash he saw the years of his life, still blank and featureless, stretching out before him with this dreaded specter of regret haunting his tracks through them all.

Back in the yard, Everrett managed to almost stop the flow of Elsa's blood as he applied pressure to his makeshift bandage. "Darling, you's gonna be alright. You's gonna be alright." Everrett didn't know if he was talking more to himself or to her.

"The men, are they—are they safe?" she asked.

Everrett nodded. "I's got to get a doctor for you." As Everrett spoke, several of Aldridge's men rode into the yard. They stopped in shock as they saw Elsa on the ground with Everrett holding her and their captain nowhere to be seen. "Your captain's hightailed it out off here afteh shooting heh," Everrett called to them.

The men continued to stare speechlessly. "Don't sit dere like a bunch of idiots. Get out of here an fetch de doctor. Hurry!" Exchanging bewildered glances, the soldiers sped off.

"I'm cold," Elsa whispered. "Please, take me inside."

Very slowly and carefully he lifted her up. A glance at the ground where she had been lying told him she had lost a good deal of blood, but not quite as much as he had feared. He brought her into the house with as little jostling as possible, but he could still see her wince with every step.

"I want to go to bed."

"Dahling, it will shake you's too much if I's carry yo up de stairs."

"I just want to go to bed." Her voice was getting weaker.

Everrett wished so desperately that he knew what he ought to do for her, but he really didn't have a clue. So he took her to bed as she asked. He sat down on the edge and laid his hand firmly against her side, as he could see that she had started her to bleed more as he carried her. With his free hand he gently stroked her hair back from her face. "I love you," he said.

She reached up and clutched tightly onto his hand, as if afraid that he would disappear. "I love you, too," she breathed.

"I'm sorry. I'm so sorry, Elsa," he went on huskily. "I's always said I's would protect you. And I didn't. I's should never have left you."

Elsa could see there were tears in the corners of his eyes. She turned her head and kissed his hand. "You have never failed me. I'm sorry. I'm sorry to leave you."

"No." He tightened his hold on her hand. "You's ain't goin' to leave."

Elsa closed her eyes. "I'm so cold," was all she said.

Everrett covered her with the quilt. "You's can't leave me. You's can't leave," he murmured to her as he bent over and kissed her forehead.

"I will try not to." Her voice was barely audible. She was going into shock and stopped responding to anything he said, but he could tell she was still breathing. It seemed an eternity that he sat there bent over her, listening anxiously for each breath. At last he heard a knock on the door. Perhaps the soldiers had gone for a doctor after all. Reluctantly he loosened her grip on his hand and stood up. He ran down the stairs and jerked the door open. Everrett let out a long breath of relief.

"Thank God," he said as he pulled the doctor inside. "Shey's upstairs.

Shey was cold. Shey wanted to go to bed. Shey's hurtin' bad. You's gotta help heh. Hurry, dis way."

The doctor followed as he bounded up the stairs.

*   *   *   *   *

"Something's not right." John's voice was strained. "We must have been sitting here for a solid hour. Something has happened. Everrett shouldn't have gone back to the house. Maybe they did something to him."

Connly nodded. "It has been way too long. It's possible the Rebs were just very insistent on looking for us. But if they haven't found us by this time, it seems they would have moved on."

"And it's so deathly silent in here," John added. "I haven't heard so much as a squirrel going through the trees, much less a man. I think we should sneak out. Something is going on, and I can't sit here another minute and do nothing."

"I feel the same," Connly agreed.

John stuck his head through the vines covering the entrance and cautiously peered out. "Nothing," he said. The two men crawled from the cave, and John helped Connly to his feet.

"Should we get the horses?" Connly wondered.

"Let's just sneak around a little and see what is up first. If we have to hide it's a lot easier without a horse."

The two men edged their way to the verge of the woods. The sun had fully risen by now, and the meadow before them was bright and inviting. All was still except for a few birds singing as they flitted back and forth catching their breakfast. John and Connly proceeded towards the house, walking along the tree line and continuously scanning for any sign of something out of place. As they approached the yard, they drew their pistols and cautiously left the protection of the trees. A small black surrey was parked in front of the house and a white horse tied to a tree.

They paused for a moment to exchange questioning glances. "There is no way to find out without going on," Connly whispered.

John nodded his consent, and they continued on into the yard.

Suddenly John stopped in his tracks and grabbed Connly's sleeve. "Look!" He pointed to a blood stained patch of grass outside the barn door.

"Oh, no" Connly groaned. "Something has happened. Hurry. Let's go inside."

The front door was unlocked, so the two men entered silently. No one seemed to be around. Keeping their fingers poised on the triggers of their pistols, they watchfully proceeded from one room to the next. The only sign of life they saw was a pot of water boiling vigorously on the stove. They heard footsteps on the stairs and froze, their eyes peeled on the kitchen doorway.

They lowered their pistols as Everrett entered the room. Everrett drew in his breath sharply. "What in hell is you's doin' here, startling me like dat?" he exclaimed.

"We're sorry," John let out his breath. "We saw blood on the ground and thought perhaps you or Elsa…"

"He shot heh," Everrett said before John had a chance to finish his sentence.

"No! Elsa? Is she alright?" John burst out.

"De doctor is with heh now. He don't know ifen she'll make it or not."

"Everrett, we're so sorry," John breathed.

"What can we do?" Connly asked.

Everrett shook his head. "I's wish I knew." He picked up the boiling pot from the stove and turned to go. "De doctor should bey done soon," he said as he left the room.

About fifteen minutes later, a tall, thin man with a neat brown beard came down the stairs. His face was serious as he looked at the dragoons. "What has happened here?" he asked. "I can't get anything sensible out of that Negro, only that he is awfully devoted to his mistress."

"We don't really know what happened," John said. "We were just riding through town this morning, and a group of Confederates started chasing us."

"We turned in here to hide, thinking this farm was abandoned," Connly explained.

"The black man upstairs, took us into the woods to hide, while the woman of the house stayed back to distract the rebels." John went on. "After a bit he went back to the house to see if she was alright, and when he never returned, we became concerned and came back to see what was wrong. That is all we know. But tell us, how is she? Is there anything we can do for her?"

"So that is why a group of Confederates came pounding on my door this morning and refused to tell me a thing. Blasted rebels," the doctor sighed, "when will we ever be rid of their infernal presence?"

"Yes, yes, but how is she?" John insisted.

"The wound is severe. She seems to have been shot at close range, and has lost a good deal of blood," the doctor stated solemnly. "However, it is not necessarily fatal. If we can prevent infection, she may recover. I have done all I can for her now. The only thing you can do is to stay with her, get her to drink as much as you can, and if she begins to burn with fever, as I expect she will, keep it down as much as possible with wet cloths. I left some medicine with the black man to help with the fever if she develops one. I'll come back in the evening to change the dressing. I feel sorry for that woman's husband," the doctor added. "More than likely he'll come back from the war to find his wife dead."

"But you said it wasn't necessarily fatal," John reminded him.

"Not necessarily, but she doesn't seem very strong. I doubt if her body has the resources to fight off an infection. Time will tell." The doctor shrugged. "I'll be back."

After the doctor left, Elsa, very faint from loss of blood, began to doze off, and the men had no option other than to speculate on what had transpired during their absence. Everrett said over and over that he never should have left her, while John and Connly said over and over that they should never have come. At last Elsa woke up and tried to get out of bed. Everrett, who was sitting next to her, quickly reached out and stopped her from moving.

"Darling, you's must lie still. You was shot dis mornin', remember?"

Elsa's expression suddenly changed from bewilderment to despondency as her eyes filled with tears. "Why did it have to be him? Of everyone in the world who could have come this morning, why did it have to be him?"

"Who? Who was dat man?" Everrett asked eagerly.

"Captain Aldridge," she whispered, while the tears which had been threatening, began to spill out of her eyes.

"Don't cry, darling." Everrett caressed her face with his hand as he kissed her. "But tell me what happened."

"If it had been anyone else I could have handled them, but not him," Elsa said tearfully. "Everrett, he wanted me to lay with him, and he would have gone away if I had. I knew I must not make him angry, so I thought perhaps it-it was the only thing to do, but I just couldn't. I bit his lip to make him stop kissing me, and then-then he was furious." The effort of crying and talking where making Elsa lose her breath, and she paused for a moment to catch it. It was then that she noticed John and Connly, standing at the foot of the bed. She gave half a smile. "You are both alright? I'm glad of that."

"I's should neveh have left you," Everrett moaned.

"No, it's not your fault, Everrett," John insisted. "We should never have come here."

Elsa had stopped crying now, and she closed her eyes and said softly. "I am so glad you are all safe. That is what I wanted."

The day progressed very slowly. Everrett would not leave Elsa's side, and John and Connly stayed with him much of the time. One minute Elsa would seem alert and to be feeling better, the next she would be confused or unresponsive. She did not want to drink, although she did take some tea as all three men were continuously offering it to her.

At first Everrett was a little uncomfortable with John and Connly's presence, but their concern for Elsa was almost as great as his own, and they wouldn't think of leaving if there was anything at all that could be done for her. As the day wore on and Everrett could see her condition was not improving, he became grateful for the fact he did not have to keep his anxious watch alone. As one after another the hours slipped slowly away, the dread they shared formed a bond between them. In these moments of tense waiting everything else dissolved, and they were nothing but three men, hovering restlessly over a woman they all wanted desperately to save.

Around noon, Everrett noticed that her face was beginning to get damp with perspiration. Their anxiety increased as they watched her fever rise throughout the afternoon. Since Connly's personal involvement was the least, he actually proved himself the most capable in caring for Elsa's well-being, preventing Everrett from pouring the entire bottle of medicine down her throat at once and John from drenching the bed in his zeal to continuously change the wet cloth on her forehead.

However, by the time the doctor returned in the evening, Elsa's hair was soaked with sweat. All three men waited impatiently at the bottom of the stairs. When the doctor came down he was very serious.

"How is she?" John asked. "Will she be able to pull through?"

"To be honest, she could hardly be doing worse. She is simply too weak to fight the infection. I won't say there is no hope, but I would be surprised if she lives past tomorrow evening. If she has any family in the area, you should send word to them."

"Is dere anything we's can do foh her?" Everrett asked.

"She is starting to get very restless," the doctor answered. "If she tosses too much she will start bleeding again, and she can't afford to lose anymore blood. You might tie her to the bed to keep her still."

Everrett watched the doctor darkly as he left. "What kind of advice is dat? Tie heh up. Like I's would tie my own wife to de bed. Ain't he got nothing betteh to say then dat?"

The doctor's visit had roused Elsa, and when the men returned to her room, she seemed more alert than in the last several hours. No sooner had Everrett sat down next to her than she said, "Who was that man in here? He was extremely disagreeable and smelled awful. Will you get me my letter?"

"What letter?"

"You know what letter, the one from the woman you hate." Elsa's eyes were bright with fever, and she was just close enough to delirium to not care what she was saying. "Everrett hates a lot of people," she said, looking at John. "And who is this man with you? Do I know him?"

"This is my friend, Connly," John answered.

Everrett returned with her letter from Ingrid and handed it to her. "This letter is from Aunt Ingrid." Elsa caught hold of John's hand. "You can read it. I wish so much that someone would help her. She is sick and can't sleep." Elsa turned her attention towards Connly for a moment and then went on to John, "Your friend is very handsome, but I do like black men better, don't you?"

John swallowed hard before he choked and said soothingly, "Of course, everyone does."

Elsa looked perplexed for a minute. "Do they? They don't act like it."

She tried to roll over, but John and Everrett both reached out to stop her. Connly handed Everrett a fresh towel wet with cold water. He began to wipe her face and then moved on to her arms.

"Don't do that," she objected.

"But, Elsa, you's so hot. Don't you's want to get cooled off?"

She shook her head vigorously. "That's not what I want."

"What do you's want, darling?"

Elsa pulled Everrett's head down to hers and whispered something that made him almost smile for the first time that day. "Leave us alone foh a bit," Everrett said to the soldiers.

Everrett gently raised Elsa's shoulders and wrapped his arms around her. He felt her relax against him. "Why did dis have to happen now, jest when I's thought our lives was gonna get betteh?" he said sadly as he brushed back the wet locks of hair sticking to her forehead.

"Am I going to die?" Elsa asked.

The only answer Everrett gave her was a kiss. She leaned against him and shut her eyes. After about five minutes she said, "It's alright if I do. Not that it doesn't scare me, it does. But I've done something good now; I haven't failed at everything. He shot me, but he didn't find out where you and the men were hiding. I feel somehow—content."

"But I's love you, Elsa. I's don't want to lose you."

"It would be better if you never had loved me," she whispered. "But when you said that to me for the first time last night, you'll never know how much happiness you gave me."

"I's wish I hadn't waited so long to tell you. I wish I's had a hundred years to tell you so every minute of every day," Everrett replied, and this time he didn't try to hide the tears in his eyes.

"I'm so sorry, Everrett." Elsa placed her hand on one of his large arms and could feel the tension in his taut muscles. "If I had stopped to think how it would be for you, I would have left you alone. And I can't stop thinking that if I had married Captain Aldridge like he wanted, none of this would have happened."

Everett put his finger to her lips. "Don't say sech things. I's can't bear to hear dem."

"Let me say them. I may never have another chance. Don't misunderstand me, Everett. These past few months I have spent with you have been wonderful, and if I could have what I wanted, we would just go on like this forever. But we both know that even if this hadn't happened, things couldn't go on just the same. What would our lives be like? Always trying to hide our marriage, and if we had children, how would it be for them?"

"I know, but why do dey have to go dis way?" he moaned, holding her as tightly as he dared.

Elsa sighed. "It hurts to die." She stopped looking at him and stared out into space. "I do want to go to heaven and—and see my parents. But—but it hurts. And I want—I want to talk to you, but I get so hot, and I can't think, and it just hurts, and hurts, and there's you, and Aunt Ingrid, and Clara, and Captain Aldridge, and my father, and you're all here, but I'm alone. I hate to be alone, and I don't want to leave you, and now— now it's happening again. I just started to talk to you, and now I can't think."

"It's alright. It's alright," he soothed. "You's not alone. I's hehe, and John and Connly are hehe, and you's won't be alone foh so much as one single second. And when you can talk, we'll listen, and when you's can't, we'll still bey hehe."

Elsa drew several deep breaths. "I want to talk to John now," she whispered.

"Don't you's want to rest foh a spell? You's wearin' yourself out."

"If I don't talk now, I'm afraid—I'm afraid I won't be able to later. And I need to talk to him alone. Go and take care of yourself for a minute. You haven't eaten or drank or done anything for yourself today, have you? But let me let me kiss you first."

He bent his head down to hers, and they gave one another a long caress. Two tears dripped down onto her face. "Don't cry, Everett." She laid her hand on his head and stroked his hair.

"You's have no idea, Elsa. I said to you so many times dat I's would protect you, and I's haven't at all," he groaned.

"Everrett, look at me." When she saw she had his full attention she went on. "You have to believe me when I say this. You—you have given me everything I wanted. You want me, and you love me. You have always thought the best of me, even when—even when I thought the worst of myself. You haven't failed me. I mean that. The only reason you left me this morning was because I insisted on it. The captain is a cruel, hateful man, and that is not your fault. Believe me, Everrett. Believe me. You have been a very good husband. I love you with all my heart." Elsa gasped, trying to catch her breath. "Now I really must speak to John."

Everrett laid her down very gradually and stood staring at her for a bit. So many thoughts were running through his head, and he couldn't sort them out, but worst of all he felt terribly helpless. He crossed to the door and beckoned for John to come in.

"Shey wants to talk to you." Everrett said huskily and rushed down the stairs before they could see he was losing his composure.

John hurried over to the bed and sat down carefully on the edge. Elsa's eyes were closed, but she held out her hand, and he took it.

"I'm so sorry, Elsa," he said. "You've never done anything but help me, and I've never done anything but cause you trouble."

"Can't you men do anything but blame yourselves?" she murmured with a weak smile. "I want to talk to you, just give me a minute to catch my breath." Her voice was so low John could barely hear her.

He picked up the towel lying in the wash basin next to the bed, wrung it out and laid it on her forehead. His mind reverted back to the first time he had seen her. Just waking from unconsciousness, he had been terribly alarmed at her presence, but she had been so sweet and eager to help. With a wistful smile he recalled how much she had not wanted to relinquish him to Everrett's care.

But most of all he remembered that afternoon in the little forest bower, when he realized just how much she cared. He had wanted so badly to tell her that he would come back to her, but he couldn't, so he had just kissed her instead. What wonderful kisses they had been too. Although John knew he could not really have done differently than he had, he could not escape the feeling that he had failed her in some way.

He gently stroked back her wet hair as he thought, "You poor thing, you would be so much better off if you had never met me in the first place." Aloud John said, "I owe my life to you—twice now. I will never forget it."

Elsa opened her eyes and smiled at him. "Did you read that letter I gave you?" she asked.

John nodded.

"What did you think?"

"What did I think? Well, it was sad. Your aunt sounds very desperate," he said slowly, not quite sure what answer she was looking for.

"I wish so bad that I could help her. She wants help. She needs help."

"I thought your aunt was terrible to you. She kicked you out of the house, so you had to marry Everrett."

"She has been a hard, cold woman all her life. But things are changing now, and she—she needs help as much as anyone. John," she squeezed his hand and looked into his eyes, "I know—I know I'm dying. There are only two things I am worried about—Everrett and Aunt Ingrid—will they be alright?"

"You're not going to die," John contradicted.

"Just let me talk," she pleaded. "I can't do anything for my aunt even though I want to so much. And Everrett hates her. Not to mention, that being the woman she is, she would never be able to think of him as anything but a servant. But the war is almost over, and when it is, perhaps—perhaps..." Her voice faded out.

A look of comprehension suddenly dawned on John's face. "You want me to check in on her. Why didn't you just say so?"

"Oh, John, would you please?"

"Of course I will, if that's what you want."

"Will you? Will you really?"

"If that's what you want."

"That is what I want," she breathed. "Thank you."

"No, Elsa, don't thank me." John squeezed her hand.

Elsa sighed contentedly. "You have taken a weight off my mind."

John leaned over and kissed her cheek. "I wish there was more I could do for you."

By the end of these conversations, Elsa was completely exhausted and lay almost motionless until nightfall. Her fever was somewhat abated, and she seemed to be resting peacefully now. The men began to glance at one another with just a little hope in their eyes. Perhaps there was still a chance she would recover.

Valley of the Shadow

It was a clear night. John stood at the window, staring at the stars as they appeared one by one, till all at once the sky was full of them. He picked out familiar constellations amid the sea of twinkling lights and thought of the ancient tales they told. He wondered if the zodiac had not yet been recorded, what stories and fortunes men would find written in the sky today. John spun around as Connly give a little gasp behind him.

Connly was saying to Everrett, "Feel her skin; it's absolutely on fire." Without warning, Elsa's fever had spiked. Her skin was so hot it was uncomfortable to touch, and she began to thrash all over the bed almost convulsively. She was mumbling frantic fragments of sentences which made no sense to John and Connly, but Everrett could tell that she was reliving the night of her father's torture. He began to understand why the doctor had suggested they tie her down.

By turns, she thought Everrett was her father and Connly was Captain Aldridge, and then that John was Ingrid and Connly, John. Then she knew who John was, but thought Everrett was Clara and that Connly was one of the night riders come to carry her off. She scratched his face so viciously she drew blood. Then she thought Everrett was someone, they were never quite sure who, but at any rate she tried to gouge his eyes out, realizing who he was just in time for him to save his vision.

For a moment Everrett's worry was drowned in his consternation.

Was this really his gentle Elsa? If any of them so much as leaned over her, she pulled their hair or slapped them with a desperate ferocity. It took all their concentration to keep her still without hurting her or giving her the opportunity of hurting them.

Finally worn out, she simply laid there moaning and mumbling incoherently, sweat streaming down her face like tears. Everrett buried his face in his hands. "Damn it! I's can't bear to see heh like dis. And I's wasn't even able to kill de bloody bastard dat did dis to heh. But I will. I's will hunt him down and kill him ifen it's de last thing I's ever do."

If the day had seemed interminable, the night was much more so. No matter what they did, they could bring no relief to her burning body, or what was acutely worse, her tormented mind. For brief moments she would be with them, only to be jerked back by the tortured phantoms holding captive her perception.

The three men reasoned, whispered, shouted, soothed, all to no avail. At last words ran dry, and they could only watch in silence, feeling her pain burning into them like a brand.

John shook his head wearily. "There has got to be something we can do to calm her down. What haven't we tried yet?"

"Well, after I lost my foot, you gave me a lot of liquor," Connly said. "I don't know if it helped the pain much, but it made the time go by faster."

"You's think we should get heh drunk?" Everrett asked.

"I don't know." Connly gave a helpless shrug. "It's not gonna help her, but it might make her more calm. On the other hand, it could make her more confused than ever."

"I don't really think it is possible for her to be any more confused than she already is," John said. "I think it's worth a try, but it's up to you, Everrett."

Everrett regarded her for a minute. Too exhausted to be violent, Elsa lay there like a crumpled rag doll, softly moaning and crying and murmuring to herself as she spasmodically clenched and unclenched her hand in the long tangles of her sweat soaked hair. A sudden vision of the glorious creature he had made love to only the night before, flashed into Everrett's mind, and his heart took on such a leaden weight he would not have been surprised had it fallen from his chest and crashed on the floor at his feet. From that moment on, the rest of the night, and many nights after, took on a trancelike quality for Everrett, in which he no longer felt a man, but a numb spirit enslaved in a body of flesh.

He spread his hands in an ambiguous gesture. "I's got a little whiskey. Let's try and see ifen she'll drink it or not." Everrett disappeared down stairs and returned with a half full bottle. He gently raised Elsa up, and with considerable coaxing and patience, John succeeded in getting her to drink about half a glass.

Elsa was not used to strong liquor, and since she had eaten nothing all day, its effect was immediate. Her head slumped against Everrett's chest, and within minutes she got very quiet. She reached up, clutched onto the half open front of his shirt, and lay against him, motionless.

"At last," Everrett said. He kissed her burning forehead and looked up at the dragoons. "Shey's not gonna make it," he said sadly.

"I know," John's answer was soft.

"What did shey want to talk to you's about?" Everrett asked him.

"Her aunt. She's was so worried about her."

"Shey's still thinkin' about heh at a time like dis?" Everrett shook his head incredulously. He laid his cheek against her wet hair. "God only knows how much I's gonna miss you, woman."

He sat there holding her for about an hour. John and Connly sat down on the bed, and aside from Elsa's breathing, the room was soundless. Everrett moved a little to adjust his position, and she opened her eyes.

"Everrett?" she whispered.

"I's hehe, dahling."

Elsa looked straight at him for a second, and he could see recognition in her gaze. "I-I love—you," she said very slowly. She kept staring at him, but the expression in her wide eyes turned vacant, and then he realized she had stopped breathing.

Elsa's eyes had always said so much. He had looked into them whenever he had wanted to know what she was thinking, but now they just stared up at him blankly, and he knew they would remain expressionless forever. Never again would they reflect fear or pain, longing or dread. But neither would they radiate the trust, devotion, or love which is too deep for words to speak. Everrett could not bear their distant emptiness, so he laid her down and tenderly shut them.

Everrett picked up the whiskey bottle, still sitting open on the bureau, and drained it. He turned back towards Elsa, lying there peacefully, lost in a slumber from which he could never wake her, and wished with all his soul that he could share her sleep.

After John and Connly left to get a coffin, Everrett lay down beside Elsa and drew her still warm form into his arms, just as he had drawn her to him so many times before. His head was beginning to get hazy from the whiskey, and he must have dozed off, because when Everrett awoke, he was dead.

*   *   *   *   *

Before noon that day, they solemnly laid her in her final resting place, beneath the graceful boughs and trailing fronds of the immense weeping willow at the corner of Elsa's favorite horse pasture. The tree under which, she had once told Everrett, she used to play dolls as a little girl. After the men had thrown in flowers and filled the grave with dirt, they stood around awkwardly, staring at the brown mound they had just made.

"It seems like we ought to have minister or something," said John.

"Shey wasn't needin' one," Everrett responded. "Shey was harder on hehself dan de Almighty will be. But ifen you's want to say a prayer, well, she'd like dat."

John thought he would asphyxiate. His mind reeled. What was he to say? He glanced helplessly at Connly, who was standing in stiff reverence, his hands clasped in front of him, eyes on the ground. John cleared his throat.

"Lord, now let Thy servant depart in peace according to Thy word." He paused, groping for words, trying to remember what he had heard from chaplains praying over the graves of soldiers. "Receive Elsa into Your heavenly kingdom, and bless her always in the light of Thy countenance as she has blessed us so much. Give and it shall be given unto you. Lord, she has given so much in her life and she hasn't had a chance to receive nearly as much as we think she ought to have, so now that she's gone to Your country of peace, where she can never again be touched by war, or hate, or violence, see to it that she receives a good reward. In Christ's name, Amen."

"Dat was nice," Everrett said huskily.

The men stood silent for a few more moments, and then Everrett suggested that John and Connly probably needed to leave.

"Are you sure there is nothing more we can do for you?" asked Connly.

Everrett shook his head. "Dere is nothin' more to bey done."

Connly took John by the arm. "We should be returning to the army, Lieutenant," he said.

"Good-bye, Everrett," John placed his hand on Everrett's shoulder. "We can't tell you how sorry we are." His voice choked, and he couldn't finish what he wanted to say.

"Thanks." Everrett said the word to be polite, but there was no feeling to it. He woodenly shook hands with them both, and they slowly walked away towards their horses.

For many long minutes which stretched into hours, Everrett stood at the grave—stiff, erect, motionless—staring, sometimes into space, sometimes at the moist dirt at his feet. He did not speak and he did not cry. He simply stood, with his burly hands knotted into fists at his sides and the muscles in his arms taut, staring.

A Promise to Fulfill

The bloody war was almost over. The nation had been rent asunder till there was nothing left to tear. Victory would ultimately go to the North— that was apparent now—but when? Lee and his worn, hungry soldiers held on with unbelievable tenacity.

Near the end of March, Lincoln met with Generals Grant and Sherman at City Point to discuss the progress of the war and if it could be won without the horror of another pitched battle. Both generals were dubious; they must not underestimate Lee.

But then, only a few days later, at the Battle of Five Forks, Grant finally managed to break through Lee's defense and seized the railroads. This spelled doom for the key Confederate cities of Petersburg and Richmond. Upon receiving the news, Richmond flew into a riotous panic and fell easy prey when the Union troops marched in on April 3rd.

It was a proud day for the Yankees, and John and Connly were only slightly less joyful than the rest. As soldiers they had learned to carry resilience close to their hearts, leave the past where it was, and keep their eyes focused on the future.

But the war was not yet over. Lee hoped to salvage his army by merging forces with those of General Joseph E. Johnston in North Carolina. This, Grant was determined to prevent. John and his men were immediately dispatched, along with scores of similar cavalry groups, to raid supply wagons and cut off stragglers. Meanwhile, Grant led his strong, healthy, well-fed infantry to bar Lee's advance. He finally cornered the haggard Confederates near the village of Appomattox Court House. Realizing it was cruel to ask more of his bedraggled men to spill their blood for a lost cause, on April 9th 1865, Lee surrendered.

Although Grant himself professed sorrow at seeing the downfall of so valiant a foe, it was a time of intense rejoicing for the men who had fought so long and hard for this day. They had left family, friends, and home, they had suffered and bled, they had endured tortures of mind as well as body, they had staked everything dear to them, and now at last came the consummation of their efforts.

But their Southern brothers had fought just as hard, left loved ones just as dear, suffered and bled just as much, and staked their all on their hopes for victory. Now they were left with nothing but a devastating feeling of defeat as they returned home to nurse their wounds, rebuild what was left, or simply nurse their bitterness.

One man's joy was bought for another man's sorrow. One man's freedom was paid for with another man's life. Every shout of victory was followed by its echo of grief. They were inseparably intermingled.

There were those like John, who suddenly found their career ended and looked into the future with doubt and uncertainty. There were those like Connly, who faced the grim reality that their youth had been stunted in its prime, like a bud bitten by the frost, and their bodies would never be whole again. There were those like Everrett, who after having been the victim to cruel inhumanities, were left with nothing but bitter pain. And there were those like Lester Aldridge, who could find no place to run from their failure and guilt.

But at long last the time of destruction was over, and the season of rebuilding had come.

"Lieutenant! Lieutenant!"

"Yes, Tommy." John stepped to the doorway of his tent and smiled as he watched the eager young man running towards him.

"D-Did you hear the new, sir?" he panted. "General Lee is surrendering today at Wilmer Mclean's farm."

"You bet I heard," John grinned. "Look, here comes Sergeant Connly."

Tommy saluted. "Did you hear the news, sir?"

"Lee's surrendering!" Connly finished for him.

"Yes, sir. Excuse me please. I'm going to tell the others." Tommy threw another quick salute as he dashed off.

"Has it sunk in yet, John? Can you grasp what it means? The war is over. We won!"

"We sure did, Connly."

The two men threw their arms around each other in a bear hug. As they released their embrace, John put his hands on Connly's shoulders and held him out at arm's length. "We can both go back home—be with our families again. Ahh, but I'm gonna miss your face, Connly." John's voice was deep with emotion.

"Not anymore than I will yours," Connly answered. "So what is the first thing you'll do when you get there?"

"Well, I'm not going straight back to Maryland. First I'm going to check on Elsa's aunt like I promised her. So I guess it's more of Virginia for me."

"I'll go with you," Connly offered.

"Will you?" John was pleasantly surprised. "I don't know what I am going to do when I get there. Kind of dreading it actually, but I promised Elsa so I want to keep my word. It seemed like this was really important to her."

Even though it was not until May that the last segment of the rebel army surrendered in Louisiana, the war in Virginia was over. On April 28th, Lieutenant John Fairfield and Sergeant Arthur Connly were discharged and free to return home. While most of their comrades headed north, John and Connly saddled up and started out for an old plantation in the heart of Virginia.

They reached their destination mid-afternoon several days later. As they rode past the fierce stone lions guarding the gate, they tried to picture what they would find inside. Neither of them had ever seen Ingrid, and everything Elsa had ever told John about her had painted the mental picture of a very dour woman.

John had kept the letter Elsa had given him, and they read and reread it in hopes of preparing themselves for what they were about to encounter. But they still felt completely ill-equipped when John lifted the heavy brass knocker and banged on one of the double doors in the front of the house. No one answered, and before knocking again, the men paused to take in their surroundings.

The house was an enormous brick mansion. Six white pillars supported the balcony overhanging the long porch they were standing on. The yard had at one time been beautifully landscaped, although now the grass was long and the flowerbeds overrun with weeds. There was a large burnt circle on the ground and the ruins of a stone foundation where at one time a barn had no doubt stood.

"She might not be here," Connly said as he surveyed the desolation.

"I know," John replied. "She might have found relatives to go live with, or something like that." John look down towards his feet, where the contorted features of a gargoyle grimaced up at him. He grimaced back and knocked again, much louder this time. After several minutes, he thought he heard faint footsteps, and then the door creaked open just a crack.

The face peering out at them was pale and deeply lined. She looked them up and down and said in a dry, raspy voice, "Why are you here? There is absolutely nothing more to take."

"We haven't come as soldiers, ma'am," John answered. "We already won the war. We're here to see you, assuming you are Ingrid Chesterfield."

"What do you want with me?"

"Well, we'd like to come in first," he said.

The woman in the doorway hesitated. Finally, with a powerless look on her face, she stepped back from the door, but did not open it any farther. Taking this was as much of an invitation as they were going to get, the men proceeded in.

The house was dim and dusty inside. Broken pieces of furniture were strewn on the floor. The grand marble fireplace set into the wall beside them was cold and contained nothing but ashes. An oil lamp was set on the mantle, but the chimney lay in a pile of shattered glass on the floor.

John wasn't sure which was more pathetic, the havoc which had been reeked on the house or the fact that no attempt had been made to clean it up. Then he turned to study Ingrid and decided she was the most pathetic of all.

Her gray hair hung over her shoulder in a long, matted braid. Her sunken cheeks and the dark circles under her eyes made her appear much older than her forty-seven years. She was dressed in light green silk, which had no doubt been lovely at one time, but was now dirty and crumpled and hung loosely on her thin frame. The look in her eyes was one of unmitigated gloom and disillusionment.

"What do you want with me?" she asked again. Her tone was cold, but not without a hint of fear.

"Your niece sent us," John replied grimly.

"Elsa? Elsa sent you?" It was quite apparent how amazed she was. "Why?" she added hesitantly.

"Well, first let me introduce myself. I'm Lieutenant John Fairfield and this is Sergeant Arthur Connly."

Ingrid nodded. "If-if you want to sit down, there are a few chairs in the drawing room which are not broken," she said, somewhat collecting herself.

John and Connly followed her into the next room, and after they were seated, John said, "You may have heard of me. I'm the lieutenant whose life Elsa saved. I believe you banished her from your home on account of me."

Ingrid's face turned even paler than it already was. "And Elsa-Elsa sent you here?" She looked down at her lap and nervously twisted her hands.

"She did." John regarded her silently for a minute, trying to determine what Ingrid's attitude was and how hard he should be on her. He certainly felt like being very hard on her. But then he had come here at Elsa's request, for the purpose of helping Ingrid, although at present he was taking much more satisfaction in the thought of tarring and feathering her.

"How is Elsa?" Ingrid asked slowly.

"She is dead."

Ingrid looked up as her mouth dropped open. John stared back at her without saying a word.

Ingrid whispered, "Is she really?"

Both men nodded.

Ingrid put her hand over her eyes, and when she finally spoke, her voice was full of remorse. "I was so cruel to send her away as I did. She never did anything to deserve that. What happened?"

"She was murdered," Connly said. "By a Confederate Captain—a Captain Aldridge."

"Captain Aldridge?" Ingrid exclaimed. "Lester Aldridge? But-but he was in love with Elsa."

"He didn't act like it," John said severely.

"He killed her?" Ingrid was still in shock. "And to think that I tried to force her into marrying him," she moaned.

"It was an atrocious thing for you to try to do," John replied. "You realize that if you had not sent Elsa away, she would still be alive now?"

Ingrid nodded miserably. "So why are you here?" she asked again, and this time there was more than just a hint of fear in her voice.

"Because," John pulled Ingrid's worn letter out of his pocket and extended it to her, "Elsa gave me this. It was her dying wish that we see if you were alright and offer you assistance if you had need of it. We have come at her request. Believe me, there is no other reason I would be here."

Two tears ran down Ingrid's tired face. "From the day I brought Elsa to this house, I was heartless towards her. When she was grieving her father's death, I didn't even try to comfort her, and I always belittled everything that was dear to her. And I did try to force Aldridge on her, even though I knew she feared him. And…" Ingrid's voice broke, and she buried her face in her hands for a minute.

The ink on the letter lying in her lap began to run into unreadable blotches as her tears dripped onto it. After a moment, Ingrid composed herself and went on. "And it's like you said." She looked at John. "When I found out how she had helped you, I sent her away, and with nothing. I could have given her some money or something, but I didn't. She always wanted my approval, but I never gave it to her. And then she became friends with this black woman, Martha. She was the sister of Elsa's nurse, who had really been a mother to Elsa. And dreadful things happened to

Clara. I never gave Elsa any sympathy about that either. I just told her to forget about it, but she couldn't. So she became friends with this Martha. I always knew she was looking for a substitute mother. I could have been that to her, but I didn't even try," she said bitterly. "I could never forgive her father for seducing my young sister, and I treated Elsa as if it were her fault."

"Martha," John said. "Did you know she had a son named Everrett?"

Ingrid shook her head.

"Well, she did, and after you sent Elsa out with nothing, she married him."

Ingrid's mouth dropped open even further than when she had heard of Elsa's death. "A—a black man?" Ingrid breathed the words faintly as if afraid of anyone hearing them. "Oh, what have I done? Did I really force her to such depravity?"

"For pity's sake, he was half white," Connly said sharply. "We stayed with him while Elsa was dying, and he told us all about it. His father was a white plantation owner just like yourself. Only his mother, Martha, was black. Elsa loved him. And you should have seen the way he cared for her after she'd been shot, and the look in his eyes. No full blooded white man could possible have been more tender or more devoted to her. And I think it's despicable the way you act like it was some dastardly crime that she should have been with him. He gave her a lot more love than you ever did."

"I can imagine what you must think of me," Ingrid said. "An ugly, withered old woman, who has been nothing but cold and selfish all her life, now getting what she deserves. If the tables were reversed, I know I would feel nothing but contempt."

"Well, it doesn't really matter what we feel," John responded. "I came here at Elsa's request, and I intend to act as I believe she would have wanted."

Ingrid stared at her hands in her lap for awhile and finally said, "I would like to offer you some tea or something, but I don't have any."

"So what have you been living on?" Connly asked.

"What does it look like? We had one group of raiders after another. I hid some wine from them, so I lived on that for awhile. I even go out in the woods sometimes and see what I can find. I've eaten things that I thought nothing but a goat would eat. It still doesn't seem possible. My whole life I have had so much, and now, absolutely nothing."

"I'm surprised you haven't tried to clean it up in here. I'm sure you could have found some useful things in all this mess," John said.

"What's the point?" Ingrid shrugged. "Every time I started to try to salvage something of my life, they came again. I don't care anymore. I just want it to be over. I didn't think I would have lasted this long, but I underestimated the body's will to survive. I would have killed myself if I thought it would bring me any peace of mind, but I wonder if the thoughts which torment me will be silenced by the grave."

"What if you had a second chance? What if you could start over now and live a completely different life?" John watched closely to see how this question would affect her.

It was evidently a thought which had never suggested itself before, and she ran it through her mind carefully. "On the one hand, I really have no desire to live. I loath my very existence. For me, to live without pride is worse than death. But like I said, I have no assurance my torment will not continue beyond the grave, and for that reason I would embrace an opportunity to atone for a wasted life. But it's too late. I am defeated. There can be no such opportunity for me."

"But if you had such an opportunity, what would you do with it?" John pressed.

"I would endeavor to do it justice," Ingrid said slowly.

"Alright then, that settles it," John said with decision.

Ingrid and Connly both turned towards him with questioning looks. "What have you decided on?" inquired Connly.

John looked at Ingrid as he answered. "You are obviously doing most wretchedly. I promised Elsa I would look out for you, and I keep my promises. I am also going back to Maryland. So that leaves only one option; you will have to accompany me."

"Oh, no, I couldn't," Ingrid exclaimed. "Me go to Maryland with you? That is perfectly preposterous. I could never consent to such a thing."

"Excuse me, Madame, what part of what I just said is not clear to you?" John's tone was harsh. "Did I ask for your consent? Or did I inquire as to your opinion on the matter? Believe me, I find no more pleasure in the thought of your company than you do in mine, but as I told you, I gave Elsa my word. And I keep my word. I can not leave you here to waste away in, to use your own words, 'this God-forsaken house of ashes'. You are getting a chance for a second life. I will take you to my mother, and I'm sure she will be able to help us find some situation suitable for you. You can begin again, and the people in my home town need not know who you are or what your past has been. I just hope you will keep your word and endeavor to do this opportunity justice."

Ingrid simply stared at him and shook her head in mute astonishment.

John stood up. "We will leave first thing in the morning," he said, and before Ingrid had a chance to say anything more, he left the room with Connly close behind him.

The Journey Home

John and Connly spent the rest of the afternoon poking around what was left of the out buildings, until they found an old carriage in what they thought was repairable condition. It took them until dark to put it into something resembling working order. But even when they decided they had done all they could, they both eyed their handiwork with a good deal of pessimism.

John purposefully avoided Ingrid, partly because he really found her distasteful and couldn't look at her without thinking she was as responsible as anyone for Elsa's death. No matter how he tried, he couldn't stop wondering how different things would be now if only she had not disowned Elsa or tried to coerce her into a marriage with Aldridge. Elsa would most likely be alive and right here at this very moment, and everything would be so different for all of them.

John was also avoiding Ingrid because he didn't want to give her the opportunity to argue with him about going to Maryland. He wasn't sure if he could really compel her to come should she decide to be obstinate, and he was determined to return home immediately. But he was equally determined to keep his promise to Elsa. It had seemed simple enough when he had made it, yet now he almost wished he had come up with some way of avoiding the commitment.

As it was getting dark and he and Connly were concluding their work on the carriage, Connly asked, "Don't you think we ought to talk with Ingrid and make sure she is actually willing to come with us?"

"She's coming," John said, "even if I have to drag her the whole way myself."

Connly gave him a doubtful look. "This isn't the army anymore, John. You can't just assume someone will do something because you tell them to."

"Well, alright," John conceded, "if she won't come willingly, I'll have to think of some way of frightening her into it."

"Do you want me to talk to her?" Connly asked.

"Knock yourself out. Better you than me. Meanwhile, I'm going to town and see about scaring us up some dinner. I'm starved."

After John left, Connly proceeded into the house, and unable to locate Ingrid anywhere downstairs, made his way up the immense staircase, which was carpeted in a lovely light blue covered with dirty boot prints. He wondered how many soldiers just like himself had made their way up and down these stairs during raids. For the first time, Connly tried to imagine what it must feel like to be on the opposite end of a raid.

He began to search the second story. There were so many rooms. He tried one door after another, each opening into a scene of total devastation. He and John had never left a house looking this bad. Everything which had not been taken, had been broken. Even most of the windows were smashed.

The library contained several Confederate flags lying torn on the floor, and judging by the smell, they had been urinated on. Books were scattered far and wide, and hundreds of pages had been torn out and hurled about the room. The glass doors of the beautiful mahogany gun case were shattered, and there were bullet holes in the floor. No wonder in their songs the South always referred to the North as tyrants.

Connly shut the door and proceeded on. He finally found Ingrid in her bedroom. Her bed frame had been broken and the mattress torn open. Goose feathers were scattered everywhere. She was sitting on a stool facing the window and staring out at the western horizon where the faintest glow of sunset was still visible.

Connly cleared his throat to announce his presence. She slowly turned around to look at him. Her face was expressionless.

"I'm Arthur Connly," he said for lack of anything better.

"I know." After a minute Ingrid went on, "So why are you really here? And why does that Lieutenant Fairfield want me to go to Maryland with him?"

"I don't understand the situation all that well myself, but apparently your niece cared about you a good deal," he answered. "She was quite disturbed over that letter you wrote her. And Ingrid, when she was lying there horribly wounded, she couldn't stop worrying about you until John promised her he would come here and see after your well-being. As I'm sure you can see, I've lost my foot. Believe me, it hurt more than you can possibly imagine, and that fact that Elsa thought of you at all at such time should be sufficient proof that she loved you deeply."

"But Lieutenant Fairfield does not like me in the least," Ingrid objected. "I don't blame him for that. I hate myself. Why, for heaven's sake, does he want me to go somewhere with him? And why is he convinced that I will? I don't know him from Adam."

"I realize you don't know John, but I do, and let me tell you, of all the men I've ever met, there is none more committed to duty than he is. Everything in his entire life is about duty and honor, even down to who he marries. For that reason alone he will keep his promise to Elsa. But beyond that, John cared about Elsa in a more personal way. He felt he owed his life to her, and let's just say, if all of this hadn't happened, and if Elsa was still alive and here with you, it wouldn't surprise me a bit if John came here for the intention of taking Elsa away and marrying her himself. Her happiness was important to him. So if he promised her as she was dying, that he would come here and see after you, there is absolutely no way in the world that he won't keep that promise. Now you can be stubborn and refuse to go, but you won't get rid of John. You won't get rid of me either for that matter."

"I don't know whether to appreciate what you men are trying to do or hate you for it," Ingrid said shaking her head. "But look at me, Sergeant Connly. It is too late for me. I cannot start a new life no matter how many second or third or forth chances I am given."

"Well, you're in a better position to judge that than me," Connly said with a shrug. "But it's like I told you, John promised Elsa, and he is not going to stop giving you those second, third, and forth chances and forcing you to take them, so you might as well at least try."

They were both silent for a moment, and then Connly said, "And what about Elsa? I can tell you feel terrible about her death, as do we all. This was what she wanted, for you to try again. She wanted you to be happy and have as good a life as possible."

"I can't imagine why," Ingrid said gloomily.

"Do you want me to tell you about how she died? John and I were both there with Everrett and her."

Ingrid didn't answer.

"Well, I'm going to tell you about it. It is something I think you ought to hear." Connly proceeded to explain the circumstances leading up to Captain Aldridge shooting Elsa, in as full an extent as he knew. Ingrid listened with rapt attention.

"So after the doctor left, we all went to the bedroom and sat there with her that whole day and night. Of course all three of us tried to do everything we could think of for her. But, Ingrid, I truly wish you could have seen Everrett. He didn't want to leave her even long enough to go outside and use the convenience. He was so afraid she would need him, and he wouldn't be there. We kept telling him we'd take care of her, but he wouldn't leave the room until the doctor came back in the evening and ordered us all out. And since he couldn't have the doctor knowing he was her husband, he did as he said.

"Ingrid, imagine being married to someone and loving them with all your heart, and yet in front of the world having to pretend you're nothing more than their servant. I dare say, there are very few men or women in this world who would willing put themselves in such a position. I know what your thinking; I can see it in your face. You think he came upon her in a time of need, saw his opportunity and took advantage. John thought the same thing at first. But if anyone got the short end of the stick in this deal, it was Everrett. He spent nine short months with Elsa, and now he's going to miss her and grieve for her for the remainder of his life. If that's not a raw deal, I'd like to know what is.

"So after the doctor left again, Elsa was awake and wanted to talk with Everrett alone, and when she was done, she insisted on speaking with John alone. All she wanted to talk about was you, how much she wished she could help you and how sad she was about your unhappiness. And she couldn't rest until John promised her he'd come when the war was over."

Ingrid's cheeks were wet as she listened to Connly. "I don't know why. I don't know why," she murmured.

"Everrett said about the same thing when he found out why she was so anxious to speak to John," Connly said dryly. "But after she got done talking with both of them, she got this terrible hot fever all of a sudden. I have never in my life felt a person that hot. And Elsa was so small. The doc said she just didn't have what it took to fight something like that."

Ingrid held up her hand to stop him. "You've said enough," she moaned.

"No, I haven't. I'm going to tell you the whole thing. I know you want to hear it even less than I want to tell it. But I'm going to tell you the whole thing, and even after you've listened to every word, you'll only have the faintest idea how painful it was.

"So when Elsa started burning up like that, she got awful delirious. She started carrying on something dreadful. She didn't know who any of us were, and she kept crying and saying things like, 'No, don't. Stop, please, stop. Let him down. We'll give you anything you want, just stop. How could you? How could you?'. I don't know what she meant, but she was absolutely desperate."

"I know what she meant," Ingrid said tearfully.

"Then she got afraid of everyone of us, even Everrett, and starts trying to hit, and kick, and scratch us to pieces. The doctor had said we had to keep her still so she wouldn't start bleeding again. So we had to hold her down, but every time we'd touch her, she'd scream like we were the devil come to carry her off. Oh, Ingrid, it was horrible. She was so afraid, and no matter what we said or did, we couldn't convince her she was safe.

"Poor Everrett just put his head in his hands and keeps saying it's all his fault for leaving her alone. And actually he is the least responsible for what happened. So finally none of us could stand it anymore, so John got her to drink a glass of whiskey, and Everrett took her in his arms, and she just slumped against him and was knocked out. And he sits there for a solid hour, not moving a muscle for fear of waking her up, and when he finally moves, she opens her eyes and says she loves him. That was the end."

When Connly was finished, all was quiet in the room except for the sound of Ingrid sniffling. His leg was hurting from standing so long, so went to lean against the wall and waited for Ingrid to compose herself. When he started talking again, his voice was gentle. "You probably think I told you all this to hurt you, but that's not the reason. I want you to understand the hell she went through, and we went through with her, so you will know what I mean when I tell you that it was her dying wish for you to be helped. John promised her that he would, and every dreadful minute he spent watching her suffer reinforced that promise until it was forged into his very soul. If you have any regard for her memory at all, you will help him to keep it."

Ingrid bit her lip as she nodded. "It is a completely ridiculous idea, but I'll go. Now, please, leave me alone."

Connly slowly thumped his way across the floor and shut the door quietly behind him. He went out to the porch and sat down on the steps to wait for John.

The plan the men devised for their journey, was to travel by carriage as far as Kentucky, assuming they could hold it together that long. When they reached Connly's home, they would abandon the old rig and leave the horses with Connly while John and Ingrid continued on to Maryland vie train.

The first part of this course of action they accomplished successfully, although it did take longer than either soldier anticipated, and by the time they reached their first destination, they were all exhausted and rubbed rather raw by each other's company.

John and Ingrid did come to the mutual understanding that the other was not a devil, but that concession was about as far as their relationship progressed. Being able to spend a few days in the haven of Rebecca's smile was a welcome change for all of them.

Connly's parents accepted Ingrid's presence as if she were a relative they had never met, while she found the attention his sisters paid her quite diverting, if somewhat annoying. Every experience that had happened since she met John and Connly was like something brand new. Ingrid couldn't say she had any happiness about the prospect of a new life, but it was happening nonetheless, and now that all of her preconceived ideas about people and life in general no longer proved any support to her, she found the world quite a different place.

Since she was no longer viewing people through the glass of haughty prejudice, it seemed everyone she met was unlike any she had known before. It was a very overwhelming time to say the least. Ingrid no longer even knew who she was and thought she had probably shed more tears in the last several weeks than in the entirety of her former life.

John and Connly made no secret of the situation surrounding Ingrid's accompanying them, and Everrett's name came up in conversation with a frequency Ingrid found very disturbing. Of all the people in the world, he was the one she wanted the least to think about. One evening after dinner, when they all had retired to the parlor to relax a little before bed, the topic came up again.

Rebecca had made the comment, "He is a man whose pain must leave him with nothing but emptiness."

Anna, whom they did not think was listening to the discussion, looked up from the paper dolls she was playing with in front of the fireplace and said, "How can pain be empty? If it was empty that would mean it was all gone and wouldn't hurt anymore."

"But pain isn't like that, Anna," Connly explained. "When I got my foot blown off, it hurt like blaz—well, it hurt an awful lot. But then I came home to all of you, and I was full of hope that it would heal and plans for all the thing I was gonna do when it did, so my pain wasn't empty. Do you see what I mean?"

"Kinda," she wrinkled her small nose.

"But for Everrett it isn't like that," he continued. "Elsa is dead, and he knows that no matter what happens, that is not going to change. He is all alone, and I doubt if he sees anything in the future to be hopeful about. Now that is an empty pain, and that is the worst kind there is."

"I know what that is like," Ingrid said despondently.

287

"Then you have something in common with Everrett," John replied.

Ingrid looked startled. The supposition that she might actually have something in common with a former slave, was entirely new to her and not particularly welcome. "Our situations are vastly different," she countered.

"The circumstances of your lives are vastly different," Rebecca assented, looking up from her knitting, "but different processes may end in the same outcome. Your life has been shattered, as has his, and you both find yourselves in a position with no option other than to begin again. I think pain speaks a universal language and bears no regard for class."

Ingrid ruminated on the idea without responding.

"I have been planning to call on him before we leave for Maryland," John said slowly. "Perhaps you would wish to accompany me."

"I do not consider that a good plan," Ingrid objected. "What could I possibly say to him?"

"What can I possibly say to him?" John asked.

Ingrid reflected a moment and finally said, "What can anyone say to him?"

"John, why don't you invite him to dinner?" suggested Rebecca, who thought the state of the world would be vastly improved if everyone where to sit down and eat a delicious meal together.

John looked at Connly. "Do you think he would come?"

"One way to find out," the younger man responded.

As the two men rode over the next day, they speculated on what Everrett's reaction would be to seeing them again. But when they finally found him in the barn, he did not have much of a response to their greeting at all.

He nodded to them and said, "Lieutenant. Connly." That was all.

For a moment there was nothing but an oppressive silence filling the barn. Everrett was in the middle of mucking out Charcoal's stall when John and Connly entered and after acknowledging their presence he just stood there, holding his pitchfork and looking their direction but not straight at them. John and Connly walked a little closer but then stopped, unsure what the proper etiquette was for such a situation and not wanting to violate it if there was any.

"The war's finally over," John said slowly. "Your people are finally free now."

"Are dey?" he asked.

"Yes, they are," John answered, unsure what to make of the question.

"Does you think my people will eveh *truly* bey free?" Everrett asked rhetorically.

John drew a long breath while Connly replied for him. "You mean free from hate and prejudice, not just from their masters?"

"Will we eveh bey able just to live ouh lives like anyone else?"

"I sincerely hope so," John said, stepping a little closer.

Everrett shook his head. "We's marked people, like a thief or a murderer with his crime branded onto his fohehead, or like dose whores who's had to wear de scarlet letteh on dere breast. We's can't escape it. Always we will bey punished foh a crime we's didn't commit. And anyone who dares to treat us like an equal will beah de punishment too."

"Someday," Connly said. "It has taken a long time for us to get this far, but someday, little by little."

Everrett gave half a shrug. "Too late foh me. And too late foh her." He stared out the open barn doorway. "Askin' her to marry me was like signin' her death warrant. If only I's neveh had, shey'd bey alive now, and den you's could'a married her." Everrett looked at John, and before he could object, went on. "Don't deny dat thought entered youh mind. You's might think I's a stupid black man, but I's seen de way you's looked at her, and I's seen de way you's looked at me. I know what you was thinkin'. And maybe you was right."

"Don't blame yourself for what happened," John objected. "Of all of us you are the least responsible."

"I know. I know. But you's don't undehstand. I's always promised her dat I would protect her. I knew I's couldn't give her money, or social standing, or any easy life." Everrett shoved the pitchfork through the dirty straw and into the boards of the barn floor as far as it would go. "But dat was de one thing I's thought I could give her, and it was somethin' shey wanted vehy much. I's should have made heh come with us back to de cave. I's should neveh have left her. I's should neveh have been born with black skin foh dat matter. Can't you's see? If I wasn't black, I's would have stayed at de house, Elsa would have taken you's to de cave, and dat damn Captain Aldridge wouldn't have had de chance to kill heh."

"But Elsa loved you, and she wanted to be with you," Connly reminded him.

"Shey did. And I's brought her happiness, but," Everrett's voice turned from gloomy to fierce in that one word, "but, it was all foh nothin'."

That simple statement encompassed so many thoughts he couldn't bear to put into words. He had never really loved anyone before. He had cared about Martha a good deal, but it wasn't the kind of love that eats your heart out. And there had been other women before Elsa, slave women who admired his manly body and hoped that if they slept with him they could find their way into his heart and he would eventually buy their freedom. He had enjoyed some of their company, but none of them had ever won his affection. And when he finally had the money and used it to buy Martha rather than one of them, well, their ardor wasn't quite so strong anymore.

He was never quite sure how he had gotten up the courage to ask Elsa to marry him. It wasn't love, but in addition to caring about her well-being, there was something he found strangely attractive about her. Perhaps it was lure of the forbidden. Perhaps he had wanted to prove to himself that he could if he wanted to. At any rate, he hadn't really expected her to say yes, but she had, and then there they were.

And he certainly didn't have any complaints with the arrangement, especially after she made it clear she wanted physical intimacy with him. To be wanted by anyone is always quite flattering, but perhaps more so because he had always been told no possible way in the world a white woman could ever desire him. But she did, and it was quite pleasing. But even when he realized he was growing very fond of her, the possibility of truly loving her never occurred to him. He didn't think he was capable of it.

And then it had happened. He didn't know when, and he didn't how. But at some point he realized that what he felt for her went far beyond physical desire, or fondness, or caring. There was something very passionate inside him that wanted her so much, while the desire to protect her and make her happy was so acute that it felt almost as if it would kill him if he couldn't. And he didn't ever want to be apart from her for even one single day. He wanted desperately to take care of her and be there should she ever need him. When he began to be aware how hard she tried everyday to please him and how much his approval meant to her, it only made that passion grow to even more overwhelming levels.

But even then, he didn't think he would ever admit it. Somehow putting it into words made it too dangerously real, and he wasn't ready for that. But then that night when Elsa couldn't sleep and was so dejected, although it frightened him, he couldn't help but tell her. Seeing how happy it made her only heightened the intensity of his emotions. But then, the very next day she was taken from him. Admitting that he loved her did make it real, but as soon as it was real, she was torn away. By then it was too late, the heart he thought he didn't have, was smashed into a hundred different pieces, each one of them hurting desperately.

Love was some vicious monster, trying to seduce him into its trap. His whole life he had escaped it, clinging to hate as his defense and building so many walls around his heart he no longer thought he even had one. But somehow, a siren's song had permeated through all his defenses and beguiled him. And the very instant he succumbed, the trap sprung and he was crushed.

"Well, I'm on my way back to Maryland, and I wanted to see you before I went." John's voice broke into his thoughts. "Connly's mother was hoping you'd come over for dinner."

Everett looked startled. "Me come oveh foh dinner?"

"We would be much obliged if you would," Connly answered.

"I's don't know," Everett mumbled.

"Come on," John urged. "You said you wanted to just live your life like anyone else. That's what we want for you too. Now just come over and for one evening try to think about something other than all the tragedy that has happened."

Everett gave an "I don't care" shrug. "Alright, ifen it strikes your fancy."

"There is one other thing," John said. "There is something I think you ought to have."

Everrett watched silently as John unbuckled the black leather holster from around his waist and handed it to him. "Elsa gave this to me. It belonged to her father," John went on quietly. "It is a very fine gun; it's served me well."

Everrett slowly pulled the pistol from the holster and studied the gleaming silver eagle inlaid in its handle. He didn't know why, but his hands began to tremble at the sight of it.

Seeing his agitation, John and Connly excused themselves.

As soon as they were gone, Everrett sunk down onto the straw covered floor, his back leaning against one of the massive timbers supporting the barn. He turned the gun over and over in his hands, and although his eyes remained dry, his broad shoulders began to shake with silent sobs, till his hands were quivering so badly the pistol slipped from his grasp. Everrett shut his eyes tightly and pressed his back hard against the stout beam as tremor after tremor of unrelenting grief shuddered through his frame.

Dinner Conversation

A great hustle and bustle ensued in the Connly household. Rebecca was one of those wonderful women who finds meaning to her life by taking care of others, and perhaps more importantly, had aptitude for doing so. But even she felt somewhat overwhelmed by the difficulty of how to make Everett truly feel welcomed, but it was a challenge she was ready to rise to. She wanted everything to be very nice so he would feel they considered it an honor to have his company. Then again, she wanted everything to be very casual so he wouldn't feel uncomfortable.

Every single detail had to be considered. For instance, the seating, she wanted to be sure to place Everett and Ingrid in such a way that neither of them would be obliged to look at the other throughout the course of the meal, should they choose not to do so. She also had the feeling that Everett might want to be positioned in such a way that there was a clear path between him and the door, so as not to feel trapped.

Ingrid wanted to help with the preparations but realized she knew absolutely nothing about cooking or housework of any kind. But she did demonstrate for Anna and Muriel how to fold the napkins into unique creations, resembling fans, crowns and flowers. When they were done with that, Muriel taught her how to churn cream into butter, while Anna showed her how to peel potatoes.

She felt so foolish. Simple things that even a child could do, and she, a woman in her forties, had no clue. She watched Rebecca with amazement mixed with envy. She was so capable, so kind, and apparently so happy. Ingrid had always been quite proud of her education and breeding, but now she wondered how her whole life she could have thought she knew so much when she was actually ignorant of such rudimentary skills.

It wasn't that she didn't want to learn, but the process was so humiliating, and she felt so painfully out of place, that she really began to wish she had stayed back in her desolate Virginia mansion and never allowed John and Connly to cajole her into coming with them. This feeling suddenly grew much stronger after she commented to John, "It comes as quite a surprise to me that Everrett Trenton is willing to come anywhere where he knows he will be forced to endure my company."

"Well, I might have forgotten to mention that to him," John admitted.

Connly looked at John sharply with a smile lurking behind his lips. "We didn't *forget* to mention it."

"It seemed too much to say all at once," John explained. "You know, one thing at a time."

Ingrid stared at John in shock while her wan complexion turned even grayer. "What were you thinking? Lieutenant, ever since I met you, you have been unbelievably full of bad ideas. Everything from me coming with you, to riding all this way in that dreadful carriage, to suggesting I speak to that man at all, but I thought even you had more prudence than this. What do think to accomplish by this evening? It will be nothing but disastrous."

"I had thought perhaps you might tell him how sorry you are over Elsa's death," John replied. "And how much you wish you had the opportunity to do things differently. Those are things you really ought to say to him."

"And perhaps I would if I thought he was willing to speak to me," Ingrid said. "But next to Captain Aldridge, I am most likely the last person on the face of the earth whom he wishes to see. You should not have invited him over while withholding the information that I would be here. I am extremely angry with you."

Ingrid felt so impotent and somewhat afraid. Anger was the strongest defense she knew. She was so used to commanding people and having them fear her wrath, but now even that didn't seem to mean anything, because John just gave her the terse response, "Go ahead and be angry then; a lot of people are these days."

Ingrid rushed from the house and into the backyard. The air was cool for April, and the sky overcast. A slight wind flapped her billowing skirts about her legs, but she didn't notice. Ingrid walked briskly away from the house until she came to an old apple tree behind the barn. It was a little past the peak of its bloom, and the ground beneath was covered with velvety, pale pink petals. She knelt and began to scoop them up and watch them float back down as they sifted between her open fingers. The scent of the blossoms was sweetly soothing, and as its gentle touch soothed her jaded emotions, Ingrid stopped trying to quell the tears that wanted to come.

Her life had turned out to be such a horrible disappointment, and she was sorry for so many things. She missed her husband, Albert, more than she had ever admitted. Ingrid had always wanted to be married. She had always wanted to be beautiful, admired, and loved like her younger sister. But she never had been. Then finally, when she thought she was destined to be an old maid forever, Albert had asked her. But then there had to be a war, and after so short a time she lost him and was alone again.

There had been Elsa, she could have been friends with her. But she couldn't admit to being lonely; she couldn't admit to needing anyone. She was strong, and it was so much easier to be proud then to be hurt, so much easier to be domineering than to be vulnerable. But now all her pride had turned to humiliation, and she wasn't strong anymore, while she was dreadfully lonely.

Ingrid was sorry, and she would do things differently if only she could turn back the hands of time and undo the past. John said he was giving her a second chance, but this wasn't the chance she needed. The only chance that would do her any good would be an opportunity to change what had already been done.

She wasn't aware of anyone's presence until a sweet voice said, "What's wrong?" Ingrid looked over her shoulder and saw Anna standing there. "I didn't mean to sneak up on you," the young girl went on. "I came out to pick some apple flowers to put on the table. But why are you crying? Did you get hurt?"

Normally Ingrid would have scolded the girl for intruding on her, but now she simply nodded. "I did get hurt, and what is worse, I hurt other people. I wish I could take it back, but it is too late. And I don't want to see Everrett tonight."

"Why not? Is he scary?"

"He is to me."

"Why?"

Ingrid couldn't believe she was discussing such things with a little girl, but it felt good to talk with someone—someone who wasn't judging her—someone who didn't have distain written behind the politeness in their eyes. "Because," she said sadly, "Everrett had a wife named Elsa, and she died."

"I know. Arthur told me about that," Anna interjected. "You're crying because you're Elsa's aunt and you're sad she died?"

"Elsa used to live with me because her mother and father were dead," Ingrid said slowly, "But I wasn't nice to her. I was quite mean really. And now I wish I could take it back, but I can't."

"And you think Everrett will be mad at you because you were mean?" Anna asked.

Ingrid nodded miserably. "I'm certain of it. And John wants me to go to Maryland with him, and I am sure those people won't like me either. I have always been ugly and mean, and people have never liked me." As she listened to her own words, Ingrid felt like she was a small girl again, watching her pretty little sister get all the attention, while she vowed to herself that she didn't need anyone.

"I like you," Anna said. "I don't think you're mean. Muriel likes you too. And we think your dresses are very pretty, except for the black one," she added in the interest of truthfulness.

Ingrid smiled slightly. "I am glad you do not find me mean."

"And I like showing you how to do things. I've never taught a grown up lady anything before. I wish you could stay here and not go to Mary's land with John. I like John, but he isn't half as much fun as Arthur. Arthur's my brother, you know. Oops, I 'most forgot to pick the flowers.

296

You could help me," she suggested, " 'cause the prettiest ones are too high for me to reach."

Ingrid stood up and dried her eyes. "I would like to help you," she said softly.

It was quarter to six, dinner was ready, and everyone was speculating as to whether or not Everrett would really come. The sky was growing darker, promising rain soon. Perhaps Everrett found the weather a convenient excuse not to venture out. All day, Rebecca had been trying to imagine herself in Everrett's shoes. What was he thinking? How would it feel to him to enter their home and eat with them? Perhaps it was too much. He certainly couldn't be blamed if he distrusted everyone.

"Someone's coming in the lane," Anna announced from her position, peering out the window. "He's black, and he's riding a black horse."

"That's wonderful, Anna, but do come away from the window. It's not polite to stare," Rebecca said.

"And once he comes inside, don't stare at him then either," Muriel added as she gave her sister a helpful tug away from the window.

John, Connly and the latter's father, stepped out onto the porch to greet Everrett, while Ingrid disappeared into the kitchen. In a few minutes the men entered, minus Connly who was taking Charcoal to the barn. Anna couldn't help but stare a little bit. After as much as everyone had been talking about Everrett, she was very intrigued. What did a man with an empty pain look like?

From a discreet distance she studied him. Everrett was not terribly dark for an African. But his eyes were a brown so deep they were almost ebony. He was very tall, and his shoulders exceptionally broad. He had lost weight during the last several months, revealing with stark definition each muscle stretched over his large frame. He had not cut his hair recently either, leaving it to stick out in unruly curls like a thick black mane, increasing the wild aura surrounding him.

Anna watched with fascination the way she could see each tough sinew in his arm and neck move with him as he turned. She didn't think she had ever seen a man like him before. Connly and her father were both strong enough, but slightly built. John on the other hand was taller, but not so broad. Everrett was a giant built of nothing but bones and muscles. Anna could have stood there all evening, riveted to the floor, just watching him, but her mother's voice summoning her to come sit down, called her out of her trance.

From the kitchen doorway, Ingrid was also studying Everrett. She observed all that Anna had, but it was his face that interested her the most. It wasn't friendly, but then again it wasn't unpleasant to look at either. From a completely objective point of view, Everrett was a fine specimen of the masculine body. It was not completely unthinkable that Elsa had been attracted to him she decided. But try as she would to read his body language, Ingrid could tell nothing. He remained uniquely expressionless. She had not expected that.

The group was congregating around the table. Everrett had not seen such a dinner since his days with the Quakers. Next to Anna's pitcher of apple blossoms in the center, was a large platter of crispy fried chicken. There were heaps of creamy mashed potatoes set beside the fresh churned butter, salad made with greens picked fresh from the garden, canned corn, and Mrs. Connly's specialty, fluffy baking powder biscuits served with spiced plum preserves. As everyone began to find their seats, Everrett noticed Ingrid. He had been introduced to all of them except her.

Rebecca saw them looking at one another and hurried over. "Everrett, this is Ingrid, she has been staying with us for a few days." Ingrid gave him a very slight curtsey, although it stabbed her like a knife to do it. Never, even in her nightmares, had she thought the day would come when her humiliation would be this complete. She kept her eyes lowered to avoid the intent stare he was directing at her.

"Ingrid," he said slowly. "Dat is not a vehy common name. Where did you's come here from?"

Ingrid gave John a sharp glance, and he stepped over and placed his hand lightly on Everrett's arm. "This is Elsa's aunt," he said in a low voice.

Everrett's posture was always erect, but it suddenly became much stiffer, while the muscles in his arms visibly rippled as he tensed them. "Why is shey hehe?" He directed his question to John.

"You remember the letter she wrote Elsa," John replied. "And when

Elsa wanted to speak to me that last day, I promised her that I would see after Ingrid. It was terribly important to her. You know that."

Ingrid could feel Everrett's dark eyes boring right into her. "Damn you!" he said. His voice was low, but there was no mistaking the burning passion he was restraining behind it.

Rebecca turned towards her daughters. "Girls, take the potato peelings out to the chickens and check to see if they've laid anymore eggs. Hurry now." She shooed them off. Anna stood up reluctantly. She wanted so badly to see what Everrett would do. He was larger than life, a fierce, dark giant of strength. She kept her eyes fixed on him as Muriel grabbed her hand and pulled her out the door.

Ingrid didn't reply to Everrett's words, so he went on. "You's think you can spend youh life carin' foh no one but youhself and treat Elsa like a piece ob dirt until de moment you's in trouble, den you turn to heh with youh sad letteh and youh tears. You's knew what Elsa was like. You's knew shey was kind and gentle and easy to take advantage of. And dat's all shey was to you, something to use when you's could and toss away when you's couldn't."

"But I regretted the way I lived my life. That is why I wrote Elsa." Ingrid objected to his scathing remarks.

"You's knew you could make Elsa believe dat. And you's knew shey would give you anything shey had. But you's didn't count on me. You hoped shey was alone, and dat afteh you's kicked heh out like shey was scum, dat shey'd come back and take cahe of you. And shey would have too, but I's can see through a woman like you."

Everrett's words enflamed her, and before Ingrid realized it, her former instincts had taken over. How dare a Negro speak to her like this? She drew herself up haughtily, although it was useless, for there was no possible way that she could look down on Everrett. "And you think that you were her saviour?" Ingrid burst out, "that you protected her from the wiles of an evil woman like me? How dare you ever have touched her? I know you are free now, but once you were a slave, the son of a slave, an illegitimate son at that, and Elsa, the niece of a Chesterfield. And you presumed to marry her. You should be grateful you haven't been hung for that."

John groaned inside. Things could hardly have been going worse. What had he been thinking? Promise or no promise he should have left this witch in her ruined castle.

Everrett reached out and took Ingrid by the shoulders, jerking her forward so her face was only about eighteen inches away from his own.

Rebecca was about to intervene, but Connly stopped her. "He won't hurt her," he whispered.

Connly was right. Everrett's hands were as rigid as steal clamps, but he wasn't squeezing Ingrid. "I hate you," he said. His words were calm and deliberate, but so cold Ingrid shivered involuntarily. "I hate you foh de way you treated heh. I hate you foh tryin' to marry heh to de bastard dat murdered her. But most of all I hate you foh de way you's tried to control her and fill her with guilt so dat even in de last hours of heh life shey couldn't rest. And de only reason you's in one piece right now is 'cause, only heaven knows why, shey loved you. But I hope you burn in hell." Everrett released Ingrid and stepped back.

It was when Everrett said that Elsa had loved her, Ingrid's resentment suddenly cooled, and she regretted the words she had just spoken. She covered her face with her hands. Everyone just stood there like so many statues. Everrett's blood was coursing through his veins with the force of a waterfall, but he did feel a sense of relief now that he spoken some of the words which had been blazing inside his mind ever since the day Elsa died.

Ingrid lowered her hands. "I know you won't believe me," she said contritely, "but I am sorry, sorry that Elsa's dead, sorry that I tried to marry her to Aldridge, sorry that I've lived a self-absorbed life. I will never be able to countenance the inter-marriage of races, but I had no right to speak. I am certain you were better to Elsa than I ever was. If I could do my life over, I would live so differently." Ingrid looked pleadingly into his face. "I really would. I hope you can at least believe that."

Everrett looked at her contemptuously, but said nothing more.

The girls burst back into the room just as a downpour started outside. They all turned to look out the window at the rain spattering against the glass. Rebecca turned towards Everrett, "I know you're upset, but do stay and eat with us anyway. You don't want to go out in rain like that. Ingrid will sit on the other side of me, and as plump as I am, you won't be able to see a thing of her."

Everrett hesitated. He felt very much like leaving right now, and he didn't care a hoot about the rain. But dinner did smell very good. It had been years since he ate such a meal. On Christmas Elsa had attempted to cook up something resembling a feast, and it had been satisfying to them, but she really didn't know how to cook.

"Come on," Rebecca took his arm. "Look at you. You're so thin. It would be a crime if I didn't feed you." Everrett looked down at her and was arrested by her warm, motherly smile. It had been so, so long since anyone had looked at him like that. And he couldn't resist.

The Future

The next day John boarded the train for Maryland—alone. Anna had spoken to her mother about Ingrid, and Rebecca convinced everyone concerned that was best if Ingrid stayed with them for awhile. Ingrid felt considerable relief with the prospect. She liked Rebecca and the girls, and if she must learn to begin all over, she could think of no one she would rather have as teachers.

It was late evening by the time John's train arrived in his hometown station, and before it had barely halted, he was leaping off. Not a fragment of the anxiety that brooded over the wooden platform the last time he had occasion to walk it, lingered there now as he eagerly scanned the sea of expectant parents and siblings, wives and children, who were gathered to greet their returning loved ones.

Was that his mother over there? Her hair must have turned completely gray. But there was his father standing beside her—no mistaking his tall frame. John joyfully elbowed his way through the crowd.

"Johnny!" His mother's arms flew around his neck. Her eyes were glistening like two stars. "God has answered my prayers and brought you back safe and sound. Oh, John!"

John rubbed her back as he planted light kisses on her forehead.

"Welcome home, son! Welcome home," his father exclaimed, punctuating his greeting with hearty claps on the shoulder.

John caught his father's hand and pumped it vigorously. "Oh, Dad, Mother, it's so good to be with you again. Boys, how have you been, fellows?" John turned his attention to his younger brothers.

"Howdy, Lieutenant." Curtis' voice had grown amazingly deep during his absence. John hugged him. "You've grown like a weed. You'll be as tall as me soon. What have you been eating while I was away? Must be better than hard tack and beans. Oh, but Lawrence, don't tell me you forgot how to talk while I was away," John said as he caught sight of his youngest brother hanging back shyly. Scooping him up, John thumped him heartily on the back, an indignity which the boy tolerated only because John was at present a household celebrity.

"Daisy had a calf," he suddenly blurted out. "It was a bull. I named him John, and Dad said we don't have to butcher him with a name like that but can save him for breeding since Hector's 'most too old. I named him that so that if you got shot we'd have something to remember you by. Oops." He clapped his hand over his mouth. "Mother said I wasn't supposed to talk about you getting shot."

"My goodness, all that out of a boy that I didn't think could talk. If I had only known that my name would be perpetuated by the bovine species, I would have rested much better all that time I was away." John erupted into laughter, and the rest of his family joined in.

When their merriment had subsided, John noticed his mother's attention was diverted across the platform. He followed her gaze, and it led him straight to Elizabeth. She looked more grown up than he remembered her. She was wearing a tight brown bodice and skirt, the lines neatly tailored to fit her curves. Her hat was green with a long feather, and she was flushed, making her face look very alive against the dark brown backdrop of her dress. She was watching him, obviously uncertain as to whether to approach or not.

John quickly began to elbow his way through the crowd again. She met him halfway. Their eyes met, and for a second they both froze. "I didn't know if I ought to come, but I did want to see that you'd returned safely," she said.

Her voice ran over him like cool water, sending tingles up his spine. It was absolutely beautiful. How could he have not noticed that before?

"I don't want to interfere with your reunion with your family," she continued. But before she could go on, John pulled her into his arms and began to cover her wonderful face with kisses. It was the first time he could ever remember making a spur of the moment decision based on passion rather than logic, and it felt unbelievably good.

For weeks John was a family and town hero, but somehow he didn't seem to fit back into life on the farm. Curtis had grown into his shoes as his father's right hand man, and John was fast discovering how little his affinity for cows really was, including his namesake. No matter how his family tried to make room for him, John knew the spot he had once occupied had long since vanished. After being gone four years, life could never be as it had been. But then he really didn't want it to.

So John turned to his old hobby of wood working and soon took a job with a carpenter. He had the patience and precision necessary for the work, and it wasn't long before he was turning out tables, chairs, chests, and desks in fine style. In time he went into business for himself.

During the four years he had been gone, Elizabeth had never once turned her attentions to anyone else and was more than happy to accept when he began courting her in earnest. It was only eight months after John laid by his uniform forever, that the church bells rang out merrily across the countryside, announcing John Fairfield's wedding day.

It was a bright December morning just two weeks before Christmas. Elizabeth's brown eyes were sparkling as brightly as the snow diamonds dancing in the sunlight over the white earth. Inside the church, all was spit and polish, pine boughs and candles.

As John slipped his silver ring onto Elizabeth's finger, it seemed as if it had always been meant to be there. Its chaste simplicity and honest charm were descriptive of the woman standing beside him.

"Thank you, dear. Thank you for waiting for me so long," he whispered as he bent his head down to hers.

Elizabeth didn't say anything, but her answer was written on her face, and John knew that he had found a woman whose faithfulness and love he need never doubt. A feeling of contentment and rest enveloped him as he realized with certainty there was no one else in the whole world he would rather spend his life with.

*   *   *   *   *

Back in Kentucky, Ingrid was surprised by how fast the Connly's home began to feel like her own. Rebecca's ability to spread comfort and graciousness was unparalleled, and little by little Ingrid began to change, to find out what it meant to be loved and what joy there was in giving it.

Much to her surprise, the day would come about two years later, when she was no longer the pupil but the teacher. She took a position at a girls' academy in Richmond, where she did credit to her profession and was always quick to spot when a bitter, love-hungry girl entered her classroom. Drawing from the memories of her own cold, hungry soul, she became both friend and mentor to many. During the holidays and summers she always went back to Connly's family, who had now become her own. She watched Anna and Muriel grow into lovely young women and thanked God she had a second chance to be a kind and loving aunt.

Rebecca took a special motherly concern in Everrett, doing everything within her power to bring a ray of happiness back into his life. But while Everrett liked Rebecca very much, and developed with Connly about as close a friendship as he ever did with anyone, the pain in his eyes did not recede, and as the summer slipped away, the ache in his heart only grew deeper with each passing day.

Anna and Muriel did not warm to him either as they had to John and Ingrid. They always remained a little awed in his presence. And it wasn't because he was black. There was something about him which remained always frigid and distant. He never let down his guard.

Occasionally he would go spend the day with the Connly's, shoeing their horses and such, and Arthur frequently returned the favor. One day near the end of Autumn, Everrett had decided the barn needed a fresh coat of paint before winter, and Connly was over helping him apply it, when out of the blue Everrett asked. "Has you's eveh thought of gettin' youh own fahm?"

"I would really like to get my own horse farm some day," Connly answered. "You know, breed and sell really top quality animals. I've always wanted that."

"What about dis fahm? Would you's eveh want to buy it? I's would give you's a good deal."

Connly dropped the brush in his hand, spattering red drops of paint into his glossy black curls. "Everrett!" he exclaimed. "This is quite a nice farm. You would do well to hang on to it. You've worked hard on this place all year, and now when it's really starting to get nice, you want to sell it? This place could be so prosperous and so beautiful. Just picture all the things you can do with it."

"You's can," Everrett said glumly. "You's can picture sech things. You's can see hohses running in de fields and flowers bloomin' everywhehe, and folks in de house laughin' and carryin' on." Connly nodded, and Everrett went on, "But I's can't. When I's look out across dese fields, all I's see is things dat crush my heart and feeds my anger. You know," Everrett's voice dropped to barely a whisper, "I's still hear heh voice. Elsa told me once, dat house was haunted to heh. I's know now what shey meant, 'cause it's haunted foh me now. Whenever I sit quiet, I's can hear her jest in de next room oveh, and I's go look, but no one's dere. Crazy talk, I know." Everrett gave a long sigh. "I's will stay through de winteh, but when spring comes, I's leavin'."

"If it's what you have to do, it's what you have to do," Connly said.

"But I's would like foh you to have it. You's would make it beautiful hehe, and I's would know ifen I's eveh wanted to come back and see heh grave, I's could."

"But where will you go, Everrett?"

"I's don't know whehe. But I's goin' to kill dat Captain Aldridge. I said I's would, and I's can't rest until I do. I'll go west, I'll go south, I'll go across de ocean ifen I's have to, but I's will find him, and I will kill him. Afteh dat..." Everrett ended with a shrug.

Connly eyed him intently. "Are you sure that is what you want to do?"

Everrett nodded, and the look in his eyes could have melted through steel.

In the end, Connly did purchase the farm with financial aid from the senior Mr. Connly, who was delighted to see his son set up so close to the parent tree. With the almost magical touch of his enthusiasm, Connly transformed it into a buzzing hub of activity and life. And as he throve on the work he loved, none the worse for wear, wooden leg and all, Connly's dark, sparkling eyes, wavy black hair, and the wide, white-toothed grin which flashes so often across his face, began to turn the heads of more and more eligible young ladies

*   *   *   *   *

The stars were fading one by one from the sky, while delicate tinges of pink were seeping up over the eastern horizon, as Everrett led Charcoal out of the barn and carefully fastened his saddle bags for the long ride ahead of him.

"Bey patient now, old boy, we's got plenty of time yet to spend togetheh. I'll wager you's will be wishin' you'd seen de last of me befohe we's done," he mumbled as Charcoal restlessly chewed on his bit.

Everrett hung the reins over a fence post. Turning away from the empty house, he strode through the morning twilight to the familiar corner of the first pasture. As he stepped beneath the willows drooping boughs, a morning breeze shook the leaves, and some of the moist fronds glided across his cheek, dropping small tears of water behind them. The tree was shedding for him the tears he could not.

All through the winter Everrett had come here—as the leaves died and fell from the tree, leaving it bare and naked, as the rain and sleet fell in icy sheets, as the north wind shook dead twigs down over the cold dirt mound which was slowly sinking into the earth. And while he never said a word, he had moaned deep within himself. And at night when he lay alone in bed and heard the wind scream around the corner of the house, it had seemed the silent cries within him had at last found a voice. "Why? Why? Why?" they shrieked.

"Why can't the sunshine last forever? Why must summer's daylight fade away?

The flowers wilt and turn to mold, as storms of winter come to stay.
Why is death triumphing over life? Why is summer's grasp so weak and pale,
While the dread of winter's breaking all that is fair and soft and frail?
Watch the darkness close in around you, swallowing all in its mouth of pain—
Broken leaves and frozen flowers, cold and wind and tears of rain.
Where's the meaning? Trees without leaves, day without sunshine, night with no moon,
Only the wind o'er the empty fields, whispering loud its chilling tune.
Life is fleeting but death is final. Love is uncertain while pain is real.
Why hope for springtime's promise, when stabbing hate is all you feel?
Although the sun may shine with fervor, darkness' eerie spell will quench its flame.
Is not growth for some great purpose? So in constant death, where's the aim?
Happy labors of the summertime, all swept away in a fearsome gust,
Leaving behind a silent shame, bare and naked it stands in dust.
Evil darkness, angry winter, these phantom voices which to you are real.
A scar, but without its glory, a hidden wound that will not heal.
There are no doves on wings of silver, and there are no diamonds in the sky.
But as you shiver in the blackness, ask alone your question—Why?"

Slowly the screams of the wind had faded to low echoes, and now spring was here. Young shoots of tender grass had turned Elsa's grave into a verdant living couch. The tree had put on a gown of new leaves, while sparrows built a nest in its branches. Sometimes when the sun shone warm and caressed the old tree and the new life sprouting from it, and the zephyrs fluttered the fresh leaves into shimmering waves of yellow and silver, Everrett fancied he could hear the tinkling laughter of a little girl playing with her dolls or her soft voice singing a lullaby as she rocked them to sleep.

Everrett thought of all these things as he stood there for what was perhaps the last time, but nothing he thought of eased the pain in his heart at all. Presently he knelt down, and pressing his hand firmly into the yet pliable earth, left its imprint there. In all the echoes and dreams which would pass over this place as the seasons came and went, repeating over and over again their saga of death and birth, pain and joy, he wanted always to be a part. Then following an old custom which dated back hundreds of years into his African roots, from a time when people lived much closer to nature, he knelt down and kissed the earth.

Everrett stood up and without another backwards glance, hurried to the yard where Charcoal was impatiently waiting. He swung himself up and headed towards the long lane. He pulled Charcoal to an abrupt halt as he saw a woman step out from the shadows of the trees. It must be his imagination. He had worried about the possibility of losing his mind. Was it really happening now?

The woman was dressed in black, and her face was hidden behind a dark lace veil. Elsa had worn a dark lace veil when they rode over to Joshua and Lydia Trentons on the day they were married. He rubbed his hand over his eyes and looked again. She was still there. She had come a few steps towards him and then stopped, waiting for him to approach her.

He rode slowly forward, stopping when he reached her.

"Arthur told me you were leaving this morning," she said. The voice was somewhat familiar, but he couldn't quite place it. Elsa was all he could think about, and the voice sounded like an older, harsher version of her.

Everrett stared at her. Finally he said, "Please take off youh veil."

Slowly the woman brushed her veil halfway aside then let it fall back down again. It was Ingrid. He had not spoken a word to her, nor she to him, since that awful dinner when they first met.

"Arthur also told me why you were going, although I would have supposed as much without him telling me."

Everrett didn't say anything.

"So I came over here to bring you this." Ingrid slipped an envelope from her pocket and held it out to him. Everrett accepted it gingerly as if he expected it to explode. Ingrid was speaking again. "Inside is the address and directions to where Captain Aldridge's family lives, where he lives, or at least used to. Also his regiment, company, his favorite saloon, everything I know about him. I thought it might help. God forgive me, but I hope you succeed in your aim."

Everett's expression remained unreadable, but after awhile he said very quietly, "Thank you."

Ingrid turned and stepped back into the shadows. Everett watched her leave before lightly tapping Charcoal with his heels and heading out.

He was setting out to seek vengeance, setting out to seek answers for the songs the winter winds had sung to him, setting out to seek the thousand pieces his heart had shattered into, setting out to seek, he knew not what. But in that brief moment where his life transitioned to flow into a new course, he dared to hope that he would find a water that would quench the flames which burned within him and a food to satiate the hunger which was devouring his soul.

The
End

Printed in the United States
73654LV00005BA/48